Goodreads Reviews fo

The Darkening Sky (4.44 Stars)

'I have read many a crime book, but this book was different. I never for one moment guessed how the story would unfold.'

'Brilliant. Very much enjoyed – a new detective series based in England.'

'This was quite a read. Greene brings a lot to the table in this with great details on psychiatry, forensics, medicine, society, cars, and countless other small details, yet they are delivered with ease and purpose. As for the strengths? For me, the dialogue wins it. It's natural. It has wit without heavy punchlines. Greene handles the reveal superbly and leaves you hanging until the end. Sign me up for more Power and Lynch.'

'It is a good crime and psychological thriller and will keep any reader interested to the end. Well written, with great development of characters; I felt that I knew Power & Lynch personally. I look forward to further volumes in this highly entertaining and somewhat edgy series. Hugh Greene is a writer to start paying attention to in my opinion. Highly recommended.'

The Fire of Love (4.62 Stars)

'Good plot and enjoyable read – away to locate more books in this series.'

'This is a gripping story, I was hooked from the first page.'

'A well written book with a well-thought out storyline, I enjoyed it very much and definitely want to read the next one.'

'There are lots of twists and turns and complex characters to keep the ending from you and difficult to guess.'

'After the first chapter I could not put it down.'

'A good read that I would recommend to anyone who enjoys crime novels and psychological thrillers. The writing is constantly good and interesting.'

'Another great and gripping read from Hugh Greene.'

The Good Shepherd (4.38 Stars)

'There was drama and suspense and a nice twist at the end. It was quite compulsive, I felt I had to read more to see what happened next.'

'It is a very enjoyable and intriguing read. Well-written, it evokes the spirit of the times, the mid-nineties.'

'I enjoyed this book. The characters were interesting and I felt the book was well researched.'

'The story builds well with excellent attention to detail paid to the places that the main characters visit.'

'The pace of plot was gripping, and makes me want to know what is next.'

'An excellent read, loved it.'

'I was hooked from the first paragraph.'

Dr Power's Casebook (4.3 Stars)

'Hugh Greene the Author conveys the nineties in a way that helps me to look back fondly on that era. Dr Power's character is developing in a way that I am enjoying and I want to find out more. I cannot wait until the next book.'

'This is a little different to the novels but it is entertaining and well worth reading. I enjoyed all the stories but 'The Dark' has to be one of the best short stories I have ever read.'

'The more I read of Hugh Greene's stories the more a fan I become. These short stories are written in his own inimitable way and as always the dialogue flows seemingly effortlessly as the stories unfold.'

Schrödinger's God (5 Stars)

'The best of the series so far. Hugh Greene never fails to deliver thrills and new insights.'

'Greene is one of those artists who manages to make everything seem simple and effortless, but the more you look at it the more detail you see, and the more you can't help but admire those delicate touches. His characters are human. They don't have a storytelling veneer, they are people. Plausible, recognisable, everyday people. An incredible piece of writing. And the more I think about it all the more impressive it gets. I strongly encourage you to walk the path of this book because it delivers.'

'Another brilliant Power and Lynch tale, this time taking us on a pilgrimage through Spain. The balance between the horror and the beautiful descriptions of the places along the way, the night sky and the food and drink combine to make a superb read.'

Also by Hugh Greene

The Darkening Sky
The Fire of Love
The Good Shepherd
Schrödinger's God

Omnibus of Three Novels in a Single Volume
The Dr Power Mysteries

Short Story Collection
Dr Power's Casebook

Non-fiction
Dr Power's Meditation & Colouring Book
Hugh Greene & Judith Eddles

Son of Darkness
A Dr Power Murder Mystery

Hugh Greene

Illustrated by Paul Gent

ISBN: 9781979126403

First Edition Published Worldwide in 2019

A catalogue reference for this book is available from the British Library

Typeset in Cambria
Proofreading and typographic design by Julie Eddles

www.hughgreene.com

twitter: @hughgreenauthor

Son of Darkness

Prologue

The silver wings sang as they sliced through the shivering-cold night air, designed to soar at an altitude of thousands of feet, they were hurtling down towards the earth they had only recently left. The hard edge of the wings clipped the top of the trees with sounds like whip cracks. Unrestrained by any impacts with the willowy trees, the left wing collided with first the chimney and then the gable edge of the stout, slate, farmhouse roof.

The roof top offered more resistance to the falling wing than the tree tops, but still the plane hurtled on past. The roof, sliced through by the wing, had exploded into a shower of slate fragments, rafter splinters and brick dust. A cloud of debris rose to cover the final descent of the Cessna 182 as it finally collided with the earth. Metal burst asunder from metal with a crashing, tearing sound. The fuel tanks, nearly full with a complete journey's Avgas – 100 octane petrol – ruptured and showered the farmhouse outbuildings in a glistening film of petrol that shimmered like glass for the briefest instant before igniting.

A vivid arc of yellow flame illuminated the scene in an incandescent ball of light. The grey trunks of the trees around the farmhouse were suddenly lit by the sheet of flame and seemed to leap up into the night sky in alarm. Smoke gathered, clustering into a thick column that climbed up above the flame.

The occupants of the farmhouse, surviving only because they had been in a room downstairs, stirred into unbelieving panic. They surveyed the fireball through shattered windows, amidst a cloud of brick dust, through tumbled down walls and saw bright flame against a night sky where ceiling and bedroom and roof should have been. Their world had been shattered forever. In the immediate aftermath of the crash they knew for certain that the emergency services would be coming. And for that reason they knew that they must flee their home of many decades, without delay.

Chapter One

"Is that you, Andrew?" asked Inspector Beresford. The Inspector's voice was deep and had a precise edge to it that belied his underlying mild-mannered nature.

"Yes it is, good afternoon to you," replied Andrew Lynch. The phone call had interrupted his work on a cold case, a case which was new to Lynch, but which had accumulated a decade's worth of files in another Police Force. Lynch's leather-topped desk was strewn with yellowing paper reports, receipts, and bank printouts. Lynch had just been reading the case files by the window overlooking Chester Castle. His office was on the first floor of an eighteenth century sandstone building, just by the Chester Law Courts. From his window Lynch could see the vacant Agricola Tower that used to form a gateway to the Castle. He was now, he thought every day, working on and surrounded by history.

"I was wondering if I was going to speak to Holmes himself," Beresford continued.

"What do you mean 'speak to Holmes', Beresford?"

"Your organisation's details on the web – the page says you are a 'consulting detective'. It sounds like Sherlock Holmes."

"That was not the intention," said Lynch. "It's merely a description of what I do. I am a detective and I act as a consultant."

"Not a private detective then?"

"No," Lynch actually shuddered at the jibe. "I work for the Foundation. The aim is to provide justice where there has been none, and not screening prospective employees, or snooping on people to find out their grubby infidelities. You know this, I explained it all when I resigned from the Force."

"Yes, I know," said Beresford, alert to the irritation that had crept into his former colleague's voice. "I was only teasing, Andrew, I'm sorry."

"Is this a social call?" he asked. "I am available for lunch, or dinner any time."

"Well, sort of. It would be good to go for lunch some time . . ."

"But?"

"Something's come up, Andrew, a case. To be frank, we need some help."

"Hmm?" Lynch was suddenly interested. "You want me to do some consulting work?"

"Not quite," Beresford sounded mildly embarrassed. "I'm the SIO for this new case and we'd like your input of course, but it's Dr Power we wanted – to ask his psychiatric opinion on a murder case. He's helped so many times before and he's on the Foundation website too."

"I see," Lynch tapped on the desk with the end of a pen. "So now you're the SIO, the Senior Investigative Officer, on a case . . . how time passes . . . and *it's* Professor Power now, of course. Since the University elevated him to those dizzying heights."

"Professor Power," said Beresford, playing with the novel idea of the words as he said them. "Prof Power. Professor Carl Power. It doesn't sound quite right, does it? Dr Power . . . now Dr Power sounds right."

"Agreed," said Lynch. He pushed the files to one side and focused his keen attention and interest on the phone call. "What is this case? Why do you want a psychiatrist like Dr Power involved? Has it just happened, has it been in the news? Do I know it?"

"No, you wouldn't know this case, Andrew. It's new. And it's an unusual case. And it's also an old case, a historical case, but one that's only now come to light. Well, I say case, but it's more than that. Much more. We discovered some human remains. It hasn't been in the news yet, but it will be, and it will be news . . . well, it will be news for months I'd guess."

"I can certainly find Power for you," said Lynch. He wondered where Power might be – in his clinic? At the University or reading a book over a pint of beer and a pub lunch? "Are there some funds to pay for his consultation?"

"There are consultancy funds, Andrew," said Beresford. "That's how they seem to want to manage things these days. Make the more senior full-timers redundant. They're too expensive to keep on. And when they realise they've no longer got the expertise in house, they have to call for help. A lot of our cases are failing in court because of junior errors – mistakes that you or I would never have made when we were juniors because we were supervised. But now, there aren't enough supervisors."

Lynch paused. He wanted to ask if he was being invited to be a consultant on the case too. He hesitated because he knew that Beresford was, by now, more than senior enough to handle an important murder case. He wondered how to phrase his enquiry.

Beresford broke the silence himself. "There's some funds for your involvement too, Andrew, your 'reasonable fees'."

"It would be the Foundation that would invoice for our time," said Lynch, anxious to demonstrate that he wasn't seeking personal gain. Lynch was secretly delighted to be asked and eager to know more, but he merely said, "I'll have to give it some thought, though . . . and I can't speak for Dr Power. He'll have to agree himself."

"Oh," said Beresford. He sounded disappointed. "I'm at the farmhouse, the crime scene. Actually, we need you both, now. Right now. It just can't wait."

"I see," Lynch was bursting with curiosity. "Then I'll find Power and get back to you right away."

"Thank you," said Beresford. Lynch thought he sounded relieved. "Thank you, Andrew."

Lynch put the phone down and stared out into the Castle courtyard beyond his window. What had frightened his old pupil so much that he had come running to his retired Superintendent?

* * *

Although it had been an hour ago, Laura's slamming of the heavy oak front-door had still been reverberating in Power's ears when he heard the phone ring. He had hoped it was Laura so they could make up. He knew some people thrived on conflict, but Dr Power hated arguments of any description. The row with Laura, his partner, had been brewing for weeks over a subject that neither liked to mention. The echo of the door slamming still hovered in the air. He had tried to dispel it by putting on some music, but the second movement of Shostakovich's second piano concerto, although beautiful, was mournful. He had tried to write a presentation on medical ethics for the students at the University. However hard he tried, though, the subject of autonomy as exemplified in the Hippocratic Oath was not sufficiently interesting to divert him from his anxiety about the argument. The recurrent and disproportionate worry that Laura might never come back could not be drowned out by such dry fare.

The basic theme of their argument was as follows; after several years of trying there was no baby. What was wrong? Whose fault was it? What should they do? Both of them lacked the adult courage to tackle the matter. The unspoken anxieties simmered, like a malevolent pot on their stove. Around the pot other meals were prepared in other pans, put on plates, consumed, and put away. But this particular pot kept on simmering, somehow contaminating everything around it, until every so often there was a volcanic eruption. The argument would billow out from the pot like a searing cloud of steam. And then one of them, (today it was Laura), would storm out of the room, or house.

The tyres on Laura's Mini had screeched and screamed their way out of the drive and onto the Macclesfield Road and down the hill into the village of Alderley Edge and beyond.

Dr Power was just about to hurl his lecture notes across the study in frustration, when the phone rang. It was Lynch.

* * *

The air itself was scorched, somehow charred with the recent fire. The day was cool, but the acrid air around the house burned the nostrils. The ground was blackened to a crisp and here and there strewn with white and grey ash, which crunched under Dr Power's feet. He had found it difficult to park on the main road because of a fleet of media reporters' cars and their news vans, antennas trained upon the skies and waiting to transmit any gobbet of information that the police or fire crews might give them.

The news bulletins had been reporting the aftermath of a light-aircraft crash with no survivors, the destruction of a house and a great fire in a wood that, in the night, had been seen for miles across Cheshire. The vans had been booked for a morning at most, to transmit the reporters' interviews of eye witnesses. The initial reports had been filed, but then, just before they were about to depart the reporters had had tips that something else happening at the farm. A new team of police officers had arrived, far more numerous, to swell the ranks of air accident investigators that were combing over twisted aircraft wreckage and the fire crews who were finishing their night's work, freed up to go now the flames had all gone with the onset of dawn. The mangled, charred corpses of the pilot and his sole passenger had been taken away hours earlier. The news scene was going cold, and the media caravan was about to snake and wend its hungry way elsewhere. And now? Things had changed in the last hour or so. There was the scent of another story, something altogether more sensational and far, far darker. An incident headquarters was being set up, and teams of white-gowned scene of crime scientists were beginning to assemble on the fringes of the crash site, like hooded white monks in plastic gloves, blue overshoes and masks. A thin woman with fair hair carried a pair of Nikon police cameras past them and the reporters eyed these cameras enviously, not for the equipment itself, but for the images they would contain. A tabloid journalist shouted out to her, "I've got a cheque book here and your name's in it!" She waved him away and turned her back on the reporters and got on with her work.

Dr Power had passed the pack of reporters earlier with his head down, eyes fixed on the ground. They had still recognised him, though.

"That's Power, the psychiatrist; best in England – they call him in for murder," muttered one, before shouting out in his turn, "Professor Power, can you tell us why they've called you in?"

Power tried to walk on as if he'd heard nothing, but despite his attempt to appear nonchalant his walk became involuntarily more awkward and self conscious. He could hear a reporter talking to camera in the distance, he slowed to eavesdrop: "Emergency services were called to Lindow Moss just before 1 a.m. following reports of a crash landing near the Moss and nearby woods. The pilot, a man in his fifties, and a male passenger in his seventies were pronounced dead at the scene and there were no other casualties found. The Air Accidents Investigation Branch has rushed a team of inspectors to investigate this accident to a Cessna 182 aircraft. They are on site gathering evidence and conducting interviews to try and establish a cause for the crash. We understand that later today the aircraft remains will be taken to their facility in Farnborough where a detailed examination can take place. However, even though the fire is now out and the occupants of the plane have been taken to hospital, we can see that a new team of police investigators has descended on the house that was damaged as the plane crashed into its roof, and so the mystery of what is happening here at Lindow Moss continues."

Power was conscious that the camera was moving away from the reporter and towards the scene of the shattered farmhouse, which he was standing in front of. Power turned his back on the lens and trudged on to the house through silver-bedewed grass. Eventually the wet grass gave way to the charred ground of the crash site. Power always avoided the camera's lens. He did not want any fame or what came with it.

With his back strictly held to the cameras Power paused a moment and took in the scene before him. A hundred yards ahead was a red-brick farmhouse which once had a grey Welsh slate roof. The farmhouse had stood two stories high in a narrow space within a clearing in a wood. What remained of the farmhouse suggested that for many years the farm had been neglected and left to go to rack and ruin. Faded green paint was peeling off the window shutters. Overgrown shrubbery had crowded over the path that led to the front door. The door was open, but Power could see that panes of glass in the door had been replaced by old plywood, which was nailed into place. The overall impression given was one of desolation, even before the crash.

Now, the slate roof had been ripped open by the collision with the plane in the night. Bare roof timbers stuck up into the sky, like shattered bones poking out of lacerated skin, cauterized by the engulfing sheet of flame. Shards of roof tiles had showered over the farmyard and its outhouses. Grey fragments of slate lay mixed on the ground with shattered glass from the windows and pulverised bricks from the walls of the upstairs bedrooms. The ground had been scorched by the fire from the Cessna's petrol tanks. Bushes and trees were crisped to black skeletons by the intense heat. The ash-strewn ground still felt warm through the soles of Power's shoes. Some of the distant outhouses remained, and others had burned to nothing. In one outbuilding that was still standing Power could glimpse a rusted tractor, that listed to port on long deflated tyres. Although the plane had driven its own wide path through the trees, Power noted there was no driveway leading up to the house and farm buildings. What might have been a farm track once had long since been reduced by undergrowth to a mere path that only one person could walk along. If the plane had not carved out its own path, the farmhouse could not have been seen from the nearby roads, and even off road if someone had walked past only a hundred yards away the old farmhouse would have been completely hidden by the trees. The plane's tragic descent, as it scythed through everything, had exposed what had been hidden for decades.

Power mused over the sight of white-clothed people clustered round the twisted metal of the plane. He didn't like to approach too closely. The smell of burning and the thought that this was a place of death troubled him and made him feel queasy. Power seemed altogether preoccupied when Inspector Beresford came out of the farmhouse's front door and hailed him.

"Carl Power! Am I glad to see you!"

Inspector Beresford made Power put on a similar white-hooded suit to his own, a mask, a pair of blue plastic overshoes and a pair of vinyl gloves. "In case you touch anything," he said.

"I don't get that close," said Power, pulling on the gloves. "I wouldn't touch anything. I wouldn't touch a body. It is a body isn't it? One of the farm people?"

Beresford knew Power was squeamish, and he now doubted that Lynch had passed on all the details of what had been found to the Professor. "There are human remains, yes, and we haven't moved anything – so you can take a look – but we don't think it's the owner of this place," said Beresford. "It's all a bit unusual. We think that the man who lived here escaped with his life, and he was very lucky to survive a direct hit to the house, but he left as soon as he could after the plane crashed. There's evidence he had just cooked a meal before the crash, and he left it half-eaten." Beresford led Power into the farmhouse kitchen. Fine ash from the incinerated trees outside was floating in the air and was coating the red-tiled kitchen floor in a grey powdery coating. Power was glad of his mask. There was a half full pan of mushroom soup on the table with a white, bone china bowl containing a thin layer of congealed soup beside it.

"Just one inhabitant?" asked Power.

"We think so," said Beresford. "At least, we've only found the remains of one bed in the house but the upper rooms have been largely obliterated."

"Who lived here? Who's the property registered to?"

"The house is registered to a man called Heaney," said Beresford. "But as he was born in nineteen hundred and four, I don't think that's his soup. He'd be about a hundred years old . . . the house hasn't been registered to anyone else. I mean, I think we can safely assume that old Mr Heaney has left this mortal realm, and so I think maybe a squatter just living here?"

Power had opened a cupboard and retrieved a sample of two or three cans. The cupboard was crammed with dozens of tins of Co-op beans and soup. "A limited diet, but whoever he was, your squatter certainly didn't mean to go hungry. Although, he'd be a bit vitamin deficient if he didn't have another food source than these tins, I'd guess."

"There's a small kitchen garden on the other side of the house," said Beresford. "Some potatoes and cabbagey looking things, I can't tell. I'm not a man of the soil. But there was a freezer. And that's why I asked for you. Do you want to see?"

Power suddenly felt a marked reluctance to move from where he was standing in the kitchen. He looked out of the kitchen window at the sky. A thin sun was piercing through the clouds, and a finger of sunlight pierced the gloom of the kitchen, falling onto the draining board and ancient Belfast sink. Power imagined that view wouldn't have been visible to whoever had occupied the house the previous day. The plane had changed all that by its devastation of the wood. Maybe the sun hadn't shone in this room for many years.

"The body, then?" asked Power. "It's in the freezer?"

"Yes," said the Inspector. "The freezer. Electricity's the one utility bill that was being paid, under old Mr Heaney's name, of course. Paid in cash at different post offices hereabouts."

"Show me, then," said Power. "If you must."

"It was the police on duty that noticed it. They came into the farmhouse whilst the fire officers were tackling the plane fire, and the fire in the wood. It was all a bit warm you see, so this one constable decided to look for some ice cream in the freezer. I ask you! Policemen are guided by their stomachs, not their heads, or hearts. He's been told off, but I suppose his actions did turn up the crime." They had reached a large white chest-freezer sitting under the angle of the stairs. Power was aware of a group of white-suited police officers and scene of crime officers standing in what he took to be a living room that was off the hallway. He felt uncomfortable as they were standing silently watching him. "It was dark, and he didn't want to switch the main lights on . . . the fire people had told him not to. In case of sparks, and gas, or fumes," said Beresford. "The constable just had a torch, he opened the lid, saw a tub of Granelli's best vanilla and hoiked it out and started eating. When he had enough and put it back, well then he saw something else in the freezer and he called it in.

"Are you ready?" Beresford put his hand on the chest freezer lid.

This was when the memories and images of similar past shocks came clattering back into Power's mind. These are the ghosts that haunt us all. His vision swam and he felt detached and slightly sick. He heard himself say, "Go on then. Open it."

Chapter Two

The chest freezer was in a dark, triangular space at the back of the dingy kitchen, under the open, wooden stairs. Inspector Beresford gave Power a torch to hold. "You'll need some extra light."

Power flicked the switch on the torch and pointed its cone of light towards the freezer. Beresford lifted the lid with his gloved hands.

There was a seated figure in the freezer, naked skin against the white ice crystals. Her knees were hunched up to her chest and her sunken, open eyes stared back at Power. The eyes were dull with death and no longer reflected any light. They stared blindly at Power. He shivered. Power thought that the woman was in her twenties. Her neck was twisted to the side and Power observed a line of brown, running up the side of her neck and face. It looked as if someone had painted it on as far as her temple. He imagined a watercolourist using a fine sable brush to apply a smooth line of burnt umber paint. Underneath the streak of brown was a small incision in her neck, and below that a thin, indented line in the skin that wrapped itself like a collar around her neck.

"Has the Home Office pathologist been?" asked Power.

Beresford nodded. "We thought we'd wait till you saw her. Then we will send her off to the morgue, and examine the rest of the freezer for clues."

"What's she sitting on?" Power peered in to the chilly depths. He could hear the freezer humming as it carried on its work dispassionately.

"Some kind of tarpaulin, I think," said Beresford. "There are bits of food packed round her. Some Birds Eye peas, and some fish fingers for God's sake. And a tub of ice cream on her lap. That's what the police officer pulled out first. He'd got overheated, the fire in the woods was still blazing. And he came in here, saw the freezer."

Power inspected the pale body further, observing the marks of rope pressure marks on the victim's ankles.

Beresford could hear the doctor whispering and mumbling to himself and thought he could hear the repeated phrase, "Somebody's daughter. Somebody's daughter." Beresford wondered if the doctor was about to lose his composure. Power used his gloved hands to prod around in the freezer, shifting some food and pulling ineffectually and repeatedly at the tarpaulin. "What's this covering up?" Power asked again.

"Some more food?" said Beresford. "How long do you think she's been dead?"

Power looked up. "What did the pathologist say? I don't want to be caught out you see, I'm a psychiatrist, not a pathologist. I'd defer to . . ."

"But you are a doctor," chided Beresford. "So what do you think?"

Power hesitated. "Two or three months?"

Beresford nodded. "That's what she said, too."

"I'm glad I passed the test. What did she say the cause of death was?"

"She said she wouldn't make guesses and wanted to perform a full post mortem. She rather thought the girl would have been drugged and abducted here, before ending up in the deep freeze."

"I see," said Power. He looked at the woman's fingernails. No nail polish. They were white as ivory, and bitten to the quick. "She was garotted. See the thin line around her neck? The wire was removed when she lost consciousness. See this line running up her face?"

"I wondered about that," said Beresford.

"She was hung up by her feet immediately she was dead, or unconscious. Her carotid artery was incised, and the blood drained off. The line on her face is blood running down whilst she was hung up. That's why she is so pale. No purple marks of lividity, because her body had no blood in it to settle and make any marks." He stood up. "Any idea who she is? Were any of her things left around the place? A handbag, or a purse?"

"No trace of her clothes or any personal effects." Beresford was watching Power, who had switched the torch off and was looking up at the ceiling in the kitchen. "What are you looking for?"

"The hook," said Power. "The hook he hung her from." He frowned, annoyed he couldn't confirm his theory. "There isn't one here".

"Maybe in one of the outhouses?" suggested Beresford. "Why would he drain her blood?"

Power was looking at the floor and pushing the fine powdery ash about with his foot. There were clouds of ash forever moving into the house from the yard, blowing across from the incinerated woods outside. The billowing clouds, moved along the ground, moving about constantly, covering all in a fine grey dust. As soon as it was swept away it simply re-accumulated. "There's a ridge here, a line, can you see?" Power pointed to a fine line, two foot long, in the mess on the kitchen floor. He noticed a small beetle scuttling along the line, waggling back and forth across it. Power peered at it. It had a bulbous antenna and what looked like comical large joints. Its carapace was yellow and black stripes. He had never seen one like it before. It was almost as if the beetle was dancing to highlight the line in the flooring.

"It's just a line in the flooring."

Power stamped on the floor around the line. One side sounded hollow. "Can we see if there's a hatchway?"

"There's no cellar," said Beresford. "My officers have checked."

Power stamped on the floor some more and frowned.

"Better take the hint and do what the good doctor suggests," said a voice behind them. "I've found it saves time if you listen to him."

It was Lynch. Ex-Superintendent Lynch, and Power's long time colleague.

Beresford sighed and called his one of his officers to do just this. "Sweep the floor and check again for a hatch." He was mildly irritated, but his irritation was mingled with a degree of pleasure at seeing his old supervisor. He shook Lynch's hand in greeting. "Andrew, it's good to see you! You couldn't keep away?"

"No," said Lynch. "Curiosity overcame me." Lynch noted that Beresford had just picked up the Investigation Policy File and was hugging it closely, as if unconsciously he somehow imagined Lynch might wrest it from him. As SIO on the Investigation, Beresford was supposed to use the file to log all his strategic decisions as officer in charge. It was a bound file, with sequentially numbered pages. Lynch turned away and nodded over at Power. "This is Cain's lair then?" he asked.

"Yes," said Power, who suddenly felt obliged to summarise some of his thoughts now there were two senior officers in the room. He felt slightly embarrassed, like he was a medical student again, presenting a patient's history that he had clerked to a senior consultant. And dressed in their smart pinstripe suits the Inspector and the ex-Superintendent did look remarkably like old-school consultants. However, Power did not want to appear the nervous youth he had been as a student doctor and so he paused to compose himself. Straightening up, fixing Beresford in the eye, deepening and steadying his voice to appear authoritative and in control. "The man who was living here, and I say man because it is, sadly, and predictably, men who statistically perpetrate violence upon women. The man who probably murdered the girl . . . hurriedly took the opportunity to escape when the plane crashed. No doubt it interrupted him and unsettled all his plans. This was his safe place. Hidden away in the trees. He made sure there was no contact with anybody nearby. No regular visitors. A lair, and as you say, Andrew, like a predator's den. When the plane crashed, apart from realising how lucky he was to survive, he also knew that the emergency services would be here in minutes, and that there would be questions upon questions and that this wolf's den of his was not a safe place any more."

"So what did he leave behind for us? Who was he?" Lynch asked Beresford.

"He left us very little information," said Beresford. "I think perhaps that he had things already prepared so he could take flight at any time. Maybe he even had a bag prepared with all the things he'd need to take in a hurry; money, passport, credit cards. An escape kit."

"Who is registered as the owner of this place, the old farm?" asked Lynch.

Beresford felt compelled to answer his ex-superior officer, but Power jumped in. "I believe there was a Mr Heaney, who would now be about a hundred if he was alive. And yet, even though he must be dead, he still miraculously keeps on paying his bills," said Power. "Whoever lived here used the old man's identity like a shield – probably to keep his name out of records associated with this place."

"How did he find this place, then, and how did he assume the privileged position of prolonging Mr Heaney's life?" asked Lynch. But he already guessed that no-one could answer his question yet. He was merely trying to order his thoughts. "And tell me, what was he doing that the plane crash interrupted?"

"Maybe you should take a look in the freezer for yourself," said Power. He deliberately moved away across the kitchen and hovered near the doorway into the living room. By standing here he could avoid any sight of the freezer's contents. He had no plans to do so ever again, unless compelled.

Lynch took the torch and lifted the lid with gloved hands. He shone the torch inside. "I see an ice maiden," he said softly. "And she's surrounded by this man's frozen food?"

"I don't think he was fussy," said Beresford, watching his ex-Superintendent peering inside the humming coffin. "Hygiene wasn't his thing." He still felt some irritation at himself at how quickly he had slipped into the role of second in command. It was his first investigation as SIO. He had really just wanted Power's insights, and here was Lynch, unconsciously adopting the role of his superior. It felt so natural to let him take over, and it made him feel uneasy. "We are about to send the body off, I don't think there's much else to be learned from her where she is."

"What's she sitting on?" asked Lynch, echoing Power's previous question.

Beresford tried not to show frustration. "A tarpaulin, I think."

"Have you looked under it?" asked Lynch. He had peeled back the stiff canvas, and was peering at the food beneath.

"It's food," said Beresford, unable now to hide a hint of resentment from his voice. Power noticed it if Lynch did not.

"I don't doubt it's food," said Lynch, poking about some joints of meat in clingfilm. They rattled around in the bottom of the freezer like stones. "Carl, can you take a look at this?"

"Really?" asked Power. "Do you really want me to?"

"Yes, I rather think it would be for the best, please," said Lynch.

Power walked over, keeping his eyes on the floor till the last moment. He stepped round the officer who was sweeping the kitchen floor as Beresford had requested. Power looked gingerly down into the belly of the freezer. Lynch pointed the flashlight onto some pink joints of meat under the tarpaulin. He saw rock hard joints – pink-skinned, white-fatted exteriors, wrapped around the brown meat of animal muscle.

Power had been vegetarian for years. "Enough to cater for a year of Sunday lunches?" he said. "A leg or a shoulder of lamb guaranteed for every week."

"Look at this one," said Lynch. "Closer, please, Carl."

Power edged a bit closer. "It's got hair left on the skin," he said.

"Well, I wouldn't recommend the butcher," said Lynch. "But for an amateur I suppose it wasn't too bad a job, professionally speaking." He looked at Power and saw that the doctor still didn't appreciate what he was saying. "Carl, is this supermarket beef, or lamb, or something else?"

"Ah," said Power, taking a step backward and looking round for the sink.

"If you're going to be sick," said Lynch. "Go outside, please, Carl. This is a crime scene."

The doctor hurried outside, hand to his mouth.

Beresford had a sense of unease. He realised he and his officers had missed something important. "The joints of meat – they aren't proper meat, are they?"

Lynch shook his head. "Well, nothing you could get in any reputable shop. It would require cellular analysis to be sure, but I would have to say that this meat looks uncommonly like a man's calf; hairs and all."

* * *

It was Beresford who came outside to find the doctor. He found him on the edge of the wood a few hundred yards from the farmhouse. Beresford lit up a cigarette under Power's mild, but disapproving gaze. "They calm me down," he said half apologetically. "Are you feeling all right?"

Power chose to ignore Beresford's polite and well-intentioned enquiry about his response to Lynch's gruesome discovery. He did not want to admit to his own weakness, and instead Power asked, "Was Lynch getting to you?"

"Oh, you know . . . you think you're old enough, a grown up, and capable of running your own show, and then the old boss breezes in and you feel like a newbie again. And he goes and spots something I've missed straightaway." Beresford let out a big sigh.

Power did not want to disclose that he had just been sick in the bushes. He didn't feel up to reassuring anybody much. "Well," said Power with a wan half-smile. "He just wants to be useful, and if you reflect on it, you were the one wise enough and mature enough to bring in some outside eyes to look at things."

"That's kind of you," said Beresford.

"No," said Power. "It's vital to get another perspective, whatever your job. I ask for respected colleagues' second opinions all the time. And if you just stick to one-line of thinking . . . like when the detective in charge of the Yorkshire Ripper case got diverted by a hoax tape. He was convinced the hoaxer, Wearside Jack, was the actual Ripper. Maybe it was the taunting voice on the tapes that needled the lead detective, Oldfield. Maybe he lost his objectivity there, because he was riled by the taunts. He thought the hoaxer's Wearside accent would lead them to the Ripper and he diverted his resources away from Yorkshire where the real Ripper was."

"Yes, but it still feels like a bit of a failure to have to call in help from outside," said Beresford. "The truth is, they've pensioned off the senior officers. Not just Lynch. Many others as well. A cost cutting exercise. So then, when something like this happens, when something altogether . . . unusual . . . then there's nobody senior left inside to ask. So I'm left calling in the 'private consulting detective'. Playing the naïve Lestrade to clever Lynch's Sherlock."

"Well, I'm not Dr Watson, playing second fiddle, as ever, to Holmes, and Lynch himself is as far as you can get from a cocaine-addled social misfit, don't you think?" Power turned back to gaze at the land surrounding the wood. "Anyway, Conan Doyle was a locum doctor who just pinched his winning formula from Poe. Read Poe's *Murders in the Rue Morgue* and see what you think." He paused, and pointed into the distance. "What's that land over there?"

"Well, it looks a bit of a wasteland to me," said Beresford. "But I'm assured it's a site of special scientific interest. For voles, and bog plants, and special insects, and the like. It's Lindow Common, a landscape 'untouched since Celtic times', they say, except for the peat cutters, and a million dogs and their dog walkers."

"I didn't even know it was here," said Power. "And I only live three miles or so away."

"There's the lake, Black Lake, just behind the trees. And of course they found the bog man's body here, buried in the peat."

"What?"

"There was a body discovered in the nineteen-eighties. Lindow Man they called him. His remains were found in the ground dug up by the peat cutters. They found half a body. The top half. Head, and shoulders, and torso. And a foot . . . Where the rest was, I don't know. They found a bit of foot first off, then the body. The rest was probably taken off in the peat they'd already cut and it probably got mulched into someone's back garden. They use the peat for compost you see. The police were called when they found the foot, but they soon realised the body was really old, I mean really old. Like two thousand years old; in fact he might have been killed at the same time as Christ was crucified. That old. Once they realised he hadn't been killed recently they called the archaeologists in."

"Ah," said Power, memories beginning to stir. "Lindow Man. I think I saw him once, in a museum. They reconstructed his face. He was young. In his twenties. They'd done his eyes a bit oddly, so he looked kind of startled."

"Well, he was killed," said Beresford. "So you'd allow him a bit of alarm, wouldn't you?"

Dr Power felt obliged to agree, and Beresford continued his summary. "So here we are, years later, at a farmhouse hidden in a wood, on the edge of a boggy Common. And the farmhouse is the house that time forgot. It has electricity, but otherwise might be straight out of the nineteen-sixties. With electricity for cooking and lights, and er, freezer. But no telephone. A black and white television. A transistor radio – a Roberts original. A Dansette stereo with some records by Mario Lanza and Johnny Cash. A scratched 78 of Shostakovich's Fifth, conducted by Stokowski from nineteen thirty-nine. Here we are in the distant past."

"What was life like for the man who lived here?" wondered Power. "Did it get so he was frightened to venture outside his den, or was he only too glad to escape and immerse himself in life outside?"

"And where is he now?" asked Beresford.

Power thought about where such a recluse might run to and

decided he didn't have any ideas. "I need to look round the rooms in the farmhouse that still exist," said Power softly. "They might tell me something."

"There's a photo book," said Beresford. "A family photo book. Decades old, and I don't know if it's relevant, because it got left behind. It might not be an album of any family that we need to know about."

"I'll take a look," said Power.

A detective from Beresford's team appeared at his superior's side. "Sir, Superintendent Lynch would like to talk to you. We've found something else."

Beresford frowned and restrained himself from reminding all concerned that Superintendent Lynch was no longer with the force. He was no longer a Superintendent at all. "We'll be there directly. And can you find the photo album for Dr Power to look at, please? I'm sure I don't need to remind you to use gloves when you look at it, Professor Power."

The detective nodded but clearly wanted to add something, and as he joined them for their walk back to the farmhouse he spoke up. "The media are asking when there will be a statement, sir."

"Tell them late afternoon," said Beresford. "I want a bit of time to think first."

Lynch was waiting for them at the front door of the farmhouse. He was tall and filled the frame completely, leaning against the upper woodwork of the doorway. "Under the ash and dust, is a hatchway," Lynch said. "They wanted to lift it, but I thought we'd better wait until you got back. It is not my investigation, after all."

Inside the kitchen, with the tiled floor swept clean, the edges of the hatchway were abundantly clear. "How do you think it can be lifted?" asked Beresford. "There's no handle, or any gap, just the line of the edge."

The beetle that Power had seen before scuttled across the floor in front of them and began its waggling dance along the edge of the hatchway, as if it too was looking for a way in. "I saw that earlier," said Power. "I've never seen one before. It must be a foreign insect." He thought its yellow and black back was very distinctive.

"It's called a Sexton Beetle, I believe," said Lynch. "Sexton, like a church sexton. It's native to this country."

"Never seen anything like it," said Power.

"I've seen it before," said Lynch. "But only at crime scenes. It's not what you'd call a good sign." Lynch reached into a kitchen drawer and found a carving knife. "I have a feeling there's a trigger mechanism to find." He pushed the blade into the crevice of the line, roughly half way down one edge. There was a click and the trap door swung noiselessly upward on its hinges. "Found the trigger first time," said Lynch. "That's lucky." He took the precaution of fixing the hatch open with an improvised prop. "We don't want it closing on us," he said.

Power looked down into the dark below. The blackness seemed to reach out to him, as if it remembered him like an old friend. He was frightened of its touch, of it being all around him, enveloping him in its silken smotheringness as it had in the past. The blackness of the hatchway seemed total. He thought, 'I can't go down there. Maybe I can leave this to them.' And there was a place in his own home that he ignored, that he tried to forget about. A doorway down into the rock, deep below his own house. He could forget about it if he tried. If he thought about it he felt the panic of being lost down there. Once upon a time he had ventured down there, into the tunnels, and his lights had failed him and the dark had claimed him. Since that time he had locked the door against the dark, and even avoided that part of his kitchen where the door was. If he pretended enough, he could forget for most of the time. And yet here was the darkness before him now. Here, he was on the threshold again.

They were finding searchlights to go down. There was a commotion around him. Power remained silent and wondered if he could suggest he stayed in the daylight, and look at the photo album, whilst they descended into the dark without him. He could see the people moving round him, but such was his panic it was as if he couldn't hear them. As if they were far away.

Lynch touched his arm. "It'll be all right, I will stick by your side." Power felt Lynch's eyes on him. "You will be all right," his friend said reassuringly.

Power nodded dumbly and took the offered flashlight.

Beresford waved the flashlight down into the Stygian gloom. "I can see a floor, some way down. Maybe ten foot below us, and there's a wooden ladder to climb down there." He turned round, reached his foot down onto the first rung and began to climb backwards down the ladder. When his chest was level with the kitchen floor he wrinkled his nose up in distaste. "There's a musty smell and a smell of something else. I don't know what." He disappeared into the darkness below them.

"What can you see?" asked Lynch.

Beresford answered, his voice was muffled. "A corridor, and shelves, like tall racks of supermarket shelves, with aisles between. Stacked with jars, like provisions."

"I'm coming down," said Lynch, and lithe as a cat he swung himself over the edge of the hatchway and disappeared quickly into the cellar.

Lynch called behind him to encourage Dr Power. Power was still standing on the threshold of the hatch and displaying marked ambitendence. Eventually, he too turned and began to descend. His feet and calves felt like they were encased in lead diving boots. He imagined himself in a Victorian diver's suit, entering a cold, watery, subterranean world. Heavy brass headpiece, air pipes with pumped air, and lead weights on his chest. He half wondered if the wooden rungs of the ladder would support the weight of him and his diving suit. He imagined his boots crashing through the rotten wood.

As he clumped to the bottom of the ladder, Power felt somehow distant from everyone around him and he could hear his own breathing, which sounded loud and ragged. The words Lynch and Beresford were speaking to each other in the cellar seemed somehow far away, muffled, and even in a different language altogether. He could see their torchbeams, distant from him, and occasional glimpses of their shadowy faces lit by the beams of light. Power looked down at his own torch. The battery was drained and the light was faltering.

Beresford found a light switch on the furthest wall and suddenly five or six naked lightbulbs burst into brightness. The cellar was flooded with light. The contrast between pitch blackness and actinic glare was absolute. Power gasped and shut his eyes until he became accustomed.

They were in a cellar, which was certainly larger and wider than the house, its floorspace almost double that of the kitchen and living room above. Lynch suspected that the cellar ran under the outhouses as well, and wondered about other hatchways.

The cellar was filled with heavy, freestanding steel shelves that reached up to the ceiling. From where he stood under the kitchen hatch, Power could see at least four rows of shelving with aisles between.

On the shelves were all manner of hardware, coils of oiled rope, nets and farm equipment; shears and scythes. And on some of the shelving there were dozens of rows of shiny tins and bottling jars. The bottling jars gleamed under the bright lights, pink and red and plum-coloured. Power peered at them. What was in them? Peaches, he wondered? Some had fallen from the shelves and smashed on the floor. He assumed that the whole house had shaken when the aircraft slammed into the roof and upper floor. Or maybe it had been that someone rushing past in panic had caught them with an arm or a backpack and knocked the jars to the floor. Power looked into the shadows where the glass jars had split apart. The content that had flopped on the floor did not resemble bottled fruit, and rather than a sweet smell of surrounding syrup there was an acrid smell that was both acid and foetid. Power shuddered.

"There's another door," called Beresford, who was standing by a wall in the distance, beyond the shelving. "Shall I open it?"

"Wait," said Lynch. "We need to check. There may be a trap set or he might be waiting behind it."

Beresford looked at his old boss, weighing up the risks. "He might have left this way. We could find him."

"But still," said Lynch. "Maybe we should check for explosives. There could be a tripwire or a deadfall."

"We're losing time," said Beresford. "Surely he didn't have time to set anything up . . ."

Lynch shrugged and raised his hands in a gesture that left the decision to Beresford.

"Stand back, then," said Beresford, and waited till Lynch had retested as far as Power, who was still looking at the mess on the floor in an attitude of some perplexity.

Beresford took cover by the wall and pulled the door open. There was no explosion. There was no ambush. There was only silence beyond. The open door merely revealed a long rectangle of darkness, and nothing more.

"If he came this way, he's long gone," said Beresford. "And I think I can see a brick wall at the end anyway. It's like a big cupboard."

"You know," said Power, who had been silent for a good while. "I've heard the phenomenon of serial killers being described as like an infection. Each victim is found in the location of the murder, scattered through a city maybe, and each victim is like a new outbreak of the infection. And you triangulate the locations of the victims to find the living centre of the infection, the host in his lair. You journey inwards to the perpetrator's home. Well, somehow we've stumbled on the centre of the infection. We're here, at the centre. We don't know where the victims came from because we're at the centre of it all. It's all turned on its head. Our problem is that the focus of the infection, the perpetrator, has escaped. And as emergency teams moved in, the infection spread out."

Chapter Three

Dr Power excused himself. He felt ill again and needed more air. Lynch and Beresford watched as Power climbed up the ladder and disappeared into the kitchen.

As he passed by, one of the police officers waiting by the farmhouse door asked, "What's down there, Professor?"

Power didn't look at her, he was looking at two more of the Sexton Beetles as they scurried along the edge of the cellar hatch. "More and more work for the pathologist."

"What do you mean?" she asked.

"I'm sorry," said Power, as he brushed past into the outside air. "I can't talk. I need a walk." He tugged the white hood off his head and took deep breaths as he removed the white protective clothing. The extra baggy layer, although light, had sealed an extra layer of air round Power and had made him overheat.

"Keep to the left on the Common," said the officer. "If you go towards the road you'll get reporters calling over. We've sealed the whole of the Common off from the public. You can get a bit of air there."

Power nodded and, head down, started walking, sucking in the clear fresh air as he strode. He walked briskly through a group of ash trees and then out into a clearing beyond. Lindow Common lay ahead, a sprawling scrubland of grass, marsh, peat bogs, trees, and bushes.

This was an ancient landscape, once spreading thousands of acres, now corralled by housing developments and the edge of Wilmslow town. Power's house, way up on the Edge looked down on this place and what was left of the wilderness. There had once been peatcutters here, part of a working tradition that stretched back centuries. Now there was a nature reserve and a site of special scientific interest. An assortment of ditches, trees, scrubland, and mosses, lay in front of Power as far as his eye could see. He paused by an information board that promised sight of buzzards and dragonflies, bats – pipistrelle and noctule, shrews, and newts. The board encouraged him to look for plants too, bilberry and romantic sounding species like Hare's tail Cotton-grass.

The natural world around him contrasted with the internal anxieties and fears churned up inside him by the day's experiences. As the police had sealed off the Common they had inadvertently rendered the mossland even more still and quiet than usual. There were no cagouled dogwalkers or amateur runners on the land, and for a moment Power saw how he might begin to feel at peace here if he were left alone for long enough. He wandered aimlessly for a few minutes and sank into a dreamtime. He found himself by a wire fence overlooking a broad lake, green and still, without a ripple. Here was silence, untroubled by any human life; just the sky and the water fringed by rushes – immobile sentinels that stood silently in the still air. There was no sense of the modern day. This was how the lake had always looked, frozen in time like an old photograph captured in silver salts on an old fashioned Victorian glass plate. Power's life, too, seemed to have stopped for a moment that seemed to last forever. Then the wind blew and the rushes rustled, and a plane droned overhead. The spell was broken. Flies and bees buzzed in the air, and two geese cried out as they landed in the water with a swoosh of spray.

* * *

Beresford looked down at a text on his phone. "They want to send someone from the Force Media Department to co-ordinate and script my appeal to the media."

Lynch looked up from his paper cup of coffee. They had moved out of the house and into a small office in the mobile 'business unit' – a large vehicle full of spaces, IT and phones that had arrived to co-ordinate the initial investigation. The great police trailer that housed it had been set up in the Common car park. Beresford's SIO office was little bigger than a cubbyhole, but it was a relatively private space to talk without being seen or overheard.

"The 'media appeal'," said Lynch. "A mixed blessing at best."

"We need to talk to someone who knew this farm and its owner," said Beresford. "But you're right, it will wake up and provoke all the usual nutters who have nothing to do with the case, just lure them in and then muddy the water, wasting hours. But I suppose there might be a needle of gold for us to find in the haystack . . ."

"Have you started the house to house inquiries?"

"Only the houses nearest, to see if they know anything. We need to draw up a questionnaire for something more systematic and snowball it."

"And what did the neighbours say?" asked Lynch, putting the black coffee down. It was too hot to drink or hold in comfort and had burnt the roof of his mouth.

"They were mainly out. The neighbours are rich. Mostly middle class commuters. Away during the day at work, home at night to draw the curtains and relax with a Merlot. From the few we found in: nobody took notice of the farmhouse hidden in the trees. Nobody saw anybody coming or going. No cars ever come or go. No lights are ever seen on. As far as they knew the farmhouse had been deserted years ago. The farm is 'the land that time forgot'. They don't know anything about it, and they didn't care up till today. They'll care when the TV starts reporting the bodies found here. They'll care when they can't sell their houses . . ."

"And you've got enough officers working on the TIE?" The acronym TIE stood for Trace, Implicate and Eliminate. A system to populate database with suspects.

"There's not much to put in the database yet," sighed Beresford. "Our suspect is male, probably white Caucasian. What fingerprints we have managed to rush through analysis match nothing on NAFIS." He was referring to the national fingerprint database which then held fingerprints of people convicted of a crime in the UK.

"Ah, NAFIS," said Lynch with some fondness at the familiar term.

"We need something better than NAFIS," said Beresford. "Something bigger and quicker."

"Oh," said Lynch. He had a sense that time was changing the once-familiar landscape of the working environment he had known. "So perhaps the murderer doesn't have any past convictions? That's a blow. Maybe the DNA will help?" and fumbled for some familiar terms. "Then maybe you can begin to set up the parameters for HOLMES?"

"Hmm, we use HOLMES2 now," said Beresford distractedly, as if in passing. "We've taken some DNA from the sink in what's left of the bathroom. There was a toothbrush in the wreckage. That might yield something, but there's going to be the DNA of the victims, smeared everywhere. It's . . . it's a logistical nightmare and it will take days to get anything back from Bramley and his FSS in Birmingham. I mean it will take days even to sort out all the . . . body parts. There's going to be so much noise in this case it'll be difficult to hear the signal, even to hear yourself think. No past convictions or vehicle registration information to short cut us to the murderer, nothing to help. I mean there's the freezer with parts in . . . and the jars downstairs . . . how many people, Andrew? How many people? Who were they all?"

They lapsed into silence. Lynch noticed that Beresford's hands were shaking. The case was bigger than either of them had seen before. It dwarfed their joint experience. Lynch wondered if Beresford needed some time alone to think and gather himself for the days ahead. And he realised he didn't know where Power was. "I'll go and find Carl and bring him back, see if he's got any thoughts that might help." Beresford nodded without making eye contact and Lynch slipped quietly from the office.

* * *

In the Common car park the police trailers housing the temporary police business unit were hives, buzzing with activity. Lynch heard the office manager and analysis manager bickering over space. The office manager was arguing that a category A+ Inquiry merited two trailers not one. The analysis manager was sighing and asking for some peace and space to complete her chartwork. She had a large whiteboard partially set up with divisions. Lynch read the familiar terms: 'Geography/Vicinity, Subject Profile Analysis, Suspects, HtoH, Timelines, Trace/Interview/Eliminate, Incident Analysis, Operational Intelligence, and a question written in red, PoLSA? Search parameters?'

On the table, Lynch noted a series of Post-it notes with details released by the Air Investigation team, to be inserted on another board – the Aircraft Accident Investigation Branch had released a flight plan which listed the two occupants of the plane as a Mr Daidalos and son. Daidalos had been a Greek inventor and the plane had been on a heading towards Malta as its eventual destination. Nearby, the crime scene manager was speaking on the telephone, organising for a great tarpaulin marquee to be set up round the farmhouse 'with floodlighting inside', to preserve the roofless scene from the elements. Lynch overheard that SOCOs were apparently sifting through the debris in the ruins of the upper storey. In a cubicle at the far end of the space, Lynch could overhear someone talking about the initial HtoH inquiry; he paused, leaning on the plasterboard wall and watched Beresford's team with more than a little nostalgia. A figure appeared at the doorway. Another officer climbed the steps and made the space inside even more crowded. He carried a tagged see-through plastic bag and caught the Analysis Manager's eye. "We've found a photo album to add to the materials. Can you accession it for us? Might help us establish the occupants of the farmhouse." The bag was handed over. Lynch craned his neck to see it.

"Superintendent Lynch," said Deborah, the Analysis Officer. "I almost didn't see you there. I heard you'd retired. Was that wrong?"

Lynch nodded to her in acknowledgement, "Hello, Deborah. I'm no longer on the Force, but I've been asked to advise on this case so I'm sort of on the payroll. That photo album . . . can I ask for a photocopy for Professor Power and myself? When it's processed of course?"

"I don't see why not, seeing it's you?" said Deborah. "I suppose it's OK with the SIO?"

"By all means check," said Lynch. "But I'm sure it will be sanctioned. Have you got any further with the name of the occupant of the farmhouse?"

She shook her head. "The official sources – Electoral Roll, Council Records just list a Mr Heaney as the owner and occupant of the farm. But he was born nearly a hundred years ago."

"Hard to track people who cover their traces. Was anybody claiming his pension?"

"No, that stopped being claimed in the nineteen-eighties."

"And any death certificate?"

"We checked. There is no death certificate or cremation form on file in the UK. No death has been registered in the UK. He could have emigrated, but I doubt it. I think maybe someone has been keeping his identity alive after he died . . . but not for his pension . . . and where his body is, well, who knows?"

Lynch grunted in acknowledgement and, deep in thought, stepped down from the trailer and looked about, sniffing the Autumn air. There was a slight breeze and a brief shower of rain had made the air seem fresher than before. He strode off into the scrubland beyond the farmhouse, searching for Power. He knew that all this land would have to be visually searched. The Common would be closed for days.

* * *

There is a golden hour in the field of Medicine. After the individual is traumatised by stabbing, collision or injury the body fends reasonably well for itself for a little while, signs remain relatively normal, and during this 'golden hour' surgical intervention often meets with the best results. Beyond the 'golden hour' the body unwinds faster, vital signs sputter and death becomes imminent. The great Victorians knew that their hospitals should be placed near factories and important engineering projects to maximize the chances of getting accident victims to surgery as soon as possible. The originator of the surgical term 'golden hour', a Dr Cowley, had said: 'There is a golden hour between life and death. If you are critically injured you have less than sixty minutes to survive. You might not die right then; it may be three days or two weeks later – but something has happened in your body that is irreparable'.

As in medicine, there is a 'golden hour' principle in policing – that special time just after a crime has been committed. Intervention as soon as possible after the crime may catch the criminal in the process of leaving the scene, or attempting to cover his tracks. Crucial witnesses might still be near the scene, and their memories might be sharp still; they might provide that unique and critical lead that could be followed direct to the murderer.

The psychiatrist, Carl Power, was musing over this 'golden hour' as he stood on Lindow Common. Who knew when some of the crimes attested to by the freezer and cellar in the farmhouse had been committed. Maybe they had been committed weeks, or even years, ago?

The 'golden hours' in this case had long since ticked their way into history. The perpetrator of these crimes had vanished soon after the plane had come crashing into his world. Amidst the flames, the confusion of noise and screaming from within the wreckage, the perpetrator had soberly gathered everything together and fled into the dark, leaving nothing but quiet sorrowful mystery behind.

Dr Power had been thinking on the theme of lost time, standing by the Black Lake, when he heard footsteps crunching on the gravel path that circled the water. He looked up to see Lynch advancing towards him. Lynch was clutching a bundle of paperwork to his chest.

"Are you all right? I know you usually go a bit pale at these scenes."

Power nodded a greeting. "I dreaded the anatomy classes and pathology practicals at medical school. Just now, I think it was a combination of things – the smell downstairs in the cellar, the heat of the white over-suit. I felt trapped underground again. Out here my head is clearing." He pointed out to the Lake. "I've never been here before. I didn't even know it was here, and it's only a few miles from home. The boards say that the Celts called it Llyn Ddu, or the 'Black Lake'."

"It is an old place then?"

"So the notice boards around the Lake say. It's acquired various legends over the years. There were records of 'prehistoric people' living here on the moss, amidst pools in the peat, in huts made of bent branches on the scrubland, even into the eighteenth century, they were said to be short and dark, with heavy features. Like Neanderthals or something! Do you think such ancient people could possibly live into recent times? I doubt it. And then there's the legend of 'Jenny Greenteeth' apparently – an ogress who lived in the bog – and children were warned, 'Don't go near the water, don't fall in or Jenny Greenteeth will get you and pull you through to another world.' Another world lying under that still, green water." Power gestured again at the lake's surface.

"They are going to do another house to house – a wider area to try and find out if anybody knew the man in the farm. They'll probably put together a team to search this land to see if they can find any trace of him," said Lynch.

"Where does the door lead?" asked Power. "The one under the house?"

"They will look into that too, the tunnel probably doesn't go very far. If the land is boggy, it's probably too damp to contain tunnels."

"I don't know," said Power. "Under the peat is probably sandstone. The Edge is honeycombed with natural caves and mining shafts for cobalt and copper and all sorts – they go on for kilometres."

"The ground's too boggy," said Lynch, reiterating his point. He held out the plastic wrapped, bundle of paper. "The Analytic Manager got this copied for you. It's a photograph album they retrieved from the farmhouse ruins. Perhaps you can take a look later on?"

Power took it and put it under his arm. "Are they very busy over there?"

"It's really complex, even when the crash investigation team and wreckage goes it will be busier than anything I ever saw. Poor Beresford! One half of me envies him the privilege and the challenge and the other half is glad the burden is not mine. Just bagging and tagging the specimens to go off for pathology and DNA is a couple of day's work for a couple of officers."

Power thought of the ice-hard contents of the deep freeze; pink, butchered portions of limbs prepared individually in plastic bags. He thought of the rows of jars of skin and flesh in the cellar. He shuddered.

Lynch went on, "There will be hundreds of samples; at least a couple of full days of STR work for the lab in Birmingham. And then they'll be able to compare the results with the national database and we can see if we can get the names of some victims."

"But surely the database is limited to samples from convicted criminals?" asked Power.

"It's not everybody, but there are two million names on the database with all their DNA results. It's a terrific resource. And with all those names there should be some overlap somewhere with the victims in the house," said Lynch.

Power looked at the ash trees scattered over the mossland. There was little sense of the bustling suburban community just beyond the treeline. "It's like some kind of isolated piece of the past, something left over from the Ice Age. I half expect to see a Mammoth barging through the undergrowth, followed by hunters in skins throwing their spears." He paused. "You know, that's who we are looking for here – I think we're looking for a hunter."

"Maybe," said Lynch.

Power clutched the photo album he'd been given to his chest and sighed. "I'd better get off home, Laura was cooking something tonight. I'm suddenly hungry again."

"That sounds a bit more like you," said Lynch.

"Andrew, will you ask them to do something?" asked Power.

"Yes, what?"

"Can they drain the Black Lake?" the doctor asked.

"Whatever for?"

"I think they'll find things there. The hands and feet. And that's where he put the heads too."

Chapter Four

Some part of the human self or soul is not subject
to the laws of space or time.

Carl Jung

They were hand in hand together, standing on the Edge; on the rocks of Stormy Point, six hundred feet above sea level. They stared out over trees and hedge fringed fields to Mottram, and beyond Cheshire into Derbyshire. Laura sighed and squeezed Power's hand.

"You've lived here a long time," she whispered.

"Forever," said Power.

"You walk amongst the trees every day, tell me their names?" she asked.

"How do you mean?"

"Well, what kind of tree is that?" Laura pointed to a tree about fifty yards away.

"That's a beech tree," said Power. "And there are oaks in Dickens Wood and Clockhouse Wood. And that over there, that's birch, and that over there, horse chestnut. And the birds of this area – jackdaw, blackbird and rook."

"And magpies, don't forget them," said Laura.

"Who could forget the magpies?" said Power.

He looked at Laura, and just for a moment her eyes were wild and she seemed to merge into nature, as if, apart from her deep blue eyes, the rest of her was camouflaged into rock and tree and leaf. For an instant she became a force of nature. "Every day I go out and I see something new. There's Brimstone butterflies and green tiger beetles, honey fungus and marsh violets. We have to make time to look, because so much of the real world just passes us by . . . and this is a special place with its own folklore," he said. "Did you ever hear of the 'spirit bottler'?"

"No, no, I didn't," and she seemed to soften as he pulled her to him. "It's a ghost story."

Laura looked up at the darkening sky. The gloaming gathered around them. "Do you really want to be telling me a ghost story at this time, in this place?"

"It's only a short one," said Power, putting his arm about her waist and drawing her close. "About a gamekeeper, a man who knew all the trees, and birds and insects, and scurrying things. He had a cottage on the Edge here. And a wife, a pretty young wife. And he was old, and he knew that she had her eyes on another. And his jealousy burned inside him like a hot red coal. And maybe it was the worry that consumed him, but he became ill, and he knew he was dying. So he made her promise and swear on the old black family Bible that she would never, never marry another. Well he died, and she married the lover. But on their wedding night as they were sitting round the fire in the gamekeeper's cottage, a third chair drew itself up by the fire, scraping its way across the flag-stoned floor. No hand could be seen moving it, but by the firelight there grew a shadow that wavered and then became solid and its angry profile was unmistakably that of the gamekeeper.

"They didn't sleep that night. When they went to bed in the same room, the shadow from the firelight stayed there and just watched them silently. They shivered under their blankets even though the fire was red hot. As dawn broke, the newlyweds sprang out of bed and hurried down from the Edge to find the church and the parson. The parson in turn went to see the blacksmith and got him to make him a bottle, made of iron, with an iron stopper. That night, the parson called round to their cottage just as the gamekeeper's ghost was beginning to appear as a grainy, writhing shadow on the wall, and muttering a prayer and making the sign of the cross, the parson forced the spirit into the iron bottle. Just before he pushed the stopper in, the gamekeeper's ghost tried to bargain; maybe he could come back as a magpie, or as a shiny Sexton Beetle and just sit on a branch or under a cupboard and watch his pretty wife from afar. But the parson was having none of this and he screwed the iron stopper in the iron bottle as tight as he could, and then he threw it into the deepest part of Radnor Mere. And that was that. The spirit bottler. His story."

"Thank you for my bedtime story, Carl." She squeezed him tight. "I hope I don't have nightmares about it tonight." Laura looked at the rising moon and shivered. "I think we'd better be getting back. You know, that story doesn't make any moral sense at all. I feel that the poor gamekeeper was a bit badly done to . . ."

"Who said a story had to make moral sense? Real life often doesn't make any sense . . . so why should a story? After a day like today . . ." Power let out a great sigh.

"What happened today?" asked Laura. Power had absolutely refrained from mentioning anything to Laura about his visit to the crash site or what had been found there.

"Do you really want to know? If that little ghost story might affect your sleep, I wouldn't want to tell you worse . . ."

"You know you can tell me, Carl, what happened?"

They were by the sandstone wall that encompassed Alderley House. The wall divided the garden of Alderley House from the woodland of the Edge owned by the National Trust. There was a padlocked iron gate that Power unlocked for them both and he locked it carefully, as always, after they passed through into the garden. In the gathering dusk, the bushes and their shadows were as dark and forbidding, as they were equally bright and tranquil during the day. In the dark, their joint footsteps on the shale of the path seemed to crunch more loudly than in the day.

"I was called out to a murder scene near Wilmslow," said Power.

"Oh," said Laura. "Where? Who was it?"

"Just down the hill, really, a few miles away. A farm on Lindow Common."

"My friend walks her dogs there every day, round the lake," said Laura. "Wasn't that where the plane crashed?"

Power grunted assent. "The very same place. Where the two people died in the crash; but the plane hit the farmhouse as it crashed, destroying the upper floor and while they were investigating the crash the police went into the farmhouse. It was deserted. Well, only just deserted. Whoever was there left just after the crash." Power unlocked the back door of the house and they walked through to the bright, warm kitchen. "They found evidence in the farmhouse of several murders. Well, I think many murders really."

Laura sat down at the kitchen table. Power started making some tea for them both, placing the heavy iron kettle on the Aga. She cut two slices of the apple cake she had made earlier.

"You say 'many'. How many?"

"I don't think they know yet," said Power as he placed two mugs of tea down in front of them and sat by her. The photocopy of the photo album from the farmhouse was nearby on the table, next to the book Laura had been reading earlier in the day; *The Curious Incident of the Dog in the Night-Time.*

Power pulled the photocopies nearer to him. "The bodies were in bits you see. There was . . . er . . ." He paused at the memory. "There was a body – an entire body – of a young woman with fair hair, in this chest freezer. She was sitting in the ice crystals. Underneath her there were cuts of meat. Like frozen New Zealand lamb or something, sawed into joints or portions. But you could see they were portions of thighs, or calves or upper arms." He shuddered. "Can I go on, or do you want me to stop?"

"I don't like hearing about what you've seen, but you've fascinated me – you've made me curious. Do you think that these joints had been prepared for . . . eating?"

Power shrugged, "Maybe."

"Where's the murderer? Did they catch him?"

"No," said Power. "Whoever he was, he was incredibly lucky to survive the plane crash – it hit the upper part of the house and devastated the upper floor. He must have been downstairs when it hit. It would have been a terrific shock for him. And because the plane had just taken off from the airport it was full of fuel, which drenched the yard and the nearby trees. It was an inferno outside within seconds. He probably just escaped after the plane hit; he would have known the emergency services would be all over the wrecked house. There was probably no doubt in his mind that they would be crawling everywhere and his secrets would be discovered. He had to run."

"Poor Carl," she squeezed his arm. "You hate this part of your work, don't you? Did you cope?"

"I had to get some fresh air," he said. "I felt . . ." Power saw Laura was holding some cake and was about to eat and modified what he was going to say. "Anyway, I coped. But I haven't told you everything. There are more secrets in that house. There was a trapdoor down to a cellar." Power noted that Laura had looked involuntarily over to the dresser in their kitchen. It was partially drawn over a hidden doorway to some stairs that went down below Alderley House. Power had once explored the stairway and the cave beyond and never done so again. Power went on, "There was a ladder down into a properly equipped cellar with equipment and shelving. There were bottles on the shelves, like jars. Like Kilner jars, you know?"

"My Mum used to bottle damsons and plums in those. She used the same jars again and again every year. Some were very old, she just kept buying new lids and rubber seals and re-filling them after every harvest. The fruit would be good in pies and suet puddings through the winter."

"Yes, well, this man, he bottled other things."

"Like what?" asked Laura.

"Well, I'm not a pathologist."

"Body parts?" asked Laura.

Power nodded, reluctant to say more and make the thing real again.

"What body parts?"

"I think they were genitals."

"Women? Men?"

"Both," said Power. "And there were dozens of bottles. Enough to keep the pathologists and DNA people busy for weeks."

Laura had put her cake down and was gazing at her plate, frowning and silent, trying to comprehend. Eventually she spoke, "You're sure they were from humans?"

Power nodded. "I am a doctor, I would know."

"Sorry, but I can't quite believe . . . why would anyone? Why would . . ." she struggled to formulate her ideas. "Why would anyone do that? Dozens?" Power nodded. "Wouldn't we have heard of all the missing people? Where did he find his victims?"

"I don't know, but I guess that's what they will be asking me before too long. That's what they will pay the Foundation for. Any ideas on a postcard . . . gratefully received . . ."

"But we would have heard about this!" Laura was still protesting. "Dozens of people can't just be murdered and put in the deep freeze or bottled. Not in this country."

"I don't pretend to understand what I've seen, but it was very real and I've been trying to get my mind round it all day. We do know that thousands of people go missing every year, though."

"Not that many, surely not," said Laura. "Britain is only a small country."

"No, unfortunately, you're wrong," said Power. "About a quarter of a million people are reported missing every single year. So perhaps he could be preying on the missing, or maybe he could find other ways to build his collection. Maybe he works with bodies in a funeral home? But either way he seems to be a collector, of sorts." An image of the serried ranks of jars flashed unwanted into his mind. He remembered the reflections from each glistening jar shining under the bright electric lighting. The contents looking like bottled white peaches. His body recalled the shudder of realization that the content of every bottle was human flesh. Like the alcohol-filled pickling jars Power had studied in the medical school pathology museum as a student. He recalled a whole swollen arm in a tall glass container on a shelf in the pathology museum – an arm swollen with lymphedema that seemed to threaten to burst out of the jar. His memory was interrupted by Laura squeezing *his* arm.

"Are you all right?" she asked.

"Yes, yes, of course," he held her hand against him.

The moment was interrupted by the telephone. The ringing clamoured for their attention. Power rose and went to the landline in the darkened hall, wondering whether he was on call for medical duty after all. It was late and he did not relish the thought of a journey to some far flung emergency department.

"Hello? Dr Power speaking."

"Hello, Carl. It's your father. Your old Dad." The voice seemed to wish to project a breezy attitude.

"Dad? Hello. Is everything all right?"

"Yes, yes. Don't worry. I was just phoning to say that I'm going to a clinic in town tomorrow. Outpatients. Just phoning in case they keep me in for investigations or anything."

Power paused to see if his father would disclose anything more. "A clinic? What kind of clinic?"

"Chest clinic, I think. GP wanted me to have an X-Ray. A cough that won't go away. Don't worry, son. It's probably nothing."

Power thought. His father had always smoked cigars. Refused to give up. A childhood image occurred to Power of his father in white shirt-sleeves, standing over a vast angled desk covered in blueprints, painting in his plans of walls and roofs with liquid watercolour on a sable brush. Cigar clamped in the corner of his mouth. Power, as a boy, had watched the brush, the reflective blue wash filling lines and rectangles. The watercolour had shone in the window light, until the moment it dried.

"Do you want me to come with you?"

"No, no. You're too busy. There's absolutely no need. No need at all. I just wanted to let you know."

"Thank you. I could come if you like?" There was a pause. Power thought, "Erm . . . are you coughing up any blood?"

"No," said his father.

Power thought he was lying, because he had answered 'no' too readily, and then wondered if he should challenge his father. He decided to stop asking questions like a doctor. "I'm happy to accompany you."

"It's quite all right," his father said.

"Are you sure?"

"Of course."

"I'm sure it will be fine," said Power. He felt a kind of dread settle on his heart though.

"You think so?" His father was seeking reassurance.

"Of course," said Power, wondering if his voice carried any conviction. "Will you let me know how you get on?"

Power returned to the kitchen and Laura was observing his frown, when he saw something and suddenly darted to the window. "What is it?" she asked.

He seemed not to hear, attention focused on something beyond the glass, in the dark. "I thought I saw something out there. By the trees. Something moving."

She joined him and they stared into the night, seeing nothing but the inky black silhouettes of trees against the murky darkness of the woods. She pulled the blinds down and locked and bolted the sturdy back door.

"There," she said. "That's the night shut out. Another cup of tea?" She motioned him to sit down again. "Was that your Dad?"

"He's not well," said Power. He looked even more preoccupied now. "He's going for investigations and I'm worried."

Laura nodded, and pausing for a while, waited to see if Power wanted to talk more, but he was silent, eyes fixed on the table-top.

For want of anything to fill the space in the conversation, Laura asked, "What's all this, then?" and pointed to the pile of photocopies.

Power stirred himself to talk. It was difficult to move his mind on. "Lynch got them for me. It's something they found in the farmhouse."

"The farm was in Lindow, you said? . . . where they found the Lindow man all those years ago? The body from the peat bog that they had in Manchester museum? He was killed as a sacrifice and chucked into a pool? I remember going to see him with school."

"The very same Lindow," said Power, unwrapping the bundle of photocopies and taking it out of the plastic cover it had been resting in.

"We got taken round by the Professor of Archaeology. I was very impressed by her. I even thought of being an archaeologist like her, and then someone said the course was very dull. And the work was difficult to get and it was mainly brushing away microscopic pieces of mud, with great care. Then brushing away some more mud. Then some more . . .'"

Power was looking through the photos. The photocopier had reproduced the colour photos, but some early ones were just in black and white. He shared the pages with Laura. "What do you think? Tell me your impressions."

"When were these pictures taken?" she asked.

They were looking at monochrome photos of a man standing in a rainy street. A thickset man, with combed-over hair swept over heavy brows, all buttoned up in a Mackintosh. The coat seemed too small and he resembled a sausage bulging in its skin, about to explode in a frying-pan. His black shoes looked sharply pointed and they curled slightly at the toes. His mouth smiled but his eyes did not. They seemed small and piggy and cold. Power imagined his brow might have a sheen of perspiration on it. The traffic on the street behind him seemed light. There were bull-nosed Commer vans. Power thought one of the cars with angled rear lights might be a Ford Zephyr. There was a light-coloured Austin Cambridge estate. In the distance, across the street, a sandstone archway with a quadrangle beyond. "I think this looks like the nineteen-sixties," said Power. "How old do you think he is? You're better at ages."

"Late forties, maybe fifties," said Laura. "It's difficult to tell, when you look at people back then, they seemed to look older, younger, if you see what I mean?"

"Maybe the smog, or cigarettes, or surviving the Second World War aged them. Or eating loads of fatty bacon or tripe," said Power. "Do you remember the mounds of tripe in the butchers? Lying there like a pile of white carpet underlay."

"No, I don't remember that," said Laura. "I'm younger than you, remember?"

"You didn't miss anything much," said Power. "Except the Moon Landing. That was good."

"I never saw any of the men on the Moon," said Laura. "It was all over years ago by the time I started school. Did it even really happen? Or was it faked in a film studio."

"I saw it live," protested Power. "I watched Neil Armstrong climb out of the Eagle as I sat on my father's knee." He smiled. "I remember that." He looked at the fat man in the street again. "I don't think I'd like him as my Dad. He looks . . . unpredictable."

They turned the pages. Laura pointed at a colour photo. "Christmas?

Lindow Moss style?" There were three people seated round a kitchen table in the photo. Two wore paper hats. The third person was the man in the black and white photos. He was joined by a much younger, thin woman. She had curly black hair and blue horn-rimmed spectacles. She wore a pearl necklace with a turquoise dress made of some synthetic fabric. There was a child sitting between them. A small boy with round NHS glasses looked directly and challengingly out of the photograph at the observer. Of the three people only the woman wore a smile, and that smile did not reach her eyes. "Has she got a black eye?" asked Laura. The feast on the table in front of them looked sparse. A chicken, rather than a turkey, roast potatoes, and carrots. There were the remains of three pulled crackers on the wooden table, but no other visible signs of Christmas. "Who took the photo?" wondered Laura.

"Maybe the camera was on a timer," said Power. "Dad is sitting a bit away from the others, like he's just sat down after setting the camera."

"He looks like he'd rather be elsewhere."

"To be fair, no-one looks like they want to be there. I wonder if that is Mr Heaney."

"Mr Heaney?" asked Laura.

"The farmhouse is still registered to a Mr Heaney, but Mr Heaney would be over a hundred if he was still alive. I wonder if that's him in the photo?"

"Aren't there neighbours or relatives you could ask?"

"Not a trace. Mind you, the farmhouse is hidden away in the woods. The nearest house is hundreds of yards away. The first house-to-house enquiries have turned nothing up. No one knows anything about who lives there. Everyone kind of assumed it was derelict."

"Maybe it was," said Laura. "Maybe your murderer is a squatter . . . and these photos are just snaps of people who lived there and left years ago."

"Maybe it is a red herring," said Power, peering at the photo again. "I think you're right. The wife has got a black eye. No wonder her smile is fake."

"It can't have been happy there," said Laura. "It feels a bit intrusive looking at these . . ."

"Didn't you say you were curious?"

"Of course – I'm nosey," she said as she turned the page. There were pictures on the next page that were out of focus, askew. A picture of some hens scurrying across the farmyard. A tractor. A rust-pocked Ford Cortina. "The boy took these," she supposed.

They turned the pages, one by one, companionably side by side. Occasionally one would make an observation. Power might say, "Look at this one," or Laura might comment; "They never smile much do they?"

After several pages, Laura asked Power, "Have you noticed there are no school uniform photos? There are always photos of a new school uniform, but as this boy gets older, you never see him in a uniform."

"Maybe he went to a trendy school that banned them," said Power. "Some schools did in the seventies as an experiment in socialism or something."

"No," said Laura. "And look at the photos of his birthday parties. The same three people getting older year by year. Each one has a card with his age on, and a cake, but it's always the same three people at the party. Mum and Dad and their son in the middle. No friends. Ever. No party with his school friends."

"So maybe he didn't go to school?" said Power. "Wouldn't the school attendance officer be round and putting Mr and Mrs Heaney in jail?"

"Or maybe he was schooled at home? And it was all above board," suggested Laura.

"I suspect these people were well off the grid, even before you could be off the grid, even before the grid existed . . ." said Power.

"There was something I read," said Laura. "It's in the study, I'll go and get it." Power watched as she darted into the hall and down to his study. She returned with an old, slim, blue, cloth-covered book. She was leafing through the pages to find the passage she wanted. "Look here it is . . ." and she described what she had found. "This was written about Lindow Common by William Norbury in the eighteen-hundreds – he talks about there being a 'peculiar' race of people who dwelt on the edges of the peat bogs. He felt such people were of a 'very ancient race, totally different from their neighbours' and that they had had marked physical peculiarities and peculiar habits and ways of life. He says 'they are often buck-stealers, poachers and fishermen' and that 'their handicrafts', pointed to them being 'a primitive people' . . . 'using twigs or osiers, in making besoms from birch, also in making straw work, and bee hives'. He talks about them being 'very sly and suspicious' . . . 'apparently very harmless but not so safe as they appeared to be.'"

"He does make them sound like Neanderthals," said Power. The paragraph was familiar to him.

"Well, I agree he talks about them being some kind of throwback, separate from other country folk," said Laura.

"Look at this," said Power, leafing further through the Lindow farm photo album. Laura looked over his shoulder. "The boy seems to have had some kind of accident." There was a picture of the boy in a hammock, between two trees. He was staring with his usual sullen look at the camera. Power wondered whether it was Mr or Mrs Heaney who was taking the photo. The boy had an enamel mug of tea in his hand, rested upon his chest. His other arm was in a sling made of old curtain. Underneath the sling protruded a white plaster cast, which was thick and lumpenly applied to lower arm, extending across wrist and elbow, up to mid upper arm. "I've never seen a cast like that."

"You're not an orthopaedic doctor," chided Laura.

"Still, look at it," said Power. "It's no work of art, and it's across both key joints." He tutted to himself and turned the page.

These were the final pages of photos. One further birthday and one final Christmas photo. Yet these family meals were different. Although all three family members were present, the face of the father had been scored out by the heaviest handed ballpoint pen work. Power imagined the unseen hand clenched with hatred and running back and forth, back and forth, digging into the photo, obliterating forever the face of Mr Heaney from history.

"Well," said Laura. "That was that. What happened to Mr Heaney in real life then?"

"No one knows," said Power. "Yet."

The final picture was a portrait of the son alone, possibly in a city park or square. It was a grainy black and white photo. Power thought the boy looked about sixteen or seventeen. He wore a wispy moustache, and a T-shirt. There seemed to be an unaccustomed grin on his face, evidence of some positive emotion although the smile was a pale, wan thing. In the background was a statue under a masonry canopy. Power recognised it as Prince Albert. "Maybe this is Albert Square in Manchester?" he mused.

"I should imagine there are statues to Albert in every city of the British Empire," said Laura. "But he does look a bit happier, doesn't he? Off to University perhaps?"

"Maybe he never came back," wondered Power. "He flew the lonely nest he'd grown up in and spread his wings on a University course studying computer science or sociology. They were big in the eighties."

"Eighties?"

"Yes," said Power. "There's a figure there in the background – a girl with big hair and a T-shirt with 'Virgin Prunes' on it. Has to be the eighties, I'd say. And the photo album stops there. Maybe he abandoned the farm and his parents."

"Hmm, he always sat next to his Mum in the photos. I don't think he'd abandon her."

"Maybe you're right about that, his body language was closer to her," said Power, putting the photocopies away. "Did he scrub out his father's face? Or did his mother?"

"You think his mother was beaten by his father, and that the son scribbled out his father's face?"

"Yes, that's what I was thinking." said Power. "How did you know?"

"I know you," said Laura. "And I saw you frown when we found the photo of her with a black eye at Christmas."

"Ah, I gave the game away?"

"I can read you. But maybe there's another explanation. Maybe this boy was a difficult child. You think that he was a badly done to child, kept away from the world for all his childhood by his cruel parents. But maybe he was a child who was autistic, who hated other people, who craved the sameness of his family. Maybe he had been violent to other children and maybe he just couldn't function in school."

"I hadn't thought of that," admitted Power. "I just assumed . . ."

"What can we really tell just from the photographs? Maybe the boy had an anger outburst when he was being dressed. Maybe he lashed out with his arms and accidentally hit his mother in the face, causing the black eye, not on purpose. Maybe Dad had nothing to do with it."

"You're right. There could be other explanations. What would I do without you?" said Power.

Laura suddenly kissed him.

A long and passionate kiss.

"What's that for?" he asked.

"Do you want to go to bed?" She slipped a hand into his shirt and stroked his chest.

"My mind is so full of this stuff," said Power. "The things I saw . . ."

"I suppose . . ." she understood what he was saying. "But it's the right time, if you see what I mean."

"I know," said Power. "But everything will happen when the time is right. You worry too much."

"And maybe you don't worry enough," she pulled away. "It's getting so I walk out of shops if I see someone is pregnant. I feel jealous, and I don't like this me that I've become. It isn't happening . . . and I feel it's my body's fault."

He shook his head. "Now isn't the time to go through this . . ." He was suddenly so very tired.

"When? When is the right time, Carl? If you want someone else . . . if you want a child . . . maybe I should stand aside and let you find someone else?"

"Stop! Stop that now. That's not what I want. That is not and never has been the way I feel."

Laura burst into tears. He reached out to her and put an arm round her shoulders. She did not pull away. He drew her to him.

"Come on," he said. "It's late, let's go upstairs."

Side by side, her head on his shoulder, they walked from the kitchen and switched the lights off behind them as they progressed to the stairway. "I'm sorry," she said. "I'm getting all twisted up inside myself." He kissed the top of her head.

She stopped at the foot of stairs. She was frowning. "Oh, I've just thought of something. I'd better say it before I forget. To do with the jars."

"The jars?"

"The Kilner jars you told me about. There are collectors of those jars. I saw a programme on daytime TV that had the collectors on. The jars all have their own characteristics. They changed the manufacturing through the years. You can date the jars to within a few years."

And that having been said, they fell silent as they climbed the stairs together. They did not speak again till morning.

Chapter Five

Inspector Beresford was simultaneously annoyed and panicked. He had misplaced his own Policy File in which he had assiduously been recording all his actions and strategies during the Investigation. He had clasped it to him almost all the way through the many hours he had been at the Lindow crime scene and its Incident Room. He recalled placing it down only once, in his office, when he was taking a phone call from the ACC. When he returned to his office, minutes later, the Policy File was gone. He had racked his brains trying to think if he was mistaken. Had he left it, perhaps, in the farmhouse? He hadn't been in his own car for hours. The book couldn't be there. He wondered about asking the office manager, but he didn't want to appear like an SIO who was not in total control. He dithered. Eventually, he barked out a question to the incident room office. "Who's got my Policy File?" People looked round.

"I've got my own File here," said the Crime Scene Manager.

"Has someone taken it?" asked Beresford. Blank looks all round. Some head shaking. "Has anybody seen someone with it?"

More silence.

The silence enraged Beresford. He was tired and anxiety lent his voice a clipped and bitter tone. "Has anybody noticed anything unusual? Maybe an officer they didn't recognise? There's a lot of folk on this investigation. Has anybody noticed an officer they've never encountered before?"

"I'm sure we're all accounted for," said the office manager, taking the implication that the Incident Room was not secure, very much to heart. "Everyone's signed in and accounted for."

"Erm, there was that man just now," said Alan, the House-to-House co-ordinator. "I thought he was one of the crime scene photographers at first, but now you mention it, I don't think he was. But he didn't particularly look out of place. He didn't seem nervous. He seemed confident."

"Did you challenge him?" asked Beresford. "Ask him what he was doing?"

"No, he looked so assured. I assumed he . . ." Alan's voice trailed off, realising that perhaps he had put his head in a noose of his own making. "I mean everyone must have seen him. I wasn't the only one surely. He went in every room."

"Every room," repeated Beresford. "What did he look like?"

"Tall man, sandy hair. Had an eyepatch."

"A fucking pirate, was he?" Beresford was frustrated and furious. "He's a journalist. Now equipped with every detail of this Inquiry. 'A stranger with an eyepatch'. How much more could he fucking well stand out? Why didn't any of you . . .?"

"I didn't like to challenge him," said Alan. "He was disabled and he looked like he knew what he was doing. I didn't want to appear rude."

"Keep digging your pit, why don't you?" shouted Beresford. "Everybody stop what you're doing. Find him. I want that File back. He can't have gone that far. Go! Now!" The people in the room scattered towards the door. Beresford caught the office manager's arm before they exited. "Except you. Except *you*. I want you to put a team to look through every bit of CCTV footage from the site. I want a picture of this man. There must be some recording of this intruder somewhere. And I want you to get me a new book, or better still, set up something on HOLMES for me to type a replacement file up. Christ! What a day!" Beresford went into his office and slammed the door behind him.

* * *

"I'm meeting a friend here," said Lynch to the landlord of the Dysart Arms. "He probably booked a table for lunch, Professor Power is his name."

The landlord consulted a list behind the bar. "We have a Dr Power booked in at noon. Is that him?"

"Yes," said Lynch. "Typical of him. He doesn't like to use his full title."

"He's already in the snug. Can I get you a drink?"

"I'll see if he wants one too before I order," said Lynch, and ducked next door.

Power was sitting in a wing-backed armchair sipping a Glenrothes whisky. He was reading the *Guardian*, but folded it as soon as he saw Lynch.

He greeted his friend warmly and indicated the pint of fresh bitter he had bought him, which stood on the table. "I took the liberty of ordering a beer for you, I hope you don't mind. You usually do have bitter, and the Dysart keeps a good one."

Lynch was happy with the choice and slumped down in the chair opposite Power. The doctor resumed his seat and folded his newspaper away. "I was going to order Power's whiskey, but you can't get it here. You couldn't get away from the stuff in Dublin, but here . . . no chance."

"How's your day been so far?" asked Lynch.

"I gave a lecture on the diagnosis of affective disorder to students at the University, and then came straight here. I was early so I took a stroll to Bunbury Mill, the watermill, and then round St Boniface's Church. It's a nice little village. Then I thought I'd read the newspapers in the pub. President Bush is visiting his idiot poodle in London. And there's going to be a demonstration against the war. I feel like protesting myself."

"You don't like our Mr Blair much do you?" Lynch grinned.

"No," said Power. "Not at all. Taking the country to war on a tissue of lies."

"But Saddam Hussein needed to go, didn't he?"

"He wasn't worth a war," said Power. His eyes were flashing with annoyance. "If he had really had weapons of mass destruction, well perhaps, but it's blatantly obvious he did not. It was obvious we were being lied to, and I can't bear that. I simply can't."

Lynch decided he didn't want to debate this matter with his friend, and pulled the menu over to himself. "You bought the drinks," he said. "Lunch is on me."

"Mightn't the Foundation afford us a working lunch?" asked Power.

"I never charge food or drink as an expense," said Lynch. "I'll charge travel for big journeys that I can justify are work, but by and large, I avoid using expenses. It's simpler that way. If your employers ever want to get rid of you, they always look at your expenses . . ."

"Hmm . . ." said Power, looking over the menu. "Well let's limit it to a main course then, if the Foundation isn't stumping up." He chose the vegetarian option, as ever, which was a cauliflower and sweet potato biryani with lime pickle. Lynch returned to the bar to order this along with scampi and chips for himself.

When Lynch returned, Power went back to the theme of the Iraq War. Lynch hoped just to listen, in restrained silence.

"We are being lied to all the time," Power said, warming to his theme. "That poor man, the weapons inspector, who was supposed to have killed himself, what was his name?"

"Dr David Kelly," said the detective, then took a deep draught of his beer to mull over as Power launched into a tirade.

"Yes, Kelly. When they were spinning this tale about Weapons of Mass Destruction, he pipes up as a UN weapons inspector and gives evidence that there were no nuclear weapons, no biological weapons, no gas and no other weapons or missiles that can reach us in minutes. And then he's threatened with the sack and losing his pension, for nothing more than telling the truth. And then he disappears. Conveniently. And dies 'by his own hand'. Again conveniently."

"He was a quiet man," said Lynch softly. "A conscientious man. Plunged into the spotlight, unwillingly. He foresaw ruin. Surely he ended his life while 'the balance of his mind was disturbed', as they say."

"That is what we are meant to believe," said Power. "That in July he goes to a beauty spot and he lies down, cuts his wrist, and fades away from all the stresses and strains of public life. Kelly had no history of past psychiatric illness. It is very rare for someone to develop a severe suicidal depression aged fifty-nine. It makes no sense to me, for various reasons medical and psychiatric. Like the way he is said to have cut his wrist, using his non-dominant hand." It occurred to Power that all this talk of the cutting of arteries was far from the best of appetizers, when the lunch they were both looking forward to would shortly be making an appearance and he hastened to say, ". . . but enough of that." And then more jovially, "better to worry about things we can change rather than things we cannot."

Lynch had heard Power's reply, but his mind was really still focused on the word 'depression'.

"Carl, I wonder, changing the subject . . . I wonder if you could pop in some time and see . . . my wife?"

Power looked puzzled for a moment. Lynch's comment didn't seem to fit with his deconstruction of the current news. Power struggled to understand. "See Pamela?"

"I'm a bit worried about her. I'm sorry, you mentioned depression before, and it reminded me that I needed to ask you about her."

"You think she's depressed?"

"I know she is," said Lynch. "Pamela's been depressed before. When our son died. For months and months. She just sat, staring at the wall. She's been like that again, sitting on her bed, staring ahead, not moving for hours."

"I didn't know that, I'm sorry."

"I get home and the house is quiet, still, and dark. Sometimes I put music on, to cure her like David helped Saul, but I don't think she hears it."

"I'd be glad to come round in the next few days," said Power.

"Good," said Lynch. "Now, I don't want to talk about it any more. Or it gets me down too." He looked out of the pub window for a moment and gathered himself. "I could tell you about the news in our current case, couldn't I?"

"If it helps?" said Power.

At this moment their food arrived, interrupting their conversation as it was placed, steaming before them. Power smiled. His stomach had been rumbling at least half an hour whilst he awaited Lynch's arrival. Lynch's blue eyes watched appraisingly as Power picked up his knife and fork.

"Laura's tip," said Lynch. "About the Kilner jars. Proved to be excellent advice. Such apparently insignificant details can be key in these kind of investigations. You can tell her Inspector Beresford was very grateful for the hint. Of course, I'm sure somebody on the team would have stumbled on it eventually, or maybe not . . . The type of jar has a very long history, back to Victorian times." Lynch watched Power's onslaught into the food slowly subside as he thought back to the contents of the jars from the cellar. Power's chewing didn't halt altogether, but he suddenly looked rather pensive. For a moment the future of the cauliflower and sweet potato biryani seemed in doubt, and then he steadied himself and began to eat again. Lynch continued, "The jars had a Ravenhead mark as well as the usual Kilner mark. This marking was only present for a short while during the jars' long history. So we can perhaps assume that none of the bottled body parts were from before nineteen seventy-seven. And we know that the body parts are all human too. Almost exclusively pudenda at that, both sexes."

These last few words sealed the fate of Power's cauliflower and sweet potato biryani. Power pushed the plate away and took a sip of table water and mused for a moment on the word that Lynch had chosen. Pudenda. A singularly odd word. An image of rows of shiny jars with what looked like grooved pink cling peaches inside. Strange fruit. 'By their fruits shall ye know them', Power wondered?

Power's eye was caught by a sudden movement outside the window to his right. He raised himself out of the chair to peer outside.

"What is it?" asked Lynch. He looked outside into the garden in front of the pub but could see nothing himself.

Power shook his head, "I thought I saw a figure outside, someone looking in at me. I'm sorry."

"Maybe they recognised you from the news," said Lynch as he speared another ball of scampi. "Pamela saw you on the six-thirty local news. Film of you walking about at the crime scene."

Power dimly remembered the journalists calling to him as he wandered about trying to find the farmhouse. "I don't need publicity of any kind," he said. "I don't want to be recognised. I don't want any more cranks or stalkers, thank you," and more vainly, "I hope I didn't look vague or stupid. I didn't quite know where I was going."

"Pamela said you looked very thoughtful," said Lynch. "It was one of the only comments she made to me all day. Anyway, the detail about the jars does let us date the crimes until some time after nineteen seventy-seven."

"I'm sure that's not much help," said Power. He watched as Lynch polished off the last of the scampi with a dollop of tartare sauce. His own part-finished plate stood as a testament to his squeamishness. Power explored the remnants of his own hunger and wondered if he could eventually stomach a pudding when his thoughts resolved themselves. Perhaps if he finished the gruesome details with Lynch he could then stabilise his queasiness and face the second half of the meal. He gathered his courage, "Did they drain the Black Lake?"

"They have both drained and dredged it," said Lynch. "And the latest tally is five heads, three hands and seven feet. Each head was garotted. The twine was still in place. They have even catalogued the type of knot he used. Possibly some more body parts have been missed. Maybe more will turn up. They were pretty thorough, though. Nothing adds up. I mean, nothing does. There are no full sets, and too many examples of certain parts. The jars, for instance, reach into dozens. Well, there aren't dozens of heads to match up. It's like the farm was a junkyard for body parts. Like a motor scrapyard with three engines from Minis, ten right doors from Morris Minors and two left doors from Ford Sierras. Incredibly complex. Poor Beresford. The case of a lifetime, and he feels, well, overwhelmed, but he can't afford to show any weakness or they will simply take it from him.

"For example, yesterday he asked me how I managed to cope with interference from the ACC, ringing up morning, noon and night. I answered that when I had a difficult case and I got pressure from a superior officer I just spoke to his superior in turn. Beresford asked me if I meant I spoke to the Home Secretary and I said no, I prayed to God. He has no superior. Well, it helped me face the pressures, but Beresford gave me an odd look. I wasn't mocking him, though. I was being sincere. Prayer does help."

"I hope we can help Beresford ourselves," said Power. "This kind of pressure can profit your career or sink it. Are they making any enquiries of local undertakers? Has anybody noticed . . . anything missing?"

"Why do you ask?"

"Maybe the son worked at an undertakers. That would give access to bodies in the embalming process. I ask because you say that the number of parts exceeds the number of bodies that have been found. As you said, things don't add up. So where would he find the . . . excuse the term . . . spare parts? We might not like to acknowledge death in our society, but undertakers are there all the time, amongst us. And this might be the source."

"I'm sure somebody will have followed that line of enquiry," said Lynch. He saw that Power had raised his eyebrows at that assumption. "I will check," he said, without making eye contact. "They have been making some enquiries in the local area. Even when prompted with the photographs from the family album the local houseowners do not recall either of the parents. Mind you, they are all young professionals. They aren't local people who have been in the area for years. Goodness knows where the old types that lived here have been spirited away to. You know, farmers, workers, people like that. I suppose none of them can afford houses round there any more. One home owner, of a gargantuan house, is a footballer from Manchester City, just aged twenty-four. High walls, locked gates. He has a Polish housekeeper who says he's hardly ever there. There's this spotless house with a swimming pool almost the size of a football field. The house is empty apart from her, all day, every day.

"One of Beresford's officers, reasoning that the occupant of the farmhouse must use some public transport, especially if he didn't have a car, went and spent some time at the railway station talking to the commuters. No joy. Then he hung around the bus stops at rush hour.

And one woman, in her twenties, said she had seen the son. She recognised him from the photos. She has even spoken to him."

Power suddenly seemed to focus acutely on Lynch's last words. "Tell me. What's he like?"

"This young woman works part-time in a firm of solicitors. Fifteen hours a week. An office girl in Manchester, Miss Ellis. Gets the bus on the road near the farmhouse around lunchtime to get in to work in the afternoons. She saw him a few times at the stop. He looked to be in his twenties or early thirties. At first, she said, he ignored her. Then once, when the bus to Manchester was delayed, he picked up the courage to speak to her. She described him as tall, about six foot two, and with a kind of stoop. She said he 'loomed' over her. When he had the confidence to speak, he came too close. He didn't smile. He didn't make eye contact. She said he smelt 'musty'. He was clean, though; tidy, dressed in a T-shirt and jeans and with a grey canvas rucksack over one shoulder. He spoke softly and he said that as the bus probably wasn't coming would she like to come back for a coffee? He didn't say where."

"Did she?" asked Power.

"Maybe she wouldn't be alive if she had done," said Lynch. "She said no; that if she missed the bus she would be late for work and that people would really mind. He blushed, apparently. Then she saw the bus down the road in the distance and he moved away. She got on the bus and sat deliberately close to the bus driver. He went to the back. She never saw him again."

"She met him once," said Power. "Passed a few words in conversation, and yet she still remembers it. She was afraid and no doubt the emotion anchored her memory. On the surface, his words could be taken as friendliness or even an attempt to make a pass at her, but she sensed something deeper, and she has it burned into her memory. Did she not see him again at the bus stop?"

"Never again," said Lynch. "Maybe he realised that he was hunting too close to home. Maybe he became more afraid of her than she was of him. Maybe he avoided the bus stop or changed the times he travelled."

"When I was lecturing to the medical students, this was some years ago, I videotaped an interview with a man who was thought disordered. It's where language is all fractured and disrupted. Someone once described it as 'word salad'. Well, I was all fired up because I had got this video to show them the most perfect example of thought disorder. And I was showing it off in a lecture about how to examine people with psychosis. But I noticed something about their reactions. Some of the male students just laughed at it, at him. They thought the man, in his illness, was just funny. They probably went on to be orthopaedic surgeons . . . but the reaction amongst some of the female students was different. They weren't laughing at the word salad. (I mean as in the concept of *wortsalat*, by Forel, which he was exhibiting). The female students watching him looked worried or frightened. And I asked them why. They said that the patient made them uncomfortable. I looked at the tape – his eyes were focused on me. It was a video of me interviewing him. Just two people sitting in armchairs together. He was staring at me, eyes like the glass eyes of a teddy bear. No expression on his face. Muttering away with a kind of paranoid intensity, using odd words, neologisms, like 'albigisty'. I couldn't see what was frightening about him, but I was focused on the academic beauty of his thought disorder. They were tuned in to something else altogether."

"And your point is?" Lynch was looking at the dessert menu. Somehow both he and Power had conveniently discarded the idea of confining themselves to one course.

"He skipped the hospital the next day after my lecture. Moved back home to London. Some further contacts with services and psychiatrists down there. Then he developed some odd ideas about his poor mother. Specifically, that she was a witch. Delusions arose about her evil nature. And he merged these with some Bible quote about not letting witches live."

"Exodus 22.18," said Lynch automatically.

"Anyway, the next I heard of him he was in a secure unit after he had murdered his mother."

"What are you saying?"

"That like the females in my lecture, watching the video and being alarmed by this patient, Miss Ellis picked something up about Mr Heaney, some non-verbal clue that wasn't right. Some little thing that warned her. She protected herself too by saying that she would be missed immediately. That would alarm him."

"You mean she used the fabled female intuition?" asked Lynch. "Are you being sexist now?"

"Guilty as charged," said Power. The waiter was hovering, waiting for their potential dessert order and after Lynch reeled off his choice, Power pointed at random to a dessert on the menu and the waiter nodded approvingly.

"Well, Laura's hint about the Kilner jars was useful," said Lynch.

Power grunted in response. "I'd like to go and see the farm again," he said. "Get the feel of the place, now it's less busy, I presume?"

"It will be, relatively speaking," said Lynch. "The park round the Lake is re-opened. The dog walkers are back. The incident trailers are about to be taken away. The incident room itself has moved back to HQ. The farm is screened off though, and guarded. We don't want the reporters filing inside and turning it into a shrine celebrated on the Internet for everybody to visit."

"If it's quiet now, then a re-visit would be useful, I think."

"All the evidence has been taken away, though," said Lynch.

"But the place," said Power. "You can appreciate how people might have thought and felt if you spend some time there. See things from their point of view."

The desserts arrived. Lynch smiled at the sight of a sticky toffee pudding surrounded by a moat of custard. Power's fruit salad of strawberries and pineapple was topped by candied fennel. He tasted it and sighed with pleasure. "Bliss," he said. And he was silent until he had enjoyed the last mouthful of fennel-flavoured syrup.

"Did the DNA tests show anything?" asked Power after a while.

"Absolute confusion," said Lynch. "As you might expect from a crime scene where there were so many victims. The jars . . . all the DNA in them is novel. No traces for them. There are many fresh traces of a male in the house, and older traces still of a male and female, related to him. A confusing welter of them all, as you would get in a family house. We assume they were his mother and father. So it would seem that the son – the one in the family album, was living in the farmhouse. Possibly on his own. And other less frequent traces in the house, in the downstairs and basement. Mainly female. Possibly from spilled bodily fluids. And some faint traces on crockery. Maybe he had entertained his victims to a cup of coffee beforehand? Upstairs . . . well there wasn't much left to test from some rooms after the air crash, things were scattered and burned, so we don't know about DNA in the bedrooms, on the sheets and so forth . . ."

"What happened to the mother and father?" asked Power. "You said older traces . . . how old? Are they both dead?"

"You'd know more about DNA than me, Carl. Forensics can use DNA from fifty years ago. In the Boston Strangler case I believe they used DNA from the nineteen-sixties. Of course, DNA degrades with time, but the half-life of DNA is around five hundred years. But we are focused primarily on the son. And this man is very much a lone wolf, living his solitary life, following his own code in his own ways," said Lynch. "Don't you think he's a loner? How could he hide his murderous ways from a mother? The jars, and a freezer full of human meat. He has been brooding alone and hunting alone for years. No, he's a loner and has been for years. Mothers know if you do the least little thing wrong; at least mine did." Lynch chuckled to himself.

"Did he kill Mum and Dad?" wondered Power. "Or did he kill Dad because he was beating up Mum?"

"You're speculating again," said Lynch. "Dad probably died of old age."

"Is there a death certificate?"

"No," conceded Lynch, grudgingly.

"Did the body parts in the Lake or house match the father's DNA? Did any of the DNA of the dead people appear to be related to the son?"

"No," said Lynch. "No, they didn't."

"So," Power asked, as much of himself as anybody. "What did he do with his parents?"

Chapter Six

The Lynch family had lived in the suburban village of Handbridge for years. Andrew Lynch had bought the house when his family was young. A conservative semi-detached house with three bedrooms had nurtured them all through his career as he steadily rose through the police ranks. He had never been an ambitious man, but his superiors had always deemed his meticulous detective work worthy of reward, despite the absence of any quest for favour. In truth, his superiors were sometimes in awe of him. They found his religious faith curious and daunting at times, although Lynch was scrupulously careful never to make any show of virtue of it. When he had retired from the force his annual salary had been over £70,000, and yet he had never sought to move from the same suburban house, behind its neatly trimmed privet hedge.

Handbridge was a polite and genteel village, separated from the city of Chester by the River Dee. Many of its houses were quarried from the same red sandstone that the Romans had used to build Chester's city walls. The Romans had worshipped their gods there, with temples to Minerva. Nowadays, there was a large bank headquarters overlooking the river, a modern day temple to Mammon. The Welsh called the village *Treboeth*, the burnt town, as they had torched it many a time trying to invade Chester over the bridge. Later, during the Civil

War, Handbridge had been burned to the ground again and the bridge destroyed, to impede the progress of the New Model Army, who then had to march ten miles upstream to ford the river.

Lynch lived on Meadows Lane, across from the green playing fields of a High School, which his daughter had once attended. Nearby there was a tavern and a Chinese takeaway, but Lynch never went to either. On Sundays he would walk through the village to the Old Dee Bridge and climb up through the city streets to the Cathedral itself. His wife, not sharing his religious zeal, would lie in bed reading the Sunday papers until she rose to put the family lunch on. Such had been the weekly pattern for decades, through the childhood and teenage years of their only daughter, and continuing long after she left home for University.

Power parked his old Saab on the road. It being a Saturday there was a game of hockey being played between school and visitors on the fields opposite Lynch's house. Power watched the game in the distance somewhat absent-mindedly, then shook his head and made his way to the white render and red-brick villa that Lynch called home. He squeezed his way between a privet hedge and Lynch's battleship like Audi and rang the doorbell.

Lynch answered the doorbell, pulling the white front door wide open. He was dressed in a thick pullover and dark blue jeans. Power had rarely seen Lynch dressed in anything other than the sharpest pinstripe suit. Lynch wore a smile and seemed expansively welcoming. His eyes betrayed an inner anxiety, though.

Lynch showed his friend into the front room and gently, and silently, withdrew, closing the door softly behind him.

Mrs Lynch was sitting in semi-darkness. The curtains were half-closed. A thin shaft of light percolated through the velvet of the curtains. Dust danced in the sunlight. The motes of dust were the only things that seemed to be moving in the room. Mrs Lynch sat immobile in a green moquette-covered armchair in the corner. She stared at some point in front of her, seeing nothing. Her face was drained of colour and her brow was furrowed.

Dr Power took a place on the sofa by the television. He absorbed the scene and the atmosphere in the room. There was a tray of untouched sandwiches and a half-full glass of orange juice on a side table by her chair. The air felt still and strangled. He began to feel anxious. There was a sense of silent, stony panic and despair that radiated from her, and seemingly had transmitted itself to him.

When she spoke it startled him. "So he's asked you to see me?"

"He was worried," explained Power.

"I won't do anything. I don't know why he's worried about me. It's me that's worried about him," she said.

"What are you worried about?" asked Power. Through his shoes he could feel how soft and deep the pale blue-green carpet was. He wondered if his shoes were clean.

"I feel everything is . . . very mortal, and I feel that Andrew is running out of luck." She looked deeply into Power's eyes. "The things you both get up to," she said. "I used to reassure myself that although he was dealing with dangerous men – criminals – he was part of something bigger, part of an organisation, something that could cope. So if he was in trouble, he could just pick up the phone and call for backup. Armed Response or whatever. And now, there seems to be just the two of you. Working on your own."

"We have reserves, the Foundation can commission support and help for us."

"But it's not on tap, is it? It needs arranging. Andrew gets into trouble and who's going to come running?" She gave him an appraising look. Power was young enough, but he was no fighter. She didn't need to say more. "He has responsibilities to me, and to our daughter." She looked at Power again and said nothing. Power was acutely aware that she meant to contrast Lynch and his family with Power's own unmarried childlessness. He felt like protesting that he and Laura very much wanted a child, but Power wasn't sure who he was protesting to.

"What does Andrew say, when you raise these concerns with him?"

"What he always says; that he fears no evil for the Lord walks with him. He says it that often, that even this heathen body knows he's quoting Psalm 23. Well, the Lord may walk with Andrew Lynch and comfort him, but He doesn't comfort his wife." Her voice was as bitter as wormwood. Power saw her hands were trembling and, seeing that he saw, she hid them under a blanket she had round her knees.

"How are you sleeping?" he asked.

"What sleep?" she countered. "I don't sleep. I dream of telephone calls bearing bad news and I wake in panic. I see the dawn through my bedroom curtains every day."

"And your appetite?" asked Power. "Are you enjoying your food?"

"Food tastes of nothing these days, but then, I can't be bothered to cook and Andrew has never aspired to more than boiling an egg." Lynch had always enjoyed his wife, Pamela's, good home cooking, and she had always sent him forth from their house smartly besuited and with a silk handkerchief in his jacket.

"Are you losing weight?"

"Who cares? Probably." Power thought Pamela looked thinner than he had ever seen her. Her hair was too long and hardly combed at all.

"What do you like to do during the day? Do you enjoy doing anything?"

"Nothing. I look at the wall, and time passes. I don't know how it passes so quickly. But it does. Hours go by and I have not moved."

"What do you find yourself thinking about?"

"Nothing mostly. Sometimes I think of Bobby." Bobby was the Lynch's son who had died in childhood. "He would be a man now. I suppose I'll never have to worry about him the way I've worried about Andrew."

"How did he die?" asked Power.

"A cancer in his kidney. Something like William's tumour."

"Wilm's tumour?" suggested Power.

"Clever doctor. It doesn't matter what it's called though, does it? It did its wicked work without ever knowing its name. I remember when Bobby was four he complained of a headache one day. He came in from playing in the garden with Katy Smith. I put a hand on his forehead and he seemed to be running a temperature. I thought it was too much sun, or some virus. I put him to bed with children's paracetamol and a glass of lemon. I thought it would get better overnight, but it got worse. It never settled. And then we brought in the doctors. He never went outside to play with Katy again. I heard all these new words; ultrasounds, and CAT scans, and staging, and vincristine, and doxorubicin. And I always promised him that some new treatment would do the trick and cure him. Most children with Wilm's get better, but my Bobby didn't. But nothing shakes Andrew's faith. He just keeps on going," she said angrily and quoted lines she'd heard from Lynch. "He persists like Job, constant in the Lord, despite a plague of boils in his life ..."

"You are still angry," said Power.

"I'm sorry to still be so angry with . . . everyone. I wish I wasn't; I wish that I could forgive and move on. But I can't forget and forgive anyone."

"Including yourself?" asked Power.

"Everyone, including myself," she said. "I . . . I can't take any more losses."

"When did you last feel well? When did you last feel that you could cope?"

"I don't know, months ago. I thought it would wear off, but it hasn't. Are you going to write me a prescription for a legion of little pills to fight my depression?"

Power grunted, "Well . . ."

"I thought so. Men like their neat little solutions, don't they? How can your pills help fill a gap inside me?"

"It wouldn't be just antidepressants to help you, although they work far better than people suppose. I think, maybe if I find the right person for you to talk to, over several sessions, to explore some of the feelings that you have held so close inside all this time . . ."

* * *

Lynch was in his den at the back of the house. He had decided to occupy himself with the case whilst Power was seeing his wife. As ever, Lynch was using the opportunity to work as a distraction, a form of occupational therapy. He sat in a comfortable Ercol Windsor easy chair from the nineteen-sixties. Its upholstery was shamefully threadbare, but Lynch felt it was the most comfortable chair in Christendom. The den held a gothic oak bookcase, a roll-top desk, and a pinboard with maps and Post-it notes all over it. There was a simple wooden cross on the wall opposite the chair. Lynch sat with a phone receiver clamped to his ear. The phone cable led to a squat device with an aerial that was plugged into his home telephone socket. A voice on the other end of the phone line was lecturing Lynch on the whys and wherefores of the device – where he could use it, under what circumstances and what the arrangements were for use of the contract that the Foundation now had with the contact at GCHQ.

The voice at the other end seemed interminable, squeaky and obsessed with its own importance and the intricate detail of the scrambling device. "Every analogue audio wave is digitized and encrypted at the same time. The salt is changed every time the device handshakes with the GCHQ mainframe, and is altered every ten seconds. The system is altogether impenetrable, even though it uses the public telephone infrastructure. The dual contact with the aerial means that we can, if necessary, randomly alter the salt. If we need to go to this altogether higher level of encryption the little red light will flash and you have just three seconds to confirm you are still present and key in your PIN. Failure to do so and the contact will cease and not be resumed until you are verified, in person, at a GCHQ regional office." Lynch remembered the baffling interview he had endured in Liverpool. "You won't want that inconvenience, so keep an eye out for that light at all times. If you need more than two personal verification interviews at a regional centre your security clearance will be revoked permanently."

Lynch felt altogether daunted by the security, but then he felt daunted by online banking. It had taken him three months to arrange a service level agreement with GCHQ and this feat had been described as a 'miracle' by a Home Office minister who at first had dismissed the possibility altogether. But the Foundation's sponsor was not only extremely rich, but also extremely powerful and had, at his command, the global resources and contacts that only very few individuals on earth were blessed with. The Foundation sponsor, Mr Howarth-Weaver, was also blessed with infinite patience, and had worn down every opposition to his Foundation securing ministerial level access to the most classified information system available. Only the Secretary of State and the Prime Minister were said to have higher levels of access. Even so, thought Lynch, the Service would not part with all its secrets, elected officials may accord themselves great pomp, but elected officials always come and go, while the Service and its secrets endure.

"The Foundation is, of course, most grateful," said Lynch diplomatically, as he tried to interrupt the torrent of technical information. "Maybe we can pause, just to introduce ourselves? My name is Andrew Lynch, I wondered . . ."

"I can't introduce myself," said the voice. "Protocol. It will, of course, usually be me that you talk to over the next six months, then another officer will take over. That's just routine to avoid any problems of bias or favouritism."

Lynch thought the male voice had an educated, London accent, maybe Indian parentage, he wondered. Perhaps early thirties? He wanted to try and form a working relationship, but this seemed the thinnest of possibilities.

"And you mentioned your name just now, that's not done I'm afraid. You must use a Service handle if you use anything, but not your name. Never your real name."

"I'm sorry," said Lynch. "But if we are on an encrypted line . . .?"

"Layers of security may save your life. May save other contacts' lives. For your information your Service handle is Dovedale."

"What if I don't like Dovedale as a handle," asked Lynch. "What if I want something a bit, well, more me."

"It's a randomly generated name. It's not meant to be 'you', to avoid compromising your identity. A long time ago agents might be given names their handler dreamt up, like Olivier for someone who was an actor, after famous thespian Laurence Olivier, you know?"

'I know," said Lynch, and tried not to sigh.

"Or perhaps handlers used some kind of in-joke or humour in dreaming up a contact's name . . . well that humour can be guessed. Knowing the handle, Olivier, might lead others to second guess it referred to an actor. So Dovedale is it for you."

"Oh," said Lynch, without enthusiasm.

"So now, I think we should check the failsafe – do you see the red light blinking on the interface?"

"Yes," said Lynch as a small red light started blinking by the side of a numerical key pad on the top of the device.

"Well, don't just look at it, you've got three seconds to input your PIN."

Three seconds is not long to recall or retrieve a keycode and punch it in. As Lynch completed the task, the red light stopped blinking. He half expected an empty line when he asked, "Are you still there?"

"Yes," said the voice at the other end. "2.9 seconds, Dovedale. Not bad, considering it is your first time."

"Don't do that again, please," said Lynch.

"Can happen randomly at any time, as well as when your handler wishes to challenge you. So be prepared, Dovedale."

Lynch swallowed his irritation. "I would like to ask for a 'Pattern of Life' analysis on a suspect in a murder case. Can we proceed?"

"Can't the police information officer on the case help you?"

"I know precisely how good or how bad such officers are," said

Lynch. "They are inevitably slow, whatever their competence level. Weeks."

"A pattern of life analysis. OK. Well, we do have a superior system to HOLMES2, I have to admit. Ours is called CALIBAN for future reference. I will need the name, date of birth, address and any telephone or vehicle details please."

"This is a man who lives off the grid, who was born to parents who lived off the grid."

"Do you think we need a challenge, Dovedale?"

Lynch continued as if he had not heard. "The surname is Heaney, probably, we're not one hundred per cent sure. His age would be around late twenties or even early thirties." Lynch then gave the address of the farm near the Dark Lake.

"Christ, could you be more vague about someone? Twenties or thirties? Probably Heaney. Not even a first name?"

Lynch frowned, but his displeasure could not be seen by the handler on the other end of the phone. "I'm sorry if the details are a little sketchy; it's why I have asked for your help."

There was a pause. "It is curious, Dovedale. Curiouser and curiouser. It is highly unusual. What detail we don't have on this individual is remarkable."

Lynch was not clear if his handler already had a summoned file in front of him. "Don't you need time to check? To verify the known unknowns to paraphrase Mr Rumsfeld?"

"Well, you were correct in preferring the Service to the police intelligence officers. We are much quicker. We have a 'Pattern of Life' program that is very fine compared to theirs. There is a file on a Mr Heaney in his twenties. His first name is Joel. I have a date of birth for you; 4th May 1979. I have no place of birth recorded other than his home address. No hospital birth. His mother, who is, or was called Mary, drew child benefit for him until he was sixteen. He attended a local primary school in a town called Wilmslow, for two years. If he attended secondary school there is no record. Maybe home schooled, but no Local Authority Record of this. I have a National Insurance Number for him, which is DI 573888. But there are no NI contributions associated with that number. He has never worked or he uses a different NINO. I have no GP health records to access. There is nothing at the Criminal Records Bureau, he does not have a passport and has never applied for one, he has no driving licence, the property has no television licence or insurance cover. He has no entry on the electoral roll. He has no bank account associated with that name or address. He has no credit card and no credit reference status. The property is still registered to his father, Arthur, at the Land Registry, and Arthur's name was used for the local council tax authority. I have nothing from the insurance fraud bureau, there never has been any telephone landline registered there. The property's water, electricity, and gas use, does reveal some consumption. However, light use of electricity and possibly heavy use of the water – maybe there is a leak, or has been, as it's an old property. There is no vehicle associated with Joel.

"There is no meta data file associated with a mobile phone and usually we can look forward to everybody's details like the date, time, and duration of calls over the past two years, plus details of all movements with an accuracy of a few hundred metres, and payment details, so we can link the phone to an address, bank or credit card.

"The absence of all data that would make this man someone we would normally be interested in if we thought there was a terrorist connection. I mean, the absence itself of the data is highly suspicious. Will you keep us informed about this individual?"

"Don't worry, you'll get to know," said Lynch, thinking of the story which was swirling around in the media. To date it had been difficult to keep the more gruesome details out of the press, nevertheless, the most unsavoury details including the sheer numbers of victims were inevitably bound to break soon.

"Thank you for your help, we now have a few more details thanks to you, and it is helpful to have some of the known unkn . . ."

"Please don't allude to that clown Rumsfeld again," interrupted the voice, shutting down Lynch's quote about Iraq from the previous year. "Now, if that's all, I will bid you good day, Dovedale."

"Bye," said Lynch. The machine hummed as it turned itself to standby mode and then Lynch disconnected it and packed it away methodically. He thought how the CALIBAN program has condensed what once would have been weeks of police work into a few seconds. And yet its results had only intensified the mystery of Joel Heaney. In his short life Heaney had left so few traces that he might have been a wisp of blue-grey smoke, twisting and curling in the air.

There was a knock on the door, it opened and Power's head

appeared round it. "Finished?" He had purposefully waited until he heard the murmur of Lynch's voice saying goodbye.

"Yes," said Lynch. "The man we seek is called Joel, Joel Heaney, and he is little more than a ghost. No substance to him at all. He was born at the farm and he has lived a life, and that is about all we can say about him. There the trail goes cold. I have never encountered a person, or a family, like this in my entire career. It must have been a conscious decision by the family to avoid everything in officialdom. A decision to hide him away, taken at the beginning of his life, by his parents. And what kind of monster have they bred?" And then he brought his attention to his friend and returned to the main source of his worry. "Enough of all that. I was just filling in the time, while you . . . how is Pamela? Will she be all right?"

"Yes," said Power. "At least I hope so. She is very depressed, though. But people with depression usually recover, if they are properly treated. We have agreed a way forward together. Pamela will begin treatment; medicine and talking therapy. I will arrange it with her GP's assent. Belt and braces."

Lynch's whole body seemed to relax. "I've been so worried," he said.

"You worry about her and she worries about you," chuckled Power.

"What can I do to help?" asked Lynch.

Power thought for a moment. "Think of some things you can do together, spend some time together relaxing." A thought crossed Power's mind as he wondered whether to tell his friend to shut down the Foundation he had just started building and to retire early, because his wife was petrified for his safety, but he decided that might be meddling too much, and he wondered whether retirement would ever suit Lynch. Some well-intentioned advice can have unforeseen consequences. Power did, however, decide against telling Lynch where he was proposing to drive after seeing Mrs Lynch, in the certain knowledge that if he did Lynch would insist upon accompanying him.

As Power was just about to leave he espied a small colour photograph on Lynch's desk, it was of a four-year-old boy with blue eyes, and a cherubic and beaming face. "Is that Bobby?" he asked.

"It is," said Lynch, who looked at the face thoughtfully. "That's him. His birthday is this month. Um . . . yes." He nodded. "Ah well."

"Do you have a picture of your daughter?" asked Power.

"Jenny? Yes, in the kitchen, I think. Taken somewhere like an ashram, I think."

Power nodded, but made no comment.

* * *

It took him the best part of an hour to get back to the shattered farmhouse. He drove up the overgrown driveway to find a police constable waiting for him under an umbrella, which dripped relentlessly under the remorseless rainfall.

The drive over had been conducted under this same endless downpour of rain. Power had watched water trickle in at a corner of the venerable Saab's windscreen as he drove. A tiny rivulet of water had trickled over the dashboard and drips plopped onto the sodden footwell carpet. Power had wondered about getting a new car, a present to himself. He had mused on how this would be safer for any child passenger, then felt a wrenching feeling in his belly as if a serrated knife were being twisted round and round. Sometimes the thought of not having children affected him this way. It was all right if he didn't think about it, but his mind had tricked him into wondering about child safety in the battered Saab and this had started a cascade of thoughts. The thought of starting the formal process of medical investigations into their infertility flickered into his mind and he tried to snuff out the flame of its existence. He couldn't bear the finality of any findings. He was trying to switch such thoughts off when he had turned the Saab into the farm's driveway.

The police officer motioned to Power to stop the car some thirty yards or so from the farmhouse door. He came over to the driver's window. Power wound it down. Rain spattered into his face. "Professor Power," he said. "I arranged to come round. I spoke to Inspector Beresford, the SIO."

The officer leant down to talk. His face was craggy, and a five o'clock shadow obscured his chin. His breath smelt of coffee. "Ah yes, Professor Power, you want to look around the property. I can let you in, but I can't accompany you. Someone has to stay outside to watch the perimeter. The journalists and glory hunters are pretty non-stop. Wanting to get inside for photographs, and maybe take away a souvenir of the murders. Can you believe people?"

Power climbed out of the car and locked it. Together, Power and the officer hurried under the shelter of the vast awning that covered the property.

"I suppose," said Power, "that the farmhouse will be pulled down eventually."

"I think it will be razed to the ground before the end of the year," said the officer. "Like the terraced house that the West's had in Gloucester. Although it won't stop the sickos. They have bus loads visiting the site of West's house, and there's nothing there but flattened ground. You know they found nine more women beneath the West's house when they were demolishing it? And now they have tourists. Black Tourism they call it. The people flock round like flies. They'll do the same here, when the truth gets out. I think it should be demolished right away."

"I went to Berlin for a holiday last year with my partner," said Power thoughtfully. "We went past a group of people just standing in a muddy car park, listening to a tour guide. Later on I found out the grotty car park was the site of Hitler's bunker. It's become like a shrine for some people." Power looked at the officer who was pale and shivering slightly. "Are you all right?" Power asked.

"Could be better," said the officer. "This place creeps me out. The silence. And knowing what went on. On this side of the property the trees have grown up round the place like Sleeping Beauty, all along the drive. You can't see anybody till they're almost on top of you. On the other side, where the trees were burned by the plane crash; they've built a high fence so the place can't be seen or photographed. So there's only one way up to the farmhouse, along the driveway, and muggins is covering it." He produced a door key and flourished it. "Here you are. Do you know how long you will be in there?" He unlocked the door and it swung open.

"I don't know," said Power. "I'm not even sure what I am looking for, but last time I was here, I couldn't really focus – the place was so crowded. So I'm hoping a bit of time in there, with peace to think, will help."

"I will be out here. Make sure you switch the lights on in there. It's very gloomy at the best of times."

"Don't worry. I'll switch every light on that I can find."

"Two things, before you go in. One. There's a blanket rule that no cameras or smartphones are allowed on the property. And secondly, I'm afraid that I have to lock you in. Protocol. The SIO says . . ."

"You mean DI Beresford?"

"Yes sir, the SIO, DI Beresford, doesn't want any photos taken by anybody. There are some hacks offering over £60,000 for good quality shots."

"You want me to leave my phone with you?" asked Power reluctantly.

"If you wouldn't mind," the officer sounded apologetic, and Power handed the phone over with an appearance of good grace.

And with that the officer pocketed Power's phone in his jacket and pressed the Velcro tab securely over it. Power went into the mouth of the doorway. Did he want to be locked in here? And he thought of all the times he had gone into locked wards and prison cells and had the door locked behind him. Of all the threats he had braved, he had never felt like this on the threshold of the Heaney house. The officer saw Power hesitate on the doorstep. Power was ambitendence personified.

The white-painted pine cladding of the short entrance hall opened straight into the kitchen. Power saw immediately that the floor had been swept free of dust, and that the freezer was gone; removed in its entirety to the forensic labs in Birmingham. There was a brown patch on the tiled floor, where it had stood. The brown patch was the residue of a pool of liquid. Power peered at that brown stain in morbid fascination. Was it rust-laden water from condensation inside the chest freezer mechanism or was it the residue of melted blood that had dried on the tiles? Power couldn't decide and shivered.

He looked round the lounge. There were a few scattered newspapers – he noted a mixed reading; crumpled copies of the *Daily Mail* and the *Guardian* from 2002. There were a few yellowed paperbacks on a shelf along with some knick-knacks, including a bronze Eiffel Tower. Power noted the spines of the books – *The Cruel Sea* by Monsarrat, *Hangsaman* by Shirley Jackson, and an orange and white paperback of *The Catcher in the Rye* alongside an empty Maltesers box. Power sat on the sofa opposite a massive ancient Sony colour TV.

Was this where the family had sat through a visual diet of situation comedies and soap operas? The sofa sagged under him. The springs were well past their prime. He had hoped by visiting the farmhouse to try and see things from the murderer's point of view. But sitting here in this room, Power could not know what the murderer Heaney watched, nor whether the murderer even watched television. Had Heaney been watching this very TV when the plane crashed into the farmhouse roof, practically obliterating the upper storey? Power wondered whether the police had searched under the seat cushions and supposed that they must have done such an obvious thing. He wondered about pushing his hand down into the crevices of the sofa and felt afraid. What if he touched something? What if someone else's fingers grasped his? He tried to reason with himself that life was not a horror movie. Power brought himself to fish down the side of the sofa and brought out a fifty pence piece. Had the police really searched properly, he wondered?

The building was still. There was no noise of any kind. Even so, there was no peace in this place. The air seemed full of something, as if a hundred voices had been speaking all at once, and he had ventured into the space that was just a pause in all their conversations. At any moment the babble of squabble of voices would re-commence, louder than ever before, incensed at his intrusion. Power felt like he was being watched. He stood up. The sofa cushion beneath him had been damp. He switched all the lights on in the lounge and kitchen to dispel his anxiety. He lifted all the cushions on the sofa and on a deep armchair that reeked of ancient cigarette smoke. There was nothing new to be found.

Power walked around the edge of the living room. Dust and grime everywhere, but was it from the aircrash or evidence of Heaney's minimal and negligent housekeeping?

The vast fireplace that sat across the space between the chairs and the TV set was occupied by a cast iron range. The grate had remnants of a few charred logs around a pile of soft, white ash. Power imagined the old man, Arthur Heaney, warming himself in slippers by the fire. From a high overmantel a pair of white Staffordshire china dogs stared sniffily down upon Power. Their glazed blue eyes glared at him wherever he moved in the room. They didn't help his anxiety and, irrationally, he felt like reaching them down and then smashing the Blenheim Spaniels upon the cast iron grate. He turned his back on them and moved into the kitchen.

With the utmost caution, Power lifted the hatchway door up and peered into the darkness beyond. A draught of cool air caught at his throat. He folded the hatchway back, and given he was on his own, with no phone, made absolutely sure that the trapdoor could not fall and close him in by weighting it back and putting a broomhandle across the inky maw of the cellar, so that it would never be able to close unless he chose to close it when he returned.

This was the part of the visit he had dreaded most. He had brought two torches. He had taken the precaution of putting new batteries in before his journey and tested them both now, and both worked. He stowed one carefully in his coat pocket and shone the other into the cellar to locate the switches for the lights. He had been trapped in the dark before, under his own house, and wasn't about to repeat his past errors.

And thus equipped, Power descended into the space below the farmhouse. His first act was to switch the lights on and so defeat the darkness and calm his own fear.

The shelves, whose contents had alarmed him so on his last visit, had been cleared and packed and sent *en masse* to Birmingham in a refrigerated container lorry along with the freezer from the kitchen. Power thought the empty shelves were reminiscent of the kind in a small corner shop. The painstaking cataloguing of each jar and its stowing away in a transport box, would have been like the work of a supermarket shelf-stacker in reverse. He could see the shape of each jar where it had been left as a ring of dust on the shelves. On the floor beneath the shelves were two brown chemical jars full of a liquid, which was clear. There were no pickled contents. Power inspected the label; '500ml diethyl ether.' Had they used this for steeping the body parts in? He would have thought formaldehyde more usual, but he thought nothing more of it. Without the stacked bottles and their fleshly contents, Power could see through the shelves into a corner of the basement he had never seen before. He moved behind the rows of shelves into this larger space. There was a window light in the corner of the ceiling. Perhaps light from the farmyard outside had once filtered through it. Someone had painted it black, probably decades ago. Maybe to keep light from shining into a Luftwaffe filled night-sky? Or maybe to stop anybody from taking a chance glimpse into the world of the basement?

His first glance at this room made Power think that this might have once been intended a bathroom, and then he imagined it more as a food preparation area or scullery. At one end there was a white-tiled cubicle with what looked like a shower head in it. The white-tiled floor was subtly inclined towards a prodigious iron grid. This grid set into the floor suggested that the place had a different, almost industrial function. And where there might have been a washbasin and cabinet in a bathroom, there was instead a vast enamelled table on four chromed-steel legs. The white surface gleamed as though recently polished. There were radiating grooves on the surface of the enamel that led to a drain or hole in the surface. A galvanized bucket sat below it to capture any liquid that fell from the table. Power was troubled by an intrusive memory from his medical school days. The table was remarkably like the ones in the anatomy department.

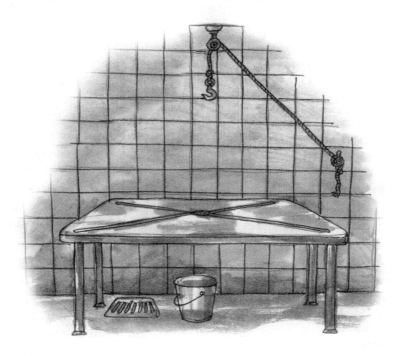

A dissection table. A sudden memory of taking a girl for coffee after a morning in the anatomy department. Power had intended to make a romantic gesture and to ask her out to a concert by Joy Division at Mr Pickwick's in town. He had been about to ask her, when he noticed a dehydrated flake of somebody else's skin in her long black hair. Power assumed she had been standing over the dissection table, staring down, when her hair collected the object. The romantic moment had been pricked and dispelled like a burst bubble. Power had later attended the concert on his own. Each ticket had cost two pounds he recalled.

He looked back at the shower cubicle. On further inspection, what he had taken to be a shower head set into the ceiling was nothing of the sort. It was a pulley, with a hook which could attach to something, which could then be drawn up and suspended. Maybe the pulley could be attached to a rope tightly wound around the feet, wondered Power.

Then the thought became too much for him and Power turned his back on the spotless white-tiled room. But just turning round could not obliterate the horror. He was now facing a place where Heaney had stored a mop and bucket next to a tap with a black curled hosepipe attached, presumably to enable the whole area to be sluiced clean.

Power wondered whether Heaney's defence lawyers, assuming he could ever be brought to trial, might argue in court that this area was no more sinister than an area where a farmer might prepare farm-fresh pork sausages. He tried not to shiver, or else there would be no stopping his fear. There was a radio-cassette player on a ledge on the wall opposite. Power switched it on. He wanted to hear something that might link or tether him to the world outside. There was a song by the KLF playing on the radio. A repeated lyric sounded like 'Time is a Turtle'. Power smiled wryly, but as hard as he grabbed at this potential source of humour it could not displace his anxiety. He briefly wondered why the police had not removed the radio for fingerprint purposes. Why was it still here? But then, he reasoned, there must have been a surfeit of fingerprints everywhere. The police had removed everything else, though. The basement, otherwise, was an empty shell. Perhaps the police officers had listened to the radio as they removed the jars and it had been forgotten?

Power had been thinking about the door in the corner of the basement, that he had briefly seen previously, and he moved round the shelving towards this next.

There was no key in the white wooden door, and when he turned the handle the door just opened easily with a puff of cold air from the velvet black space behind.

Dr Power stood back a moment before entering the darkness. There seemed now to be no bulb in the light fitting hanging down from the ceiling just ahead. He took the torch from his pocket and shone it into the void.

It was as Beresford had described the space to him. A passageway with brick walls covered in lime or whitewash which smelt of damp. What was the cold space beyond used for? Storing meat? He shone the torch on the floor. Concrete, pale grey and without any stain of blood. Towards the end of the tunnel, water had gathered into a glossy black puddle that entirely filled the end of the rectangular space. The surface of the puddle shimmered with the moving air. Reflected ripples of light created by his torch danced on the bricks of the end wall.

Power looked at the ripples, mesmerized for a moment, then switched the torch off and shut the door behind him.

He walked to the foot of the ladder and switched off the lights. The basement went dark behind him. He realised then that he'd forgotten to turn the radio off, but somehow he couldn't bear to be bothered to re-light the cellar and go to silence it. He climbed up the ladder to the sounds of Orbital on the radio behind him and emerged gratefully into the relative warmth of the kitchen.

Dr Power removed the broomhandle and the weight that he had used to keep the hatch open and softly closed it on the nightmares below.

Power then chose to look around the kitchen and remembered the questions he had hoped to solve by searching the place again. He was acutely aware that the police had by now removed everything they thought would be of value in identifying the murderer and his crimes. The son of the Heaney family was the main suspect. A woman at a bus stop had potentially identified him as being near the property in recent times, but was it really Heaney himself who had lived here and murdered again and again?

Power imagined if it had been Heaney living in the farmhouse, how he might have felt during those moments when the plane hit his world. Shock, terror, fear at the sudden events, fear for his life and then maybe a growing realisation that the farm would be the centre of a major rescue operation, and then, a frenzied scramble to escape from the farm and the services who would inevitably and quickly descend upon the farm. Heaney might never have imagined the plane crash happening in a million years, but knowing his guilt and the likelihood the police might descend on him at any time, might he always have been prepared to leave suddenly? Had he always been on a type of alert to escape with a key selection of items at any time? Maybe he had stowed his entire life – a pay to go phone, key identifying documents and money – a survival kit – in a rucksack near the front door? Maybe he had scooped this kit up as he left and ran, forgetting to take the photo album with him? Maybe that was the only mistake he made? Maybe he had a secure safe house or location to escape to? Or maybe he had never lived here? Maybe this was just a place he used during the day, like a butcher's shop, and empty at night? Maybe he had not actually been here at all when the plane struck? Maybe Mr Heaney had not lived here in recent times or no longer existed? What if the entire family from the photo album had only been here as body parts in the freezer and their murderer was the man the police were seeking?

Power felt more perplexed by the unknowns in this case than he had ever felt in any other investigation.

He reasoned that if it was Heaney who had lived here and escaped, clearing out, and removing any clues in those vital few minutes after the plane hit, then the downstairs would be devoid of any vital leads. It was the upstairs, hit by the plane that he would not have been able to get back to and visit during those brief moments before the services arrived.

There was a stairway at the rear of the kitchen, to the first floor. The stairs themselves were boxed off behind white-glossed tongue and groove pine boards. Power opened the screen door to the stairwell, and the draught flooded past him. There was little left of the roof and anything upstairs now. The combination of impact, flame and a need to remove any teetering piles of brickwork and rafters that might fall on investigating officers had led to the obliteration of most of the upstairs rooms. Without the protective awning the stairwell itself was open to the sky. The stairs were covered in sodden russet-coloured carpet, scattered with plaster dust, ash and black charred debris from the rafters and eaves. Power had been hoping maybe to visit bedrooms, snoop on beds, rumpled bedclothes, bedside reading, look at choices of cosmetics and toothbrushes and clothing to gauge some profile of the murderer, but he was faced with buffeting wind, swirling ash and damp, windblown leaves. There were two framed prints on the stairwell walls. Their frames rattled against the walls in the wind, and fragments of shattered glass glinted in the fading daylight. Power looked at the mildewed prints; they seemed to be pages ripped from some ancient library tome of anatomy. An imperfect delineation of the cranial nerves on one stolen page, and on another a lateral depiction of the left cerebral hemisphere with the optic nerve and single whitened eyeball below the frontal lobe. A singularly odd choice of interior decoration, Power thought.

Power chanced to look at the scattered wreckage of the landing beyond; ripped and scorched wallpaper, dusty tumbledown brick walls, laths sticking out of shattered plaster like broken white ribs. He receded back downstairs and closed the stairway door. There was no point in venturing further aloft.

He turned his attention to the kitchen. The cupboards might contain some clue as to the daily life lived by Heaney. No matter how you approached the task of exploring another person's kitchen, the organisation always seemed unique to the individual. Cupboards that you as an individual might think an obvious to place put crockery might be full of herbs in another's kitchen, cupboards you might put cleaning fluids in might be full of dried noodles or pans. And the risk of exploring this kitchen was that it might prove even more surprising, given what Power knew of the contents of the freezer to have been.

Power decided to focus on the oven first. At least the purpose of that could not be in dispute. The glass oven door creaked as he pulled it down to peer inside. There were some dirty, blackened roasting tins. Maybe Heaney was never in the habit of cleaning them. Perhaps Heaney reckoned that to clean the blackened trays would be to lose vital flavour, as some cooks maintained. Power's oven dishes at home were shiny and spotless. To Power's further disgust there was a thin film of white grease in the belly of each oven dish.

Power stood up and, as an idea brewed in his mind, fumbled in his pocket for his phone, only to remember that he had given it to the officer outside. He was quite alone here in the silence.

Power reached in his jacket pockets and withdrew a fountain pen and a piece of blank white paper to write himself a note:

Phone Beresford. Urgent. Ask if scientific officers swabbed the oven interior for DNA? Would heat destroy any DNA. Look out paper on degradation of DNA after fire exposure. Check if human DNA in oven. Important for prosecution case.

He stowed the note away in his breast pocket.

There was chipped, blue and white family crockery in the wall cupboard nearest the sink. The bottom of one of the plates had a Winfield trademark on it. Everything about the design betokened the nineteen-seventies. Power assumed there should originally have been four of everything. With the passage of time there were some items missing; of the soup dishes and cups only two of each remained.

There was a cupboard with sauces like congealed Heinz tomato ketchup and jars of faded brown beetroot and brown red cabbage, floating in an excess of vinegar; like pathological specimens in formalin. He noted several more modern packets of herbs; sage and rosemary. Power found three packets of Paxo stuffing still within their best before date range, two jars of instant pork gravy and two jars of apple sauce. He shuddered.

Power rifled through drawers upon drawers, cutlery drawers, drawers with tea towels, drawers for utensils: all seemed superficially so very domestic and suburban. He yanked open another drawer and found inside a tube of hand moisturiser, faded from use: what was it? It smelled feminine. What did it smell of? Roses? Absentmindedly he wondered if it had animal fat in its composition and turned it over to look at its faded ingredients.

The hairs on his neck suddenly stood on end.

Over to his left, Power realised that he himself was being inspected.

The world seemed to go into slow motion.

The trapdoor on the cellar had been lifted.

The head and shoulders of a man had risen from the depths. His eyes were focused on the doctor. The eyes were set in a long, pale face that ended in a small chin with a wispy brown beard. His torso was covered in a tight-fitting, red, rubber jacket of some sort.

In an instant, Power launched himself across the kitchen and grabbed hold of the upper edge of the hatch, wrenching it from the hold of the stranger. A terrified Power slammed the heavy lid downwards with both hands. The bottom of the hatch collided with the stranger's head with a sickening 'clonk' and both the head and the body underneath it collapsed, falling downwards into the cellar, with all the grace of an inanimate sack of potatoes. The hatch slammed back down flat into the kitchen floor. Power couldn't quite believe what he had seen or done. Had he killed someone by acting in sudden panic?

Dr Power tried to get out of the farmhouse by opening the front door, but as luck would have it, the officer who had been standing guard just outside had needed the toilet and had made his way into the remaining trees and shrubs that surrounded the old farmhouse. He had deemed it prudent to lock the front door to prevent any strangers from getting into the farm. However, by doing so, he had also locked the good doctor inside. Power hammered on the wooden door, but the officer was not there to respond.

Power looked back at the trapdoor in the kitchen. He was frantically worried that it might suddenly rise again. He went to one of the drawers he had just searched and took out the sharpest looking knife. As he did so, he wondered whether this was the best weapon to choose. Was there anything else?

A few moments passed as he waited for something to happen, but there was no noise from the cellar. He realised that the silence around him meant that the stranger below had, at some time, switched off the radio that Power had put on in the basement. Power hadn't noticed the change. When had the radio gone off? Just now? Or earlier when he had been rummaging through the drawers? It mattered. If it had only just gone off it meant that the stranger had survived the blow to his head.

Who had the stranger been? The man had maybe looked like an older version of the boy in the photo albums. Power wasn't the best at recognising faces, though. What if it had been a scene of crime officer somehow returning to the farmhouse? Had Power killed a police employee? But then where had he, be it police or the grown up Heaney, come from? The only entrance to, or exit from, the farmhouse known to Power was the front door and this was locked fast.

Power leaned over the closed hatchway in the kitchen floor. He shut his eyes and tried to focus on any sound from the basement below. All was silence. There was no sound betraying any movement whatsoever.

Power picked up the handle set into the hatch with trembling fingers. Slowly, and extremely cautiously, he began to lift it up. He held his breath and hoped that the hatch would not creak or groan as he raised it.

As soon as there was enough of a gap to see downwards, Power peered into the cellar. The lights were on now. He expected to see the crumpled body of Heaney lying on the cold concrete with a bleeding skull. There was simply, nothing.

Well, thought Power, there wasn't quite nothing, for the floor was graced with a glistening dribble of water. It reflected the harsh light of the lamps above. Gradually the water was sinking into the porous grey concrete, though, leaving a dark grey stain.

Power let the hatchway fall all the way back and gingerly looked as far as he could below. Heaney wasn't waiting with any weapon to strike at him. As far as he could tell from his particular vantage point in the kitchen, the cellar below was now empty. He sighed with some relief, but somehow the inherent curiosity in his personality made him want to verify that the cellar was completely empty. The sudden shock of Heaney's appearance and the puzzle of his disappearance had elated and energised Power with a burst of adrenaline. And this burst gave him courage.

He climbed down the wooden ladder as silently as he could and stood at the bottom scanning round the basement for a glimpse of Heaney's head or red jacket. Perhaps he was crouching, or lying injured behind the shelving, or behind a corner in the alcove area where the dissection table was. Power's eyes darted round and fixed on the floor. There was a set of tracks. There were grey footprints on the concrete, and the prints were fast disappearing as the concrete sucked any moisture up. The single set of prints led to and from the ladder and tracked all the way back to the cupboard doorway at the far end. Was

Heaney hiding in there? There seemed no other explanation for the tracks.

Power tried to make no noise as he walked along the path of prints towards the door. When he reached it, he stood to one side lest it burst open and slam into him. He listened carefully. The cupboard beyond, seemed as silent as the grave. All was still, without even the merest hint of sound to suggest a breath being taken. Power took the precaution of switching a torch on, and then suddenly wrenched the door open and shone his torch into the blackness. The cupboard seemed entirely empty.

Power cast round the cellar again to see if Heaney had somehow hidden from him and was behind him, but it was all as empty as the cupboard and Power began to wonder whether he had imagined the event in the kitchen as some kind of illusory episode brought on by apprehension and fear.

He walked through the door into the brick passageway.

The shallow puddle on the ground at the end rippled and cast reflections on the wall. Power looked into dark surface of the water and saw nothing but obsidian blackness. He thought of the Black Lake on the common.

Power knelt by the water's edge.

He reached a hand to the surface and touched the coldness.

He dipped his fingers into the puddle. He expected to touch the concrete floor underneath. Even when the water was up to his knuckles, however, he could still not feel any ground beneath.

Power leaned forward and peered into the water, trying to divine its mystery.

His hand was into the black coldness up to his wrist. There seemed to be no bottom to the puddle.

Then a hand grabbed his hand, and with alarming grip and strength, pulled Power forwards and off balance.

Power fell full length into the freezing cold darkness and, suddenly immersed, could not breathe.

Chapter Seven

Take the most accomplished combatant you can find; throw them into deep water and their skill will instantly dissolve. Dr Power could not remotely be described as a combatant, let alone an accomplished one. He had had no chance to take a last breath before he was submerged in the watery depths. An unknown hand had gripped his and dragged him head first down into the cold darkness. The dark water folded over him like icy black velvet.

Power was plunged into a monochrome world, where his senses were dulled, vision blurred, and sound muffled. In the distorted shadows his lungs screamed for life and his heart spiked with fear. Head down, his nostrils full of water, he looked up beyond his feet to a vague light above. He was still being pulled down and he tugged his hand out of Heaney's grasp. He punched out with his fists and his skin collided with the reptilian sleekness of Heaney's wetsuit. Action and reaction. The two struggling bodies parted for an instant. Somehow, Power's head was down in the region of the water where Heaney's feet were, the result of his headfirst fall into the water. Power's thick jacket was filled with water now and dragging him down. It had only taken an instant but the deep pool was suffocating him. Heaney needed to do nothing further to kill Power, the water would drown him for sure. Cold was numbing his feet; he was dying from the edges inwards. He was suddenly afflicted by the thought he would never feel Laura's warmth again.

Heaney was moving closer, trying to grab Power's legs to hold him and stuff him down further. Power pulled his legs up towards his chest, into a semi-foetal position, and in the icy amniotic fluid of the pool kicked his heavily booted feet up. The sole of his right leg connected with something hard. The flurry of Heaney's limbs seemed to stop for an instant. Had Power's boot connected with a human jaw?

Free at last, Power waved and flailed his arms to right himself, tilted his head up, and kicked upwards towards the light.

As Power streamed past, Heaney lunged at him. Power felt a sharp icy pain in his shoulder.

Power's whole being focused on moving up towards the distant glow of light. He streamed up and breached the surface of the pool and kicking frantically and with such force he launched himself out of the water and onto his belly on the concrete floor of the cellar. He forced his legs backwards and his feet connected with the brick wall at the end and he pushed his torso and hips forward onto the safety of the cellar floor. Gulping in huge gouts of air and intermittently gasping and coughing, Power slithered forwards so that he was wholly out of the water. He knew he could not pause, though, and he pulled his legs round so that he could face the surface of the pool to be ready for Heaney.

But Heaney did not come and the surface of the pool, still choppy from Power's emergence, became ripples that slopped against the wall, and then relaxed into smaller ripples that diminished altogether into stillness. The deep pool that Power had delivered himself from, now looked altogether the same as it had done before, like an innocent, thin puddle; a mere sheet of moisture on a concrete floor. Looks were deceiving, for this was clearly a portal into a different realm; Heaney's world.

* * *

The officer on duty was alarmed at the sudden banging and thumping on the inside of the kitchen door, and even more alarmed by the appearance of the bedraggled and drenched doctor. Power tumbled out of the farmhouse and fell to his knees.

"He's in there, he's in there!" he gasped, and pulled at the officer's yellow hi-vis jacket.

"I'm sorry, sir?"

"Heaney. He was in there, down in the cellar! Just now."

"I can assure you . . ."

"The cellar has a pool in it, at the end, there must be a tunnel beyond. A way in and out."

"Should I go and see? Is he still there, Doctor?"

"I doubt it," whispered Power, sinking onto his haunches. He had wanted the officer to do something, and quickly, but this didn't seem to be happening, and he realised that probably Heaney was truly gone. "You'd better check, though." The officer made to go into the house, but Power stopped him. "My phone, please. While you check, I will phone."

When the officer had gone into the cellar, Power stood up and found

Beresford's number on his phone. Shivering, Power suddenly realised how very numb with cold he had become. He staggered to his car and let himself in. He started the engine for some warmth. There was an old blanket on the back seat that covered an ancient jagged rip in the Saab's upholstery. Power shrugged off his wringing wet jacket and shirt and wrapped the scratchy woolen rug about himself. When he got through to Beresford it was all he could do to stop his teeth chattering.

"It's Carl," he said, as Beresford responded. "I've been to the farmhouse."

"And did you find anything my officers had left undone?" Beresford's voice sounded slightly cynical. He had half-regarded Power's trip to the farmhouse as a waste of time.

Power was not in a mood to be diplomatic. Circumstances would not allow him to sugarcoat his words. "I found Heaney," he said bluntly. "Or rather, he grabbed my attention. There's a pool in the basement. Looks like a puddle on the concrete floor. In that cubby-space behind the door. It's not a puddle. It's a pool that connects to somewhere. Heaney has been able to come and go all the time using it."

"I don't understand," said Beresford.

"The pool is deep – like a u-bend or something . . . it probably connects to another space further on. To be truthful I didn't stay to find out, because he was there. He attacked me."

"He attacked you? Are you all right? Are you there now? Where's the police officer?"

"I'm trying to get warm in my car," said Power. "You'd better send some back up. He's gone in alone. I think Heaney went as soon as I escaped. You'd better find some divers too."

"I'm coming over. Wait there."

Power was shivering and wanting to go home. He didn't want to wait, shivering in his car. "Before you go, can you answer me one thing?" He was still thinking of the memo he had written himself. It was probably just a sopping piece of paper in his sodden pocket now. "Did anyone test the inside of the oven for DNA?"

"I don't think so," said Beresford. "The heat would destroy anything surely."

"Maybe worth a try," said Power. "Looking for human DNA."

"Stay there," said Beresford. "I'm about fifteen minutes away from you." And he ended the phone conversation.

Power sighed, the Saab's heating was only just beginning to kick in. His teeth were chattering and he wondered whether it was part cold and part shock. Why had he asked Beresford that detail? There were more important things – he had just survived an ordeal, why focus on a tiny detail at this time? He looked at his jacket on the seat next to him. Drips of water were falling from a corner of it, one by one, into a puddle on the rubber floor mats. He pushed the whole thing on to the floor. No sense in ruining the seat. He didn't think he'd want to wear the jacket again.

The blanket round him moved over his shoulders as he pushed the jacket to the floor. The wool of the blanket seemed to be stuck to his upper arm and it hurt when he tried to peel it off his skin. He looked at his bare flesh. His flesh had been cut down to the deltoid muscle and dark blood was oozing from the sliced skin. It was his own clotted blood that had made the blanket adhere to his skin. He looked at the jagged cut with some disbelief and as he did so his mind began to acknowledge the pain. During the underwater struggle Joel Heaney had stabbed him, and dragged the blade across his muscle and skin.

* * *

Power had been taken to the police station, and after Beresford had loaned him some of his clothes from his own locker, been debriefed and seen a doctor who had put three stitches in the deep wound in his muscle. Now with painkillers and a tetanus booster inside him, Power was limping home in his old Saab when his mobile rang. He was passing through Alderley village and pulled over into a rare parking space outside Wienholt's bakery. Power usually visited here at a weekend to buy cheesecakes and sweet sesame buns.

He scrabbled awkwardly for the phone in his pocket, reaching across his body with his unhurt arm.

"Hello, Dr Power speaking."

"Professor Power! Thank you for speaking to me." The false jollity in the voice irritated Power.

"Who is this, please?"

"You don't know me, but . . ."

"How did you get my number?" Pain was making the doctor uncharacteristically brusque.

"Somebody wrote it down for me. I'm John, Professor. I have an offer for you, don't hang up. It's a very good offer."

"John who?"

"John Lovett, a writer of sorts. I admire your work and want to write a profile."

"A journalist? You're a journalist?"

"More of a crime writer, with several published books. Not with the newspapers. Not a hack. I have awards."

Power didn't say anything. He was wondering about ending the call. Only the pain was distracting him, somehow, from doing this. He could hardly concentrate on what Lovett was saying.

Lovett went on talking, "I've followed the cases you have worked on and I wanted to feature you in a book, and there would be an advance from the publishers to reward you for your co-operation. Five figures. Which is why I'm wanting you to really consider this and say yes."

But the breakthrough pain was now lancinating. The stitches felt too tight. Could he drive as far as home? It wasn't far, just up the hill on the left. But maybe walking would be better than moving the gearstick and turning the steering wheel.

"Perhaps we could meet to discuss the proposal? Can I suggest that pub that you like? Tomorrow at noon?"

"You want to know about the case I'm working on now, don't you?" said Power. "You want to bribe me."

"No, no, you're wrong, please hear me out," the voice pleaded and wheedled.

"I don't know how you got my number," said Power. "There's something about your voice. I can hear it in your words. You're lying."

"I'm making you a really good offer. Just meet me tomorrow."

"No," said Power, and switched off the phone. He felt sick and opened the car door. Passing drivers blared their horns at him suddenly throwing the door wide open. Pain was destroying his concentration. He locked the car and began the journey home on foot, walking uncertainly and shivering, watching every footfall he made as if from some remote distance. It felt like his feet belonged to someone else.

* * *

"You've been in the wars," said his father, who peered at him from within a cloud of hospital pillows that had gathered round his head.

His father's white hair seemed almost like gold in comparison as he lay against the starched bright whiteness.

Power was wearing a yellow cotton sling that Laura had contrived for him. His arm still hurt two days on from Heaney's underwater attack. Power tried to smile as best he could. "It's nothing," he said. "A scratch."

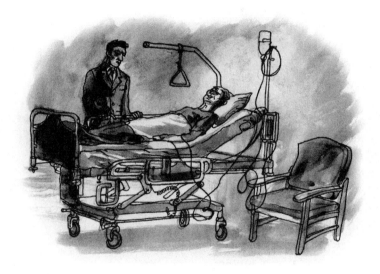

"I don't believe that for a second. I saw you wince just now." His father's coal-black eyes glittered in the afternoon sun coming through the window. "Your work, I suppose. Too dangerous. You should stop it. Retire."

"Retire? How old do you think I am?"

"You've money enough," said his father. "Your aunt left you more than enough. And the house as well. Why do you risk your health, Son?"

Power looked deeply at his father. How changed he had become in the last few months. How had such a strong man shrunk to this? His father tried to appear cheerful. They were both playing at the same game. Power thought his father's skin was pale, almost translucent, and tinged with yellow. He gathered that the 'tests' which had kept his father in hospital for several days were not good.

"Your job was not entirely without risk," said Dr Power.

"Architecture? I spent all my days hunched over a drawing board. At least that's what we used to use before the CAD computers came in." Power remembered his father using shiny trays of watercolours to paint in the lines on vast sheets of paper.

"You sometimes went up to the rooftops. I went with you once to the very top of a tower; the wind nearly blew us to eternity. You took me everywhere."

"Did I?" And he quoted from the reserves of his memory, *"Architecture is the learned game, correct and magnificent, of forms assembled in the light."*

"Le Corbusier?" asked Power.

His father nodded to confirm. Power wanted to ask something he had been wondering about. "Dad, did you ever survey my house? When Aunt Jessie was alive, maybe?"

"From top to bottom. I was a student and I wanted to see how a master did it. It was designed by Waterhouse, you know."

"I know, but did you find anything unusual?"

"How do you mean? Waterhouse liked to put all means of conceits in his designs . . . little animals carved into the masonry. There's a Liver bird on the front elevation of your house. Waterhouse was born in Liverpool, you see."

"No, below the house, I mean."

"Below?" his father frowned. "What have you been doing?"

"I was decorating . . . this was a few years back," said Power. The way his father was looking at him seemed to kindle some kind of guilt inside him. Why did he feel guilty? It was his house, but his father could make his son feel guilty with a simple frown.

"You don't want to go playing down there," said his father.

"I'm not a child, Dad. Did you know about the steps and the archway?"

His father broke eye contact. "Yes, a very fine curved stone stairway and an archway into the caverns under the hill. The arch had exquisite turquoise tiling as I recall. Like the blue malachite you find in the old Roman mines below the Edge. And there were sturdy iron gates in the archway he designed. Perhaps Waterhouse imagined the Victorians going for a stroll underground after their Sunday lunch with oil lamps, I don't know. It was a bit of a folly if you ask me."

"The gates had fallen when I went down there."

"You shouldn't go down there," said his father. "A man could get lost forever. There are many cases of men being lost down there. There are natural caves and mineworks all through the sandstone on the Edge. There are miles of mine shafts for copper and cobalt and stuff. Vertical shafts hundreds of feet deep. It's not safe."

"I know," said Power. "But why did my aunt hide it all away?"

"Not safe," said his father. "She didn't want visitors like you, when you were a boy, going down there. That was her practical mind speaking. And she also didn't want ghosts coming up from the tunnels. That was her being impractical, I'm afraid. She was inclined to be fanciful. But she cared a lot about you, I think. She didn't have her own children so she wanted you safe."

"I see," said Power. "That makes sense. You've never mentioned it before, you see."

"Well, maybe I didn't want my son going down there, either. There are some things best sealed away."

Power paused and changed tack in their conversation, "We've been trying for a baby. Laura and I."

"That's good," said his father, smiling. "Perhaps it would be a shame if the Power family line ended. Your saying that is a bit of a comfort to me. In these days particularly."

"But nothing seems to be happening, Dad. We've actually been trying for a while."

"Ah," said his father, who was nonplussed. After a moment he asked, "Have you seen a doctor, Doctor?" Power shook his head. "Are you afraid to?"

"Yes, I am. Afraid of making things real."

"Well," said his father. "You can carry on living in hope, or you can see if your profession has anything to offer you to boost your chances. I'd like to see a grandchild, if I ever get out of here, which, to be honest, I don't think I will. I have that feeling." His father put on a resigned smile. Power reached out and squeezed his father's hand. His father looked out of the window. His eyes were suddenly full of tears. "I am afraid, Carl. Dreadfully so." Power offered his father a handkerchief and his father gave a nervous laugh as he tried to reassemble his composure. "I was trying very hard not to cry today. I didn't want to. I don't like to. It's undignified. You've always been a very good son. I've been so proud of you. Family is so very important and I've been lucky with you."

Power didn't know quite what to say. He looked round the single room with its NHS green walls and the islands of furniture, clustered together on its linoleum floor; a functional metal bed, two heavy armchairs, and a formica-topped bedside cabinet. His father sat in the midst of all these islands, a life reduced.

"I've been lucky with you too, Dad," he said at last. "Do you remember how we watched the moon landing together?"

"I remember it all, but you do as well, do you? You were so young." said his father, and coughed slightly, either through his anxiety or physical need. "It was about 4 a.m. in England when they landed; I had to wake you up. You couldn't miss that. You know, I think only twelve men ever walked on the moon. And we saw two of them together."

They talked a little while longer, but Power could see his father was getting weary and his eyes looked heavier and heavier. His voice slurred ever so slightly. At last his father seemed to slip into a sleep and, rather than wake him, Dr Power stood up. He kissed his father's head to say his goodbye and tiptoed out of the room.

* * *

It was morning and the city centre shops had just opened. Dr Power was tucking into breakfast in a café on Bridge Street in Chester. He was sitting by the window, noting the pedestrians bustling along on the cold cobbles outside. The day was frosty but the café was blessedly warm. He was listening to a song called 'Time is Running Out' on the café radio. The oblong plate on the deal table in front of him offered roasted tomatoes, courgette, peppers, and mushrooms, served with seared, sliced avocado and hot, fresh rosemary focaccia. He was hungry and he was almost halfway through his meal when the café door opened and in walked Lynch.

Power stood up and greeted him. "I'm so sorry, Andrew, I started. I was hungry. What kept you?"

"Morning prayer ran on," said Lynch, by way of explanation, and sat down. Power offered a menu to him and re-started his meal.

"Morning prayer, where?"

"St Anselm's Chapel," said Lynch.

"Where's that?" asked Power as he reached to pour a second cup of tea from a mammoth yellow china tea pot.

"It's a chapel from Norman times hidden away in the Cathedral, lovely Gothic plasterwork," said Lynch.

"And who was St Anselm?"

"He was very important. He brought a bit of reason and scholasticism to the medieval church. He was a sort of philosopher within the Church – teaching people how to resolve differences in opinions. He championed making reasoned debate and using inference."

"He sounds a sensible man, very modern."

"For his time," said Lynch. "He valued an understanding of the world and believed in order that he might understand. He thought our conception of God was limited by our understanding and that what we know is but a fraction of what the Lord could be." The waitress hovered at Lynch's elbow and Lynch pointed at Power's plate. "Good morning – can I have the same as my friend here?"

"The vegan breakfast?"

"If that's what it is, then yes. It looks good."

The waitress smiled and left.

"You're having vegan too?" Power expressed open-eyed surprise. "Not your usual bacon and sausage and black pudding. Are you looking after your heart today as well as your spirit?"

"Today I don't feel like any bacon or meat. Not after . . . well, not after I talked to Beresford. He phoned me at 8 a.m. – before he briefed his team. And he said that you were right."

"Right in what way?" asked Power.

Lynch looked round to see if he could be overheard, but he and Power were the only customers in the café. "Your suggestion to check the oven for human DNA. Well, you were correct and now we have Mr Heaney's motive."

"He cooked their flesh?"

Lynch nodded and looked away. "So now Beresford wants you to tell him what it all means – what Heaney is all about. He wants to know if Heaney is mad? Is this going to be a case where the perpetrator claims 'diminished responsibility' and ends his days in a comfortable hospital somewhere?"

"I don't think I'd call the Ashworth Hospital comfortable," said Power. "Have you ever been there? Twenty-four foot high walls, five different locks between you and the outside world, some nurses who are more prison officer than anything else, jailers rather than therapists."

"Point taken, perhaps," said Lynch. "But I would prefer the man not to escape justice. Or might you argue that his cannibalism is, by definition, proof of his madness and that a secure hospital is the appropriate destination?"

Power mopped up the juice from his breakfast with the remaining morsel of focaccia and ate it with pleasure. He sighed, replete. "What a conversation for breakfast time! How we do start our days, you and I, eh? Everything depends on your philosophy, Andrew, and I suppose the ethos of the culture you come from."

"Well, our culture views murder and cannibalism as the ultimate taboo, I would dare say, so things would seem very clear indeed, without resort to philosophy."

Power sighed. "The motives of Heaney may be our keys to catching him. Now his motive to kill and eat his victims cannot be purely hunger, can it? There are much easier ways to get your calories than risk putting yourself on trial for murder. And if you want meat or flesh then society will sanction Mr Sainsbury to butcher your animal of choice and slice it to fit a neat plastic packet. You need never know your skinned chicken portion, or beef steak, had ever been a living, self-aware creature. So very easy. So the motivation to hunt people and stock your freezer with human joints can't be convenience or a desire to eat for free, because of the risk of your 'punishment through justice'. So the situation is much more complex.

"Some cannibalism might be for practical reasons, like the survivors of that plane crash who would all have died unless they ate the dead comrades. Some cultures believe in the act of eating another as a kind of ritual to acquire power or strength. A prince might kill and eat his father, the ageing king, to ensure his strength keeps flowing along the royal line. Like a sacrifice. Or there might be a sexual motive. Some cannibals describe being aroused by the whole idea. There was that German Meiwes a couple of years ago who advertised for a young man who wanted to be eaten. And someone actually responded. Meiwes kissed him and stabbed him in the neck, then over time ate him bit by bit, fried in olive oil and garlic. And Dahmer, who probably murdered dozens of gay lovers, drugging them after he lured them home. He described their fried flesh as like *filet mignon*. And there may be hatred or revenge as a motive, like the Australian Katherine Knight a few years ago who killed her lover, skinned him and cooked parts of him to serve to his children.

"By the way, do they have two people guarding the farmhouse at all times now?"

Lynch nodded. His own breakfast had arrived and he was looking at it with some bemusement. Power ordered another pot of tea. "So," said Lynch. "If his motivation is key to catching him . . . how do we know what his motivation is without talking to him?"

Rather than give an incorrect answer too early in the investigation, Power chose to ask a further question. "The body parts, were they a mix of male and female?"

"Yes, they were mainly female though."

"So, he's no Dahmer," said Power. "And a body count?"

Lynch sighed and pushed the plate to one side and Power eyed it prospectively. "The DNA analysis finds tissue from over sixty different humans."

"And the divers – what did they find?"

"The pool doesn't extend far underground. Swim down a few metres then swim horizontally under a rock and you are in a very short tunnel. It can then be traversed in ten seconds or so of swimming underwater. Not much of a feat if you can hold your breath for thirty seconds or so. Then you come up onto a sandy ledge. And there are two tunnels or mine workings branching out from there. One leads up to a hatch in fenced off ground near the lake. The other goes deep into the mines. They think he used the hatchway to escape up into the open air. That would seem to be the obvious thing to do. They think he meant to take you through the tunnel for some purpose, or else drown you in the water. Do you think he knew who you were, did he recognise you?"

"He looked so surprised to see me when I first saw him there. I thought I had killed him when I brought the hatch down on him. As for whether he recognised me from the news? Who knows? I try to stay out of the public eye, but they keep on writing about me. Maybe he has seen something or read something. But, I don't know."

"Well, we know it's Heaney we are looking for. He is confirmed, I think, as the prime suspect. No need to seek anyone else."

"You're probably right," said Power. "But all the victims, we need to find out who they were and how he chose them."

"There's a team working on it, Beresford says."

"I've been thinking about something, the whole body, the girl, alone in the freezer. The butchered portions. The jars of bottled flesh. All different. Different methods, different motives? The iced cuts, stored as what? Roasts? The bottles preserved for a long time. What as? As trophies?"

"You can bottle meat for eating," said Lynch. "It might just all be meat for the table."

"Ugh, bottled meat?"

"Sure, Pamela once bottled some venison in a pressure cooker."

"There's something I don't remember," said Power. "The broken bottle, the one that fell off the shelf. Did it have a smell of formaldehyde? You couldn't eat meat preserved with formaldehyde."

"I don't remember any smell either," said Lynch, remembering the smashed bottle he had seen on the floor. He made a note in a slim black diary to check this point with Beresford.

"Do you want the rest of your breakfast?" asked Power.

Lynch pushed the plate over to him.

"You are what you eat," said Power.

Chapter Eight

Lindow Man

Lynch had been sitting on his own, waiting in the undertakers in Wilmslow. He had, he thought, been waiting too long. The floor and walls were a calming pale grey and even the air about him was still. Something about the room seemed to suck sound from the environment and so Lynch could not even hear his own breathing. Indeed, he began to fear that he was not breathing. He glanced around at the display window that had a feature with dried flowers, a yellow drape over a mock brick wall and in front, two engraved headstones to announce to the world outside the nature of the funeral directors' business. The interior of the office had some armchairs, and a sofa, and a more conventional oak veneered desk with upright metal chairs clustered about it. Lynch was sitting by this desk. There was a framed black and white picture of a single dandelion head on the desk. The photograph had been taken at the moment a fluffy seed was parting company with the main dandelion head.

The numbing ambience of the office was such that Lynch did not even notice the entrance of the small bespectacled man who was suddenly sitting opposite him across the desk.

"Superintendent Lynch?" he asked. "I'm Mr Jacob, I gather you are making some enquiries. Can I help you, perhaps?"

"Good morning. I am a retired Superintendent, though, but I am undertaking some current enquiries on behalf of the local Force, at their recent request. I can show a letter of confirmation to that effect if you would like?" Lynch reached into his pocket for the letter signed by Beresford.

"That's quite all right, we are happy to help, but we seldom see anybody from the police. Have we perhaps done something wrong?"

"I've been seeing all your colleagues through the area to see if anyone can help us. It is in relation to a murder enquiry." And at Dr Power's sensible suggestion, thought Lynch.

"We are only ever involved after a formal death certificate or Coroner's certificate is produced, I don't see how . . ."

Lynch did not want to explain the nature of the murders, and had been very careful in all his previous approaches to other funeral directors. The police still did not want some details of the murders to be revealed, although there had been some leaks and also breaches in security, the largest of the latter being the deliberate theft of Beresford's log book. And yet no details from this had appeared in the UK media. Lynch had speculated on why someone would steal all the details of Beresford's initial thoughts and contacts, but not publish them.

"There are two lines of enquiry I wish to make," Lynch continued. "The first is to ask you if you can identify one or more persons, maybe as employees. The second is to ask about your procedures . . ." Lynch fished in his pocket for a sheaf of papers and spread three A4 prints on the desk in front of Mr Jacob. "So first off, do you recognise any of these three people?" Lynch was careful not to mention the names of Mr Arthur Heaney, his wife or their son. "Have you perhaps employed them in the last ten years as mortuary technicians or reception staff, or drivers or . . . you understand me?"

Jacob took out a pair of golden *pince nez* and, with irritating affectation and delay, placed them on his nose to peer at the cropped heads and shoulder shots that the police had resurrected from the family photograph album. He concentrated. He pondered. Lynch had to give him credit for full consideration. But at length, Mr Jacob sighed and said, "No, I don't think so. We are a small family firm. I would know."

"Ah," said Lynch. "You were my last and best hope amongst the funeral directors of the area, because you are closest."

"Is this about the plane crash at Lindow Moss? There's been a lot of . . . speculation. That the plane carried more than two people, for instance. That dozens of people were killed by terrorists shooting down a plane with a surface-to-air missile. Or that the plane was carrying diplomats and spies, and other ideas, that the farm was a tomb of double agents' bodies executed by MI6 during the war."

Lynch raised his eyebrows. "Is that what people are really saying?"

"People say all sorts of things," said Mr Jacob, as he removed the *pince nez*. "I'm aware that the truth is probably more prosaic. But clearly," he gestured at Lynch. "Your presence would suggest something out of the ordinary, indeed, something extraordinary. And nobody believes the papers, or trusts the police."

Lynch's professional pride was hurt and he felt somewhat rankled. "The plane crash was an unhappy tragedy with two victims. Father and son. That in turn coincidentally led to the discovery of a set of crimes in the farmhouse."

"By these people?" The undertaker gathered the papers together and offered them back to Lynch.

"They are people we need to eliminate from our inquiry."

"Suspects?"

"If you prefer that term," said Lynch. "The second question is about the process you use here; I am interested in whether an individual might have access to a body to remove body parts during the process. Do you think that this kind of behaviour might be possible?"

Again Mr Jacob gave the question deep thought for several minutes. "It is never wise to say something can 'never' happen, but I think it highly unlikely. We tend to have two people working on a body. The body is weighed several times – on arrival, and before embalming, so we know how much fluid to use. And the body is weighed immediately after that, so there are checks. The weight of fluid and body should all tally. Although we don't weigh to check if anything's missing, do you see? It's all done for a scientific reason – to get the amount of fluids right, or to inform the crematorium how much to stoke the fire . . . if you see what I mean. Pardon any offence."

"Yes, that all tallies with everything your colleagues told me, but you will allow that if an employee was determined, and wanted to deceive his employer, it might be done?"

"Possible, but unlikely. The process is quite streamlined these days, and any 'mistakes' would come to light eventually."

"And none have?"

"No. No, they haven't. Such things could never happen here."

Lynch looked around the sterile reception area. "There are no markers of the Christian faith here. This is, permit me to say, a very secular space."

"Yes, deliberately so."

Lynch frowned. "This is a Christian country, though."

"It may have been once upon a time, but nowadays we do not wish to offend those of other faiths or no faith at all."

Andrew Lynch's frown became a glower of disapproval. He said goodbye as best he could and left the still greyness of the funeral directors with alacrity. He stepped into the noisy colourful street outside with a sigh. As he crossed the road to buy a coffee, he sang softly to himself, "Still be Thy care, O God, our shield; Still may Thy wisdom guide us . . ."

* * *

"Professor Power? How nice to see you." Dr Timothy Lehman stood up and shook Power's hand warmly. He guided Power to a vintage canvas metal seat, designed by Bruno Pollak, had Dr Lehman but known it.

The room was small and cold. Power did not feel he could take off his coat. The walls were whitewashed Victorian brickwork and the only window was set high up in the wall, above their heads. The window was small and arched, and the panes of glass in it were a glossy, inky black. "You've come to join me at the midnight hour?"

"I have," said Power. "I had no idea a colleague would run a clinic this late."

"Well, it's entirely voluntary, but I am semi-retired now so I will have a lie in tomorrow. Don't you do on-calls yourself, anyway?"

"A one in seven," said Power. "Still, running a psychiatric night clinic is dedication."

"We've run a clinic here in the Cathedral basement for ten years now. Since they started closing the old hospitals. It's not easy to find a GP and get pills and injections when you're on the streets. We don't prescribe opiates or benzodiazepines by the way, that prescribing proved a bit too dangerous when we first opened. So we stopped. We aim to treat plain old schizophrenia and depression; bread and butter psychiatry. And we take care of infections and other stuff too, when our people have that."

"And there's food too?"

"There's your soup kitchen, yes. Sometimes local businesses and restaurants will send over batches of unwanted food. There's a pastor on-hand for spiritual emergencies – that's to keep the cathedral on board, and some social workers who donate their time. Would you join us and give us some of your time, Professor, or do you want to study us and write a paper on us?" Lehman smiled. "We don't mind that, any publicity would help us. Did you know that the average age of death for a man on the city streets is about forty-seven and forty-three for a woman. Alcohol, drugs, suicide, respiratory and cardiovascular causes. Their risk of suicide goes up four times."

Power coughed, slightly embarrassed. "I wanted to ask for your help really."

"Go on," said Lehman, sitting back in his chair and folding his arms on the yellowed wooden table that served as his desk.

"I wondered if I could maybe talk to your patients as they come through the clinic? I'm working as an adviser to the police and . . ."

Lehman shook his head emphatically. "It would destroy our work

... we'd lose our chance to ... look, Professor, they will stay away in droves if they know you are anything to do with the police."

"Hear me out," said Power. "Please ... it's about your people. You get to know them over time, but sometimes they default, don't they, they stop coming?"

"Of course," said Lehman. "They find a place to stay maybe, or go home, or move to a different city, or get taken up by a pimp, or go into hospital – what's left of mental health care – or, of course, they just die and stop bothering 'society'."

"Well," said Power. "Who would notice if the turnover of people on the streets increased, or if they started disappearing?"

"That's difficult to say. There are some patients I've known for years, but some I see only once or twice. I wouldn't notice any disappearances, as you describe them. Because the population is shifting all the time."

"What do you know of the Lindow farm situation?" asked Power.

"That's where the plane crash was? And they found bodies in the farmhouse ..."

"Yes," said Power. "Can I trust you to keep something confidential? Doctor to doctor?"

"I thought I remembered your face," said Lehman, peering at the Professor. "They profiled you on the regional news, didn't they? You were outside the farmhouse."

"Can you keep this confidential, though?"

"Of course," Lehman leant in towards Power. "What is it?"

"The farmhouse was a crime scene unlike anything I have seen before. Nothing compares. There was a freezer with one entire body and dozens of butchered body parts in it. The parts came from a whole host of different individuals, males, and females. Dozens. And, as you know, there'd been no outcry about a sudden disappearance of dozens of people beforehand. You have to ask yourself where these missing people came from? And the obvious answer, to my mind, is that the missing people are disappearing from a group that is already missing ... if you see what I mean. If you are already missing from home, then who would notice if you go missing again?"

Lehman paused. He stood up. He blew out his cheeks and considered. He looked up at the night sky through the window. He sat down again. He looked sidelong at Power. "I'm sorry to have seemed

. . . brusque before. It's just that these folk won't trust us, won't even come and see us, if they think there's a chance the police are involved."

"I understand," said Power. "That's why I need to listen to them. Their silence . . . for understandable reasons . . . means that they are even more vulnerable. I think they have become victims for a predator who knows and benefits from their vulnerability."

"I'm still trying to take in what you said . . . about body parts. In a freezer? From how many people again?"

"I wasn't specific, because the extent of the crimes is still a sensitive matter."

"Why not be open?" asked Lehman.

"There would be panic," said Power. "Justifiable panic, but panic nevertheless. And as you know, the outcome of panic is somewhat uncertain."

"Hmm," said Lehman. "Are there more people than Shipman killed?"

"Dozens," said Power, determined to give no more information than absolutely necessary.

"And what would the motive be?" asked Lehman. "Is the predator a man wanting sex with runaway girls, perhaps with an unfortunate paraphilia involving asphyxia?"

"Some think the motivation is simple. I think it is more complex. Some think our predator is a cannibal and that his victims are women, and men."

"He ate them?" Lehman looked horrified and his voice had risen in volume.

Power put his finger to his lips. "You promised to keep this confidential. You understand now why the case is sensitive. And can I ask for your help please?"

"Yes, of course, you can stay and listen, and I will introduce you as a colleague."

And so that was what happened. Power stayed. Initially he sat in the corner of the small room observing Lehman talking to a steady stream of patients who drifted into the support centre. There was an old man, with beard but without teeth, who cackled at things no one else could see or hear and who was hallucinated. Lehman checked his records and gave him his weekly injection of a depot drug. There was a thin, middle-aged man who smelled of refuse and rodents and said that time and space had stopped, and also that there were no longer any other planets beyond earth. Lehman arranged for him to have a bath, some clean donated clothes and some capsules of fluoxetine. After Power had got the measure of the first few attendees he suggested that perhaps he could see the patients first and then present them to Lehman, as if the Professor were become a trainee again, and presenting to the Consultant.

It was around one in the morning, and Power's level of concentration was flagging. The heating in the building had gone off for the night and he nursed a cup of coffee in both hands for warmth. There was a knock on the door and one of the helpers ushered in a thin, bird-like young man who looked about him with sharp, small eyes that flitted about, taking in his surroundings. This was to be Power's next patient. He had just finished eating a reheated bowl of stew and was gnawing at the remains of a bread roll. Power wondered if the volunteers had been in such a hurry to usher him in that they hadn't even let him finish his meal properly.

"Hello," said Power. "Was the meal any good?"

"Yes, yes," the man said. His voice seemed unbroken. Power looked at him more closely for a moment, but so as not to disquiet his patient he did not let his gaze linger. He took in a young man, perhaps just over twenty years of age, with greasy brown curls, ginger stubble, and spots around his mouth. Power briefly wondered about solvent abuse. The patient was looking at Power as he finished his bread and then, having considered the matter, said, "You're different, not the same doctor."

"'I'm Doctor Power. You can see the other doctor after me if you'd like?"

"It's all right. I don't mind. He thinks I'm mad and gives me pills, because I go on a bit."

"Can I ask what you're called?" asked Power. He wanted to check the limited records that Lehman kept to see what had been prescribed for the man in front of him. Power looked at the patient again and this time took in ill-fitting trainers with no socks, ragged cargo pants, a thin grey T-shirt, and a sky-blue nylon sleeping bag draped around his shoulders like some sort of cloak. He noticed how agitated the patient was in the seat and that the man's eyes were wide open and staring. Power wondered about thyotoxicosis.

"Kyle Daniels. That's what I tell the doctor."

"I see," said Power. He didn't ask what Kyle's real name might be, but searched through the card file in front of him. A single card showed him that Kyle had attended four times in the last six months. "You're taking olanzapine? Do you take it as Dr Lehman wants you to? Every day?"

"If I have it. If it isn't robbed."

There were scant details on the medical card. Power couldn't tell what the history was from the card and didn't approve of the brevity. Lehman's note-keeping style was minimalist. Maybe the notes were a kind of shorthand purely for Lehman's benefit. "Does the drug help? Maybe the olanzapine reduces the voices?"

"I don't hear voices, Doc."

Power looked at the card again. By way of history there was only a diagnostic classification number from ICD-10. The card said 'F20.0'. "Maybe you can tell me what troubled you when you first met Dr Lehman."

"He prescribed that because I kept going on about Sky and Jay."

"Sky and Jay?"

"I kept telling everybody about them here at the refuge. The chefs and the helpers, and people didn't want to hear any more. I'd told the people I knew on the streets and they didn't want to hear any more either. They told me to shut up or they'd shut me up."

"Who did?"

"Other homeless people. We can be helpful to each other, but I suppose people have limits. They can only take so much aggro I guess. You tell them once and they sympathise, twice and they try and calm you, and three times they tell you to shut up. Four times they kick your teeth in."

"It's no fun when people won't listen, is it?" Power looked at the sheen of perspiration on Kyle's neck and suspected he might be running a temperature. He wondered if there was a thermometer in the makeshift clinic.

"The worst thing . . . the worst thing . . . apart from not having a roof and walls about you, is the time you have. The endless time you spend shifting from one rain soaked place where you are not wanted to another place where you are even less wanted. Endless effort spent in wasting time."

"Tell me about Sky and Jay," said Power. "I'd like to know."

"You want me to talk about them? No-one else does."

"Please tell **me** then," said Power.

"Sky was our friend. Jay and I were her friends. Jay was my girlfriend, on and off. We were more like mates. Slept together for warmth. Jay was from Leeds. Blonde and clever. She had got into Uni, the Metropolitan one, but had a row with a lecturer who reminded her of someone and she started bingeing on drink and drugs, and gambling to try and make up what she owed for the drugs. And she got pregnant and had it dealt with and her family didn't want to know. She'd stole from them before Uni, so they weren't going down that route again and they just kind of closed the door on her. So we were together. I stopped her being picked up by a pimp the first night she was on the streets. I wonder whether I did the right thing or whether that's what she does now anyway . . ."

"What do you mean?" asked Power.

"Well, I done what I thought was the right thing. Saving her from the dirty flesh peddlers. But was what I got her into, better? Living in doorways and pissing behind bushes? And is that what she did, go to them in the end to get off the streets?"

"You don't know where she is now?" Kyle shook his head. "And when did you last see Jay?"

"She went off to find Sky."

"When was that?"

"A few months back. I lose track of time. I have so much of it."

"And Sky then? Can you tell me about her?" asked Power.

"Sky was new to all this too. But she had a different journey. She was younger and she'd be straight out of care. Seventeen. From Rotherham and she'd been passed about by men since she was thirteen. She was in care, but they didn't care, that was the thing. No-one cared that men were picking her up in taxis waiting outside the home. No-one cared. And then when she was seventeen, she was, like, too old. Too old for the fostering or the homes, and too old for the men. You know what I mean?"

"So she ended up in the city centre with you and Jay?"

"She said we were her parents now, though the maths wasn't right, you know?" Kyle sniffed. "And then one night we saw this bloke talking to her, by the Gardens. He didn't look like a flesh peddler, though. He didn't have no fancy Land Rover. I think we saw him getting off a bus, for fuck's sake. But Jay was worried, 'cos he was leading her away, with a hand on her shoulder. And so Jay went over. And he told her that he was taking Sky for dinner, and she could have a bath and a warm bed, just this once. And he'd see she got back safe to Jay tomorrow. He said he was from a charity, but he didn't have no ID and he wouldn't look Jay in the eye. He had his hoodie up. Anyway, Sky, she was keen to go. You get kind of itchy sometimes, on the street, do you know? And what he offered tempted her I s'pose, although it was just simple stuff. So Jay asked if he'd show her his face, and he pulls his hood off and forces a smile and says, there are you satisfied? And off Sky goes. But she never came back. She left on the bus. She never came back and we just waved her off."

"You feel guilty?"

"I suppose," said Kyle. "But I sometimes like to think Jay fell on her feet, you know? But then I think about Sky and I know, I know inside, that Jay's gone and Jay and Sky are never coming back."

"What did they – Sky and Jay – look like? Do you have a photo?" Kyle shook his head. "Can you describe Sky then, please?" asked Power.

"Short, but slim. Light as a leaf. With pale, milky-white skin and the bluest of eyes. And long hair, I mean really long. Blonde hair."

Power sighed. Kyle had given a perfect description of the Ice Maiden. "And then, what happened?"

"Well, Jay wouldn't rest. She didn't sleep that night. Like she really was Sky's mum, waiting up for her. And she went on then, on and on about where Sky was, and we went looking all over the city in case she'd found a different district. But no-one had heard of her."

"Did you try the police?"

Kyle looked taken aback, but decided to ignore the question as being from a professional who was naïve in the real ways of the world. "So Jay started asking and looking for the scum who'd taken her away. But he was nowhere to be seen. And Jay rode the bus route a few times – the bus Sky had taken – to see the route and if he ever got on the bus. She never saw him."

"What bus was it?"

Kyle had to think hard. Then he asked, "Why are you asking? Are you testing me?"

"It's not a trick," said Power. "I genuinely want to know."

"You're the first one who has. That's what worries me."

"So?"

"The 130. She rode it. I rode it with her once. But we didn't see anything. And so we stopped. Then one day she thinks she spots him in the crowd. The one who took Sky, walking with a woman. And Jay heads off, sprints. Running through the crowd. I couldn't keep up. I get out of breath." As if by way of illustration, he coughed. "I couldn't catch my breath or catch her. And then when I got through the crowd to where he'd been, no one was there. He wasn't there. Jay wasn't there. And I've never seen her again." He gave a single heart-rending cry, and before another was half out of his mouth, he caught and snatched it back, desperate not to show emotion.

"And after that, I asked for her. Everywhere. I asked for Sky and Jay, but no one knew. Then I told everyone that there was this man, this scum, who would spirit you away. And because I kept on, people think I'm mad. Because I cared. Because I didn't shut up."

"But you came to see Dr Lehman, and took his prescription?"

"He listened. Less than you maybe, but he listened more than the others. And the tablets do give me some calm, some peace. And in the end, you give in, Doctor, you just give in."

Power nodded and reached into his pocket and brought out a picture of Heaney as a young man, seated at the table in the farmhouse. The picture was cropped so it just showed Heaney's head and shoulders. He showed it to Kyle. "This man, do you recognise him."

Kyle let out an unguarded cry and seized the piece of paper. "That's him, the man with the hoody, the man who took them away."

Power nodded thoughtfully. He looked at how fiercely Kyle held the page. "Do you want to keep the photo? I have copies." Kyle nodded. Power reached for his pad and wrote out an address and a telephone number. "I might want to talk to you again, Kyle. There's a place for you to stay. If you want." He handed over the address. "I work for a Foundation. Not a charity. Set up by a wealthy man, a philanthropist who was once homeless himself. If you contact that address, and ask for help, they will give it. I will speak to them for you when you leave. They will give you a bed, somewhere safe. You don't have to go, but it's a safe house, and the Foundation will help you after that." Kyle stared at Power's handwriting.

"Do you think you'll go?" asked Power.

"I'll see," said Kyle. "I'm making no promises." He stood up. "Can you get them back, Sky and Jay?" He looked at Power's face and seemed to divine what Power was thinking. "I can see it from your eyes, that no-one can. Well, thank you for listening." He moved to the door.

"Kyle?" said Power, as he stood from the desk. "Will you stay in touch, please? Try that address I gave you?"

"I'll see," said Kyle, and then he ducked out of the door and was gone.

Power paused, then instinctively he felt compelled to follow Kyle to see where he would go. The young man was walking away down the corridor and Power followed at a respectful distance. Kyle made his way across the dining hall where volunteers were still handing out day-old Pret a Manger sandwiches and enamelled mugs of tea. Power hung back, not wanting to frighten Kyle. A middle aged volunteer approached Kyle as he transited the hall. She offered him a mug of tea. He initially waved her offering away, but clearly she was insistent and Kyle grabbed the mug from her and swigged it down, staring at the grey-haired volunteer defiantly. She was thin and angular in a shapeless, grey dress. She smiled as Kyle drained the very last drop and retrieved the mug from him. He muttered a gruff thank you, before hurrying off into the darkness of the corridor leading to the exit. Power saw Kyle was still clutching the paper with the address on.

* * *

"Come in!" A cheery voice cried out in response to Power's knock on the varnished mahogany door. Dr Power twisted the brass handle and peered round into a parquet-floored office with high gothic ceiling. Around the walls were heavy wooden bench tops covered in piles of dusty Victorian manuscripts and glass cases of stuffed animals. A grandfather clock ticked away in the corner. In the centre was a roll-top desk, which was high enough to screen the seated occupant from Power's view. The desk's owner stood up, however, and held out her hand across the top of the desk. Professor Rose wore oval spectacles, had beaming rosy cheeks and grey hair tied back into a bun. "Professor Power, is it? You're spot on eleven as arranged. Are you one of those folk who likes to be punctual?"

"Well, yes," said Dr Power, as he was ushered to a wooden captain's chair by the archaeology professor's desk. Without asking him for his choice she poured him a beaker of black coffee from a thermos flask and thrust it into his hand.

"Decaffeinated, black. Is that how you like it?" she asked. Power felt he had to say yes. "I thought so," she said happily; her right eye twinkled at him, but her left seemed half-closed. "Although, of course, punctuality is neither here nor there to me." She pointed to some rugged ingots of copper on her cluttered desktop. "These were smelted from copper mines between eighteen hundred and nineteen hundred years ago in Alderley Edge. When we look at things that are thousands of years old what does five minutes here or there matter?"

Outside the room, Power could hear a group of schoolchildren chattering and laughing as their teacher conducted them on a tour of the University Museum. He guessed they would enjoy the Egyptian mummies and the skeleton of the Triceratops best. Those were the things that he remembered from when his father took him round the same museum as a child. The shrunken brown toes of the mummies had given him nightmares.

"I live out at the Edge," said Power. "I didn't realise the mine works were that old."

"Even before the Romans came to the Edge, Neolithic people cut down trees to smelt ores of malachite and azurite to make gorgeous shiny copper," Professor Rose went on enthusiastically. "There were prehistoric barrows out near Lindow Moss and the Common grounds of Wilmslow. All bulldozed now and covered by an urban wasteland of tacky houses and trivial shops."

"There are tunnels in the sandstone under my house," said Power. "Could they be mines?"

Professor Rose rummaged under a pile of paper and extracted an Ordnance Survey map. She said, "It's from nineteen thirty-six, but if you can point out the area where your house is . . ." Power pored over the map and found where his house was, near the Macclesfield Road. "No," she said. "The mine workings of the twentieth century were way over here, to the west. So your tunnels aren't recent mine workings – probably they aren't mine workings at all. Although, who knows, some shafts were centuries old, like the Abbadine tunnel, five foot high and three foot wide, driven 'halfway through the hill until the centre'. Others in the area are sharp, vertical shafts nearly two hundred feet deep. Your tunnels could probably be older than the nineteenth century. Possibly they are natural caves, not mine workings. Have you been down? I suppose you must have been."

"Only once," said Power. "I . . . er . . . didn't enjoy it. There is a way down there, from the kitchen, through a tunnel, a stairway, straight into the caverns."

"Like a *souterrain*, maybe?" Professor Rose suggested.

"Ah," said Dr Power. "I'm afraid the oceans of my ignorance have no shores . . . please, could you tell me what a *souterrain* is?"

"Well," Professor Rose took off her spectacles and cleaned them with a soft, yellow cloth. "A *souterrain* was an Iron Age invention – used in ringforts. For coping with sieges, or attacks. It's an underground hiding hole or escape route, if you like. I wonder how much good they were, as some might have led to very obvious ways out and you could be ambushed, I suppose. I don't like going underground myself, though," she admitted. "Well, what can I do for you specifically, Professor Power. What can an archaeologist tell a psychiatrist?"

"I was wondering if you could tell me about the people who lived at the Edge and on the plain below it, before the urban sprawl arrived, as you described it earlier."

"The land around your house has been farmed and worked for hundreds of years, thousands of years by the same people, families organized in strict hierarchy since Medieval times. They worked according to the old system of villeins and yeomen – giving their time and produce to the Lord of the Manor. Mainly these were illiterate people working all hours in the dirt or perhaps as servants at the great hall. Once or twice they might have a day out to the town in Macclesfield to break up the monotony. Some of them might have mined in previous centuries, for cobalt and copper. Copper was used for the hulls of ships, and coins, and brass. And blue-black grains of cobalt oxide were used, for the brilliant blue. The Victorians used cobalt to make blue glazes for pottery, and used it in the blue of stained glass. And they mined vanadium too, for making the blackest permanent ink to print patterns on their textiles. And the same old families, who'd farmed the land in centuries past stayed on to work the mines, before all the terrible changes of the Industrial Age uprooted folk and pulled them into the cities. It was like the new cities had their own kind of gravity, sucking people out of the past. But there was talk even in the nineteenth century, I gather, of some primitive folk still living down on the plain, in huts made of bent wood, down on the mosslands. Burning turf for fuel."

"Primitive people?"

"Unlike the villagers and farmers," The archaeologist replied. "A writer called Norbury made them sound like some kind of throwback – he described them as 'peculiar people' – like dangerous Neanderthals. Have you heard of Norbury's account?"

"I think I have done. The name sounds familiar," said Power.

"Another author speculated that they were savages in ragged animal pelts covered in pigments of blue malachite and azurite. They were definitely not to be approached if you were alone, and the Mosslands could never be travelled through after dusk. Norbury deliberately makes them sound like prehistoric survivors, although another line of thinking is that these folk were just ex-soldiers. I suppose they might have been invalids from the Napoleonic wars just eking out an existence on the fringes of society."

"Ah," said Power, who had enjoyed the romance about a forgotten people from the distant past managing to live into the nineteenth century rather more than the drier theory that they were marginalised ex-soldiers. "And the Lindow Man – the body they found in the peat. Is he still here, at the museum?"

"He's off travelling," she said. The Lindow Man was the preserved body of a man discovered in the nineteen-eighties by peat-cutters. "He's part of an exhibition of other bog people. Europe has a number, like Tollund Man and Elling Woman, for instance. There's an exhibition in Denmark that has gathered some of the bodies together. I suppose this new exhibition is a bit like a conference for bog people. Only I suppose they don't participate much."

"How long had he stayed in the earth?"

"Pete Marsh? I'm sorry – that's what we call Lindow Man. He'd lain there for almost a millenium. But so well preserved, at first they thought he was a freshly murdered victim."

"And I seem to remember he died a violent death?" said Power.

"Yes, he'd suffered a deal of violence before he died. There was a serious head wound, that was perhaps healing at the time of his least meal. After this meal of burned bread he had had a ligature of sinew placed round his neck and twisted and tightened using a piece of wood until his vertebrae broke, and then someone with good anatomical knowledge had slit his jugular vein to drain his blood."

"And he was found at Lindow Moss?"

"He was. Like Lindow Woman."

"There was another body?"

"Again the peat cutters found her," said Professor Rose. "They discovered a head in nineteen eighty-three. She was middle-aged. There were remnants of soft tissues; the brain, eye, the optic nerve, and her hair. Well, again the preservation was so good that the police called up a man they had always had their suspicions about – they suspected he'd murdered his wife, Malika. She'd disappeared in the nineteen-sixties. When Lindow Woman was found they assumed they'd found Malika's body and her husband Mr Reyn-Bardt actually confessed that he **had** disposed of her body there and said that after so long he thought he'd never be found out. He had lived near the Moss. And on the basis of his confession that he'd strangled and dismembered her he was sent off to trial in Chester. Only when the carbon dating from the body came back it returned a date of around 200 AD, so whoever the peat cutters had found she certainly wasn't Malika. The husband tried to retract his confession, but it stuck and he was convicted.

"We did studies on their skin, which we found was tanned after death by sphagnan, a chemical in the sphagnum moss, but also we found traces of copper, as if in life they were covered with this copper pigment." She looked wistful for a moment. "And there was a third body, a man found in nineteen eighty-seven, but the peat cutting machine shredded him . . . he had no head."

"And these people, found in the moss from two thousand years ago, they had died unnaturally then?"

"We think so, yes, the Lindow people obviously were rather violent. And Tollund Man was hanged with a plaited leather cord. The girl from Holland was strangled. Dätgen man from Germany was beheaded, and Worsley Moss Man from Lancashire was strangled. So yes, ritual slaughter or sacrifice happened throughout Europe then, we think."

"But why do archaeologists always bring religion into these things? Why is it always ritual." Power sounded a note of frustration. "What if these people were criminals and society just decided to execute them? Or maybe they were considered dangerous or mad, and society couldn't treat them, but just wanted to be rid. Or like that husband in the sixties who just wanted to be shut of his wife. The victims could have been dispatched because of motives like jealousy, or revenge or sudden rage. Why dress it up in rite and superstition?"

"Why indeed?" agreed Professor Rose. "Archaeologists want to know everything about a past world, but only have things that are preserved as evidence of that world . . . things like stone and bone. Ideas and motives are lost if they remain unrecorded – any ideas or spoken words are lost as soon as they are uttered. Only those ideas which are carved into stone persist from some eras, and how many words of mine and yours are carved into stone Professor Power?"

Power paused to consider this and then said, "I'm puzzled about the motivation behind putting bodies into the moss, I came to see you to clarify my thoughts."

"Am I helping or confusing you, I wonder? This is to do with the farmhouse at Lindow isn't it?"

Power nodded. "In confidence, yes it is."

"I don't think I've clarified anything for you have I?" she said. "You don't have to answer that. But I think the Moss may have held some significance to these people – more than just being a convenient place to hide bodies. It is after all, a place that was probably away from settlements so the victim, or sacrifice would have to be brought there. Killed on the spot. Bodies are more difficult to transport than you think. Why do all of that unless the place held some meaning. And it would have been a dark, watery place there, perhaps a place where they thought ancient water spirits lived. Spirits down in the water and swirling in the mists; maybe the marshland was believed to hold a gate to the underworld? And some of the bodies we've found are clearly well to do individuals. There's a theory that these were nobles or local kings who once they showed signs of weakness or age, were killed so that their power would flow on to the next ruler. But as you say, who knows what the motives behind these killings really were? It's just – to me at any rate – they do seem to have . . . an element of ritual to them."

Power nodded. "Well, I am grateful to you for talking to me. It has helped me. I knew of Lindow Man . . . I didn't know there were others."

He shook her hand, somewhat awkwardly and left. As he walked the parquet floors to the cast iron stairs, a new group of school children were gathering around the glass cabinets and gazing at the museum finds within. Power made his way past the gift shop and out through the café. His gaze lingered on a pile of pastries and his nose sniffed at

SON OF DARKNESS

the vapour trails of fine Arabica coffee, but he resisted the temptation and emerged onto Oxford Road into the midst of a student demonstration against proposed increases in tuition fees.

He made his way through the jostling crowd with their flapping linen banners and along the road towards the car park where he had left his Saab. He passed a blue plaque on the physics building dedicated to Alison Uttley and further on another to Alan Turing, who, Power noted, had been a reader in mathematics in the building it was attached to. Why had they never granted him a Chair, even posthumously, wondered Power?

He was nearly at the car park, when he looked left down a passageway that had once been a genuine street, and which the University had expanded over and pedestrianised as it expanded outwards in its incessant growth. There was the gothic yellow brick building of the old Victorian medical school. For a moment he stared at the doorway beneath a turreted tower, and the arched windows in the brickwork. The medical school had been disused for years, and had the air of dejection that such forlorn buildings wear once they are robbed of their purpose. Power had a sense of *déjà vu*. Why did the old building look familiar? He was sure that he had never crossed its threshold in his life. And then the sudden sense of intuition was gone and Power was left wondering what had sparked the intimation of familiarity in his temporal lobe. He shook his head and hurried back to his car to make his way to his afternoon clinic.

* * *

Andrew Lynch was reflecting on the reading he had just heard in the morning Cathedral Eucharist. It was a weekday, and he had an appointment at the Foundation's office just after lunchtime and so he was hoping that the Deacon's sermon would be brief. She walked across the nave and started to climb the wooden steps to the pulpit. She was grey-haired and owlish behind horn-rimmed spectacles; a stubby individual made that much broader by her cassock. Lynch looked up at the vaulted stone arches that criss-crossed beneath the wooden ceiling. Lynch was preparing to tolerate her sermon as best he could, but as she spoke, found himself drawn into her theme. It was, after all, about a matter that he considered most days of his working life. The Old Testament reading had been from Genesis 4 and the

Deacon had worked this into her sermon. She spoke well and clearly and her voice was compelling.

"And the first ever murderer in our world was Cain, firstborn son of Adam and Eve, who slew his own brother, Abel, in a jealous rage. The scripture tells us that Abel's blood cried out to God from the ground where Cain buried his brother, and the Lord asked Cain 'where is thy brother', and he lied to God, Cain said 'I am not my brother's keeper.'

"And the Lord told Cain he would ever more be a restless wanderer on the earth, and set upon him a mark so all would know him and tradition tells us that this mark, actual or otherwise, as a curse, was upon the sons of Cain. Because Cain had children, some monsters, and some who look exactly like us, and they are with us today, of course. Cain lived till a great age, leaving legions of his corrupt descendants to spread his evil on the earth.

"For Cain's children cannot bear mention of the Lord, and are as atheists, and deny that very God whose works are all around them, deny the evidence of their own eyes, deny that very creation of His that gives them life. Tradition has it that Cain's children build cities and make metal things, and lust for power. They abhor nature, because the Lord told Cain that the soil of the earth would never sustain him, in punishment for defiling it with Abel's blood.

"There is a legend of the Jews that Cain was conceived by Eve after a seduction by the serpent, or satan, or Samael, the archangel of death.

"And know this to be true, we must avoid the family of Cain; they are amongst us, they look like us, for they are also in the image of God, but they eschew His love. They deny Him. Know them then by how they curse the Lord.

"And know this, that though we might hate the thought, the blood of Cain may run within our own veins! Only the deluded or the criminally fascist believe in racial purity – we must by the nature of chance in the shuffling of our genes, generation by generation, have acquired a modicum on Cain's blood – some less, and some more – and we must watch for the ideas of Cain within our own hearts and pray that we become more like our maker and less like the family of Cain."

Lynch was thinking so much about these words that he hardly heard the Deacon's final prayer and dismissal. He sat silently reflecting upon her words until she herself came up to him. "Andrew, isn't it?"

Lynch was surprised at her sudden appearance in front of him, but she had been shaking hands and saying farewell to most of the small throng who had attended the Eucharist. He was surprised too that she appeared to know him, but then he did call into the Cathedral on more days of the week than not. "Did the service mean anything particular to you? You seem lost in thought."

"I am . . . I used to be a police officer. And I hate to say it, but murder was my bread and butter. You made me think . . . about the family of Cain."

"Ah," she said. "You caught a glimpse of something. God gives us these little insights. I see you have some years of experience of God's world, and I guess you know that some things in life happen just beyond your range of vision. You can only just see them, perhaps, out of the corner of your eye."

"Thank you," said Lynch. He shook her hand, bade goodbye and made his way thoughtfully out into the cloister.

Chapter Nine

The train rumbled and chattered along the points and tracks from Piccadilly Station as it sought its way out of the great Victorian city of Manchester. The dusty, deep-blue upholstery of the seat felt prickly underneath Power's trousered legs. Professor Power looked down from the windows onto lines of huddled terraces punctuated by squat superstores, islands amidst oceans of cars in their car parks. Once on the open rails to Alderley, the train gathered speed and confidence. Power thought over the conversation he'd had with Professor Rose at the museum and tried to fix on a solution to the concerns he had about the case. He was not a religious man, and he found it difficult to ascribe the murders of people to ritual or sacrifice. And yet, Power knew that just because one person didn't subscribe to a certain point of view, it didn't mean another wouldn't hold that same view as their very *raison d'etre*. How else could he explain the acts of some of his patients? Their surprising actions were sometimes founded on a certainty that was nothing more than delusion. Could the motive of repeated sacrifice to some unknown spirit really explain the series of murders at the farmhouse? Power had been struggling with the notion of ritual all the time that the curator was talking at the Museum. How could he bridge the gulf of understanding between himself and Heaney? And yet no matter how hard he tried to grapple with the problem his attention was captured by the piercing wailing of an infant opposite him in the carriage.

Power looked over and saw a mother frantically battling with an irate, red-faced baby as she struggled to send out a message from her Blackberry. Using two thumbs to type out letters on its tiny keypad was not easy for her whilst under siege from the furious child. Power watched and noted how, although the baby's eyes were fixed on its mother, the mother's eyes were fixed on the tiny screen of the phone. Almost as soon as she typed a response, there was another message to reply to. Was her text conversation urgent? Power realised he was silently judging her and scolded himself for his thoughts. The conversation might be vital, but then he wondered, what could be so crucial? The baby screamed hoarsely for attention and Power felt annoyed; he thought that he wouldn't behave so, if he had a son. If he had a son he would look into his eyes and make contact. If he had a son . . .

* * *

Lynch had struggled to find a parking place amongst the glossy black V8 Range Rovers that garnished the streets in the village. He was due to meet his friend, Carl Power, off the lunchtime train and Alderley's station car park was, as ever, full of commuters' cars. Lynch had planned to have a sandwich with Power at the Village Café, but instead, he lingered on the yellow lines outside the station entrance, hoping that Power would be able to get off the train and find him before a traffic warden issued a ticket.

He thought he had been watching the station entrance carefully enough, when suddenly the passenger door opened and Power got in.

"Where did you spring from?" Lynch asked.

"People often don't see me. I think I must merge into the background or something. Maybe it's a skill that goes with the job, or a defect of character. How are you?"

"Unusually hungry, and with lots to tell you." Lynch revved the engine and drew away from the kerb. He drove along the Alderley Edge High Street. There was still nowhere to park. "Pamela is much better, she sends you her thanks. She is sleeping well, she says, and singing your praises to her friends."

"I was happy to help," said Power. "Any time . . . weren't we going to stop for food?" he asked. Lynch was speeding away from the shops and turning left, up the hill on the Macclesfield Road.

"I'd been trying to find a parking space in the village for ages. I've quite given up on that idea. Don't worry," said Lynch. "I'll take you to The Wizard."

The Wizard was a pub less than five hundred yards from Power's house, but Power almost never went there. And Lynch had never been. Before Power could protest and offer to make them lunch at home, Lynch said, "I've never been and it's my shout."

"OK," said Power, folding his hands in resignation in his lap. He tried to settle, but caught a glimpse of a car behind them in the passenger side mirror and suddenly had the intuitive feeling that the car was following them. Power tried to catch sight of the driver, but shortly the car slowed and pulled off into a shared driveway. Power sighed and wondered how he had become so jumpy.

Lynch parked in the National Trust car park and they wandered left towards the adjacent pub, The Wizard.

They saw a group of people clustered around an urn of tea on a picnic table outside the teashop by The Wizard. The group was dressed in overalls and mostly wore, or carried, yellow hard hats. They laughed and joked as they drank paper cups full of milky tea. As they walked past, Power nodded to a grey, bearded man in glasses on the edge of the group.

"What is it?" he asked. "A Union meeting?"

"Derbyshire Caving Club," said the man and clumped his way over to Power in a pair of heavy boots. "It's a working tea break. We're clearing a roof fall in Engine Vein – some debris from an earth tremor last year."

"Engine Vein? Is that the copper mine near here?"

"Precisely, sir – just over there in the trees." He pointed over his shoulder. "A quake can sometimes dislodge rocks in the cave roof, so we're clearing what fell. Very carefully . . . we don't want any casualties. The roof can remain unstable after a tremor."

"How large is the mine?"

The caving club man took off his helmet to reveal a perfect dome of baldness. He cradled the helmet in his left arm and extended his right hand. "I'm the club secretary, Stephen."

"Hello," said Power, shaking his hand. "I'm Carl Power, a doctor, I live in Alderley House – it's about five hundred yards from here, I suppose." He pointed in the direction of his house.

"Well, Engine Vein Mine goes down around fifty metres to the Hough Level. There's copper and lead and manganese down there. It's been a mine for the last four thousand years, on and off."

"How . . . erm . . . wide do the mines extend?" He was conscious that his questions might sound naïve, but what he wanted to know, was whether the tunnels might reach into the sandstone bedrock under his house.

"These aren't big mines. Each one is quite small, but Engine Vein Mine links up to Brynlow and Wood Mine and West Mine. They don't go over that way . . ." He pointed over in the direction Power had indicated. "If that's where your house is, our Engine Vein stops far short of that. We do keep discovering new things all the time, though."

"Ah," said Power. "There's a tunnel or a cave right under my house. Instead of a cellar under the kitchen, there's a tunnel."

"Really? Is it like a worked tunnel? Are there pick marks on the walls?"

"I don't know," said Power. "I think the walls of these tunnels are smooth." He thought back to how the walls felt under his fingers in the dark.

"Maybe a natural formation then, carved by a watercourse underground. You've not explored them?" asked Stephen.

"No, no," said Power hurriedly. "I had a bad experience down there. My light went out. I thought I was lost."

"Ah, then you've experienced the dark. There's nothing quite like it, there's nothing darker than underground. Over the years many people have gone missing in the tunnels that way," nodded the caver. "And where they ended up we don't know, we've not found any bones, but there's miles of tunnels. We've only explored so far, ourselves. There are vertical shafts like Bear Shaft and Ring Shaft that are a hundred and fifty feet deep. So be careful, you don't want to take a tumble down one of those."

Power shook his head. He wasn't finding the club secretary's words reassuring. He was thinking back to how he might have stepped out into the darkness, and plunged suddenly into nothingness. He imagined falling and ricocheting from side to side to a broken-limbed death at the bottom.

"I'll tell you what, Doc," said Stephen. "You are a proper doctor, not one of these philosophy doctors?" Power nodded. Stephen disconnected the light and its battery pack from his waist. "Hold these." Power took the proffered light and heavy battery pack and held them with some bemusement. Then Stephen placed the helmet onto Power's head. It still felt warm and mildly humid. "It's a decent fit," said Stephen. "You can keep those. We have plenty. In case you want to venture a bit further along the tunnel under the house. But don't go alone, and don't go too far. If you'd like to wait, contact the club and I'll even come with you. I'd be intrigued to see if the tunnels are worked – mined – and if they connect up."

Power thanked Stephen profusely and made his way over to Lynch, who had taken up a seat at a vacant table some way off from the caving group. He was watching with some amusement, especially whilst Power received a present of some equipment.

Lynch asked, "Who are they then?"

"Cavers. Volunteers," said Power. "They have access to the mines here. I gather there was a whole industry once, separating the copper and cobalt from the ore."

"And you got a present, too," said Lynch, gesticulating at the helmet and light. "Are you planning to go under the house again? I've said I'll go with you."

"Maybe," said Power without any great confidence. "Nice of him to give me this stuff. I didn't feel I could say no."

"Well, come on, bring it with you," said Lynch. "I'm the starving one, just for once." It was usually Power's appetite that led the way.

Power's impression of the interior of The Wizard pub was that its wood beamed ceilings were low, rather like the roof of a mine and the stone flagged floor emphasized the impression in his imagination. Dried brown garlands of hops hung low above their heads. In a darkened corner was a bar and Power and Lynch both ordered a pint of bitter before sitting at a table with two menus.

"What would you like?" asked Lynch, after a while.

"Even though it's five hundred yards from my house, I've never eaten here so it's all a mystery," said Power. "Tagliatelle with kale and pine nuts. I'll try that."

"And I'll have the sea bass with asparagus and saffron potatoes," said Lynch, half to himself.

"I thought you might go for the roast beef," said Power.

"It's a Friday," said Lynch. "Fish on a Friday."

"I see," said Power. "Remind me – why no meat on a Friday?"

"Jesus died on a Friday, so no warm-blooded life can be sacrificed." Lynch said this in automatic fashion, as if his mind was occupied elsewhere. He stood up and went to order at the bar. Power watched him order and then he went out the front door of the pub, rather than return straight to the table.

Power mused on the concept of rites and rituals whilst he waited for Lynch. When Lynch did return he was frowning. Power looked up, "What's the matter?"

"Strange thing, like seeing a ghost. I thought I saw someone, looking at me, through the window behind you. I just walked all the way round the outside of the pub. No-one there."

"Who do you think it was?"

"Oh, I don't know. Just my eyes playing tricks. Think no more of it."

And Power would not have made any more of it, except for the fact that Lynch had seen fit to act on whatever he had seen. He'd taken a walk around the building. So Power pressed the point, "But who was it? You used the word 'ghost' and that would imply a return of someone you knew."

"No-one. Let's not waste time, we have so much to discuss," said Lynch, affecting a falsely breezy manner that Power saw through immediately.

"I have wondered, in recent weeks, whether there was someone following or stalking me," said Power. "An intuition, not much more than that. Perhaps some shadows in my garden that made me suspicious, or troubled by a feeling of . . . disquiet. If you suspected someone or something, you would let me know, wouldn't you?"

"Of course if I had evidence I would tell you," said Lynch. "Look, think no more of it. I checked and there was no-one."

"But there was something, or someone, who made you wonder. It wasn't Heaney you thought you saw? I didn't think it was wise to be featured on the news . . ."

"I wouldn't be sitting here if I thought it was Heaney. Just relax. It was nothing. A mistake."

Power looked into his friend's eyes, and for once he was not reassured. "I see. Then I wonder what you want to discuss today?"

"As you mentioned it, in passing, the media strategy for the Heaney case is changing. As Beresford feels he has certain facts established he wants to . . . er . . . develop the media strategy, to encourage the media to get us leads rather than discourage them from pointless speculation. To profit from their interest rather than merely serve their curiosity."

"What does that mean?" asked Power. "Do you mean he didn't quite know what was going on and didn't want to look bewildered on camera?"

"A little harsh of you, Carl. As SIO Beresford faced many unknowns; the true number of people who had died for instance and who they might be. The SIO would not want to cause unmitigated panic, and if Beresford fed the media with uncertainties he might well cause panic. The media strategy has changed to seek, rather than suppress publicity. To stage recreations and have television appeals. To find out all we can about the victims and how they may have met Heaney. To garner leads on where Heaney might be hiding. He might be working as a labourer for cash in hand somewhere, picking vegetables, or he might have adopted a victim's identity and be squatting in their flat. A neighbour might recognise him from a crime appeal on the BBC. And I think Beresford might appreciate an expert giving their general views on the case – in short, anything to keep the media's attention focused on this phase of the investigation."

"An expert. You mean me?" Power's eyes flashed.

"I was asked to sound you out," Lynch sensed he must retreat.

"I might talk to the media about a paper or a book I had written, but this . . . you know I have no wish to attract publicity here, there is no control over what kind of person could fix upon me. It might bring trouble right to my doorstep, to Laura. I am more wary than when I was younger, because I have seen what happens and how overwhelming and unjustified the hate can be."

"Well, I completely understand," said Lynch. "I did question how you might ride two horses at once – being a confidential adviser on the case, and a source of media comment. Let us talk no more of this."

There was a moment of silence between the old friends.

Lynch broached something to discuss to fill the hiatus. "The final count from DNA studies and body parts. The grand total. Do you want to know?"

"Oh," groaned Power. "You can't imagine how much I don't want to know, but go on – we must face the fact."

"Thirty-seven men, and sixty-two women. All kinds of ages, but mainly people in their teens and twenties. Some malnourished."

"Ninety-nine not out," said Power grimly. "Not as many as Shipman." He paused, thinking. "Could they say if any of the body parts were Heaney's own parents?"

"That was not a finding. In other words, the body parts were unrelated to Heaney's DNA."

"And the girl, the complete body in the freezer?"

"The Ice Maiden, as she has become known to Beresford and others?"

"Yes, was she the girl that Kyle Daniels told me about? Sky?"

"They think so. They made an identification of her against a missing persons report. Sky is a distinctive sort of name. We . . . they . . . found her parents in Dorset. The DNA matches them, but of course they were able to travel up and make a positive identification, poor souls. So, one by one, Beresford and his team are beginning to make links between the body parts and living relatives. I mean, they found Sky's parents."

"Beresford wants to interview Kyle," said Lynch. "Kyle's evidence can link Heaney's behaviour to his victim. You said you gave Kyle an address? The safe house?"

"Yes, he went off clutching it. I got the feeling he was really considering using it . . ." Power paused. "You're going to tell me Kyle didn't?'

Lynch shook his head. "He never showed up."

"He might have been frightened and run. He was wary of authority. Suspicious. He might have left the city. Moved on."

"He might," said Lynch. "But you're not the kind of person who would frighten a man like Kyle off. Beresford is searching, of course." Lynch thought about what he had just said and sought to clarify. "I do not mean that you could not intimidate if you chose to . . . I mean that you have a gentle way of asking, that would not feel like an interrogation. Effective though."

"The compliment does not cover up the fact that I have lost Kyle for the investigation and I shouldn't have. I didn't want to frighten him off. I wanted him to keep the control."

"It would be a matter of crying over spilt milk," said Lynch. "You did what you thought best at the time. You found out Sky's name, and re-united her with her parents. It's some kind of comfort to them to have a conclusion."

"A comfort that is a small and bitter one," said Power.

"To lose a child," said Lynch. "Is a deep wound of sorrow that never heals. Would that the Lord did not test us so."

Power thought of his desire to have a child. He weighed up the grief of never having a child against losing a child, and felt a cold emptiness inside.

"Here's your fish and pasta," said a cheery voice, interrupting Power's thoughts and jarring against the strands of his reflections. Two steaming bowls of food were placed in front of Lynch and Power. "Can I get you anything else? Any sauces?"

"No, not for me, thank you," said Lynch.

"Well, enjoy!" the waitress said and bustled off.

Power fumbled to detach a knife and fork from a rolled up paper napkin that seemed welded somehow to the cutlery. "It is perhaps fitting that we are not eating meat, as I wanted to discuss some ideas with you. About Heaney's motives for killing ninety-nine people. His motives might catch him out, you see. There is one behaviour – cannibalism, and that would be one motive. And there might also be some form of ritual behaviour involved, some religious purpose we cannot divine." Lynch sniffed, but did not interrupt. "And, maybe, some other reason we cannot yet understand, like psychosis – a delusional motivation that is outside our ken. I saw a patient once who ate raw pigeons, feathers and all, on the basis of a delusion, because he believed in eating a raw bird with the power of flight, he would acquire the power of flight."

"Well," said Lynch. "The oven was bespattered with the DNA of dozens. That would seem to suggest the motive of cannibalism, wouldn't it?"

"But even if it were cannibalism, things are more complex than that," said Power. Lynch was glad he had not chosen roast beef. "Because – I don't think I mentioned this before, but cannibalism itself has different motives. There is simple necessity, as in a shipwreck, where sailors adrift in a raft must survive, and perhaps drifting in the doldrums on the high seas, a dead companion might sustain the life of the remaining survivors a little longer. That motive cropped up in that twentieth century plane crash in the snowy mountains of the Andes. And then there are certain tribes who eat their enemies to absorb their strength or cunning – like the Fore Tribe of Papua New Guinea who ate their victims' brains to acquire their powers. Although in doing so they also caught kuru, a brain disease."

"Would that be an example of a delusion, then?" asked Lynch.

"What?" asked Power, his train of thought broken by the interruption.

"The idea that eating someone's brain would let you absorb their mental powers?"

"That depends on the definition of delusion. Probably not in the case of the tribespeople," said Power. "A delusion has to be an idea that is not culturally sanctioned. If I believe that a god lives in the tree next to my house, then maybe I am deluded, but if everybody in my culture believes that a god lives in that tree, well, the idea may be objectively scientifically incorrect, but the idea is not technically a delusion, because many people share it." Lynch reflected on this, but said nothing. "And then there is the cannibal who derives some sexual gratification, some arousal, from eating someone. A *paraphilia* – a fetish, if you will. It's called *vorarephilia*. And it can cut two ways, the consumer may seek out someone who is equally aroused by the idea of being consumed."

"Really?"

"It may start quite young by eating living creatures, or er . . . containing them in different ways . . . I won't go in to that. There's a character in Bram Stoker's novel, *Renfield* who eats spiders, and flies, and birds . . . and a psychiatrist, Dr Seward – who is actually quite fairly portrayed . . .

"And then there is *erotophonophilia*, where the murderer has sex with and kills the victim, then eats or keeps part of the sexual organs, like Ed Gein. I'm thinking here of the jars. Can you tell me, did the pathologist find that Heaney had sex with Sky?"

"Um . . . let me think . . . there was no semen inside her vagina. In fact, the post mortem actually suggested she was a virgin."

Power interrupted, enthused by the academic possibilities of Heaney's psychopathology. In his dissection of the academic problem he was partially oblivious of any possibility of Lynch's unease. "There's a variant of cannibalism, where the object of desire is a virgin, *pathenophagia.*"

"I was just about to say that there was some DNA from Heaney inside her. In her mouth. If you take my meaning."

"Ah," said Power. "Could the pathologist tell whether this was consensual?"

"How can . . . I don't know, Carl! You have clearly given all this a great deal of thought."

"Should I be apologising?" asked Power. "It is what the Foundation would be expected to provide as part of its consultancy. Are you uncomfortable with it?"

"It is outside . . . my comfort zone."

"And yet, we must consider every possible idea that lurks within Heaney's mind to catch him and once we have caught him, convict him. But much will depend on what he says when he is caught, if he says anything at all. We are like archaeologists – we only have the bare bones and stones left behind his crimes. We need him to speak to voice the thoughts behind his behaviours."

"And you were at the University today, seeing the archaeologist. What did that tell you?" Lynch hoped that the question might distract Power from further discussion of *paraphilias* and other sexual perversions, but he wasn't all that sure that the topic would lead far from cannibalism.

"I saw Professor Rose at the Museum, and she was helpful. And that brings us on to another motivation, really. The idea of a more local ritual. The practice of dismembering corpses and placing parts in the water or the marshes or the bog. Old practices. The old ways, practiced over generations. Pre-Christian ways. We talked of the bodies that have been found in the bogs – old Pete Marsh, and the other bodies preserved in the peat bogs of Northern Europe. What it all might mean, like there were rituals where the old king is slaughtered to pass power on to the new. Like in *Harvest Home,* maybe too, where Mother Nature must be propitiated by sacrifice."

"And were you convinced by these folk tales?" asked Lynch.

"Well, unless I am wrong," said Power. "There were body parts . . . heads . . . that Heaney placed in Llyn Dhu, in the lake?"

Lynch nodded. Now that sex seemed to have ceased its part in Power's mini lecture, he had started to pick at his food again. Power continued, "So maybe Professor Rose's local legends of rituals might add to our understanding of Heaney's motivation. Although I did get frustrated with what she was saying. Why were the previous bog bodies there because of religious rituals? Hasn't a marsh, where the body bubbles and glugs its slow way down into the dark mud . . . hasn't that always been a good place to hide a body? Nobody's going to see the body as they pass by. Nobody's going to go looking in that filth. Why ascribe some religious mumbo jumbo to it? Lakes as gateways to the land of faerie and all that kind of thing. It could just a very cunning way of disposing of a body – a wealthy woman you've robbed, or a troublesome criminal that no-one liked and no-one would miss. Why invoke religion or ancient mystery?"

"And yet, from what I remember of Lindow Man," said Lynch. "And I do remember the case. Whoever killed him went the long way round in murdering him, using many different methods. Rather more complicated than just a bash on the head with a branch or log and a chucking him into the water. Heaney's actions, despicable though they are, are in the way of a life's work, however evil that life's work is. He is, as you say, decidedly more complex than your common or garden impulse murderer acting through rage-filled jealousy or drug-fuelled hatred. Which brings me to my next point that I wanted to discuss . . ."

"But it was all her talk of ritual and religion," said Power. "Archaeologists always put things they don't understand down to religion. It's lazy thinking in my opinion."

"Maybe," said Lynch, ". . . and don't take this as criticism of your good self . . . maybe we live in an age which takes religion not nearly seriously enough. England has become a land of atheism or at best agnosticism. We are become secular." Lynch sighed a deep sigh of discontent and thought back to the impersonal and bland funeral directors. "We have lost our way. Badly lost our way. This country, our civilization, was founded on Christianity. Our prosperity, our wellbeing, our lives are dependent on it. And when we leave it behind for doubt, for atheism, for worse, then we will descend again into the darkness. I know Christianity was thought stifling by some – old fashioned and smothering – but after it goes, if our faith is allowed to slip away, the vacuum will inevitably be filled by something else. Something far worse, I fear."

Power looked astonished.

"What is it?" asked Lynch. "Have I finally got through to you? Is this your epiphany moment?"

"No," said Power. "I need to look at the photos of the Heaney family again. I think I have realised something."

* * *

Lynch paid the bill for lunch and drove them from the car park outside The Wizard for a few hundred yards along the Macclesfield Road down to Power's drive. Alderley House was basking in the afternoon sun, its walls aglow with sunlight. Waterhouse's red terracotta tiles contrasted with the verdant treescape beyond. The broad and stout oaken front door stood ajar showing the cool, shadowy hallway. Laura had heard Lynch's Audi crunching its way over the gravel of the drive and welcomed them in.

"Would you like some tea or coffee, Andrew?" she asked.

"Tea if there's any going, nice to see you," said Lynch, giving her a modest hug.

"Normal tea I presume. Do you want your fish tea, Carl?" she asked Power.

Lynch raised an eyebrow. "Fish tea?"

"It's what she calls Lapsang Souchong tea," said Power, taking Lynch through into the sitting room.

"It smells like smoked fish," said Laura. "Foul."

"Where did I put those photos?" Power muttered to himself, as he scanned the bookcases and tables in the room. "Take a seat, Andrew. I'll just try the study."

They reconvened a few minutes later with tea and the photo album that had come from Heaney's farmhouse. They looked again through Heaney's long and lonely childhood and Power remarked on how isolated he must have felt. "Was society being withheld from him, were they protecting him from the world?" mused Power. "Or were they protecting the world from him?"

Power found the photo he remembered near the front of the album. It was the man they took to be Heaney's father – a man standing in a rainy street with combed-over hair, all parcelled up inside a Mackintosh like a wrinkled sausage roll. His eyes were piggy and cold. Behind the figure, across from the traffic on the road, on the other side of the street, was a sandstone archway, with a quadrangle beyond. It was this archway that Power had seen that very morning.

"It's the University," he said. "That arch in the background is the University, and the road is Oxford Road."

"What is it that you suspect?" asked Lynch.

"We could see if there is a link between Heaney's father and the University, maybe he taught or studied there."

Lynch nodded. "Do you want me to check, or will you?"

In the hallway outside the room the phone was ringing. Laura answered it. Somehow the call itself drew Power's attention and he didn't answer his friend, Lynch. The polite voice of Laura, heard in the distance, ominously drew his attention and he could focus on nothing else. He felt cold despite the warmth of the day. "I see. Thank you." said Laura. "No, I will just get him. Please hold."

Then she was standing in the doorway.

"Carl, could you come here, please? It's the hospital wanting to talk to you." She pressed his arm as he half walked, half stumbled to the phone in the hall. "I'm sorry," she whispered.

Chapter Ten

Blessed are they that mourn for they shall be comforted.
Matthew 5 v.4

"But someone **has** looked through the files!" said the ward sister. "Many of them were just pulled out and left open on the desk." The ward sister looked at the Matron for a response, but the Matron said nothing.

The Matron was a gaunt, angular woman who barely inhabited the dark purple uniform she wore. She was so slender that the bony crests of her pelvis showed through the front of the tunic's fabric. The ward sister was about to say something else to her but Matron's sharp eyes had seen Dr Power at the doorway and she was not about to discuss any problems in front of him. "We'll discuss it later, Sister," she said.

Matron stood up, smoothed her tunic and extended a hand and a calculated, sympathetic smile to the dark-haired visitor to the ward. "Professor Power, thank you for coming in." She noted his downcast stance and how he shifted distractedly from one foot to another. "I have read some of your papers over the years and so it is a pleasure for me to meet you, but not, I am sure, for you to meet me at this sad time." Her words were finely scripted. She shook his hand. Her palm and fingers seemed moulded from ice. "A very difficult time, I am sure," she echoed herself. "Would you like to see him?"

Power nodded. Somehow his grief had robbed him of the ability to initiate any speech. He followed the Matron down the ward corridor as she walked briskly towards his father's side room. He noted how the staff nurses nodded to the Matron as she passed and mused at their deference. The Matron grade had only just been re-introduced into the National Health Service by the Health Secretary. He half expected the next staff nurse they passed to curtsey to the Matron. And this Matron seemed to revel in the status of her new appointment. To Power it seemed like a reversion to Victorian times. Power half wondered where the new grade had sprung from. Maybe the Matrons had hatched as a cohort from the ground like cicadas after an incubation of decades. The Matron paused by the side room and unlocked the door. She invited Power to walk inside with a gesture of her arm. Power looked at her arm, focused on her palm. Time stood still and a part of his brain refused to move a muscle. He could not face going forward. "Professor Power?" she spoke softly. "Is there anybody with you?"

"My partner, Laura, is downstairs in the car." Power caught the Matron raising an eyebrow. "It's not that she doesn't care, it's that she probably cares too much."

"It's quite all right, you don't need to explain," she put a hand on the door handle and opened the door. "This is it; I will leave you with him for as long as you need. He passed very peacefully, you know; I was on the ward at the time." Here now, on the threshold of this hospital room, Power observed his own ambitendence as if he was external to his body. When he eventually moved his feet and calves they felt like lead.

His father was lying in his bed of pristine white bedclothes. His eyes were closed and his pale face expressionless, but seemingly calm. There was a metal chair by the bedside and Power collapsed on to this as his legs gave way. The Matron closed the door softly.

His father's head rested on the pillow, floating in an imperceptible fashion, making no indentation, as if when he died he had somehow lost all the weight of life.

The room was still and silent, but imbued with a pale light from the sky outside. On the bedside table was a week-old card from himself and some flowers that Laura had picked from the garden at Alderley House the day before. Power looked at his father's narrow form lying in the bed. Everything seemed frozen in a permanent stillness. Power was motionless too, like a figure in a faded monochrome photograph; as fixed in time as an insect in amber.

And the thought that his father would never call him 'son' again, either in anger or in love, shook Power to his very foundation. The man who had taken him to school, applauded at his graduation and visited him during his long nights on call as a junior, bearing sustenance and a kind word; that father no longer existed. Irreversibly lost. And now Power's heart suddenly ached with longing.

Power decided to approach his father more closely and stood on his trembling legs. He looked into the pale, lined face. An older version of his own brow and jaw. The eyes were sunken. Power was just about to retreat back to his chair when he noted the skin of the face was not uniformly white and in places was flecked by a handful of small broken blood vessels. His mind struggled to find the term to describe them. 'Petechiae,' he whispered to himself. He reached out a hand to touch his father's eyes, to pull the lids back.

"I wouldn't advise that," said a voice behind him. Power jumped involuntarily and turned. The Matron had re-entered the room, noiselessly, and stood almost at his elbow. "It's just that after death the eyes look . . . well, you are a doctor. You know they don't look like they do in life."

Power nodded, they would be shrunken and clouded by now. He didn't want to remember his father that way.

"Matron, he has these marks on his skin. Petechiae."

"Those are very common, Professor. We see them all the time. Surely, you . . ."

"I'm no pathologist," said Power.

"You are welcome to stay a bit longer, of course, but we would like to move your father to the . . . chapel area soon. The pressure on beds, you know."

Power understood. "I just wanted to see him as quickly as possible. Thank you. I have finished. It was all very sudden at the end."

Matron heard the catch in his voice and placed a hand on his shoulder.

"It is always a shock in a way. You must get some rest."

"I can't quite believe it," said Power. "How can someone be there one minute, and then gone . . . forever." He looked away from the Matron. "Thank your staff for all their . . ." He left the room and the ward very suddenly; almost breaking into a run. He couldn't bear to break down in front of people and so he took refuge in the corner of a deserted stairwell beyond the door of a fire exit. His shoulders moved with his chest's ragged breaths as he sobbed into a handkerchief.

* * *

Forever afterwards, he would not recall the journey home. Laura had driven him through the evening traffic in her Mini. She would have maintained a respectful, but sympathetic silence. She might have reached over occasionally and squeezed his hand. But his mind was far away and not registering the world around him.

When Power next came to, he was standing on the gravel outside his own front door. Laura was putting the key into the solid oak door and saying something about a pot of tea. She sounded very far away.

Power stared up at the carving of foliage in the sandstone lintel above his front door. He realised that he had not really focused at the face peering down at him for years, and yet there the face was, as it had always been, hidden in the midst of the carven leaves. There were two benign eyes looking down at him. A mane of curling oak leaves for hair. He had a smiling mouth and tumbling from that mouth a cascade of tendrils and vines snaked all around the door's architrave. How long had he not noticed the Green Man? He had been there all time, watching Power come and go through the front door. The Green Man had been there before Power; as long as the house itself had stood. He had been there as part and parcel of the design, and before that he had been planted and grown in the architect's consciousness itself.

Laura saw Power standing on the threshold, looking upward at the foliate head. "What are you doing?" she asked softly.

"I've not really looked at this in years. How could I have ignored him? When I was a child I used to nod to him every time I came through this door when I visited my aunt . . . with my Dad. He'd tell me all about the Green Man. We'd go looking for him in churches and other buildings my dad looked after. If I found him up in the eaves or on a church pew my dad would give me a bar of chocolate."

Laura came and linked an arm through his. She glanced up at the head and then began gently guiding Power into the hall of the house. She chided him gently, "Really, ignoring the Green Man! Shame on you."

They moved into the hall and Power pointed up to the newel post, where a wooden drop also had a face carved into the base. "There he is again, look."

"You know, I'd never seen that one!" said Laura.

Power looked up at the small head carved into the wood of the stairs with writhing foliage spouting from its mouth.

"Strange how we don't see things as we did when we were children," said Power. "My dad and I would play the game when he took me to work with him. I'd run round the churches searching for carvings like these while my dad did surveys and talked with builders and his clients. Well, now we've started seeing the Green Man again we'll probably keep seeing him wherever we go. He's everywhere – if you really look."

"Come and have a sit down, I'll make you something to eat and drink. What would you like?"

Power was about to protest that he didn't feel like eating again, but was surprised to find that his stomach felt so empty and indeed he felt ravenous. "Baked beans on hot buttered toast, please. Strong tea, with milk." A childhood meal.

"I'll have to look if there's a tin, we don't usually have them."

"I don't feel anything else will do," groaned Power, sinking into an armchair and curling himself round into a ball. "Please take a look, there may be a tin at the back of the cupboard."

* * *

Ashes to ashes.

There had been a service at Alderley Church. Lynch had helped Power through the interview with the vicar, helping choose the hymns and readings. The vicar had been surprised by Lynch's insistence on portions of the 1662 Book of Common Prayer. There had been the mildest of altercations about this, but Lynch preferred the Common Prayer book with its rich language, quoting, as an example, "Come ye blessed children of my Father, receive the kingdom prepared for you from the beginning of the world." The Church of England and its liturgy was a mystery to the doctor, but Power backed his friend when the vicar asked wearily, "Perhaps we should ask Professor Power what *he* would like?"

There had been a solemn procession of black cars that wound its way to the crematorium.

There had been another short ceremony that blurred its way past

Power. He remembered events involving the sense of touch more than others. He remembered holding Laura's hand. Lynch's hand on his shoulder.

There had been an afternoon tea at The Wizard with sausage rolls, cold pastry pies, and strawberry tarts. There had been ex-colleagues of his father, the few that were still alive, who shook Power's hand and told him what a respected architect his father had been. There had been some tearful elderly ladies who professed to have been his father's friends. Power wondered exactly how close friends they had been, as they eyed each other with a certain degree of hostility, with at least as much animosity as was appropriate at a funeral.

Belatedly, Power thought to eat, but found that the vegetarian food had been scoffed by the meat eaters, and only a few spiced pork pies were left. He wondered about ditching his principles as his belly gurgled with belated hunger. He turned his back on the silver platters and asked a waitress for a large glass of wine from Chateau Camorgue, one of his father's favourites, that Power had ordered in especially. The wine was dark and dangerous, rich and chocolatey, and somehow soothed him. He made a mental note to beware of addiction in his current state.

At last it was all over. The mourners left and peace descended on the back room of the pub. Power sagged onto a seat. The room was almost empty apart from Laura, Lynch and his wife, Pamela. They sat down round him. No-one spoke. In the distance Power could see people in the rest of the pub, beyond the 'Private Function' sign, and the velvet rope across the entrance. They were buying pints and laughing noisily, irrespective of Power's grim mood.

"I will drive you back home," offered Lynch kindly, although the pub was only yards from Power's house. He led them all to his latest powder-blue Audi 6, which was parked in a car park belonging to the National Trust.

Power was very quiet as they walked to the car. He was trying to stop himself thinking about the cremation process. Maybe he should have opted for a burial, somewhere green and sunny, but cool. He tried not to imagine his father, no matter how briefly, in the intense roaring flames. He broke out in perspiration and felt jittery.

Power didn't know how he got into the hallway. He didn't remember getting out of the car and walking into the house. He became aware that the Lynch's were saying their goodbyes. Pamela was chatting to Laura. She seemed quite animated and smiled benignly over at him. He made a note that he counted her as recovering from her depression.

Lynch stood nearby, watching his friend. For want of something to say, and because he was aware he had been altogether silent for too long, Power pointed at the wooden carving of the Green Man that decorated the underside of the staircase. "I haven't really noticed this since I was a child when my Dad talked about him. Would you count it a pagan thing?"

Lynch looked up and smiled. "People think he is a pagan symbol. He's in all the best churches though. It is the face of Adam. The foliage bursting from his mouth is a symbol of fertility, of life bursting from him anew. The story is in the Gospel of Nicodemus. Somewhat apocryphal, of course, but very old, a fourth century thing. Be reassured he's quite benign."

"Ah," said Power, who was puzzled that he should be so surprised by a lacuna in his knowledge. He had thought he understood symbols rather better. He watched his friends leave and did not speak again, merely nodded in a preoccupied way and went to slump in the living room. Power stared out into the woods outside.

Lynch opened the car door for Pamela and as she got in, glanced over at Laura's white Mini and Power's dowdy old Saab. There was a piece of folded paper under windscreen wiper on the Saab. Lynch went over and plucked it from the windscreen.

The note had been printed on a laser printer and read:

How are you sleeping Dr Power? How does it feel when someone takes one of your family from you? Get used to it.

Lynch gasped involuntarily and returned to his car, still holding the paper by a finger and thumb.

Seeing his troubled frown, his wife wound down the car window and asked, "What is it?"

"Please can you find me something? In the glove compartment there are some evidence bags. Can you get one out, please?"

Pamela retrieved a clear plastic bag for her husband who delicately inserted the paper into its sterile interior.

"We have a problem," said Lynch, passing the protected evidence to her.

She read the note and understood her husband's concern. Lynch was wondering if he could reasonably leave it till the next day, before upsetting his friend further.

Lynch reached into his pocket and drew his phone out and started making the first of three calls.

Chapter Eleven

"I wonder," said Pamela Lynch. "Maybe it would have been wiser of you to tell Carl about the note." They were sitting in bed reading books. It was the end of the day and they were bathed in the soft warm glow of pink bedside table lamps. Both Lynch and his wife had their backs against the large, padded satin headboard. Outside, the village of Handbridge was quiet except for the cracked singing voice of a man wending his drunken way to the bridge from the Ship Inn after last orders.

Lynch looked up from his copy of a yellowed Alastair MacLean paperback that he had re-discovered on the bookshelf. "I just thought that he had had enough worries for one day. I didn't think he could take any more . . ."

"Yes, but he can't protect himself against the unknown," said Mrs Lynch. "How can he prepare if he doesn't know about the threat. There's Laura too. All alone in that house."

Lynch sighed the mildest of sighs.

"Don't you sigh at me, Andrew Lynch. I'm the one that should be sighing at you. I was just beginning to feel better and then all this goes and happens."

"I am sorry," said Lynch, and he was too. "I promise faithfully that I will go and see Carl tomorrow. I have taken measures, though, I didn't just leave things as they were. I had a word with Beresford. So now there's someone stationed outside on the road by Alderley House – keeping an eye out for anything unusual."

"That's good," she smiled. "That reassures me a bit." She returned to reading her translation of Ferrante's *The Days of Abandonment*. She read a few paragraphs then her attention wandered. "Because what would Laura do if anything happened to Carl? And, what would I do without you?"

"The Lord would help you forward," said Lynch.

Pamela did not comment. She gave him a look. "So do you have any idea who wrote that terrible note? Was it the man you're looking for in this farmhouse case? Mr Heaney?"

"It could be, we can't rule anything out."

"Because he did attack Carl, didn't he? Stabbed him. Nearly drowned him too, poor man."

"I think that was because Heaney was interrupted in whatever he was doing. He was probably frightened that Carl turned up there in his cellar all unexpected."

"But he could have seen the news. Carl was plastered all over it as the expert psychiatrist. That could have made him mad enough to do it. Putting him forward as Professor Power, the expert! And so Heaney has now tracked Carl down. It might well be a case of self-preservation – get the expert before he gets you."

"You'd have made a good police officer," said Lynch thoughtfully.

He dog-eared a corner of the ancient paperback and put the novel on the bedside table. He shuffled down the bed and lay down, pulling the sheets up to his chest.

"But I think this is someone we have met before. I think I even caught a glimpse of him outside a pub once. But I couldn't believe my eyes, I did think I saw him there and then when I went outside he was gone – like a ghost. It was a bit of a surprise and I didn't trust that I had it right."

"And now, maybe, you think otherwise? That he IS alive, not dead? And what does he want with Carl?"

"I'd say revenge," said Lynch, settling his head into the soft coolness of the pillow. "For what we did in Spain."

"What 'we' did?" exclaimed Mrs Lynch. "Really, Andrew, how can you go to sleep at a time like this?"

"If you commit your worries to the Lord every day, you can sleep very easily," murmured Lynch, slipping into the depths of slumber.

But Mrs Lynch did not fall asleep as easily. She had formed the idea that perhaps it was not just Power who was at risk. She had picked up that her husband had said he thought it was someone they both had met before.

She had not forgotten the idea when she woke during the night. She had a nightmare about the theme of revenge when she got back to sleep. Waking unrested she had planned her questions as she washed. Over breakfast she had quizzed her husband and had not been reassured that whoever it was Power and Lynch had encountered and wronged in Spain, had not borne Lynch as deep a grudge as well. Lynch had ploughed his way through his plate of bacon and eggs with brisk efficiency, declined toast and pleaded he must leave early for a meeting.

She was not willing to be left to worry, however, and she would not let him go until he promised to brief her on how he would address the threat to them both and also how she might protect herself in very practical terms.

* * *

Power had already started his clinic at the hospital when Lynch arrived. He had decided not to take any compassionate leave after the day of the funeral, but instead had chosen to immerse himself in work. The rhythm of seeing patient after patient every half an hour was something of a comfort, although he dreaded perhaps talking to anyone about their own grief or bereavement. The subject was too raw for him.

Lynch sat waiting outside Power's consultant office in the mental health unit, amongst the doctor's patients. He observed that should anyone pass him in that group, there was nothing external to distinguish him from them. Only *in extremis* does mental disorder become observable, in terms of behaviour, outside the confines of a person's skull. It was impossible for Lynch to discern whether the woman waiting opposite with her daughter was the patient or the mother of the patient. She sat stony-faced, but was that expression of hers a mask for depression, or just the non-committal face anyone might wear in public, say, on a tube train? Lynch mused that he could have rung ahead and avoided this sojourn in outpatients, but he had been in a hurry to escape his wife, Pamela's, forensically acute questioning. He looked at the pale-blue door that bore his friend's name; 'Professor Power.' The hospital managers had insisted on updating the nameplate when news of Power's university appointment had come through. It was an honour they were keen to benefit from, whereas Power viewed his new title with modest embarrassment. Power now had ten sessions of work during the week. Six were clinical sessions with the hospital and four were with the University. As often happens with the individual who works for two masters, Power ended up working more hours than he was contracted for.

Eventually, Professor Power's current patient left the room and the doctor himself looked into the waiting room to invite his next patient in. He saw Lynch sitting there. His face broke into a smile, and then he frowned. "Come in, Andrew," he said. To his next scheduled patient he apologised, "I'm sorry, I will try to be with you as soon as possible."

Once the door was closed behind him, Lynch did not sit down. "I need to speak, Carl, when does the clinic end?"

"Is there a problem? I'd like to know sooner rather than later . . ."

"There might be," said Lynch. "But we need a bit of time to talk. Lunchtime will be soon enough. I don't want to inconvenience your patients, I can wait."

And so they reconvened over a hospital canteen lunch. Lynch made his way through watery lamb, roast potatoes, soggy French beans and thick beige gravy. Power made do with a baked potato accompanied by a sad salad. All about their ears was a cacophony of hospital gossip, clattering crockery and slapping trays. But such was the seriousness of their topic that the chaos of the canteen melted away into insignificance.

"So, tell me now, Andrew, what's wrong?" asked Power.

"Something happened yesterday, after the funeral. I hope you will forgive me delaying this conversation, but I left it till now to burden you. I thought it wasn't right to pile anything else on you. And I did take precautions to ensure you were both safe overnight."

"What do you mean?" asked Power, hearing that his own voice seemed tinged by a note of panic.

"A note left on your car. A threatening note. I noticed it left there last night. I took measures to protect you. There's a security watch on your house and on you and Laura. You're both safe."

"I didn't notice anyone," said Power.

"They're good. That's why you didn't see anything."

"Do you have the note? I do get things like this as a matter of course. It happens in my line of work, unfortunately. Patients get odd ideas. A colleague I knew in Liverpool was stalked by a man with a delusion that she'd put machines in his armpits to make him smell of fear. He wrote letters complaining about her to the hospital chief executive. Endless letters."

"I don't think this is that kind of note," said Lynch. "The original note is with forensics. I have a copy here." Lynch reached into his jacket pocket and retrieved the note. He handed the paper to Power, who read it.

How are you sleeping Dr Power? How does it feel when someone takes one of your family from you? Get used to it.

"On the day of my father's funeral," whispered Power. Lynch saw tears welling up in his friend's eyes. Power sniffed and pulled out a soft purple handkerchief, ostensibly to blow his nose.

Lynch refrained from speaking immediately, and then said, "I'm sorry, Carl. Do you have any idea who this might be?"

"As you forge your way through life, you encounter people who will dislike, even hate you. And sometimes you just don't know why." Power shook his head. "And in my branch of medicine sometimes you have to take decisions that people don't like. Making people have injections to control their psychosis, detaining dangerous people in hospital. And, although you think you're doing the right thing by them and by society, they hate you for it, or their relatives hate you for it. I once sectioned a young man who had stabbed his father in the neck – and the father couldn't see why I did."

"I don't want to worry you, but I think this is more than your average stalker," said Lynch. "This isn't a patient."

"It's usually me who is the paranoid one," said Power. "You're the sceptic."

"There's an implicit threat in the last sentence."

"Look," said Power. "What do you know that you aren't telling me?"

"I thought I recognised someone. A while back. Just a glimpse. Watching you. Or maybe watching us both," said Lynch.

"Who?"

"Well, I saw him when we were at The Wizard, staring in at the window."

"Who?" said Power, exasperation creeping into his voice.

"Cousins, (or Doyle as he was born)."

"Risen from the grave?" asked Power. "I thought it was concluded that Cousins was dead."

"I saw a man like him, raven-haired, but shot through with grey. And with an eyepatch. My glimpse was just for a few seconds. You'll remember I rushed out of the pub to catch him, but he was gone. I don't know how."

"Are you asking me to believe in ghosts?"

"This was no ghost, Carl."

Cousins was a killer that Power had tracked once upon a time. Someone he had followed as far as Canada. Cousins had assassinated Marianne Howarth-Weaver at a dining table in front of Dr Power. In self-defence Power had stabbed at Cousins's eye socket, leaving Cousins to run away wounded, bleeding. There was no further record of Cousins. No hospital records of such an injury. No border control record of his leaving Canada.

"And we trapped his twin brothers," said Power.

"The Doyle brothers, yes, we ran them to earth. And they died. That would surely provide him with a motivation for revenge."

"An eye for an eye, the death of a relative for the death of his brother," murmured Dr Power.

With the passage of the years after their last encounter Power had just about forgotten Cousins, and now news of the man had crashed back into his life in the most unwelcome way. Cousins would be a gravely wounded man, seeking revenge for himself and his two dead brothers. "It would make sense of the note," conceded Power.

Lynch nodded. He raised a cup of milky hospital coffee to his mouth. It was tepid and he put it down again after a single sip. The lunchtime tables around them in the canteen were nearly empty as people went back to their work on the wards and in clinics.

Power coughed to clear his throat. "Andrew, there's something troubling me now . . . troubling me very much. When I went to see Dad afterwards . . ." he spoke softly. "He had these marks on his face."

"How do you mean?" asked Lynch.

"The technical term is *petechiae*. They're caused by broken vessels – like very small bleeds into the skin of the face, or even the whites of the eyes."

Lynch nodded. "Yes, I think I've heard pathologists talk of them at *post mortems* I've attended. What are you saying, though?"

Power was feeling cold, dizzy and faint as if all his own blood had settled in his feet. "My father had them. I mentioned them at the time to the Matron who was there. She was quick to reassure me that these were often seen, but now I'm not so sure. And I'm suddenly afraid." Eyes now full of tears, Power named his fear. "I think Dad was killed. Smothered. Asphyxia."

"These marks – *petechiae* – they're seen in asphyxia?"

"Yes," said Power. "But I didn't say anything. I saw the marks. The worry must have been at the back of my mind. But the Matron reassured me . . . you don't like to think . . . and she was so certain . . ."

Lynch knew there had been no *post mortem*. The coroner would have accepted that Mr Power senior was in hospital, with a fatal diagnosis, and that his death was not unexpected. The provision of a death certificate and cremation form would have been automatic. The cremation had followed as automatically and naturally as night follows day, and now there could never, would never, be any *post mortem*. Lynch and Power both knew that. Lynch could see his friend's pain.

"I understand precisely. Don't blame yourself. Leave it with me, Carl," said Lynch. "I will look into it. When you can, talk to Laura. Tell her what she needs to know to stay safe. Stay with her for now."

* * *

Power had chaired his afternoon ward round and then left the hospital. He had found it difficult to focus at work, but he had not wished to let anybody down. He felt numb. He drove home and nearly went through a red light, slamming on his brakes only just in time and vexing a taxi behind who had hoped to go through behind Power's Saab. As he waited at the lights he wondered how he was going to explain events to Laura. He somehow felt guilty for believing that his father had been killed. He felt unreal. He mused how the universe had pushed back against him. Lynch and he had acted to stop Cousins's crimes, to stop his brothers from abusing others. Power had done nothing wrong, but somehow he felt he was reaping a cruel harvest. To every action there is an equal and opposite reaction. Newton's Third Law of Motion.

There was a vigorous and repeated sounding of a horn behind him. He had failed to notice the traffic lights had changed and he roared off with stuttering progress as he mishandled the clutch. In the rear view mirror he saw that the taxi driver was waving a fist at him. The taxi angrily remained inches from the Saab's venerable rear chrome bumper as Power sped his way through Wilmslow towards Alderley Edge. The taxi turned off to the right giving Power some space, but he felt a rising sense of panic. His pulse was pounding in his neck. He pulled over into the road beside the train station and tried a relaxation method he called 'the method of threes'.

After a few minutes his pulse had slowed. "Come on," he was left to console himself. "You're almost home. You can hide away and catch your breath there."

* * *

Lynch wondered why hospital corridors were so long, and how he could never find a parking space that was not at the very furthest point or orbit, the aphelion, from the part of the hospital he wished to visit.

Lynch arrived at the ward he intended to visit, slightly disgruntled, and he walked on to the ward and announced his arrival in less than his usually courteous manner.

The ward was hot and cluttered and the office was filled with nurses absorbed in tasks upon computer screens. In the distance an elderly woman was crying out for a bedpan and a bent figure of an old man was doddering his way to a toilet, unaided, clinging with his finger tips on to a black rail that ran down the walls of the ward. No-one stirred to help the patients or Lynch.

"Excuse me," Lynch spoke in his most assertive tones. Only one male nurse looked up. "I'm here to see the ward manager."

"Do you have an appointment?"

"It's a very important matter, please can I speak to them?"

"She's very busy at the moment, could you come back tomorrow, I can set up an appointment if you're a relative?"

Lynch reached into his wallet and brought out an official identification card that had been made for him by the Cheshire Constabulary. "I haven't introduced myself, I apologise. Police. Andrew Lynch." He peered at the badge on the nurse's uniform. "Pleased to make your acquaintance Staff Nurse Beddoes. Now, the health and wellbeing of everyone on the ward depends on my seeing her. So, unless she's actually involved in some urgent, direct patient care, I'd be grateful if you could inform her, now, please, that I need to talk to her immediately. Thank you."

The nurse looked displeased and scurried off to dive into an office. He emerged a few moments later and invited Lynch into the sister's office. Lynch observed fresh sandwich crumbs on her uniform and a half-full cup of tea on the desk.

"I'm sorry to interrupt your lunch," said Lynch. "But I'm sure you will appreciate why things cannot wait once I have spoken to you. My name is Andrew Lynch, I was a Police Superintendent in the CID here, but I've been promoted to a Consultant rank." He waved his identity card at her, and made his affiliated role sound as important as it could be, without his being technically inaccurate. "I am investigating events surrounding the death of Mr Power. He was a patient on here until his death from lung cancer ten days ago."

"Hello, Superintendent?" she offered her hand, which was plump and moist. Lynch observed that her red hair was ever so slightly awry.

She looked distracted. "I'm Sister James. I didn't know the police were involved. Mr Power died a natural death, I'm sure. I believe he had lung cancer."

"For sure, that may be the case, and it may not. But a doctor has raised some concerns about Mr Power's *post mortem* appearance." By 'doctor', of course, Lynch meant Professor Power.

"I ... er ... I didn't think that there was a *post mortem* in Mr Power's case."

"Then you are familiar with Mr Power and his last admission?"

"Yes, but ... there wasn't a *post mortem* ..."

"By *post mortem*, I mean 'after death'. A doctor has raised some concerns about Mr Power's appearance after death."

"Are you from the coroner's office, then?"

"Were you on the ward at the time of Mr Power's death?"

"I was, but . . ." Sister James felt a red flush spreading over her, from her neck over her jaw line and into her face. Lynch observed the discomfort.

"But? Were you there when Mr Power died?" She shook her head; the old man had been found dead. "Was there anything unusual around that time? Anything different or unusual on the ward that day?"

"Yes, there was something unusual that day. But it's not really related and I shouldn't comment. It's purely a matter for the Trust."

"This could be a murder inquiry, Sister. You wouldn't want obstruct the police in making a reasonable inquiry, would you? Tell me precisely what was unusual about that day?"

She was blushing now. "There had been a breach of our security. We found some notes had gone missing from the ward trolley. We were just trying to find them when the new Matron arrived. In all the chaos of us trying to find the lost notes, the new Matron marches on to the ward. What sort of a first impression am I making on Matron, I asked myself."

Sister James turned an even darker shade of red and Lynch noticed a sheen of perspiration over her forehead. He wondered how long she had been in a position of responsibility. She seemed very new.

"You weren't there when Mr Power died. You were with the Matron in the ward office. So who told you Mr Power was dead?"

"An HCA, sorry – a Healthcare Assistant. Jerry actually, the man who showed you in."

"Ah," said Lynch. "And then what happened?"

"We called the on-call doctor and the relatives, and put the mortuary on standby," said Sister James.

"And it was Matron who saw to Mr Power's son, when he arrived, I believe?" asked Lynch.

Sister James nodded.

"And what is Matron's name, please? I'd like to talk to her," said Lynch.

There was a pause.

"Sister?"

"I've been told by the Chief Executive that this is really a Trust matter and not something I can . . ."

"And I explained that this was an altogether more serious matter," said Lynch firmly. "So, who is Matron?"

"Well, a new Matron **was** due to start, soon, so you can understand why I thought . . ." She looked at Lynch's unrelenting eyes. "You can't talk to her, Superintendent. She can't be found."

"Explain please," said Lynch. "I don't follow you."

"She had the right uniform and everything. We were excited to see her. You know, there's the new Government initiative to drive up quality and everything and they've re-introduced the Matron grade. And she turned up on my ward and announced herself and . . . no-one has seen her since. When I happened to talk to the ward manager of the AMU about how I'd met her he said that the new Matron wasn't due to start for another three weeks."

Lynch was beginning to understand. "So the Matron who arrived on your ward was not the real Matron?"

"That's right. And we don't know who she was."

"She was a Jacob, stealing your blessing." Lynch saw the sister frown at his words, and realised with some regret that she had no knowledge of the Biblical story. "I am sorry, I mean to say, your new Matron was an impostor. This is even more worrying."

"But who was she? Why did she do it?"

"She was with you the whole time?" asked Lynch. "She didn't venture to see Mr Power **before** she saw you?"

"She came straight to see me, I think. She breezed in off the corridor and came straight to the ward office. She was confident and assertive, and her manner was exactly right. She spoke to Mr Power's relative. She was very good with him, I must say, very convincing."

"No doubt convincing people is her forte," said Lynch. "That will be her business." He sighed, and thought in silence for a moment. "She was a distraction. No doubt the arrival of the new Matron held everybody's attention while Mr Power died."

"I am dreadfully sorry," said Sister James. She began to cry.

Lynch patted her shoulder in a comforting fashion, but he looked preoccupied and remote. "Why apologise for being deceived? I am sure she was perfect in every detail."

"Do you know who she is?" asked Sister James. "Was she like one of those people who puts on a white coat and goes round hospitals pretending to be a doctor?"

Lynch shook his head. "An unqualified impostor who boosts his self-esteem by pretending to be something he could never be? No, this woman wasn't motivated by low self-esteem and she was no amateur working on her own. She was a paid professional. And I don't know who she is. Will there be any CCTV videos of the ward?"

"We don't have it on the ward."

"You should have it, though," said Lynch. "It would help you spot the wolves in sheep's clothing."

Sister found this turn of phrase difficult to follow and was still thinking of his previous question. "There might be some video of the hospital corridor. But why would anyone pay her to pretend to be Matron?"

Lynch finally paid full attention to the need to explain matters to the ward manager. "Sister James, I don't think I've been clear enough. Mr Power's death was not natural. It was suspicious. The woman who pretended to be your Matron was an impostor. Her presence on the ward was not to act as a murderer, but to act as a distraction for you and your staff; she was there as a decoy to focus your attention on her rather than your patients, to smooth the way for someone else who didn't want to be seen. Someone who needed a distraction so he could go to Mr Power's room and smother him. And whilst you were otherwise engaged he could escape whilst everyone was running around the impostor. Now, was there anyone else on the ward around that time? Someone you didn't recognise? Someone who looked a bit ... different maybe?" Sister James shook her head. Lynch thought how clever the distraction had been and how brilliantly it had played to the fears of the staff in the presence of supposed authority.

He stood up. "I will arrange for someone from the headquarters to come and take statements from you and your staff. We will bring some photos of possible suspects, but I am not optimistic we will have a photo of this person who played Matron. She is undoubtedly a true professional and will have disguised herself perfectly. But it's the man who paid her for her performance that I want most."

Lynch asked her for directions to the security offices, and hurried on his way through the hospital corridors.

The security offices were tucked behind the switchboard and server rooms. A large room with lockers for patrol officers, and two small offices full of screens. Lynch spent the rest of his afternoon in one of these trying to ignore the stale smell of other people's sweat and traces of illicit cigarette smoke. The footage from the hospital corridor outside Mr Power's ward was captured on a disc which was wiped once in every fortnight. The disc was, therefore, only a few days away from being irrevocably erased. Lynch was just in time to acquire a couple of copies and to watch the original through for himself. He played it at twice the speed of reality. He would have played it at a faster rate, but he wanted to be sure he didn't miss anything.

And then he saw it, timed half an hour before the official time of Mr Power's death. A figure stalking determinedly down the corridor, pushing a cleaning trolley in front of him as camouflage. There was no mistaking who he was, though. Even though his face was in shadow, he was wearing a black eye patch. Lynch took a sudden, hissing intake of breath.

"Cousins," he whispered.

* * *

It was now late afternoon and Lynch had phoned Power to tell him some pieces of news after his interview with the ward sister. Any other news or suspicions Lynch had kept to himself until he was more certain. From the news he had heard, though, Power had sounded very upset and, concerned, Lynch had ascertained that he was at Alderley House. Lynch, in turn, had phoned Laura on her mobile. She promised to return home to be with Power.

Laura drove her Mini as swiftly as she could through the town and back home. She spied Power's car in the driveway, parked beside it and crunched her way across the gravel to the front door. She felt the rain on her face as she crossed the short distance between car and porchway. It was growing dark and the porchway was shadowy. The Green Man above her head was wreathed in shadow. She put her key in the lock and turned it, to no avail. Power had locked the front door, bolted it top and bottom and put the chain on. She rang the bell twice then pounded on the stout oak of the door. There was no response.

Worried, she looked through the front windows, then took the path that passed along the side of the house. She looked in the drawing room and study windows, but she could not see Power.

Then, as she turned the corner into the back garden she heard him. He was there in the gloom of dusk, oblivious of her approach. He was digging frantically at a quarter of the kitchen garden and, seemingly, also talking to himself in an angry fashion. Whatever frustration he felt, Power was clearly taking it out against the rain-glistened, lumpen clay beneath his feet. He sliced and heaved at the sodden earth with his spade, tearing the soil from the ground and tossing it over.

When he first received Lynch's call Power had retreated to the old room in the Tower, a bedroom he had once occupied as a boy when visiting his aunt. He had curled up on an old couch and pulled a patchwork quilt, that his aunt had knitted, round himself. He had lain desolate, thinking over his father's last illness, his last hours, and the closely plotted, deliberate way that the final threads of his father's life had been deliberately severed.

And as he lay there, tears blurring his vision, and conscious of the patter of rain against the tower bedroom's tall windows, he had grown more and more angry – with the murderer and his accomplice, but possibly even more so with himself. He felt angrily ashamed that he had not protected the old man when he was at his most vulnerable. He let out a cry of rage and despair and flung the patterned quilt from his body and charged outside to throw himself into a fight against the earth, stabbing the spade viciously into the soil and ripping at its surface again and again. He was there still, wetted to the skin by the driving hissing rain, when Laura found him.

"Carl!" Laura called to him.

He did not hear her.

She moved closer and risked a hand on his shoulder. He seemed to shrug it off without any knowledge of her presence. "Carl! Are you all right?" This time he acknowledged her, nodding at her voice, although almost imperceptibly. No sound escaped his lips. "Andrew phoned! Can we talk?"

It seemed to be difficult for him to cease the rhythm of digging that he had built up. He slowed to a halt, like a locomotive, pistons gradually grinding to a halt. "I'm sorry," he said slowly. "I didn't see you there."

"No, I know. You're soaking wet. You'll be cold."

"I don't feel it, I feel physically numb to the world. I could ram my head against a brick wall and I wouldn't feel it. I'm so . . . angry."

Laura shook his head. "Is there anything I can do? Come in and get dry and we can sit and talk. Have a cup of coffee?"

Eventually he said, "I am all that's left now. All gone. My mum, my aunt, my dad. That generation. All gone. And what now? What happens now?" His eyes burned and she sensed the anger within. "I didn't stop it happening. I should have . . ." He hurled the spade to one side and it clanged against a wheelbarrow several yards away.

Laura had never seen him like this. She wrapped her arms around him. "Oh, Carl, you mustn't feel like that. Come inside, I'll make you something to eat and drink. You'll feel better, I promise."

Chapter Twelve

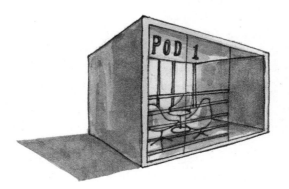

Despite Laura's protests Power had returned to work the next day, saying he needed the rhythm of his work. Laura and he had breakfasted on banana porridge and mugs of strong, Blue Mountain coffee.

They had both left home for work at the same time. Laura in her Mini, to work at a medical publishers in Macclesfield, and Power to spend a session teaching at the University on the topic of 'Hallucinations and other Misperceptions'. Before they left, Laura saw that Power had double-bolted the back door, as well as checking that every window in the house was locked. He had crunched over the gravelled drive to the front gate he now kept locked, and unchained and unpadlocked it for her to leave. He had waved to her cheerily enough. But as she drove away through the solid stone gateposts, Laura mused on the fact Power had never chained the gate before in all the time she had been living with him.

Power had settled in what the University Library euphemistically called a pod, to give a tutorial to eight psychology final year students on hallucinations.

The library had once been a genteel place with carpet and tall, nineteenth century oak bookcases filled with rows upon rows of red leather, spined law books.

There had been the welcoming silence and dust of ages. Now the University had sealed off each alcove and installed cubes built of purple striped glass, each bearing in horrendously large letters the titles POD 1 or POD 2.

In this new academic environment Dr Power was Professor Power, an academic with his research in psychopathology. But he missed teaching medical students. Sometimes he felt this was snobbish of him, but he had no real affinity with the background of psychologists or social workers. Medical students, as Power had been, dissected bodies, got covered in blood and worse, delivered babies, participated in operations, and generally worked with the very stuff of life and death. Psychologists prided themselves on their analytical skills, and endless questionnaires, but never examined or touched anyone. Consequently, Power sometimes found it difficult making them understand the difference between simple sadness that everyone feels from time to time and the profound depression that saps the will to live out of mentally ill people, rendering them incapable of speech, unable to sleep, eat or drink, and internally tortured by hallucinations that wish them ill, or taunt them with ideas of suicide. Nevertheless, Power kept on struggling to explain the difference between normal emotion and the dark abandon of pathological mood. And this was why Power had determined that he would continue to press the Vice Chancellor to consider bidding for a new medical school at the University. He remembered discussing such a proposal with Vice Chancellor Armitage at their first meeting over tea cakes. Even now, Power mused on just how many cakes he had watched the VC consume at the aptly named Indulgence café.

Power finished his tutorial with a clinical scenario to illustrate the importance of hallucinations – he described command hallucinations that tell those afflicted to do things, such as harm themselves or others, and also how some visual hallucinations are so real that they can cause post traumatic stress disorder. He told the group about a patient who had looked in a mirror and seen a nightmarish scene where he was cutting the skin of his neck with scissors, in a horizontal line all the way round his neck. That hallucination, under the influence of steroids had been sufficient to cause him PTSD.

Power observed the reactions of the students; most flinched at the story, but worryingly he noted a male student who just seemed to smile to himself.

And then the tutorial was over. Power thanked the students for submitting their essays on-line and promised he would mark them over the next week. The group started to gather their notepads and laptops and started to disperse.

Power himself was about to leave, and was closing the pod door when one of the students returned and came close to him. She was short, with dark curly hair and brown eyes. She smelt sweet to Power . "I enjoyed your talk, Professor Power," she smiled at him. "I hope you will enjoy my essay."

"Thank you," said Power.

"If there's anything I can do to improve my essay grade, will you let me know, please," she moved a fraction closer to the doctor.

This confused the Professor. "Yes, well, the essay has been submitted now, so I don't think changes are especially allowed?"

"Well, yes . . . but if there's anything I can do to boost my essay grade, just say." With this she turned on her heel, and for the first time Power discerned a distinct wiggle to her gait. This was not unattractive to him.

The conversation had taken place across the way from the lending desk, and Power walked toward the desk to renew a couple of loaned books. A bespectacled woman with long blonde hair and pale skin gave him a smile, but before he could reach the librarian's desk his progress was interrupted by a tall balding man in his forties, with an easy smile. He was dressed smartly and had just come out of a meeting, discussing figures with the Head of Information Services. Power immediately identified the man to probably be some breed of administrator.

"I saw you," he grinned. "She likes you."

"I'm sorry?" said Professor Power.

"Yours for the taking, I'd say." The man chuckled. Power gasped, and the man went on. "There's no law or University statute against seeing a student."

"I didn't . . . I wouldn't . . ." Power said in a flustered way. He meant to go on to say something about boundaries and power imbalances, but he couldn't formulate the sentences he needed before the man patted him on the shoulder.

"You're only young once," he leered and walked sprightly off towards the library exit, leaving Power wondering what had just happened.

Power walked slowly over to the lending desk. The librarian saw his frown. "Afternoon. What can I help you with?"

"I just wanted to renew these two books I've borrowed," said Power, handing over his University card.

She popped the card into a card reader. Whilst she checked the screen in front of her she looked up at him and said, "You look puzzled?"

"Yes, yes," said Power. "Do you know who that man was? The one who came up and talked to me?"

"Our esteemed pro-vice-chancellor, Dr Shacklin. You've not met him before?" She handed him a printed renewal confirmation.

"No, I'm not sure I want to meet him again, either."

"Join the club," she said. "He asked me out once. He's asked out every woman in the University who still has a pulse. He's definitely one to avoid, I think."

"I would tend to agree," said Power. "Can I ask you if I can use the computers here to pick up my University email?"

"Yes, of course," she said. "Any of the terminals in the computer room runs the University's Windows network."

Power settled himself at a terminal adjacent to the terminals of a darkly-stubbled teen, chewing gum, and a plump, owlish girl. The gum chewer was listening to an iPod that clattered tinnily. Power tried to ignore it.

He logged in and began to wade through the accumulated email detritus – a gallimaufry of invitations to edit journals from improbably faraway lands who named themselves after Cambridge or Oxford, exhortations to buy chemical reagents mistaking Power for some kind of chemist, and polite reminders that he must attend the induction course on lifting and handling that he had intentionally avoided. One email arrested his attention though, and had they been watching, the owlish and iPodded students would have seen the colour drain from the Professor's face.

The email was from a proxy. No chance of tracing it. The content ran:

You took my eye. You took my livelihood. You even went on to take my two brothers. I have nothing to lose, but you have. Tell me why I shouldn't take your reputation, your profession, your house, your partner, everyone else you love or care for and burn your house to the ground, before I then maim you and leave you to consider what you have done.

And with that, instead of fear, Power reacted with a driving anger that flooded his veins and made him slam the desk with his palm. The grey, feathery, cardiganed girl looked affronted and moved ever so slightly away from Power. The iPod imprisoned youth didn't notice Power's slamming of the desk, nor the doctor's glowering face as he forwarded the email to Lynch and gathered his things. Power practically ran through the library and off to his Saab in the car park near the University Chapel. Power's initial alarm at the email had been swiftly followed by an insistent determination.

Chapter Thirteen

Of the dark past
A child is born.
With joy and grief
My heart is torn.

Ecce Puer, Joyce, 1932.

Dr Power's on-call mobile had woken him at 5.30 a.m. Bleary eyed, Power had stumbled down the stairs to make tea so as not to disturb his partner, Laura. With the phone still clamped to his ear he spooned out two spoonfuls of tea, of a continental variety known as *Heidi's Delight*, into a warmed tea pot. He listened intently to the junior doctor. The police had brought in a wild-eyed young man, with straggly hair and worn out shoes, from the town centre in the early hours. The officers had found him wandering – he seemed confused and distressed, but not drunk or drugged.

"What's your assessment?" asked Power, sipping the golden tea and looking out into the trees on the Edge as a grey-blue dawn touched their canopy of yellowing leaves.

The trainee was Dr Proctor. Power knew her and she was one of his brightest trainees in seminars.

"Mr Susskind, the patient, says he knows that he is in Manchester, and that this is September and he knows I'm a doctor, so he is orientated, in conventional terms, but he says that he is 'unhomed', Professor."

"You mean homeless?" asked Dr Power.

"No, he doesn't mean that, in fact he has a home, and a wife – a flat in the city centre, but he doesn't want to go back there. He says his home is 'no longer familiar'."

"Can you explain a bit further?" asked Power.

"He says he first became certain something was wrong when he heard the news that Johnny Cash had died of diabetes in September. You know, the singer, Johnny Cash?"

"Yes, I have heard of him, go on."

"Well, he says that this news was how he knew that this was not 'his' universe. In 'his' universe, Johnny Cash died five years ago in nineteen ninety-eight. In Mr Susskind's universe Johnny Cash died in a car crash with his wife June. Mr Susskind says that there are alternate universes and sometimes, if the circumstances are just right, we can slip between them, like passing from one bubble into another. Everything in the alternate universe is mostly very similar, but that if you experience these slips some things are subtly different. You can rarely catch the changes, but when he heard the news about Johnny Cash he was amazed as he knew that Cash had been dead for years. And then he realised that he really had slipped through the bubble at some point."

"Hmm," said Power, thinking. "How sure is he?"

"Very sure."

"You challenged his idea? To test his conviction?" The level of conviction Mr Susskind displayed might indicate whether his thinking was delusional.

"He conceded that the idea seemed unusual, but said that many scientists accept the idea that alternate universes are theoretically possible," Dr Proctor responded. "He sounded rational. He said that he had been walking in the night air to clear his head."

"Is there anything else that might indicate risk to himself or others?" Power was always cautious.

"No, he seems a bit perplexed, but he isn't suicidal. His mood is fairly normal. He seems sober. He isn't hallucinated. He says he doesn't want to harm anybody."

Power paused. "But you're worried about him, or else you wouldn't have woken me at five-thirty with hypotheses about the multiverse."

"I don't know what to do with him."

"It doesn't sound as if we could, or should, detain him in hospital against his will. Is there anything more about him? Have you spoken to his wife?"

"That's it, he won't give permission for me to phone her. He says that everybody is affected by these slips into different Universes. That it's happening to all of us, all the time. Most times, though, we don't notice, because people around us slip past with us. We don't always notice when we slip and slide and transition between the bubbles. Sometimes all we notice is a sense of unease about the world around us, a slight derealisation, if you will. He says if we are lucky those closest to us also slip through into the new Universe at the same time, more or less, and so our feelings for them move too. The social fabric remains the same. But that sometimes, an individual slips through on his or her own. He slips into place – fitting into the new universe with a similar job, and home and family, but nobody else has changed with them, so the feelings don't fit. The family he has looks like his family, but the feelings don't match, don't marry up. And he says that's the reason love breaks down, that's why relationships suddenly break up. It's because we've slipped into another Universe and we've lost the person we were meant to slip with. The person we were meant to love forever didn't slip through with us. Lost them altogether, forever. He feels his wife in this universe is just a stranger. He will keep on living with her. He will go back to work this morning, but he is bereft. He has lost his place and his love. He feels that the news about Johnny Cash just proved that there had been a break in the universe. He went on about how these alternate universes branch at significant points in our lives. I kind of lost him. He explained it better."

"Fascinating," said Power. "Please give him an appointment to see me in outpatients, unless you feel he needs something more urgent? To check again, is his wife at risk do you think?"

"No, no I don't think so. He's really in a different catchment area to your clinic Professor, any follow up appointment would usually be with Dr Rastogi."

"I don't mind," said Power. "I'd be interested to see him."

"Thank you, Professor," said Dr Proctor. "Shall I send you my formulation and letter?"

"Thank you," said Power and rang off. Outside, the morning sky was brightening above the treeline. Power began to think about the day ahead. Firstly, he was not due in to the hospital today. He had booked the day off so he could supervise a locksmith who was refitting new, more secure locks on all the household doors and windows that afternoon. He had also arranged for a builder to visit to quote for raising the sandstone wall that ran round the perimeter of his house. He had opened the gates so that the tradesmen could get to the property. He felt good that he had arranged the visits. Power felt the need to take on any threats, and neutralise them, rather than quiver uselessly in fear.

In this spirit of actively challenging his fears, Power had, therefore, also decided to tackle one of his worst, a fear that had troubled him for years, a dread of the darkness that he knew lay deep beneath his own house. In the tunnels under the foundations of the house, he had once faced this darkness and been defeated by it. On the kitchen table he began to assemble his armoury. The helmet with its light and battery given to him in The Wizard Inn, two extra lanterns should that fail, and as overkill if all three lights malfunctioned, a pair of infra-red goggles. He also had a thick coil of twine to follow back, Ariadne-fashion from wherever the tunnels led.

Power took a pot of Blue Mountain coffee up to Laura and, after showering and dressing in old clothes, he returned to the kitchen and began unloading the heavy dresser that stood guard over the doorway to the entrance to the tunnels. He could hear Laura upstairs, taking a bath and then moving about, dressing. Power had emptied the dresser of crockery and cutlery onto the kitchen table. He hoped the heavy mahogany dresser would be somewhat lighter as a result. Power was heaving at the dresser, and wedged behind one edge of it against the wall when he heard a ring at the front doorbell.

He shouted up to Laura, "Can you get that, please? Make sure you look who it is before you unlock the door!"

Power was concentrating on heaving the heavy dresser back from the wall. It moved agonizingly slowly and scraped noisily on the kitchen floor. He was so intent on this effort that he was surprised when Laura spoke to him. She was standing by his side.

"Carl, can you stop doing that for a moment, please? There's an old gentleman at the front door. He's asking to speak to you. He won't tell me any more. He's parked his car on the driveway."

Power frowned. "Do you know who he is?"

"He was quite polite, he looks kindly, but he was clear that he could only talk to you."

"Did you ask him in?"

"Of course I did, Carl, but he was adamant about that too. He won't come in."

Power extricated himself from the tiny space he had created between the dresser and the wall. Frowning in puzzlement, he made his way through the lofty hall to the porch. The front door was wide open and Power could see a bent figure dwarfed inside a baggy, gabardine overcoat. He stood shuffling on the sunlit, gravel drive some way beyond the front step.

"Good morning," said Dr Power. He was aware of Laura's presence a few yards behind him, sitting on the steps at the bottom of the stairs. "I'm Professor Power, how can I help you?" Power offered his hand, but the old man did not take it.

The old man paused, and looked Power slowly up and down. "Professor Power? Aye, that you are. I can see the resemblance." He made no move towards Power. "Good morning to you. I've driven up from Surrey to see you, because I need your help."

Power tried not to frown any more deeply. Was this someone wanting his professional help? "Will you come in? If you've travelled all this way . . . ?"

"Your wife invited me in. But I won't keep you here long. It's about my daughter, Penelope. My name is Ferrer; John Ferrer. Her name was Ferrer, too." He paused, and Power was acutely aware that he was watching him specifically to gauge his reaction. And all Mr Ferrer saw on Power's face was an expression of confusion. "I can see that you don't remember her."

"I'm sorry, Penelope Ferrer . . . *was* your daughter?" Power had picked up use of the past tense. He was trying to recall if he had treated anybody called Ferrer. Had one of his patients died, perhaps? He saw grief in the old man's brown eyes, as well as a watery rheuminess, a deeply lined face, white hair, yellowed perhaps from smoking. This was a man bowed by life's many burdens.

"She died last year. Cancer. Ovarian. Not detected by the GP until too late. The excuse was he thought it would be unlikely at her young age."

Power relaxed just a little as he assumed that this could not be a relative of one of his patients laying their angry grief at his very doorstep, berating him for failing to prevent a young woman's suicide. Power felt he could settle his mind only just so much, however, as he sensed there was more to come. He decided not to ask a fool's question, but to let the old man tell his story.

"It was very swift for her after the diagnosis. I nursed her as best I could at home, but I am no caring mother. I am unfitted to such care. I did as much as I could. Her mother died when she was young." He scanned Power's face again for any dawn of recognition, but saw none. And the lack of Power's comprehension was an added weight to the old man's already heavy heart.

"We only get so long on this Earth, Doctor, as well you know. And a few weeks ago I got my own maker's call. I have lived my three score and ten so perhaps I can't complain. I am weary and want done with it all. But we all have our responsibilities, do we not?" He paused and looked at Power. "And I must discharge all of my duties while I still can, before I go. I have lost three stone in the last few weeks, so I know that I don't have that long."

Power could have protested that none of this was anything he could do anything about, but he was beginning to feel that in some way everything about this man's journey to see him was precisely to do with him.

The old man was fumbling inside his coat for something. Laura had moved forward and was now standing by Power's shoulder. She again offered a cup of tea or something to eat. The old man shook his head slightly irritably. "She didn't want to ask anything of you. I didn't want to either. Except . . . it seems I must now, for his sake. Damn it, where is it?" The missing paperwork he was seeking came to his hand in a far-flung jacket pocket.

"This is her will. She left me everything In Trust. And appointed me testamentary guardian. For the boy."

Power heard the old man's soft words with an appallingly clarity that resounded in his brain. He whispered to himself, "For the boy . . ."

The old man was scanning through the document, looking for the relevant sentences in the will, and seeking the exact words in the lawyer's bloated legal screed. "Here," he said, putting the page before Power's eyes. "This line where my finger is. She thought ahead. She named me as testamentary guardian. And maybe she guessed something. She named you, too." Power looked, and Laura looked over his shoulder. There indeed, where the old man was pointing, was Power's name.

"How old is he?" asked Laura, from where she was standing behind Power.

"Seven," said Mr Ferrer. "Seven years old. He lost his mother, and is losing his grandfather, but today he is gaining a father."

Laura was staring at Mr Ferrer's car. There was a boy in the front passenger seat, playing on a blue Gameboy. He seemed intent on the brightly lit screen, and the characters from Mario 3, but once, just once, he chanced a glance at the three adults on the doorstep of the big house. His face was pale and childishly round, but he also had the same eyes as his father. Laura could see that even his hair grew in the same fashion. Power hadn't noticed the boy in the car before, but he saw Laura looking fixedly at the car, and now he looked too.

"It's not through wanting to leave him here," said the old man sadly. "It's not through planning to leave him here, it's because I can't do anything else. I can't go on, I am simply exhausted and spent, and I must do what I do, while I still can. And he will have a life here. You must see that you can give him that, at least."

Power was red-faced, confused, stammering. "I'm sorry, I don't understand."

"Look at him, Carl, don't you see? The boy in that car is your son. I don't know how, but he is your son." Laura walked over to the car and the boy looked up as she approached. His eyes were large and wistful, staring up at her, and now set in an expression of some anxiety. She smiled welcomingly, and beckoned him to get out. The door slowly opened. He climbed out of the car and stood out on the drive. He was carrying a bedraggled-looking, maroon rucksack into which he was stuffing the Gameboy. "You've had a long drive," she said. "I'm Laura. Would you like something to eat and drink?"

He stared at her for rather too long, and then nodded. The boy followed her, arms crossed, his sneakered feet crunching on the gravel towards his father and grandfather. The facility of speech had still not returned to Dr Power. He watched his partner leading the boy up to him. As he passed his grandfather, the old man caught hold of the boy's arm and pulled him into an embrace. Their eyes did not meet, and it seemed to Power, at some detached professional level, that a hug was unusual between the grandfather and grandson. The old man kissed the top of the boy's head awkwardly and whispered, "Goodbye, I'll miss you." Released from his grandfather's embrace the boy sailed on in Laura's wake into the hallway of Alderley House. Echoes of a one-sided conversation about lemon cake drifted back to Power as they receded into the depths of the house.

"Your wife seems less surprised than you," said Mr Ferrer.

"Laura's my partner," said Power.

Ferrer said nothing and bit his tongue. "Come with me," he said, and limped over to the car and opened the boot. "I've brought most of his clothes and favourite things. Books, photos of his mother, that sort of thing. I can't carry them in, I can't really lift anything any more. I can't even manage climbing a few steps." Still silent, Power looked down into the boot of the car. There were some rucksacks crammed and jammed with T-shirts and jeans, a few cardboard boxes full of books and computer games. There was a Playstation 2 with its a snake-like confusion of wires. There was an orange photo album which Power picked up. Pictures of the boy as a baby. He noted that someone, maybe Penny, had noted the places where they were taken and how old the boy was. 'Jonah eating chips at Chessington, aged 2'.

"He's called Jonah," said Power.

"He prefers Jo. He won't respond if you call him Jonah. Can you take the stuff now? I'm bitterly cold. I need to get back before dark. I don't see too well." Power could see there were tears in the old man's eyes, but he was blinking them away. Power started putting the bags and boxes on the front step. When the last box was emptied from the car, Mr Ferrer slammed the boot shut and walked immediately to the car door.

"You can't go just like that," said Power. "Wait, we need to talk. You can stay the night . . ."

"We've waited for you, though. You might not see it that way and it might seem unfair, but that's the way it is. Give it some thought before you judge Penny and me." He rummaged in his pocket and took out the will. "It's a true copy. I reckon you'll need that to keep the social workers at bay. It names you as his father, like I showed. I can't do anything more."

"I mean, it's not fair on him to just go," protested Power.

"Fair? What is 'fair'? I can't stay. I've run out of time. He doesn't know . . . he's cross with me for doing what I've done today. And I wish we could part on better terms. Maybe you can make him understand when he's older. He doesn't know. It's for the best." He coughed and appeared angry, but the old man's heart was breaking. Rather than show this to the younger man, he scrabbled his way into the car, slammed the door and roared off across the drive to the gates. Gravel spun up from the tyres and the angry spray of stones peppered Dr Power's legs.

The path of Power's life had branched suddenly, changed forever and irrevocably by this day.

* * *

Power woke in the darkness. He was hot and his heart was beating fast, mind filled with uncertain thoughts, all threaded with a pervasive theme of panic. And yet, there was a sense of potential relief that perhaps the remembered events of the day had just been a dream. Nothing had changed. He lay there attempting to fumble his sleep befuddled way between fantasy and reality. The curtains were moving gently in the night air from the open casement. Moonlight from a cloudless sky flooded the bedroom carpet. Beside him, Laura was breathing softly. All was as it should be, wasn't it?

But the images of the day that wove their way back into his consciousness were all stamped with the vividness and clarity of genuine memory. He had put the boy's few belongings at the foot of the stairs and closed the front door. He had made his way back through the hallway, like he had done thousands of times. He had run through this same hall as a small child when his aunt was alive and owned the same house. He had remembered being three and running round a dining table piled high with food to welcome a long-lost uncle back from Singapore. And today, when he had stood at the doorway of the kitchen, he had seen a version of himself at the table, seated on a chair, legs hanging over the chair edge, feet swinging in the sunlight from the window. This dark-haired child, eating lemon cake and drinking milk was talking to Laura and laughing. He recalled the unsettling combination of elated wonder and profound disquiet. The potential pleasure of surprise, mixed with and tempered by shock at the abruptness of it all. Power simply didn't know how he should feel. Power felt he was watching events from outside himself.

Lying there in the still moonlight, he reflected that he had felt like an actor, moving through the scenes of the day, but without a script to guide him and so *ad libbing* reassurances which he murmured to the boy, to Laura, and to himself. Laura had seemed to enjoy herself, feeding the child, showing him the garden. Power had taken him on a walk to the see the view at the Edge in the afternoon and they had all taken a drive down to the village in Power's battered Saab to buy the ingredients for tea. Power had told himself not buy any drink – the temptation to numb any feelings of panic with a bottle of wine had been great. Lying in the big double bed Power recalled going upstairs to his old room in the square tower of the house, and tidying it for his son, making up the bed and unpacking his son's things into the cupboards, whilst Jo had lain back on the bed, carefully watching the installation of his clothes and books in the cupboards and on the shelves. Power had been formulating what to say to the questions that must be damming up inside Laura as he prepared the boy's duvet and pillows. He wasn't quite sure whether he himself knew the answers to the inevitable questions. Who was this person who had just been inserted into Power's life, forever?

Power was lying in bed, staring up at the ceiling and thinking about everything, when Laura spoke.

"You aren't sleeping. You woke me."

"I didn't do anything," said Power.

She laid a hand on his arm reassuringly. "I sensed you were awake, that's what woke me. Are you going to tell me who she was? I've been waiting to ask."

"I wondered why you hadn't."

"I wasn't ready to hear. The boy needed something . . . safe . . . we couldn't do this conversation in front of him."

"Thank you," said Power. "Thank you for thinking of him, for being kind to him. For being you."

"So . . . ?"

"It was before we were going out . . ."

"I worked that one out, I'm not conducting the Inquisition. I just need to know the facts. Not excuses."

"There aren't many facts at all," said Power. "I've been wracking my brains to recall what I do know. It's more a case of what I don't know. I don't know this boy, this son. I had never heard of him before yesterday. I didn't know there was a Mr Ferrer. I didn't know of a birth. I didn't know of a pregnancy. I'm struggling to understand what has happened."

"Tell me what you do know, then we'll work out the rest together."

Power moved closer to her in the bed. "There isn't much. I went to Dublin once, to give evidence as an expert. To the court there . . . The Four Courts. I think I stayed one night. Flew in, flew out. But I met someone, a PhD student. She was studying English, I think. Penny, she was called. An English girl studying English at Trinity College. And that's it, I flew out the next day. I didn't hear from her again."

"You didn't contact her?"

"Er, no, no," said Power. The absolute truth was that he couldn't have contacted her, even if he had wanted to. And he remembered that he had wanted to. Very much. Power kept this to himself. He had lost Penny when he lost the scrap of paper with her details on. Had he tried to find her beyond that though? Or had he got caught up in the whirl of his life and routine in England? He seemed to remember yearning for her.

"She didn't contact you?"

"No," said Power. "She didn't. Ever."

"But she knew who you were, and a doctor is easy to find, doctors are on the GMC register," said Laura. "She could have traced you, and it sounds as if her family came from Surrey. And she knew your name. She put you in her will. She didn't forget your existence." Laura paused. "Perhaps she followed you from afar. She'd have to know that you were still alive, where you were from . . . to name you in her will. She'd have to have felt she could involve you at some stage. Reassure herself that you were a safe pair of hands. In the end, she had to entrust you with her boy."

"But why didn't she ever tell me?"

"Pride? Maybe she was waiting for you, even if you couldn't contact her. Maybe she didn't know that you couldn't contact her. Maybe it was all just a total break down in communication? Or maybe she didn't want to share Jo?"

He paused, thinking. And then he spoke, with some anxiety, about the 'here and now'. "I thought that you . . . well, I was afraid that you would react badly. You seem . . ."

"I seem what?" asked Laura, and for the first time there was a warning hint of fieriness in her voice. "Don't think I don't have mixed emotions about this, Carl Power. Don't imagine I . . . that I don't harbour some . . . resentment in my heart towards you. My brain tells me that whatever happened with Penny was long before we started going out, though. Still . . ." she jabbed him suddenly hard in the ribs. "That's for the anger in my heart."

"I'm sorry," said Power. "I had no idea. Believe me. I'm sorry to you, to Penny, and to the boy. And I can't quite believe it all. It seems dream-like . . . oneiroid . . . I can't get my head around it all."

"Ah," said Laura. "Big world. Little doctor. How our loves surprise us? But still, my mind also says how this could be good for us, you and me. The Universe has sent us a son."

And with that, they embraced, and with one thing and another, their feelings merged into a shared passion. They were shedding their nightclothes and each was aware of the other's mounting arousal, when the distant sobbing of a child permeated the silence of the rest of the house. Both ceased their motion and held their breaths listening out for the sound in the darkness.

"Is that him?" asked Power uncertainly.

"Yes," said Laura. "I think you'd better go. It's an unfamiliar place for him."

"Me?" asked Power. "I don't know what to do."

"Of course you do. Comfort him. He's all alone – first night in a strange new home. Go to him, you both need to get to know each other." She pushed his chest up off her. "Go on, quickly, I'll be here when you get back."

Chapter Fourteen

A child is sleeping:
An old man gone.
O, father forsaken,
Forgive your son!

Ecce Puer, Joyce, 1932

The foursquare tower room was reached by a spiral staircase from the landing. The iron steps were cold on Power's feet as he climbed. He recalled that he had always implored his aunt to let him sleep here when he visited the house as a child. As the staircase transmitted the vibration of Power's feet up into the room, the child stopped whimpering.

"It's all right," Power called up, to reassure his son, in case the boy thought he might be an approaching monster. "It's me."

The room was still; a sliver of moonlight ran across the polished wooden floorboards. The boy had pulled the duvet up to his chin and watched Power's arrival with eyes that were wide and coal-black.

"Are you all right?" asked Power in a half-whisper.

The boy might have nodded; Power could not quite see. He wondered what to do next. He was acutely aware that he had formed no feelings towards his son. No concern. No sympathy. Just a sense of astonished bewilderment, a sort of numbness, for which he felt self-consciously guilty. This was his son, but where was the accompanying emotion, love? He supposed it was not possible to switch such feelings on. He supposed the lack of such affection might be reflected in his son as well. He was probably equally bemused by this new relationship. How had the Ferrer family talked about him? Had Power been portrayed in the family as the permanently absent father? Maybe his son harboured negative emotions? Resentment, or hatred?

Jo had seemed to get on well with Laura. Power recalled them laughing, giggling whilst watching a cartoon. With Power there had been . . . distance.

Power knelt by the bed and sat back on his haunches. "Are you all right, Jo?"

The boy regarded him with glittering eyes and a stony face. He said nothing.

"It's all so new, I know," said Power. "A lot for you to get used to. Are you missing your Grandad?"

The boy stared at him in resolute silence. "Did something frighten you?" The boy had drawn the duvet up to his chin. "Can I do anything to help?"

A pause. Power began to feel slightly frightened himself. The feeling transmitted itself. For a brief moment, a thought occurred to him, before he pushed it away. Jo could never meet his other grandfather. They had overlapped in time, but something had been robbed from both their lives and Power felt guilty. He buried the feeling and looked at his son.

The boy considered whether he should gamble and trust Power. He weighed his options and decided to say something. "It's the dark," he said. "I don't like it."

"Neither do I," said Power. "Neither do I."

"You don't know what's hiding in the dark," said Jo.

"Probably nothing," said Power, although, just after he said this he realised this comment was not as reassuring as it could have been.

"But if you listen carefully," said the boy. "You can start to hear something breathing in the dark. Something that isn't you."

"Probably that would be me downstairs snoring?" said Power, trying to make light of the situation.

"No, no. I could hear laughing, too."

"Maybe someone walking past on the road outside?" suggested Power, although he knew that at night no-one walked the Macclesfield

Road. The road passed through open countryside for miles. After dark, people either travelled by car or not at all. No-one walked past the house, which was, in any case, set well back from the road.

"The laughing was downstairs. Underneath us."

"I didn't hear that," said Power.

"Maybe you're deaf like Grandad."

"There's moonlight coming through the curtains," said Power appeasingly. "It's not totally dark. You can see there's no-one here but me." His son looked at him sceptically and Power asked, "Would you like a light on downstairs on the landing, or in here?"

"I always have a bedside lamp at home," said Jo.

"Oh," said Power. "I'm sorry we didn't think of that, I'm not used to . . . well . . . if you are used to having a light it must be very strange without it." Power felt a pang of guilt that he hadn't foreseen this eventuality. "Shall I go and fetch a lamp?"

"Yes, but don't leave me."

"But, I need to go and get the lamp, I have to leave you."

"I will come with you, silly," said Jo. And so they went and found a side lamp from the study that would act as a bedside lamp for now. As they walked though the hall, Jo said, "It's a very big house," as he peered into the dark corners of the stairwell and landing. "Anything could be hiding."

"It will be better in the morning with the sun," promised Power. "And better in your room with the lamp."

He set up the lamp on the floor by his son's bed. The lamp and its shade were oversized for the bedroom, but the warm yellow light showed the boy was smiling at last. It was, Power thought, the first time his son had smiled at him. He allowed himself a ruffle of the boy's hair. He said, "I'll see you in the morning then?"

"Yes, you will."

And without further word, lay back down on the pillows and, rolling over, turned his back on Power.

It was a beginning.

* * *

Power woke hungry. He almost jumped out of his bed, where Laura was still curled into a ball. Seeing her lying in the fastness of her slumber, Power crept stealthily from the room and then, once out of earshot, bounded down the broad stairway to the kitchen. He made strong coffee and drank two cups of this while he made dough to bake soda bread. As the bread was rising in the oven he cut avocadoes, scrambled eggs, and fried tomatoes. He was standing thoughtfully near the kitchen table, surveying the pulled out dresser. He was considering afresh when to make his long-postponed journey down the steps he knew lay behind – down into the darkness beyond, when his son entered the kitchen.

"I'm hungry," said the boy. "Is there any bacon?"

Power decided not to broach the topic of the family's vegetarianism this early in the day. "There's eggs, and fresh bread coming?"

"That'll do," said the boy. And he started walking deliberately around his father. Anticlockwise. Three times.

"What are you doing?" asked Power in bemusement.

On the third circumference of his father, the boy stopped and sat down on a wooden chair at the table.

"Three times makes you safe," he said smiling.

"Makes me safe? Am I dangerous?" asked Power.

"No, it keeps you from danger."

"Well, that's kind of you," said Power. He supposed that seven was the prime age for developing rituals. "But you walked widdershins round me."

"What's 'widdershins'?"

"You went against the journey of the sun. You went anticlockwise. It should be clockwise. That's what the ancient Celts did. You should have marched *deosil*. Clockwise. Like the sun."

Jo looked upset. He'd done a nice thing for his father, and his father was complaining. He sat down with a frown, angry, arms crossed.

"Never mind," said Power. "You got the three times right. Just do it again, the opposite way." The boy made a slight shake of his head. "I'd appreciate it," said Power. "And I'll make you some toast?" And with a slightly embarrassed expression his son got off the chair and marched solemnly round his father, clockwise, *deosil*.

"There, you're done now!" And, this task accomplished, Jo sat down. "Toast please. Peanut butter please."

"Who taught you the three times round thing?" asked Power, as he sliced some bread to toast from the loaf he had just made.

"Mum," he said softly.

"Maybe she learned something like it in Ireland," said Power. "That's where we met. She studied there at Trinity College." Jo listened to this intelligence from his father. He nodded in as wise a fashion as a boy could muster.

* * *

Andrew Lynch, ex Superintendent, was troubled by the dust and coughed every so often, in the University archive. The smell of dust from disintegrating paper was all around. Here in the gothic attics at the top of the Victorian buildings were aerial caverns filled with boxes of personnel and wage slip records. Vaulting beams of oak soared above Lynch's head as he bent over a yellowed, varnished plywood desk, reading with some difficulty by the light of a single desk lamp. The only other light came through narrow slit windows at the gable ends of the roof.

Lynch was alone. This particular archive had not been visited in years, and the University administration admitted they had almost forgotten its existence. It was to Lynch's advantage they had been in the process of forgetting, as these archives had evaded the sifting process other archives had faced, where records had been culled and decimated to free up precious space.

"But you'd be destroying evidence, by destroying any archives," Lynch had protested much earlier in the day, when he learned of the potential editing of the archives.

"Evidence of what; how much the porter John Smith was paid in nineteen sixty-eight, and when he took his fortnight's holiday? How much value is there in knowing that?" asked Emily, the young archivist, who had shown him up the narrow stairways from the ground floor, to the eyrie where Lynch now perched. "We can't keep everything."

"Mightn't it be of academic interest to someone one day?"

"There could be a case for digitising some records, I suppose. But a lot of the HR records are things like old IBM punch cards and computer print-outs. And they're faded print outs at that! It would cost too much to conserve it. Better to recycle." When they had reached the locked door for the attic repository, she handed Lynch the key and a list of the boxes in the archive. "There's a kind of order, by Faculty, or there was. Staff would not necessarily preserve that order over the years since that list was made. Workmen would just move the boxes around if they needed to access the roof. So, good luck." She chuckled as she clunked her way over to the stairs in her cherry-red Dr Marten boots.

Lynch put on a winning smile, and called out to her, "Could someone maybe help me, show me which boxes to concentrate on, please?"

"I'd love to help, but I've meetings to go to, and to be frank, there's nobody left on the staff who even remembers ever working on this archive." She paused on the top step. "Are you interested in academic staff or support staff?"

"I'm not sure, I don't think the man I'm tracing was a Professor or a lecturer."

"You'll find there are different sets of records for academic and non-academic staff. And all of them will be sorted according to Faculty – which ones are you interested in?"

"I'm not sure," said Lynch. "Medicine probably, dentistry, maybe zoology."

"Good luck," she said, beginning her descent down the stairs. "Medicine is one of the biggest Faculties. Please make sure you lock up and bring me the key before you go." And with that, she was gone beyond a turn in the stairs and Lynch was left to unlock the archive alone.

The dust had made him cough and sneeze whenever he moved the boxes of records about. He had started with two decades of records on employees in the medical school from 1960 to 1979. The black and white photograph of Mr Heaney senior seemed to be from those decades. It had taken Lynch hours to find the crate of records he needed with lists of support personnel in. Hour by hour he sifted through the stacks of heavy binders full of computer print outs, month by month.

Some time after lunch, looking through lists for May 1975 Lynch came across the first trace of Mr Arthur Heaney. There he was – a single line on the computerised personnel list. The yellowing, crinkled pages gave Lynch information on his starting date, and specified his weekly wage had been £40 a week, paid in cash on a Friday. There was a National Insurance Number, but no address. Heaney must also have given no next of kin as the relevant column was marked N/A. Mr Heaney had seemingly tried to keep the world and his family apart for decades. Lynch then followed the line on the printout all the way along the page and saw Heaney's job title; Mortuary Technician. Alongside this was the University Department Code and Name; MED5 Anatomy Department. Lynch smiled grimly and sat back with some satisfaction. His silent moment of triumph was short-lived. His stomach rumbled and he realised he had missed lunch and in synchrony with his rumbling belly, his mobile phone started to ring.

Lynch stood up and moved to the vertical window in the end wall of the roof space. He peered down at the trees in the University quadrangle below, shorn of leaves by the onset of winter. He pressed the mobile to his ear.

He answered brusquely, "Lynch?"

It was his wife, Pamela. "Andrew? I need to speak to you, now."

"Of course, what's happened?"

"I've had an email."

Lynch paused, frowned, and turned away from the window view. "You sound worried. What's the matter?"

"It's a threat. Like the note Carl got." He could hear anger brewing through her fear.

"Read it out, please."

"I can't." She sounded upset. "I mean, I don't want to look at it again. Come home."

"Don't look at it, then," said Lynch. "But tell me the gist of what it said, please. In case I need to do anything now before I head off."

"All right, it's not anonymous, it straight out says it's from a man called Cousins. He says he will punish you for killing his brothers. He says you hunted them to their deaths. He says that you deliberately pushed his brother off a roof, and that he will pay you back. I think he means to harm me or Jenny." Jenny was their daughter. "I think we need some protection. I need to know what to do if he turns up. And I need to know, Andrew – did you really kill his brother?" Lynch thought back to the last moment of a priest's life on the roof of the Cathedral in *Santiago de Compostela*. He remembered the words he had spoken and running towards the priest.

"I will be back home in about forty-five minutes," he promised. "Lock all the doors . . ."

"I always do."

"I'll take a look at the email, send it to a colleague. Then we'll discuss how to make you safe. Don't worry. You are safe, Pam. I will make sure of it"

* * *

The local news was droning out over the radio. Power could hardly be said to be listening to it as he wended his way through the house. 'There were two earthquakes felt through the night here in the North West. The first of this morning's tremors, at 2 a.m. measured a fairly gentle 3.1, and was felt across much of Greater Manchester and was followed by a 2.3 aftershock, nineteen minutes later. Further tremors may follow over the next few days.'

Power supposed he had slept through both. He shut the study door behind himself to concentrate and, here, cocooned within four square walls lined with books on oak shelves that climbed from floor to ceiling, Dr Power proposed to indulge his Professorial self and focus on the task of correcting a set of Journal proofs about the scandalous lack of hospital beds across the country.

After a few paragraphs, Power decided that he could not concentrate enough upon the dry figures and switched to reading a scuffed copy of Jaspers's *General Psychopathology*. He opened it at random and was struck by a phrase: 'Death cannot be experienced'.

The reasoning behind this contentious observation was that since an experience requires a person to consider an event from two reference points, that is to say, before the experience and after it, Jaspers reasoned that death robbed the individual of considering its experience from both points, and so it could not be experienced. Power wondered at the logic of this and what his friend Lynch might say. Lynch certainly believed in the afterlife; surely if you believed in an afterlife that would logically provide an eternity within which to contemplate the experience of death.

Power sighed the longest of sighs and his shoulders slumped. He wondered sadly, 'Where is my father?'

His attention was then further removed from the task of proofreading by the email he had received that morning from Phillip Beresford. A body had been found at the bottom of a Victorian ventilation shaft in the city centre near Piccadilly Station. The shaft had once allowed steam to escape from the new steam locomotives running in tunnels under the city streets. Steam had exploded upwards in gushing plumes of white steam, mingled with smuts and cinders erupting high up into the air from the fiery, furnace bellies of the engines. The body, however, had apparently fallen down in the opposite direction, downwards onto ancient gravel that had lain undisturbed for decades. An infrequent routine inspection of the tunnels had revealed the decomposing body of Kyle Daniels.

Power had felt a feeling of sadness overwhelm and blanket him when he read Beresford's news. At first, the police had assumed that Daniels had fallen whilst scaling the wall of the ventilation shaft (although the ventilation shaft, a towering circular wall of red brick rising some ten feet above ground, was separated from the public) after teetering on the top of the wall, plummeting inwards and down the shaft, to crumple and burst upon the unforgiving sharp stones below. And yet the Home Office post mortem spoke a different truth altogether. There were no injuries consistent with a fall. No shattered pelvis, caved in skull or broken femur. Kyle had collapsed where he was found, or he had been placed there after death. His decomposed belly, distended with gas and infested with larvae, still had stomach tissue. The contents of the stomach included his last meal of simple soup and bread, overlaid and diluted with sweet, milky tea. The residue of the tea contained *Atropa belladonna*. The taste of *Atropa belladonna* is sweet and somewhat insipid.

Power mused on Kyle's death. He thought of the moments before his patient's demise. Either convulsions or a hard, driving, very rapid heartbeat had preceded the young man's death. And before that, fear, panic and hallucinations. What kind of lonely death had Kyle experienced? Power wondered just how long Kyle had lived after the doctor had seen him in the homeless shelter clinic?

Power emailed Beresford back: 'Upset to hear of death of Kyle. I had hoped when I saw him that I was going to make a positive difference to his life. Is there any way of knowing what meal the homeless shelter made on the night I saw him? Could this be cross checked with Kyle's stomach contents?'

Something blinked past, outside the study window, just out of the corner of Power's vision. His gaze flickered to the garden just as a black and white object fell past the window.

Power felt puzzled and, for a moment, wondered if he really had seen anything. He left the warm nest of his study and went through the hall into the kitchen. He unlocked the two new security locks he'd had installed and locked the door carefully behind him as he knew that Jo was inside and, because of fatherly concern, wanted to keep him safe. He walked the crunchy gravel border around the perimeter of Alderley House and stood outside his study window, scanning the ground beyond it.

There, under the branches of an ash tree, was the still, piebald corpse of a magpie.

Power walked over and crouched to peer closely at it. He had never seen a bird plummet like that from the sky. He noticed that its neck was distorted, skewed to one side. Up above Power, in the near leafless branches of the ash tree, another magpie cawed in alarmed concern. Power stared up at the bird. It was moving about on the branch in an agitated way.

"I got it! I got it!" a child's voice shouted.

Power looked round. One of the windows in the house's square tower was wide open, and his son was jumping up and down in excited joy. Power's eyes could just make out something in the boy's hand. "What have you done?" shouted Power.

"I got it! First stone too."

"Is that a catapult? Where did you get that?"

The boy discerned real anger in his father's voice. Jo's face took on a petulant expression. It seemed his father was not congratulating him on what was undoubtedly a brilliant shot.

"It's only a magpie," said Jo. "Just a stupid magpie."

"It's a living thing," said Power. "And look, Jo!" Power pointed up at the magpie dancing in a chattering frenzy of anxiety on the branch. "That's its mate. Magpies mate for life! You've upset the balance."

"It. Was. A. Brilliant. Shot!" Jo shouted at his father, eyes screwed shut to prevent any tears from falling. Then a new idea caught the boy, and inspired him to open his eyes, and angrily fit another stone to the ammunition pocket of the catapult. He pulled the pocket back, stretching the thick elastic bands back and took deliberate and careful aim.

"What are you doing?" asked Power. "Don't!"

But the boy was beyond listening. In hurt rage he let loose the stone and it flew with a fizz through the air to strike the remaining live magpie with a minor thud. The bird followed its mate, plummeting to the dusty brown earth below.

"There!" Jo shouted at Power. "That's all in balance for you. Happy?"

The window was slammed shut.

Power stood stunned by events for a minute, mouth half open. Then he reached down and picked the bodies up. Their feathered forms were still warm and, with necks broken, unpleasantly floppy in his hands. He carried the pair to the nearby flower-beds and fetched a spade to dig a grave. The blade of the shovel sliced into the red clay of the earth, which parted and cleaved to accept the bodies.

Power fretted about the two creatures, who had gone from the element of air to earth, in minutes. As the boy had mentioned 'balance', Power mused on the idea of balance. The idea was particularly uncomfortable to him because Power had earlier been contemplating his father's death and thinking that revenge was aimed at a perceived restoration of balance. Power suspected that this 'balance' was what Cousins had sought to achieve by redress or revenge. Accordingly, Power felt a discomforting mixture of sorrow and rage as he buried the birds deep.

* * *

"I mean, I've never . . . never, killed an animal deliberately, or even felt like killing an animal," said Dr Power, still nursing a sense of shock at his son's actions even hours afterwards.

It was after dinner. Jo had been sent to bed early, straight after a dessert of stewed home grown plums and rhubarb that the boy had hardly touched. Power was sitting on the sofa in the living room, his arm around Laura. The long curtains were closed tightly, and the lamps were on. Power had lately taken to closing the night out. He preferred not to think about what, or who, might be outside lurking in the garden in the dark.

"You say you've never killed anything, but surely you must have squashed a wasp or stamped on an ant when you were little?" asked Laura. "As an experiment to see what happened, maybe?"

"Well yes, but maybe only when I was two or three, as soon as I could think properly . . . I mean, I'd open a window for a fly and usher it out. And I've never understood someone who regarded killing a living thing as a sport. Shooting elephants, or hunting foxes. How could anybody be so cruel? Why?"

"And yet this IS something that humans do. I don't like it either, but people feel they can, and so they do, kill animals."

"But, I never imagined a child of mine might . . ."

"Yes, but he's not been brought up by you. Maybe he watched his grandfather shooting or fishing. You don't know what he was taught or what examples he's had."

"No," said Power, calming down under the gentle reasoning of his partner. "But, he's seven, he shouldn't be so brutal at seven. So callous."

Laura sighed. "It's going to take time for you both to know what you expect of each other. Maybe some boys are just like this. Maybe he was brought up in the country. Some people believe that magpies are unlucky or vermin."

"Hmm, well, what do we do now? At the back of my mind I have this thought from Aristotle – 'Give me a child until he is seven and I will show you the man' – and I worry his character is maybe set, or marked indelibly. What if I can't alter or improve what has been carved into his personality?"

* * *

The next evening, Lynch had gone so far as to invite himself and his wife over to Alderley House. Power had made a Hotpot supper with red cabbage. Lynch had been contacted by the security service who confirmed they had collected facial recognition data of Cousins in London and in Manchester city centre. Nevertheless, Lynch had refrained from mentioning anything while they ate. Their visit was of a social nature, for himself and Pamela to call in on Power and meet his new son.

Lynch kept looking at the boy sitting at the head of the table, playing with his food, he was so like Power, the same dark hair, the same eyes. They even held their fork in the same manner. Occasionally, the boy looked at the men warily. He seemed to get on better with Laura.

Lynch noticed that his own wife seemed to take any opportunity she could to praise and engage with the boy. He thought Power was a lucky man to be a father of such a child, although, the suddenness of it all did seem to have thrown his friend. Lynch supposed the situation was one of those crises in life that are inescapably absolute.

There was a pudding of sponge and blackcurrants with custard, that Power had imagined his son might like, but instead, Jo refused a portion and asked if there were biscuits and cheese. Lynch was amused at the choice and half expected the child to call for port or brandy like an old man.

In contrast to his son, Power munched his own bowl of sponge and custard with the relish of a schoolboy.

There was a lull in the adults' conversation, and the boy, who had been quiet throughout, and praying that the episode of the magpies would not be aired in front of a policeman like Lynch, ventured a question he had been nursing for days. Jo looked at Power to get his father's attention and asked, "How did you get this house?"

Lynch looked up. It was a question he himself had wondered about as Alderley House was a remarkable architectural pile, probably worth millions. It wasn't necessarily the question a friend could bring up. The fact of Power's ownership was assumed, and challenging this would undermine the status quo of their friendship. But a child can ask the obvious question that no adult can.

"It was my aunt's," said Power. "My dad's older sister by some years. She would be your great aunt. Do you want to see a photo?" He left the dining room for a moment to retrieve a photo album from his study and stood by Jo's chair opening it on the table in front of him. "There she is."

Jo looked at a photo taken in the very same dining room, although maybe more than thirty years before. There was a bigger table, with a crisply starched white tablecloth on it. An ornate central display of irises was surrounded by a lavish spread of salads, cheeses, and meats. A vase of celery was clearly in focus. Jo hated celery. Around the table stood a range of adults, in purple velvet jackets, big bow ties, droopy moustaches and overpoweringly lurid orange dresses with yellow flowers as big as dinner plates all over. A woman with flowing, jet-black hair, standing in the centre of the photo, was laughing and holding her cigarette in a holder. She seemed to have been photographed in the middle of recounting some story to the assembled party. "That's my Aunty Peg," said Power. He sounded proud of her. Jo saw a little boy, caught in the same instant at the back of the room. He seemed to be frozen in the act of running around the table. Jo looked up at his father.

"That's you," said Jo.

"It is indeed," said Power, taking a closer look at himself. "I was probably your age. I think I remember that party. It was to welcome some other relative back from Malaysia. I can't recall who exactly. I was perhaps just a bit less than your age, maybe, and running around the table seemed more important. I was probably being a pest."

"Very likely, knowing you," said Lynch teasingly, peering over at the photo. "You look remarkably like your father, Jo." Pamela nodded in agreement with her husband.

Power picked the album up. He couldn't see his father at the gathering. He wondered why. Then he realised that his father had probably taken the photograph and was behind the camera. He flicked through the album. There were hundreds of photos of smiling people. Power felt he had been lucky to be part of such a family. He realised his family album was in marked contrast to the few mean photographs in the Heaney album.

"Your aunt – did she leave you the house in her will, then?" asked Lynch.

"Well, sort of. She was a widow. Her husband, my uncle, made a fortune from inventing a new kind of air filter or something for a jet engine. He died before I was born. And she lived this jet set lifestyle – flying to Mustique, (she even dined with Princess Margaret), spending months in Avignon, touring the Amalfi Coast in an old Rolls Royce . . . that sort of thing. I think she had a range of playboy toyboys. But no children. She spent all her winters abroad in the sun. She kept this house on for the few weeks in the Summer she was in England. She couldn't spend too long anywhere, I think, or the tax creatures would get their claws into her. A gardener and his wife kept the house ready for her, for any time she wanted to wing back here, and they had the use of the house. And when she died she left the house to them for their use while they were alive. I never met them. A life interest, and when they died the house was meant to go into a Trust for unwanted stray dogs. My father was not impressed. She left me some shares in a firm of tailors, instead. Hepworths or something. But they became a different clothing firm and suddenly the shares rocketed in value. Went sky high. Which gave me enough money to make an offer to the trustees. So I've always called it my lucky buy. But I suppose, in her way, my aunt left it to me. It was her money that I bought it with, after all."

"And the couple that ran it? Did they die here, then?" asked the boy.

"I don't know," said Power. "I never met them. I just dealt with the solicitor who was the Trustee."

Jo wondered about asking his father what a Trustee was, but decided the answer would be too dull. He looked down at the crumbs that were left on his plate and suddenly yawned. Laura came round to Jo, smiling, and taking his hand led him upstairs to his bed.

Waiting until the boy was out of earshot, Lynch looked at Power, studying him. "The boy looks so much like you. And you never knew, it was a complete surprise?"

"It was a welcome surprise, but it was a shock. It still is a shock. If only I had known when my father was alive. I think he would have been so pleased."

"All those years," said Pamela. "He was there all the time, growing up without you, and now you have to catch up with him and quickly too."

"And the boy's grandfather, just disappeared?" asked Lynch.

"He was very ill," said Power. "I could see that he had maybe a few weeks to live. I need to formalise everything legally. The will makes it clear I am a testamentary guardian, but still . . . I need reassurance . . . he needs everything squared. Although, I'm afraid to let people know, the authorities, in case they interfere." His fear was that the faceless social workers might take the boy away before Power had begun to know his son. Part of him could understand why the Heaneys had avoided the authorities. If your life story doesn't fit the current fashionable norms and preconceptions of the authorities, your life will be edited to fit. "I must arrange a school, too," said Power thoughtfully, almost to himself.

Pamela desperately wanted to ask about Jo's mother. How had she met Power? What was the nature of their past relationship? No one had said. She had noted, with some surprise, how easily Laura seemed to have taken to the boy. But she knew her questions were driven by her own curiosity and might be considered prurient or impolite. Instead she asked, "Would you send him to your old school?"

"The Grammar School?" wondered Power. He tried to imagine his own son in the uniform he had worn, and smiled. "Maybe, maybe. I hadn't thought that far ahead, but I must . . . it has all been such a shock."

"I wonder if Laura's reading him a story?" said Pamela. "'I'll just go and listen in, if I can."

Lynch watched his wife through the doorway as she climbed the stairs. He whispered to Power. "She's thrilled with your news. We are both pleased for you. Are you happy?"

"Bewildered," said Power. "But happy."

"We have some things to discuss, though," said Lynch. "Less pleasant matters. News on two fronts. Our two separate concerns – Cousins and the Heaneys. Cousins has been sighted. The security services keep glimpsing him on the streets with their face recognition software. In the last few days. First in London, then closer to home in Manchester. Just brief glimpses. The CCTV with recognition software isn't everywhere yet. And so there's never enough footage to track him and pin him down so they can get a snatch squad onto him. So I'm glad you've made the old house like Fort Knox."

"There's more than just Laura and I to worry about now," said Power uneasily.

Lynch nodded, but didn't comment on that. "Well, I suppose Cousins will be picked up, on the statistics of chance; one day he'll stay a bit too long in one spot when the right eyes are upon him and he'll be brought in. We just need to keep one step ahead of him. Do you know that he emailed Pamela directly . . . which has caused me some distress at home. Questions were asked. Demands made. It's a matter of outwitting and outlasting Cousins, because he will make a mistake sooner or later."

"Hmm," said Power, who didn't want to think about the subject overly much. "At least he is being tracked and there's a chance he'll be held. And the separate case, Mr Heaney? There's more news there?"

"Yes, news from Scotland. There's someone there that Beresford wants you to go and interview. A contact. He has faith in your abilities to discern whether she is lying or not. But I gather that she did mention your name to Beresford, which may have given him the idea, I suppose. She saw a clip of you on television".

Power squirmed slightly at the memory of the television appearance. "Tell me what he wants me to do?"

"This woman, she's called Mrs Kilty, says she was a friend of Mrs Heaney and that she worked with her in a cafe on Buchanan Street in Glasgow for about the last twenty years. Mrs Heaney prepared salads until she retired very recently. She says the Heaney family has been living in Scotland for decades after leaving the farm at Lindow. That Joel went to school there and everything . . ."

"But I saw Joel Heaney!" said Power. "I saw his face there in the cellar. And we know the farmhouse was occupied by the Heaneys."

"Exactly, we know all that, but now we have this contrary data. And it doesn't fit. So Beresford has asked if you and I will go up there as soon as possible and talk to her face to face, to work out if she's on the level. The lure is that she might lead us to Mrs Heaney. Who knows Mrs Kilty might even bring Heaney's mother along to see us."

"Oh, we can't possibly go all the way up there just like that," said Power. "Not at this time. It would mean a night away, probably. It wouldn't be safe. I haven't really left home for days and, now, with the boy . . ."

"I would come and stay here," interrupted Pamela. She was standing at the doorway after listening to Laura reading to Jo upstairs. Neither Lynch nor Power had heard her coming down the stairs. "I'd be happy to. I can keep Laura company. And I'd feel safer myself doing that, too."

Lynch grunted assent. "I'd be happy with that. Nobody would be alone then. I could leave the Audi with you."

There was a pause while Power thought it over.

"Do you want me to drive, then?" asked Power. "Are you proposing we travel in my car?"

Lynch frowned and said quickly, "Not at all, not at all." He did not approve of Power's collection of ancient Saabs. "We can't guarantee it would get halfway to Glasgow, let alone all the way there and back."

"Of course it would cope," spluttered Power, although he secretly shared some of Lynch's doubts.

The Saabs did require a lot of coaxing to move far and spent many days a year being nursed in the garage by Power's favourite mechanic. "What then? If we don't drive?"

"Train," said Lynch. "It's easier. Beresford will stand us first class tickets and accommodation."

"I see," said Power. "Well, it sounds as if you've thought it all through beforehand. But I am still a bit reluctant to leave home at this time."

"We'll be fine," said Laura as she rejoined them. "Pamela can have the spare room for the night." She patted Power's shoulder. "Jo's fast asleep. Good as gold."

"Hmm," said Power, mindful still of the fallen magpies.

"Now he's here," said Lynch. "At the risk of being a killjoy and being asked to leave . . . maybe you could think of getting a new car; I don't think they had even invented children when your Saab was built. Cars nowadays are safer – they come with passenger airbags and side airbags and ABS. Much safer for the boy."

Power would have scoffed at the suggestion of a safer car a week or so ago. Now, his mind was more focused. He nodded instead and, his mind predominantly elsewhere, said, rather softly, "Scotland, here we come then."

Chapter Fifteen

They lunched at noon. Laura then drove Power in her Mini to Piccadilly Station. Power had agreed to meet Lynch there to look at the abandoned tunnel where the body of Kyle had been discovered. For efficiency's sake they had then arranged to catch the afternoon Glasgow train. Power's son Jo, had been strapped into the back of the Mini. On the journey, Power had wondered about Lynch's words regarding safety and asked Laura if she would consider an upgrade to a new BMW built Mini on the balance that it would be safer. "Maybe," she said. "Would you change yours? And . . . you asked me to remind you – have you phoned the school yet?"

"I'll phone them from the train," he promised. Over lunch he'd asked Jo about his old school, and prised its name from him. Jo had not enjoyed it there and Power deduced that there may have been conflicts with his teachers. But Jo also complained that the work had been too easy and that he had too often been left bored with nothing to do while the others were still writing.

He heard Jo groaning in the back of the car and turned round. "Do I have to go to school?"

"It's better than being taught at home," said Power. "You can make friends."

Jo scowled.

When they came to say goodbye, however, the boy's sullen demeanour seemed to have lifted. As Jo and Laura said goodbye to Power on the station pavement he hugged his father tightly, and appeared reluctant to let go of him. It was the first time Power had been hugged by his son.

Lynch was already standing on the station concourse with a Network Rail manager, who proceeded to take Lynch and Power on a winding route behind modern screening to a wooden stairway in a deserted part of the station, far away from the sleek modern styling of the building. This part of the station had remained untouched for decades. It retained the smoky patina of wartime stone buildings, and reminders of a time when Manchester was an industrial city, rugged Cottonopolis personified; a time before it became a city of finance and Universities and gay bars.

Power noticed faded World War Two signage on the smoke-begrimed stone walls – battered old direction signs to an underground air-raid shelter.

They headed downstairs and through a maze of dusty tunnels to a portion of track covered by debris and piles of vegetation and leaves that had blown through from the outside. Around a solitary pile of gravel, under the opening of the Victorian ventilation shaft, was a ring of metal stakes thrust into the packed, grey ground. Police tape ran round the circle of stakes, marking out the area where Kyle's body had been placed.

Power spoke, "The way we came – is that the only way to get here? I can't see the murderer carrying the body through the station to here . . . and he couldn't have thrown the body over the wall of the ventilation shaft . . . it's too high."

"If you know the tunnel . . ." the manager waved into the gloom. Power peered into the darkness and in the distant gloom discerned the mouths of two or three tunnels feeding in towards the station. One line still had rails upon its rotten wooden sleepers. "Well, if you know the tunnels you can get in from outside. We spend a fortune blocking them up, but whatever you try – fences, railings . . . people get in. They like a challenge, some of them. In the past they've even used a lorry and a winch to pull the railings down."

"Have the tunnels all been searched?" asked Lynch, more for

Power's benefit than his own. He knew Beresford was a thorough officer.

"Twice, once by the police and once by our surveyors. They're thinking of bricking the tunnels up, but that's gonna cost."

Power was looking at the mound of gravel, the bed where Kyle had last lain. A patch of the gravel was still stained by fluids that had leaked from the decomposing corpse. There was a keen breeze blowing through the dark tunnels, and Power suddenly shuddered. "Can we go?" he asked through chattering teeth.

"I think so," said Lynch. "I will ask Inspector Beresford for the photos and forensics."

They thanked the station manager and followed him back to the bustle and relative warmth of the main station. Their train to Glasgow was at the platform waiting for them. They made their way into the blue velvet comfort of a new First Class Pendolino train to Glasgow, manufactured by Alston for Virgin at Washwood Heath, Birmingham.

A table had been reserved for them and, as the train pulled away, stewards bustled round them with tea and coffee, and promises of sandwiches and cake as an early afternoon snack.

In the same carriage opposite Power there were two older gentlemen, in tweed and corduroy, sitting hunched over a chess board. Their attention was solely fixed on the game and they tetchily waved away the stewards' offers of food and drink. They were clearly engrossed in their game and Power could not help but look at the arrangement of the black and white pieces on the board. He thought white would probably win, in three moves.

Lynch was quiet, and after the flurry of proffered drinks closed his eyes. Power looked out of the window as they hurtled north past a blur of fields and trees. At curves in the track the train tilted over towards the inside of the bend. Observing this tilting process against the tree-lined horizon made Power feel slightly queasy. He found it was preferable to pretend the process was not going on and instead keep his attention inside the carriage. He looked at Lynch. His friend was not asleep; instead his lips were moving soundlessly and Power eventually realised Lynch was praying softly. Power admired his friend's devotion to his faith, but such rituals were not for him. Lynch believed in the numinous power of prayer. Power thought that prayer had benefits, like meditation or relaxation, and that it could be an effective control for anxiety. As he observed Lynch discreetly, Power wondered exactly what it was that Lynch was praying about.

Was Lynch praying for Kyle or his family? Was it allowed to pray for the dead, Power wondered? Perhaps Lynch thought the dead were beyond the power of earthly prayer? Power certainly remembered at school they had prayed for the dead. They had all been obliged, pupils and staff, to participate in an annual Founder's Day to pray for the souls of the Founder's parents. Generations of school children on successive Founder's Days had prayed for the dead man's parents over the course of several hundred years.

Power's thoughts led him to focus on the time he had spent with Kyle. How long after their conversation had Kyle lived? Had he lived for days? Hours? Or was it just a matter of minutes? Was Power's conversation about the dead girl he had found in the freezer, Sky, the last real conversation that Kyle had had? Was his gift of an address for accommodation and help, the last act of kindness in Kyle's life? Power brought up the memory of shaking hands with Kyle and pressing the address into his hand. He struggled to remember what happened next. He had watched Kyle crossing the floor of the steamy dining hall. And then? No, Power's act of kindness wasn't the last such event in Kyle's life. Power remembered someone else stopping Kyle in his progress towards the exit. Someone had stopped him and persuaded him to accept a mug of tea. Persuading him to drink it. That was another apparent act of kindness in the last minutes of Kyle's life. The image of the mug of tea being passed to Kyle was clear in his mind's eye. Somehow, the rest of the scene was indistinct. He felt that the memory was somehow very important. The gift of tea was an apparent act of kindness, but the timing of the act was all wrong. Kyle had clearly been on his way out of the building and the tea had almost been foisted on him. Kyle had had to be coaxed into drinking it. The cup of tea was meant for Kyle, and Kyle alone, because it had the poison in that would kill him.

The train barrelled its way Northwards through the grimness of Preston and Lancaster on towards the Lakes, and Power nursed his intelligence while Lynch prayed, or slept, or both.

The train attendants kept plying Power with mugs of coffee and accordingly he kept vanishing to the toilet. On his return from one of the visits he found Lynch wide-awake, sipping tea, and poring over a folded copy of the *Daily Telegraph*.

"I thought of something," said Power, as he slid into his seat.

Lynch looked up at him through reading glasses, "What is that?"

"I remember the last time I saw Kyle he was being given a cup of tea."

Lynch put his own cup down, thoughtfully, "What do you mean?"

"I had just seen Kyle at the Shelter. He was going on his way – going out, back onto the street, going back through the dining hall. He was hurrying. Determined he was, and clutching the address I had given him. He was interrupted, deliberately, on his way. Someone had been waiting for him to leave my consulting room. And they had a cup of tea, a single cup of tea they had prepared, ready for him. I didn't think anything of it at the time."

"And you are implying that some volunteer, or organizer, at the homeless centre poisoned Kyle?" asked Lynch. Power nodded. "But why would anybody there want to do that? I don't see the connection."

"I'm sure you might if you spend some time on the idea. I've been thinking about nothing else whilst you were praying," said Power. "We've considered the theory that Heaney's victims were people who might not be missed . . . that he was preying on the homeless. Where else would be better to find victims than the homeless centre? And maybe he was right there, when I was talking to people, trying to find some leads. And when I was talking to Kyle, maybe someone there knew his information might join everything together."

"So he had to be dealt with," said Lynch softly, to himself as much as to Power.

"Exactly," said Power. "But before you ask, I can't recall a thing about who handed him the tea. I was sort of focused on the cup, and on Kyle. He said thank you to whoever it was. He knew them, or liked them, I think, or else he wouldn't have stopped. He stayed to drink the tea that they gave him, because he already knew them."

Lynch nodded. "It will come back to you. It wasn't Heaney himself?"

"No," said Power. "Or at least I think not. Which is a thing in itself."

"Exactly," said Lynch.

"You know that I've been puzzled for some time about the different types of victims we found at the farm and the different ways they were killed, and the different times they were killed – they were all killed over a matter of years – and I think there are all different reasons they were killed," said Power.

"Go on," said Lynch.

"I'm trying to make sense of why someone would kill so many people, over so long a period and for different reasons – to keep some body parts in jars, and to keep some body parts to eat and to have sex with at least one of the victims; these are all different motives. Trophies, sustenance, and sex." Power whispered the end of his sentence as he was conscious that his voice had earlier been climbing in volume, but even so at the whispered word 'sex' a businesswoman had looked up sharply from her laptop screen two seats away. Lynch too, had sensed Power's words had been overheard.

"And yet," said Lynch quietly, "we are dealing with someone who is extremely unusual, and his motives – why shouldn't they be equally complex? You seek rationality in the mind of a man who is hardly a man at all. More like a beast, or a monster."

"Animals are as rational as we are," said Power. "Just because we cannot talk to them, we infer their actions lack rationality. We share the same drives."

Lynch did not want to be drawn into a debate with his friend on vegetarianism again, and sought to find some common ground between them. He spoke deliberately, but in a quiet voice so that no-one but Power could hear. "Fine, so it was not Heaney who gave Kyle the tea. If . . . and it is an if . . . if it **was** poisoned tea. Someone at the shelter, someone who had befriended Kyle, and knew what Heaney had done, was protecting Heaney by poisoning Kyle. That might fit with your theory that there were different people behind the host of dead souls we found at the farm at Lindow. Different people with their own different motives . . . but what kind of people would conspire together to do such things or protect each other? They would have to trust each other, they would have to be very close. So far as we know, Heaney has nobody. He is a loner. His father is dead. His mother is in Scotland, and no mother would . . . well, less than fifteen per cent of murderers are women. It's very rare."

Power watched the landscape of the Cumbrian hills wash past them in the rain, and thought about what Lynch had said. Eventually he spoke, "Rose West conspired with her husband and helped him ensnare at least a dozen girls. That was a family thing. And they even killed their own daughter when she tried to leave the household."

"I remember the West case," said Lynch. The train had stopped at Carlisle and was just pulling away from the platform.

"My supervising consultant wrote forensic psychiatric reports on the Wests for the prosecutor, Leveson," said Power. "He'd been at Liverpool College with Leveson."

"I don't recall any psychiatric reports in that case," said Lynch.

"His reports were never used," said Power. "They didn't want the mental health card being played. Both prosecution and defence wanted a conviction, pure and simple."

"Ah, justice closes its eyes and ears when it wants to," said Lynch. "When you see a statue of justice, she wears a blindfold to represent impartiality, but did you ever notice that her hands are unfettered, unbound. She retains the ability to take off that blindfold or put it back on at will."

"I suppose," said Power. "That they didn't want the Wests to end up in hospital like Hindley and Brady, but wanted them punished. To go to jail, not hospital. As if they perhaps thought a secure hospital was a cushy option. It isn't. Perhaps they should open their eyes and take a look."

"Well, I suppose you have worked in those kind of settings?"

"I met Brady in such a hospital, once upon a time," said Power. "He made me toast. When I was a trainee in forensic psychiatry for a year . . . I don't consider myself a forensic psychiatrist, though. I didn't stay in that particular gang of psychiatrists," Lynch raised an eyebrow, but did not comment. "Brady shuffled in to the ward office with tea and toast for the nurses and I ate some before they got around to introducing him to me. Like all murderers, he seemed quiet, almost banal. There's a strange kind of inverse snobbery amongst forensic psychiatrists. Like taxi drivers, you know, 'I had such-and-such a famous person in the back of me cab once.' Well, like cabbies, forensic psychiatrists like to boast they saw this infamous murderer, or that infamous arsonist . . . they were all very upset when Shipman refused to see any of them. They could have dined out for years on seeing him."

"And you just mentioned meeting Ian Brady . . ." Lynch pointed out.

"Guilty, m'Lud," said Power.

Glasgow Station was a lofty, arched Victorian affair, built when Glasgow considered itself to be the Empire's second city. The train unloaded its cargo of passengers in a stream that flowed to the barrier, where officials dutifully checked tickets, before allowing the rivulet of people to cross the marble hall under the suspended wooden clock, to the sandstone arches that led to Gordon Street beyond.

Lynch confidently navigated them past taxi ranks and buskers, through the Merchant City to Buchanan Street. "The message was to meet here," he said, pointing to a doorway off the bustling street.

Power looked at the sign over the doorway, "Willow Tea Rooms? Did Beresford suggest this?"

"No," said Lynch, leading the way inside and up a flight of stairs immediately beyond. "It was the suggestion of the person we are supposed to meet."

"I was going to say, that if it had been Beresford then he was teasing my love of food . . ."

"Mrs Kilty, on the other hand, knows nothing of your penchant for culinary delights. Come on, we have to meet on the second floor."

They ascended the narrow stairway through the period tea room designed by Charles Rennie Mackintosh, and passed through the White Dining Room, with Art Nouveau features. There was the inviting clink and chink of teacups, saucers, and silver cutlery. They climbed on, up to the immersive blue of the Chinese tearoom on the second floor. It was late afternoon by now, the busy hours of elevenses and lunch were over and the room was only dotted with a few tourists and Glasgow housewives, gossiping over high tea and afternoon sandwiches.

They seated themselves at the only available table, a table for two. Lynch said, "We'll have to try and move when Mrs. Kilty arrives, or get an extra chair."

"Or two chairs?" said Power. "Mrs Kilty might just bring Mrs Heaney along, mightn't she?"

"I'm not sure," said Lynch. "I suppose she could bring Mrs Heaney along. That wasn't the arrangement Beresford agreed to. It would be useful to meet Mrs Heaney, for sure." Lynch looked around the room whilst Power addressed himself to the menu. Lynch's impression was of a turquoise-blue room, with open screens of blue woodwork made up of large blue squared frames, and rectangular black wooden chairs contrasting with white ceilings and crisply bright linen tablecloths. "Art Deco, I suppose," said Lynch.

"Art Nouveau," Power corrected him, whilst wrestling with internal decisions about afternoon tea; Darjeeling or Lapsang Souchong, finger sandwiches or a selection of cream cakes. "Mackintosh was Art Nouveau. Early nineteen-hundreds."

"And whatever is the difference between Art Nouveau and Art Deco then?" asked Lynch with mild irritation.

"Art Nouveau is nineteen-hundreds to nineteen-ten, Art Deco is nineteen-ten to nineteen-thirty. Art Nouveau is kind of flowery and Art Deco is all lines."

"Then where are the flowers here?"

"In the vases on the tables," said Power.

"Bah," said Lynch, looking at his watch. "Half an hour till she gets here. Well, at least we're here in time."

Power looked up from the menu for a moment and glanced at the blue screen on his left. "It's a recreation of the original design, from the nineteen-nineties." said Power. He returned to his first love, the menu. "There's an afternoon tea for two with gin and tonic?" he said hopefully, as a young waitress glided to their table, all efficiency in a black dress and starched white pinafore. "You get a stand of sandwiches and scones."

215

"Just a black coffee for me, please." Lynch ordered.

"Oh," said Power, slightly disappointed at Lynch's spartan order. He did not intend to be so abstemious. "A pot of Darjeeling for me please . . . and a Brie and grapes sandwich . . . and also a meringue with cream and berries, please."

The list was duly written down on the waitress's paper pad and she shimmered away, like Jeeves.

"So," said Lynch, seeking to re-focus Professor Power away from his food and on to the more pressing matter of their mission. "Presumably Mrs Kilty will lead us to Mrs Heaney. But what if Mrs Kilty does bring Mrs Heaney today, as you suggested. I know what I would ask Mrs Heaney over a cup of Darjeeling, but seriously, whenever we find her what do **you** want to ask her?"

Power paused. "It's difficult to know what to ask the mother of a suspect in a murder case. The instinctive questions might be; 'Did you know? What did you think was going on? How could you not know? Why didn't you stop him?' But those questions are likely to freeze the interview before we've even begun. I wonder what she's thinking as she travels to see us. She must be terrified or puzzled and seeking her own answers. I suppose I want to know what Joel's upbringing was like."

"I want to know when she last saw him," said Lynch bluntly. "We can tie Joel to the crimes. We know he was living there. We . . . well, you . . . have witnessed him in the vicinity of the farm. Now I want to know if we can tie her to the crimes as well."

"I guess she wouldn't come today if she was tied to the crimes," said Power. "It may be many years since she saw Joel. Maybe she and her husband left Lindow Moss for Scotland and Joel stayed on."

"If she came we would need to establish where she lives, get some ID. Verify she IS Mrs Heaney. She needs to be brought back really, interviewed under caution. We can't let her just slip away again. Beresford agreed to this meeting with Mrs Kilty only because he thought working with Mrs Kilty might be the only way of making contact with Mrs Heaney. If we didn't grasp this opportunity Mrs Heaney might disappear again. Vanish into the heather and mists of bonnie Scotland . . . and Mrs Kilty asked for you specifically. She saw you on the television apparently."

"This is what comes of publicity," grumbled Power. He brightened as the waitress laid a small tray of tea, coffee, sandwiches and scones in front of them. Lynch looked at the sandwiches as Power was beginning to tuck in and felt a pang of regret that he had not ordered something after all.

Noticing his friend's face, Power nudged a plate of sandwiches towards him. "Have one, go on." Lynch relented and took one. In the distance, they were playing Domenico Modugno's version of *Nel Blu Dipinto di Blu*. Power hummed along, thinking his own thoughts, and enjoying the food. Eventually he spoke, "I suppose I wanted to ask about Joel as a child. The photo album shows him in isolation. Were his parents separating him from a cruel world that didn't understand him. Or is he perhaps autistic and cannot tolerate the noise of the world. Or were they protecting the world against him. And if so, what had he done as a child?" He looked behind Lynch, through the window at the lights of Buchanan Street. "It's gone dark. So soon. It's only afternoon."

"The consequence of us being further north," growled Lynch, brooding deeply now on his own thoughts. "She should have been here now, shouldn't she?" He looked at his watch. "She's ten minutes late."

"That's all right," said Power. "I wouldn't worry," but looking at his friend he saw that Lynch was indeed showing signs of concern.

Their food and drink were all consumed. A waitress came over to the table, Power thought she would clear the crockery away, but she asked a question. "Is either of you Dr Power?"

"I am," said Power. "Is anything wrong?"

"There's been a phone message for you. A woman rang and said she was sorry she was running late. She missed her train from Arrochar. She will be another three quarters of an hour."

"Thank you," said Power. "Is she still on the line?"

"No, she just left her message and rang off."

"Can we order some more tea and sandwiches?" asked Power.

Lynch interrupted. "What time do you close, please?"

"Six-thirty, sir. Do you want the same sandwiches?"

"No," said Lynch. "We're not stopping. Can we have the bill, please?" The waitress nodded and went to the till to print off their bill.

"But... but..." said Power, protesting. "What are you doing? She's on her way. We could have another sandwich..."

"No, she's not on her way," said Lynch, standing up and pulling a number of ten pound notes from his wallet and putting them on the table to cover the bill. "We've got a train to catch and ten minutes to get to the station."

"But what happens when she gets here and we've gone?"

"Nobody is coming. There is no Mrs Kilty, there is no Mrs Heaney of Glasgow. Our being here is merely a diversion. Come on, we have to go. Quickly."

Chapter Sixteen

Power followed Lynch as he ran from Buchanan Street down Gordon Street, on through the great hall of the Grand Central Station and straight onto the London train. They collapsed into First Class, gasping for breath. Between ragged intakes of air, Power panted, and asked Lynch why they had sprinted as if the devil was behind them. Lynch raised an eyebrow at the phrase Power had used and held up his hand to stall Power until he had regained his own composure.

The train had pulled away from the platform before Lynch had got his full breath back. He looked over the table at Dr Power opposite. "It is vital we get back home. This mission to Glasgow was never our own mission; we did not formulate it. We did not plan it. This – this trip to Scotland – is a diversion, a sleight of hand to distract us. And I pray that we are not too late."

"I still don't understand," said Power. "Mrs Kilty and Mrs Heaney might have arrived and be standing in the café right now, and we've gone . . ."

"We could have waited all night and no-one would have turned up, Carl. I grant you there might have been a final phone message with some plausible excuse and an offer to meet us tomorrow, if we stayed overnight. Anything to delay us." Lynch brought out his mobile phone and rested it on the table in front of him. "I am sure that the idea for our mission to Scotland was devised by the same person who stole Beresford's Policy File. Using the information in that, they would know everything about the case, Beresford's thoughts and strategy would be recorded there, along with the suspects in the crime and details of us, as associated investigators. And the thief of that Policy File dreamed up a lure, some bait, or whatever you want to call it, to draw us both away from home. And he knows us well enough to concoct something that fits us . . . something that would tempt us away; a meeting in a café with a missing key player in an investigation that is preoccupying us; he offers us the bait of meeting Mrs Kilty, Mrs Heaney's friend, in a café; how ironic a proposition. See how he mocks us. There is no Mrs Kilty. No link to Mrs Heaney here."

"Well, I guess it was far fetched for Mrs Heaney to be alive and to have moved to Scotland. She's probably dead like her husband."

"If she is dead, her name's still being used by the Policy File's thief. And as for her living in Scotland? It might, in theory, explain why Mrs Heaney hasn't been found living in a retirement home somewhere in Manchester. But again, this is all a contrived situation. A diversion."

"And so that begs the question; who stole the SIO Policy File?" asked Power.

"Putting everything together," said Lynch. "Weighing all the possibilities, I'd say Cousins."

Lynch saw the deep-lined concern in his friend's face. "I'm afraid so," said Lynch. "Why did we ever accept this mission north? In retrospect, the artifice is clear, but we still didn't see it. All Cousins has, and all he has become, is hatred for you and me."

"We are on two separate quests then," said Power. "A quest to find Mr Heaney – who was uncovered by the accident of a plane crash, and a quest to catch Cousins who wants to destroy me . . ."

"Cousins intends to destroy us both," said Lynch. "I have no doubt of that. He holds us both responsible for his own tragic life and the deaths of his brothers. He won't stop until you and I have both lost."

"And Cousins has hijacked our concerns about Heaney to fool us." said Power. It was an observation more than a question.

Lynch nodded. He had been looking at his phone.

"Please give me a moment," he asked, and closed his eyes and prayed almost silently.

Power heard a few whispered words that mostly eluded him, but amongst them he just caught the phrase "... the defence of those who trust in you and the strength ..."

Lynch picked up his phone and pressed in a number. He listened as it rang, and there was a look of infinite relief upon his face when a familiar voice answered.

"Pamela, is that you? ... Is everything all right?"

"Of course," said his wife. "We're making tea. Laura and Jo and me. I've been teaching Jo how to make pizza dough. It's proving near the Aga right now."

"Aha," said Lynch. He was wondering what to say that would sound appropriate. He wanted to avoid alarm. "What are you using for toppings?"

"Olives, mushrooms and other stuff. Jo wanted some ham and pineapple."

"I see," said Lynch.

"Then we will watch a little television, and I have brought a book to read him to sleep with."

"You've planned everything," said Lynch.

"I've been looking forward to spending the night here," said Pamela. She sensed something in the pauses that Lynch left as he listened. "Is everything all right?"

"Of course," said Lynch. "We are on our way back."

"I thought you were staying over?"

"We've accomplished everything we could," said Lynch. "We're on the train and should be back in a few hours."

"Oh," there was the slightest hint of disappointment in her voice, that her sleepover might be curtailed, but she detected something else in the phone call. "Is everything all right?"

"Now I've spoken to you, yes," said Lynch. "Are all the doors locked? Could you check, please."

"I check them all the time now, just as you told me to."

"And you remember what else we talked about?"

"Don't worry," said Pamela. "I have everything under control."

"Good," said Lynch, reassured somewhat. "Well, we will join you soon. We'll stay over at Alderley House tonight, don't worry, I won't spirit you away from your time with Jo." Lynch said good-bye and looked up at Power. "Everything seems all right. She is very fond of your son, you know. She didn't want me to interrupt her stay, but we must get back as soon as we can."

* * *

Lynch had refused the tiny plates of 'dinner' offered by the stewards to First Class passengers. Power had polished off the vegetarian Highland Barley Stew just as they passed Carlisle, and then he had supped a mini bottle of claret as Lynch looked into the darkness outside the train window and tapped his fingers on the table.

"Why do we do it?" asked Lynch. "Why do we put ourselves through it, and put our families through this?"

"What do you mean?" asked Power.

"I knew Pamela was stressed by my police work. All those years I spent . . . Sometimes she wouldn't sleep at all when I was out on duty. And now I've left the police behind, and I work for the Foundation . . . what do I do? I keep on with this same kind of work. Chasing the dregs of society. Trying to put things right that will never be put right, because the evil keeps on coming. Men's hearts are stained with darkness and ever more shall be so. So why, why do we do this? Why do police and doctors fight this endless battle, against crime and sickness? Why do we risk everything for a lost cause, for strangers we will never know?"

"Altruism," mused Power. "That's what some people say. But is altruistic behaviour truly selfless? Does it help **us** to help strangers? I suppose by helping society it also helps us and the people we love? By building a safer society for everybody, we help ourselves, or people we know – friends, family. We then trust that if we help society, society will help us, reciprocally. And altruism is an attractive trait, biologically speaking, if a person demonstrates altruistic behaviour, then a potential mate might think them kind; a good provider for any children. And altruists have more life satisfaction. Research finds they are less likely to be depressed or anxious."

"1 John 4 does tell us that to love God we must love our fellow man, and that hatred of one's fellow man is the same as hatred of God, but sometimes it is hard not to hate," said Lynch. "And yet, whoever does not love does not know God, because God is love."

"I often recommend volunteer work to people with mild depression, it helps them socialise, and helps self-esteem, and . . ."

Power broke off in mid-sentence. He was thinking about the refuge he had visited. The homeless people, and the volunteers. He thought of the helper's apparent altruistic motivation to turn up night after night. Dr Lehman running a clinic every week, entirely unpaid. He thought of the woman who had handed Kyle the cup of tea.

"Isn't altruism supposed to be pure?" asked Lynch. "You make altruism sound as if it does have its own rewards. If altruistic behaviour has rewards then is it not really altruism?" He looked at Power, who seemed not to have heard him.

"I've remembered something," said Power softly. "It was a woman who handed Kyle the cup of tea. A woman."

* * *

Pamela was insistent that the dough was properly proven before they formed it into pizzas. "There's nothing worse than unproven dough for giving you indigestion," she said. They had finished watching *The Empire Strikes Back*, and an excited Jo had been persuaded to stop leaping from sofa to sofa whilst waving round a broom handle he insisted was a light sabre. The persuasion had only had an effect *after* the whirling wooden handle had dispatched a tall green and gold pottery vase to a fate of scattered smithereens. He apologised shamefacedly as together they inspected the damage.

"I don't think your father will be very impressed," said Laura.

"It wasn't a very nice vase, though, was it?" Jo was seeking reassurance or absolution.

"That isn't the point," said Laura. "We asked you to stop, and you didn't stop. You went on a rampage and this happened."

"Sometimes it is the ugly pieces of pottery that are the most valuable," said Pamela.

"If I say sorry, will he forgive me?" asked Jo.

"I dare say," said Laura. "Still . . ."

"He won't be cross like Darth Vader. He won't chop my hand off?"

Laura caught that he was referencing the film they had just watched. "No, I don't think he'll be that cross. Shall we make our pizzas now? Will the dough be ready do you think, Pamela?"

"It's had all the time that the film took to prove, and the kitchen's warm, so I expect it will be perfect."

The blessed thing for Laura, as she was desperately hungry, was that the pizzas would be cooked quickly in the piping hot oven. Once sprinkled with Mozzarella over their toppings of mushrooms, artichoke hearts, olives, and courgettes, (and for Jo, ham and pineapple), the pizzas took only twelve minutes. Laura and Pamela shared a bottle of Malbec at the kitchen table and they chatted over each slice. Jo guzzled a bottle of luminously red cherryade that Pamela had brought him.

Pamela eyed the scuffed paintwork of a door, part hidden and barred, by the kitchen's vast wooden dresser. "I haven't seen that before," she pointed at the door with the tip of a slice of pizza. "I didn't know you had a cellar."

"It's not, or at least, I don't think so," said Laura. "Carl keeps meaning to open it up and show me down there. I think he's wary or even more than that, afraid. He once went down there and lost his only light. I think he got a bit panicked in the dark. He doesn't like to talk about it. I gather there are some steps going down into a cave or something." She looked over at Jo, who was listening attentively to her words. Not for the first time she marvelled at how closely the boy resembled his father. "And you're not to go down there either, Mr Big Ears. Well, I'm not sure you could move that dresser, anyway. I can't. I don't think an average woman could shift it on her own. It took Carl all his strength to move it the first time. Anyway," she looked Jo in the eye. "Don't try!"

"I won't, I promise," he said. "I don't like the dark. Is there any more pizza?" He had been eating steadily whilst the adults were talking. The boy's plate was empty whilst theirs were still half full.

"What it is to be a growing lad," said Pamela, as she gave him two slices of pizza from her own plate.

"Can I take these and go and watch the TV?" Jo asked, getting down from the table.

"Of course," said Laura, and she watched the boy running from the kitchen with his plate.

"It will be fun at Christmas – having him here," said Pamela wistfully.

"I hadn't thought that far ahead," said Laura. "But it isn't far off, is it?"

"Christmas is designed for Jo's age," said Pamela. "I think I enjoyed the festivities up to when I was around ten. You start to see through things after that," she sighed. "I hope that Andrew and Carl are all right.

Andrew sounded worried on the phone. He tried not to show it, but I could tell. I wonder what the real reason is for them coming back early. Do you know much about this case they are working on?"

"Sometimes I don't like to know too much," said Laura. "This one is a big case, though, isn't it? Dozens of people going missing and all ending up in that house near the Black Lake. So close to here, too." She shuddered.

"I think I nearly went missing myself once," said Pamela. "Many years ago. Did I ever tell you?"

"No, no, you didn't." said Laura. "What do you mean, missing?"

Pamela pushed her plate away from her and leaned forward on the deal table to tell her story to Laura. "This was in the days before everybody had mobile phones. I was just twenty and I hadn't met Andrew. I wanted some money to go away on holiday and I thought I would take on a sort of nanny job. It was down in Suffolk, a stone's throw from this long pebbly beach and at night you could hear the waves roaring up the shore. It was a big country house, owned by some brewing family for a couple of hundred years. The house had once been owned by the old King of Jordan. Imagine! Anyway, it was passed to the diplomatic service and used by this Diplomat and his family. There was a cook, and a housekeeper and a gardener, but they lived in the village. They had accommodation available in this big block . . . it had been a stable block once, but it just housed this grotesque blue Rolls Royce. But none of them would stay at night. I was told that there was this family. The Diplomat, his wife and two children.

"I arrived on the train and expected to be picked up at the station, but no-one turned up. It was miles from anywhere. No shops or house nearby. Just a hedge-lined road into the distance. I could smell the sea and the sky was grey. It felt like it would rain. No taxis. The payphone on the station platform looked like it had been smashed to pieces some time ago. I started to walk. And then I saw there was a bus stop and I waited an hour before the coach from the nearest village came. It had rained, I was drenched, and cold. I sat there on this leather seat, dripping onto the lino of the floor. Anyway, when I got there, the housekeeper was very short with me. She wanted to get home and she said she couldn't leave the house until I got there, because of the children. As soon as I arrived she was gone. What a welcome! I stood there, like some bedraggled Mary Poppins, in the hall, and there were these little faces peering down at me from the balcony above. When I spoke, they skittered and ran off into their bedrooms. Of the wife there was no sign. I later found she'd left a week before to see some relative in Amman. That was the story I was told, anyway. I found my own room. I found the kitchen and made myself and the children supper. The lighting was supplied by a generator and nobody had told me how to keep it running. So we ate in the dark by candlelight. These glum little faces. A sad little boy and his vicious sister who kept kicking him. I put them to bed and locked the front door at ten. We went to sleep in the dark, too.

"There was a terrific banging in the middle of the night. Someone at the front door. It was this tall urbane man being dropped off by an Embassy car. He'd been driven all the way from some function in London. He had slicked-back hair, short and a sharply angled moustache. He was very, very drunk and collapsed against me when I opened the front door. Collapsed by mistake or design I don't know. He apologised for not being there to greet me and tried to shake my hand. He didn't apologise for waking me up or for being drunk. In fact, I rarely saw him when he wasn't either drunk or under the angry influence of a hangover.

"And so that was my life for a few weeks. I looked after the children, who were too cowed and nervous to be too much of a problem. I read to them and did jigsaws and we went for walks by the sea. They talked about two previous nannies they'd had. And their mother who had left suddenly to catch a plane one day. I tried to talk to the housekeeper and the cook, but they looked at me with disdain. They were only there during the week. We had to fend for ourselves at the weekends. During the week the gardener shuffled about a bit, raking leaves and trying to grow mushrooms in a shed.

"The children's father would shout at me if the children made a noise or left toys out. He once hit the boy for drawing in a book and I had a row with him. He hit him so hard he flew across the room. I said I'd call social services and he replied that he had diplomatic immunity and he could do what he liked. They were his children. The laws of this country did not apply to him. He could murder me if he liked and no-one would prosecute him. He said that in anger, and when his circulation was more whisky than blood, but it stopped me in my tracks.

"The next day I asked the cook, who seemed the most

approachable of the three servants, what had happened to the two previous nannies. One was about my age, and she'd lasted three weeks before she went to a dance in the village and never came back. Her suitcases were still in the cellar, apparently. And the other nanny, younger than me, had simply not been there when they turned up for work one day. Gone overnight, it seemed. The housekeeper overheard and told the cook off for mentioning anything. The master's business was confidential, she said. I challenged the housekeeper and asked her straight what did she know about the missing nannies, and she said that some people were just unreliable.

"That night, it was a Saturday, I locked myself in my room when I went to bed. The diplomat was out, but he returned after two o'clock, banging on the front door again. But I wouldn't go and let him in. I was frightened, I remember being so scared. I heard a smash of glass round the side of the house. He smashed his way into the conservatory. I thought that would teach him to leave his keys behind.

"And then he ran upstairs. I remember the thump-thump-thump as he ran up the stairs and down the corridor to my room and he started banging on the door. Shouting that he could hear the children crying and that I must go to them. I thought, why can't you go to them, they're your children. And so I stupidly unlocked my door, I was still a bit sleepy, not thinking right, but also scared; anyway, I went down the corridor, across the wide carpet of the landing to their room. And he was behind me, like a tiger, stalking me. I went in the room, and the children were fast asleep, or feigning sleep. He had been making such a noise. I said, they're asleep, what do you mean, waking me. And he was blocking my path, and I wasn't putting up with it. I take so much. Carl said I take too much on board, and I swallow it down and I get depressed by taking it. But I wasn't about to disappear. I ran at him, and his balance wasn't so good with all that alcohol on board, and he went flying backwards and I jumped over him and ran to my room. Locked the door, barricaded myself in.

"Then in the morning I heard him going out. He went to a café on a Sunday for eggs and to read the newspaper. I unbolted my door and went downstairs to use the phone to ring the local taxi company. They met me and my luggage at the end of the drive. It had snowed, and my feet were cold as they went into the snow, I remember scrunching my way down this long drive. For the first few steps from the house I had stepped into his footprints in the snow. So that maybe he wouldn't notice and follow me. Then where he'd got into the car and driven, his steps had disappeared. I couldn't step in them any more. I tried to walk in the tracks of the car. I must have been very frightened, I think. I felt like rabbit out in the open. And I thought, what if he didn't go to the café, and what if he is behind me and sees me, or follows any tracks I leave, I felt that he'd swoop down on me like some hawk, but of course he didn't. I took the taxi all the way to Ipswich – I didn't want to wait at the village station – and got the train home.

"And so, that was the time I nearly went missing. Do you think I read too much into it all? Was I being fickle and imagining too much?"

"No," said Laura. "You have to trust your instincts in these things. Better safe than sorry. I think you had a lucky escape."

"Yes, I do too. Thank you for listening. Strange I should still need your reassurance that I did right, after all this time. When I was low, I saw Carl, and I realise that he was right. He said I take my anger inside and get depressed. I don't trust my feelings and let it out. I should do, really."

There were clattering, banging sounds from the hallway. They both got up to investigate and found Jo at the bottom of the stairs in a heap with a dark coat round his shoulders and his makeshift light saber beside him. Jo was laughing, however, and appeared unhurt. "I was leaping down the stairs, like Darth Vader leaping on Luke in the film."

"You jumped down the stairs?" asked Pamela.

"From the sixth step," he said proudly.

"I think," said Laura. "It's probably time for bed."

"Come on, then," said Pamela. "I've got a book in my bag. I brought it from home – it was Andrew's favourite when he was a boy. It's called *The Box of Delights*. I'll take you upstairs and read it to you, if you like." He nodded. "Is that all right, Laura?"

"More than all right if the book settles him down," said Laura. "There are some pyjamas on the radiator. Maybe he can have a bath another night." She watched as Pamela, carrying her handbag tightly, led Jo upstairs, hand-in-hand.

And while Laura cleared away the dishes, restoring order to the pizza-smeared kitchen table and tidying up the trampled sofa, Pamela read aloud to Jo of Kay's adventures; a journey by steam train, the Christmas holidays, a Punch and Judy man, and buttered eggs for tea.

There was a violent hammering at the front door.

Not a polite knock. A commanding rat-a-tat-tat; imperious and alarming.

Laura heard it and paused in her tidying of the DVD shelf.

Pamela heard it and placed a bookmark in the book. She stood up and laid the book on the counterpane. "Stay here, Jo, I will just be a moment. Let me see what that is." She picked up her handbag and made her way to the top of the stairs. She called back to Jo, "Stay there in bed."

He didn't, of course.

Laura left the DVD she was putting away and made her way to the hall. She put her hand on the front door latch.

* * *

He had been outside for some time, watching with his one good eye. He had watched them through the kitchen window, making pizza. He observed them laughing as they sprinkled mozzarella on pools of tomato sauce and had sneered at their happiness. He walked around the house checking windows and doors. Admirably, he thought, all were closed tightly for security against him. He stood in the shadows, aware that if he stood too close to the windows, internal light flooding onto his face would betray him if they chose to glance into the dark. Cousins stood in the bushes, under the branches of the trees, clothed in shadow. He watched them finish their pizzas. Power's son left and he could see him jumping around in the living room. To do this he had peered through a glimmering crack in the curtains. Power's partner and the policeman's wife chatted in the kitchen whilst the boy scattered cushions and created chaos. He watched the policeman's wife stand, and call the boy to her. It must be done soon, thought Cousins; he had created this time and this opportunity, and he must seize it now. He must show no pity. He must be ruthless in these acts of cold revenge.

Cousins moved around the house. From the front of the property, he watched the hall through the windows on either side. The policeman's wife switched the landing lights on and climbed up the stairs hand in hand with the boy. He looked just like Power. Perfect. In one hand she held the boy's hand, in the other a ridiculously bulky brown leather handbag with long straps. It was a Gisele bag. Cousins judged the woman to be overly fat and too old to be attractive to him. He despised her. What did Lynch see in her? Maybe he wouldn't miss her? Cousins stood just to one side, to escape any glance from within. Yellow light spilled out of the windows on either side of the front door and through the fanlight, illuminating a carved Green Man. The Green Man's face glared ominously when lit from below. Stained glass windows on the first floor glowed red and green. The lights in the tower room came on. Was that where the boy slept? If he rang the bell now he would take Power's partner first, then run upstairs to the boy's room where he guessed the fat woman would be with Power's son. He unzipped his jacket so he could easily reach inside when the time was right.

Cousins rang the bell.

Chapter Seventeen

Laura opened the front door.

There was a man standing a few feet away on the drive, dressed in a black quilted anorak and black jeans. He wore a black felt hat and there was an eye patch over his left eye.

He smiled to reassure her, said a cheery "Hello!" and moved forward within arms length of the stout oak door, which stood ajar. "Is Dr Power in?"

"I'm sorry, he isn't," said Laura. "Can I take a message?" She held the door firmly.

"Will he be back soon? I could wait. In my car, on the road." Again a reassuring grin and then a lie. "He's an old friend from medical school, you see. I was just in the area and I thought he'd like a visit."

Pamela called down from the top of the stairs.

"Who is it?" she asked.

Cousins could hear a tremor in Pamela's voice. She was looking down into the hall but couldn't quite see. Laura was holding the door across the entrance. Pamela took a few steps down the stairs, but still couldn't get a good view of the figure at the door. Cousins temporarily placed both hands on the outer door frame, taking possession of the entrance.

Laura looked behind her, to her friend on the stairs, "Someone who says he's a friend of Carl's."

With the distraction of Pamela's voice, and because Laura was looking back into the hall, Cousins moved forward now and gently placed his left arm on the door, taking full control of it, lest Laura decided to try and swing it shut. His feet were on the threshold of Power's house. He slipped his right hand into his jacket where the shoulder holster was.

Laura looked back to Cousins and was shocked to see he was only inches away from her now. "Or maybe I could wait inside?" he asked, gently and firmly pushing the door open wide.

Laura stepped back. The door swung fully open. The cold night air spilled into the hall and stole up the stairs. Pamela felt the frigid draught swirling up the stairs and curling around her legs as she watched the man in the doorway. Pamela recognised him, and, in fear, clutched her handbag tightly to herself.

Cousins thought the arrangement was excellent. The opportunity could not be bettered. He drew the handgun, a SIG P226, out of his jacket, and he did so theatrically for his own pleasure, he was so very gratified to see the fear in the faces of both women.

The alignment of bodies was almost too good to be true, thought Cousins. If he held the gun low and angled upwards he could take out both women and might even be able to wound the boy. Power's son could be seen hovering just behind the overweight woman. The Parabellum would easily fly straight through both women's bodies. Even the overweight one he physically disliked so much. The scene afterwards – with the sprawled bodies – Cousins would title it 'The Aftermath' if he were an artist – would be a wonderful tableau for Power and Lynch to grieve over. He took careful aim, before Laura could even think to run. They were all probably too stunned to even move, although Cousins could see, with aroused pleasure, that the boy knew what was happening. He'd started to scream. The woman on the stairs had dropped her handbag.

The shot rang out.

The force of the shot threw Cousins's shoulder and whole body backwards. He was shocked. Surely the recoil was more than usual. He looked down at where his right shoulder used to be.

When the door swung open, Pamela had seen the man clearly. He had an eye patch and he matched the photos of Cousins that her husband had shown her. Lynch had briefed Pamela with the greatest care. He had been assiduous in his description of the man, and his rehearsal of what scenarios she might encounter. The angle from which she now saw Cousins, standing above him on the stairs, was almost exactly the same view that the CCTV camera had had of Cousins in the video that she and Lynch had studied together. The video taken from the hospital where Cousins had been Mr Power's last visitor.

It was grimly ironic that Lynch had trained his wife to use the very same model of handgun that Cousins had planned to slaughter her with. Pamela had enjoyed the afternoon Lynch spent with her at the firing range. She felt somehow empowered by the experience. All that afternoon Pamela had been more than a little wary about carrying the SIG in her handbag in case Jo had gone rootling in it, and so she had taken extreme care to keep it with her at all times.

Cousins had just seen the handbag fall from Pamela's grasp when she took out the gun and aimed it at him, but he hadn't understood, in that split second, what was happening. He hadn't understood, because, in his arrogance, he never expected any kind of resistance from his victims. Whilst Cousins was aiming at Laura, Pamela had an uninterrupted shot over Laura's shoulder. There was a merging of perceptions. As Pamela squeezed the trigger, she heard Jo screaming behind her, and in the same instant she heard the roar of the gun. The chain of cause and effect was almost instantaneous – pressure on the trigger, the explosion inside the gun and the blossoming flower of spattering blood and spicules of calcium from Cousins's shoulder as bony humerus, glenoid and scapula erupted in a shower of red, white, and pink fragments. Pamela watched as Cousins staggered back, shocked and bewildered. His right arm was only held on to his trunk by shreds of skin and tendon. His gun clattered onto the hall floor and he sank backwards into the darkness, like a folded feather bolster, eyes wide, face pale as alabaster, knees bending under the physical shock of the gravest of wounds.

Laura slammed the door on the man and sank onto the bloodied hall floor, praying that Cousins would die outside.

Chapter Eighteen

"Stay down!" shouted Pamela. She was sitting on the half-landing, out of view of any windows, holding the boy tightly in her arms. The handgun was still within reach, by her side. She could see through the banisters, and saw Laura below on the tiled floor. There was blood sprayed over the floor. It was darkening as the seconds went by. Some of the blood on the floor had been smeared as Laura moved through it on her knees.

Laura had intended getting to her feet to try and peer through the window of the door to see if Cousins was gone when Pamela shouted her warning.

"I just wanted to check," said Laura.

"Move away from the door, stay down and get behind something solid," warned Pamela. "He could shoot at you through the glass."

"He can't," said Laura. "He dropped his gun – it's here in the corner of the hall. I don't think he could hang on to it. His shoulder sort of disappeared." Laura looked at a mess on the front door casing; of coat fibre, with slivers of bone and splattered muscle smeared into it. She reached across the door and slid a bolt home to gain extra protection.

"He might have another gun," said Pamela. "Get out of sight."

"I think he could be dead or dying," said Laura. "He must be losing blood."

"He's wounded and dangerous till we know he's dead," said Pamela. "Is the back door locked?"

"Oh yes, Carl's been obsessive about us locking everything for weeks now, I'm sure it's locked." Laura was crawling on hands and knees as fast as she could to find a refuge behind a very solid hall table. She was out of sight of Pamela, and called up to her. "Are you and Jo all right?"

"I'm fine, my wrist and hand are smarting a bit. The recoil from the gun does pack a punch. I'm shaking though."

"So am I," said Laura. "How are you Jo?"

There was a pause. "He's here," said Pamela. "No bones broken and not a scratch on him. But I don't think he's exactly in a talking mood."

The boy was wide-eyed and dithering. "Do you want a blanket, Jo?" asked Pamela. Jo said nothing.

"Have you a mobile there? We should call the police," said Pamela.

"I think I can reach the landline phone," said Laura. She felt up above her head on top of the hall table. She could just reach the phone receiver and plucked it from its cradle. She put it to her ear. There was no dialing tone. The line was dead. "He must have cut it," Laura called up to Pamela. "Do you have your mobile with you?"

"It's in my handbag, which I dropped down the stairs. I think we should sit tight for a bit. Until we think he's gone. He'd need to get help very quickly with that wound."

"Maybe he drove off, or there was someone with him in a car to drive him away." said Laura. "He did mention a car before."

"Did you hear a car driving off?" asked Pamela.

"I . . . I don't know . . . I wasn't listening for it. I might have missed that. There's been too much to think about."

"He couldn't drive himself," said Pamela. "How could he turn the wheel when he was changing gear? He's still outside. Unless he had an automatic car, or he had a driver . . ."

"Is he still outside?" whispered Jo. He hadn't been talking before, but he had been listening acutely – to everything.

"Shall we go up to your room, Jo?" suggested Pamela. "Where it's even safer?"

Jo nodded. His nod could not have been more definite.

"Laura? I'm taking Jo upstairs to his room. I will try and have a look outside from his windows – they're higher up – I'll call down if I see anything."

Together, Pamela and Jo climbed the steep stairs to Jo's turret bedroom. She took the precaution of bringing the gun with her. She wrapped Jo in the duvet, and on hands and knees crawled first to one window and then to the other. From the first window she had a view over the front drive and the road to Macclesfield. The view forward of Alderley House showed no car now in the drive or on the road beyond. There was no body either. The other window showed her the back garden and the forest that cloaked the Edge itself. The trees were in darkness and the gloomy view held no reassurance. But at least she could see nothing amiss in the dark. No reflections on, or movements of any figure. She called down to Laura, "There's no sign of him. Do you want to come up?"

"I'm already on the first floor," said Laura. She had moved quickly from the hallway up the stairs. Pamela heard her climbing, slightly out of breath, to join them in the safety of Jo's bedroom. "Are you all right, Jo?" Laura wrapped her arms around him. All of a sudden he seemed very small and vulnerable. She reminded herself of how much Jo had lost in his short life. "It's all right, Jo, we dealt with him."

Something smelled different to Laura. She realised that she could smell the iron tang in the blood that had spattered over her clothes and had the urge to shower immediately and put on clean clothes. It must wait, she told herself. She looked at Pamela through altered eyes. "That was an incredible shot!"

"I missed," said Pamela. "I was aiming for his head." She paused. "But it worked out quite well, I suppose, I stopped him shooting anyone," she laughed nervously. She felt she should reassure Laura, after implying that she might have missed Cousins and possibly hit Laura. "And of course, you were well out of the line of fire. I made sure of that. I have had training from Andrew, you know. And I used to be in a gun club when I was in my twenties . . ."

"Oh," said Laura, not knowing how to respond. She couldn't imagine Pamela enjoying a gun club and reflected that it wasn't possible to know everything about someone else. "When will it be safe to go downstairs, do you think?"

"We should stay up here a little longer, I think," said Pamela. She looked at her hands in some wonderment. She hadn't been aware how much her hands were shaking. Her arms were also trembling, and profoundly so. "Will you let me into your duvet, please, Jo?" she asked. She suddenly felt horribly cold.

Jo offered Pamela a corner of the duvet and she crawled thankfully under it, and curled up next to Jo on the floor by the bed.

"What about me?" asked Laura, and Jo offered her a space under the duvet on the other side of him. She noticed how cold he felt. He was shivering next to her. Shock, she thought.

There was a violent banging downstairs. The front door reverberated under a sudden assault as someone battered on the stout oak panels.

"He's back to kill us," said Jo fearfully, and began to sob.

"I don't think it can be him," said Pamela. "I think I can hear two fists on the door." She cautiously reached for her handgun again, though. She held her breath as she listened to the noise in the hall below. "Yes, I'm definite that there are two fists banging on the wood. That can't be Cousins."

Then they heard Power's voice. He was shouting, the pitch was high and alarmed. "Laura! Laura, open the door, it's us."

"Why does Dad sound frightened?" asked Jo. "Has the bad man got him?"

"I think he will have seen the . . . mess . . . on the porch steps," said Laura. "I'll go and let him in."

"You'd better be quick," said Jo. "Hurry. The bad man is outside."

Laura got up and ran down the stairs to the hallway and fumbled with the door. The barrel bolt seemed to take an age to move across before she could stand and open the front door. Power and Lynch were standing in the porch. Power was looking in towards her and Lynch was standing guard, looking out into the gloom of the trees. He was peering into the shadows outside the pool of light from the houselights. Lynch scanned the darkness intently, listening for sounds of the slightest movement. Lynch held a handgun, similar to Pamela's.

Power rushed his way inside and threw his arms around Laura. "Are you hurt? Who's hurt? Is Jo all right?"

She melted against his firm body. "Everybody's all right," she said.

"There's blood on the step and on the door," said Power, voice upset. "I thought . . ."

"It's not *our* blood," said Laura.

Lynch entered more cautiously than the doctor. He walked carefully backwards, step by step, keeping a close eye on the driveway. "Please can everybody move away from the windows and go up to the first floor," he said, pushing the door to and locking it behind them. They climbed to the first floor and crouched at the head of the stairs, in such a place that they could not be overlooked. Pamela joined them. Lynch reached out and squeezed her hand, but did not feel he could relax enough to hold her as he wanted to. He quickly asked Laura and Pamela what had happened, and both he and Power listened to their account in tense silence.

Then Lynch spoke. "Has anyone called the police?" he asked.

"Cousins cut the landline, we think," said Laura.

"That would be a logical step for him," said Lynch. "Did you use a mobile?"

"The mobiles are downstairs," said Pamela. "I thought he might be watching through the windows if we went to get them."

Lynch nodded.

"If you've got your mobile up here we can phone them now," said Pamela.

"I'd prefer it if . . . or rather I recommend that . . . we don't," said Lynch. "I can see you all look surprised at that. But I think we should only involve the police on a 'need to know' basis. That is to say we DON"T phone them."

"But why?" asked Pamela. "Surely they need to know about this."

"My views on these things have changed somewhat in recent times," said Lynch. "I'm not as enamoured with the police as I used to be when I was setting out in my career, when I was bright eyed and bushy tailed. I would advocate that we contact them on a need to know basis; that is when we need them to know something and when we need them to do something for us. Trust me on this."

"But why?" Pamela pressed him on the point.

"You did all that was required and needed, to deal with the threat you faced," said Lynch. "The police could not have responded to save you better than you saved yourselves. They could not have responded in time. It is a grim reality that I have had to come to terms with. It's not that I have lost faith in all police officers, but more that the system itself has let us all down – police and public. Anyway, what use would come of involving them? What will we gain? Only find ourselves faced by a new layer of complication, precisely when we need to focus ourselves and concentrate. If we contact them, we will ourselves be investigated and we need to be free to move and do as we determine fit."

"I don't know . . ." said Pamela. ". . . couldn't they offer us protection? I always thought that you worshipped the police?"

"I worship only God. At this moment, the police I used to respect so much when I was an officer myself, can only offer us the realm of bureaucracy and misplaced interference. The 'protection' they can offer is not the protection we need. You, yourself, protected yourself and Laura and Jo, and for doing that your reward would be a police charge for holding an unregistered and lethal firearm, and also possibly a charge of grievous bodily harm for discharging it into Mr Cousins, when instead you saved three people's lives. So no, no, no; I do not think the police need to know. And before you tell me off for putting that weapon into your hands and compromising you legally; I'm glad I did. Cousins is not the kind to respect any legal niceties, and if anyone he considered his enemy hesitated to worry about the legal whys and wherefores he would be only too pleased to take advantage of their hesitancy, and just take their life, like that, without any qualms whatsoever. No, you did the right thing, Pam." And Lynch reached over and hugged her tightly. Such public displays of affection were not usual for Andrew Lynch.

"I forgot," said Power, standing up. "How could I forget? Jo, where is he?"

Laura pointed upwards in the direction of the boy's bedroom.

Power ran across the landing to the narrow stairway up into the tower room. There was a warm yellow light from the lamp he had brought Jo the night he could not sleep. The light spilled over the bedside and glowed upon the bright colours of the rumpled duvet as it lay on the floor. The windows were all glossy black with night except for the sharp bright reflections of the lamp. Jo's books were scattered around the room, on tables, chairs, and rugs. There was tray with an unfinished plastic model of a lunar landing module on his desk. Power could smell the polystyrene cement glue. Lying nearby on the desk surface was the catapult Jo had shot the magpies with. An irritating thought entered his mind that he should have confiscated it, but he dismissed it. Power stepped over to the windows and whipped the curtains across to prevent his being visible to anyone outside. The radiator under the window was red hot to the touch and the room was warm and cosy. But the comfortable room was seemingly empty – there was no sign of Jo.

"Jo?" Power called.

No answer.

Power wondered if Jo had slipped past them and gone downstairs without their seeing him, whilst they talked. Young boys can creep and prowl silently, like the stealthiest of cats, if they so wish.

Then Power noticed that the mattress had no pillows on it.

Jo liked three pillows.

Power considered this and then knelt down on the rug by the bed. He bent forwards and peered into the gloom beneath the bed; into a realm of shadowy floorboards and fluff. His son's brown eyes glittered back at him. Jo was lying on the floor, his head cushioned by the missing pillows. He said nothing, but stared, white-faced at his father.

"There you are. Are you all right, Jo?"

"I thought you might be dead," said Jo. "There was a man with a gun. I thought he had killed you and then he was coming for me."

"He's gone," said Power. He noted that the boy mentioned his fear that his father was dead first of all. A perfectly reasonable fear, he supposed, given that Jo had just lost both mother and grandfather. "I'm all right, though. You're all right, too. You can come out now, if you like?"

The boy shook his head. "Not yet."

"No?" said Power. "Can I wait here, then?"

"Yes, you guard me," said Jo.

A pause.

"Are you cold?" asked Power.

"A bit," said Jo. "There's a draught. Through the floor."

"Do you want the duvet you had before you went under there?"

Jo nodded and Power passed the duvet under the bed. The boy pushed it under himself and wrapped it round his body as best he could in the narrow space.

"You want me to stay here and guard you?" asked Power.

Jo looked out at his father and nodded in a very definite manner.

"Are you planning to go to sleep?" asked Power. "Maybe you'd be better on top of the bed?" But Jo shook his head. It felt safer to him to stay where he was. Jo could see his father shifting round to sit with his back to him. Anyone would have to get past his father to get at him now. His father would protect him. Jo felt warmer and more relaxed.

"Aunty Pamela shot him," Jo said softly. "I saw. She was very brave." Jo yawned. "I don't think I can get to sleep, though . . ." But when Power looked five minutes later Jo was snoring softly.

Chapter Nineteen

D r Power had balanced a cardboard tray of coffee and pastries throughout his walk from the café on Bridge Street to the Chester Castle without so much as losing a crumb or spilling a drop. He was pleased with himself, because such trays had proved to be a foe in the past; dissolving in the rain or twisting in the wind to spill scalding coffee on him.

Power crossed the parade ground car park and arrived at the doorway of the Foundation's office. He pressed the intercom button with an elbow. The Foundation's new administrator, Gill, came downstairs and let him in. He was grateful when she took the tray from him. "Thank you," he said. "It's not easy carrying one of those and a briefcase."

She looked at the tray and smiled. Power noted her glossy black-cherry coloured lips were delineated in another, darker, colour. Her eyes and cropped short hair were similarly glossy, but chestnut brown. "There are three cups," she said. "Is anybody else coming?"

"I got you a coffee too," said Power. "Just in case you were joining us."

"That's very kind of you," she said, and carried the tray upstairs to Lynch's office, where she deposited it on a window ledge near Lynch, who was looking at a vast Ordnance Survey map of the Edge he had spread all over the surface of his desk. Gill prised a cup of latte for herself from the tray and diplomatically slipped out of the office.

"You left the safe house before people were awake, Andrew," said Power. "Pamela asked me to bring you breakfast, so I've brought you a black coffee and a *pain au raisin* . . . or if you don't want that we could go out . . . there's a place on Bridge Street that does a good breakfast of roasted vegetables with some really light, fragrant focaccia bread." Dr Power smiled at the very thought.

"I wanted to check some things in the office," said Lynch. "Make a few phone calls."

It was two days after the attack by Cousins.

On the first morning after, (following a more or less sleepless night), Lynch had insisted that everybody move out of Alderley House. Lynch would not allow anybody to remain at risk from Cousins by staying put. It seemed unlikely, but if Cousins was still alive, he might return. So Lynch arranged what he called a 'safe house' near the Castle, close to his resources at the Foundation offices in Chester.

The 'safe house' had proved to be a pair of linked flats above a firm of solicitors on White Friars Street. They had deliberately left cars and mobiles behind. Such things are easily traced. And so, Lynch had provided everyone with brand new, cheap 'pay-as-you-go' mobiles. He had forbidden Pamela to return home to pick up anything, even a change of clothes. She had protested, "My own home is a few miles away from here. Why should I go through with this pantomime?"

Lynch had explained that even if Cousins was out of commission; he had the contacts to arrange for another person to visit in order to finish what he had begun, and that only when they knew exactly where Cousins was could they begin to relax.

Power protested that he had work to do – patients to see, papers to write, essays to mark, court reports to dictate – and that all his files were at Alderley House. Lynch had stared him down.

Laura had entered into the spirit of the adventure. She enjoyed wearing a paisley headscarf and sunglasses on her brief trip with Lynch to buy immediate groceries from Tesco. Jo had spent the day glued to a game console that Lynch had brought back.

Now they were on their own, Power again made a plea to be allowed to return to Alderley House to 'do some work'.

"I can't stop you," said Lynch. "You're an autonomous human

being, but obviously if you go then Laura will follow, and it is less easy to keep everyone safe. Can we stay put, please? Just until we know a little more?"

And so Power said he would abide by this, but inside his heart there was still a spark of resistance. The bribe of coffee and pastries had obviously been too feeble to overcome Lynch's determination. "So, is there any news of Cousins? Has he been picked up at an emergency department?"

"Security services say he that if he is alive, he is probably still within UK borders. No track of his passport since he re-entered the country some weeks ago. No vehicles associated with him have been tracked by ANPR. I used my Developed Access to search for him on bank card facilities. No transactions. No NHS trace. If he did live long enough to get medical help, it must have been private. There are private trauma facilities that such people as Cousins use in circumstances like these. And you can find independent surgeons with the ultimate levels of 'confidentiality' and 'no questions asked' for certain clients. No doubt he could access such a service – he probably did after he survived the incident in Toronto. And I've only checked for the identities we know he has. What else has he got?"

"He would lose so much blood, and quickly, after a shoulder gunshot wound," said Power. "Laura said his shoulder just dissolved as it exploded. She could feel the spray of his blood on her face."

"Well," said Lynch. "He undoubtedly has had help. Who knows what contacts he has, or resources he has built up access to. They are still plugging holes in the finances at the Howarth-Weaver Pharmaceutical corporation where Cousins worked. Simon Howarth-Weaver stopped up some leaks and diverted some of those funds to start up this Foundation, our Foundation. Nobody can yet work out where the original finance streams Cousins had set up were flowing – money running like underground water – shifting through offshore accounts, seeping from a shady company account in a Panama bank to a holding company in the Turks and Caicos Islands banking sector . . . permeating through layers upon layers like water percolating through so many different strata underground. So, if our Foundation could be financed on just one of those tributaries leaking from the Howarth-Weaver Corporation, then it follows that Cousins could well have set up many more streams and built up a whole lake of finances over a longer time. And that, Carl, is precisely why I think we should stay put. Use our safe house, employ every resource we have, because who knows what resources Cousins has at his finger tips. In fact, right now, the way I feel, I think the Foundation should have our own armed team."

Power looked at the vast map that lay over Lynch's desk like an untidy canvas tablecloth. "What's that for? Are you planning a military campaign?"

"Almost," said Lynch. I've been working on our other case – considering the area between the farmhouse at Lindow and the surrounding land. Trying to work out where our other problem, Joel Heaney, could have holed up. Beresford has had resources for a couple of door-to-door enquiries, and some searches, but he has a big area to cover, and although he is under immense pressure to solve the largest serial case in the county in living memory, he keeps being criticized for wasting public resources. It beggars belief," said Lynch.

"I met him here last night; he is desperate for a breakthrough from us, and I wish I could help. Beresford is being sidelined politically – you know when they have an important meeting about your case – the high-ups – and they don't invite you . . . you begin to sniff in the air that a change is coming. Finding the body of Kyle means the killer is still active, and looking at it academically, although it might bring us closer to finding Heaney, politically it is just evidence of our failure – and so naturally, questions are being asked about Beresford's competence and the newspapers unkindly point out that even Inspector Morse would have been sacked at this body count. That is, of course, an unfair comparison and television detectives are, by and large, monumentally incompetent. But then, Beresford has always faced prejudice. At promotion, non-white officers are universally heralded, because they help combat the idea that the force is institutionally racist, but after the initial trumpeting about their appointment they face the usual suspects who actually want them to fail. Like women police officers . . . who are given more than their fair share of toxic child abuse cases to cope with, or moved to duties that cannot be combined with family life. There is a shiny surface of political correctness, but it is a wafer-thin veneer."

"You would have thought that modern day civilisation wouldn't have such prejudices," said Power.

"One day you're made to feel wanted and special and the next you are surplus to requirements. Like me – I like to think I was the model police officer, but then, suddenly, I was seen as 'different' – too religious maybe? Too old and too much of a salary burden? And so, one fine day, you find your face no longer fits. And now Beresford is also the model officer. A high flyer who is given a massive case that provides a singularly sensational story for the newspapers. Scores of victims over the years. A cannibal to scandalise their readers. And, of course, Beresford ran the Heaney investigation precisely according to the book. But . . . no arrest. Nobody could have run the show better, but . . . no arrest. Nobody in custody. And suddenly his face doesn't fit. And they scrutinise his actions, looking for something, some tiny little thing they can criticise and which can provide the hook they will hang him on."

"And have they found the hook?" asked Power.

Lynch did not say, but instead, he suggested they go and find some lunch. He stood and put his coat on and together Power and Lynch left the office and began to walk into the city. They crossed the old parade ground in front of the castle, strolled side-by-side past the old regimental headquarters and down a side street, on to St Mary's Hill and then to Grosvenor Street.

Lynch continued their conversation in hushed tones. "The hook will be the Policy File book, the one that I believe Cousins stole, and which gave him the detail to construct that lure to get us away from home to Glasgow. The loss of that File will give the Chief Constable the justification he needs. The File is the key document that the Senior Investigating Officer must keep and guard. They will argue that the file he lost contained vital information – information that would have shortened the investigation and produced an arrest."

"But they don't know that," protested Power.

"True, they can't prove their case with evidence. And equally well Beresford can't prove otherwise. All they need to do is cast suspicion and that will provide them with enough political capital to depose him. If only we could help Beresford," said Lynch.

"How?" asked Power.

"By providing him with Joel Heaney."

"And that we haven't been able to do."

"No," said Lynch. "Despite Heaney's picture being splashed over every national newspaper for weeks. He has just gone underground."

They turned down Cuppin Street and passed a newsagent. Seemingly to illustrate Lynch's point a newspaper board outside had a blown up-front page pasted onto it and Joel Heaney's unremarkable face stared back at them. The newspaper headline was 'Find Cannibal Jo.'

"His name is Joel," said Power. "I suppose they thought Cannibal Jo had a better ring to it than Cannibal Joel. The media never letting facts stand in the way of their chosen reality. I wish they could have called him something else."

They were walking across the cobbles of the street, when Lynch suddenly stumbled. Power reached out to support him, but Lynch waved his arm away.

"Lose your footing on the stones?" asked Power.

"No," said Lynch. "Didn't you feel the ground lurch?"

"No?" said Power.

"Like it shifted," said Lynch. Power shook his head. "Maybe another aftershock?" Lynch wondered. Power did not quite understand what Lynch was alluding to and decided not to query it further.

They were now standing outside a small bistro called Francs. Lynch was inspecting the menu absent-mindedly, and still talking to his friend about Heaney. "Where is he?" asked Lynch. "He must go out to get food or money. Why hasn't he been spotted?"

"Maybe no-one reads newspapers these days?" suggested Power. "Or maybe people just aren't very observant any more – walking around in a daze staring at their phones. Or he looks different to the photos we have of him? He could have changed the length of his hair, dyed it a different colour, shaved it off, grown a beard, hidden behind sunglasses, or maybe only goes out at night with a hoodie on. Perhaps he gets food deliveries rather than visiting supermarkets. Society isn't that close any more. People don't care about reality any more. They are more interested in virtual friends on Myspace or Messenger than the flesh and blood of their neighbour. *Anomie* rules."

"Do you think this place will do for lunch?" asked Lynch.

"I've been here a few times over the years," said Power. "It's OK if you like steak and frites."

"Well, I would like exactly that," said Lynch, "but I guess you wouldn't . . ."

"I'll find something to eat," said Power, "Don't worry."

Power and Lynch went in and found a small table at the rear of the dining room. The linen was crisply starched and white, the cutlery polished and solid, and the service prompt. Cool spring water was poured into glasses and orders taken for drinks. Lynch ordered a bière from Alsace, *Licorne Authentique*, Power ordered a lemon pressé. He had plans to see patients that afternoon, although he hadn't told Lynch, in case he challenged the wisdom of Power making an appearance in clinic.

Lynch ordered Soupe du jour, Steak au poivre, green beans, and Frites. Power ordered Tarte du chèvre (pastry tart with green asparagus, goat's cheese and seasonal leaves) as a starter and then Tagine aux legumes – a spiced spring vegetable Tagine served with pea and mint couscous.

When Lynch's Frites eventually materialised on their table, Power felt a pang of envy. The thin fries glistened like gold and were speckled with salt. Lynch attacked them with relish and as he munched he asked his friend a question, "So Carl, I don't often ask you to organize your thoughts into a profile, but could you profile the killer in this case? It might help."

"I expect that Beresford has already had the 'benefit' of the usual profiles from well-meaning psychologists," said Power. "But I'm not a psychologist. I listen to people. I don't try and reduce people to types or push people into categories. Everybody is different."

He went on, "A profiler of a serial killer always seems to start by asking if the murderer was organised or disorganised, that's what they usually consider first off; well isn't everybody a mixture of the two things? A butterfly collector might organise the trophies in a regimented way on his boards behind the glass of a frame, he might be a meticulous lepidopterist at a museum, but impulsive alcohol binges might interrupt his ordered existence every now and then. So – is he organised or disorganised? A person with anorexia may be stringently rigorous about his diet, but impulsively sleep with different men every night from a gay bar. Is he organised or disorganised? From a certain point of view, I suppose that Heaney is organised – he lives without leaving traces – he has no bank account we can detect, the house is kept free of any evidence that might help us – such as letters. It's not easy to live without leaving traces, and especially without leaving evidence of yourself in your own home – and yet his home – the farm – was always kept that way, so that even if there was a sudden event like a police raid, nothing could be found to link him. Even when a plane crashed into his farm, he could escape with no paper trail."

"There would be DNA evidence though," said Lynch.

"Who can live somewhere without leaving traces of spit and snot and whatever," said Power. "He organised everything he could, and that day I met him in the cellar, perhaps he was coming back to remove the one piece of evidence he'd left behind; the photo album. So he was, and is, organised, but what does that tell us? Maybe some of his victims were stalked beforehand and their abduction, their murder, was carefully planned. He targeted homeless people that maybe he knew something about – making sure they were lonely, isolated people? New to the street? And then when he knew they were truly alone, he'd invite them back for a meal, a warm bed? Or sex? But sometimes he may have risked a departure from that careful approach. He might have craved the risk, the thrill of deviating from that plan. The girl he met at the bus stop. Maybe he'd only seen her once and thought he'd try it on."

"Do you think Heaney might be driven by psychosis?"

"Well, classically I suppose, psychosis destroys the ability to organise, but some psychoses can have well-defined boundaries – a monodelusional psychosis for instance, like a man who believes his arm has been infested with a maggot, and believes this wholeheartedly despite his doctor's reassurances. He can go to work. He can play five-a-side football, and take the kids swimming, but he still believes that somewhere inside him there is a maggot that never comes out, except maybe when he is asleep. He can function, and nobody knows, he never says it in public, because it's socially unacceptable to be infested, so why tell anybody? But in this one particular delusional belief, if you ask him a specific question, he will answer that, yes, he has a maggot living inside his flesh. So this man, he has a psychotic symptom, but in an isolated fashion – is he disorganised? And then there are other presentations, I suppose, like *folie a deux* – a couple, maybe, where only one is ill – only one has the psychosis – and they in turn convince the other of the validity of their beliefs, so both live under the thrall of this illness. Detach one member of the couple from the ill one, and their joint 'folie' is broken. Was Joel Heaney brought up in such an environment? Was his father ill? Was Joel brought up according to the delusional rules of a sick family? I'm not sure, but the organised/disorganised question that the profiler typically asks about serial killers is too simplistic a model in this case. I just don't think these rigid classification schemes work.

"And then the profiler always tries to make *thematic inferences* – looking at the dominant themes of the criminal style – like looking at how a serial offender, say a rapist, forces entry into the victim's home in a certain way, always takes precautions not to leave fingerprints and, steals from the victim leading to the conclusion that the perpetrator might have prior convictions for burglary; and this inference guides the police in extrapolating from known convictions to find their offender. And yet in this case, we can see varying themes. Heaney selects victims that are male and female, mature and young, from different locations – and the victims we've traced are from the city and also from elsewhere. Some are killed at the farm, some are killed elsewhere. And the motives . . . the objectives of the crimes? What are they? Trophy taking? A twisted exercise in power? Heterosexual gratification? Sadism? Cannibalism for sure, but not in every case. Some of the bodies are literally butchered for storage as meat. One body, the Ice Maiden, is kept intact. Was she selected for another purpose? It's all so complicated that the profiler's routine tool of *thematic inference* is no use here.

"I believe that every person is different, so every criminal is different, so every motive behind every crime differs that little bit and so divining the solution to the problem is different in every case. If you want a solution you are required to think both consciously and unconsciously. Believing you can reduce it all to categories and typologies is to lose the very edge of keen thought. Dividing crimes into organised and disorganised is to try and cut out an answer with the bluntest of blades.

"You know *Twin Peaks*? In *Twin Peaks* Detective Cooper takes his inspiration from a lady who talks to a log or by playing a game of throwing stones. It's absurd nonsense, of course, but what the director of the series meant was that it's really about opening the unconscious mind to imagine the solution. These days we trust in computers like HOLMES to understand crimes, which are perpetrated by people. Computers think in series, they can't process two or three ideas at once. Only the human brain can think in parallel."

"Are you saying that finding the solution is in some way also an unconscious process?" asked Lynch. "I think you've lost me. I just don't follow you."

"No," said Power. "I'm not sure I'm saying that." Power paused and wondered how he could formulate what he meant more precisely.

"Well," said Lynch. "Let me help. I certainly hear you saying that the crimes in this case have a variety of motives and so the usual profiling of an individual wouldn't work?"

"The approach presupposes an individual with a predictable mind, and here I see so many motives that I can't see behind them to one mind. It's like a philosophy Heaney is adhering to, but is it just his philosophy?"

"I don't understand," said Lynch.

"Joel Heaney had a disordered childhood. Was that by virtue of his being unusual and kept away from the public, like a family hiding him in misplaced shame . . . or shielding him from prejudice . . . or was his life designed to be that way? Did his parents *always* intend him to be brought up in isolation, and if so, why? Is all this *their* way of life? Is this way of life; feeding off others . . . the culture of a family?"

"Surely no parents would ever . . . ever . . ." Lynch was truly shocked. "Isn't it more likely that Heaney killed both his parents and became more extreme as he grew without their influence? Or that his mother did move away to somewhere like Scotland leaving him to his grisly habits?"

"Hmm, it's difficult . . . I can see that you're hoping that the horror of his way of life was confined to just Heaney's own mind. It seems less uncomfortable to believe that only *he* is responsible, rather than to admit the alternative – that Heaney was the son brought up according to the rules of a horrific family – that he was subject, over the course of his upbringing, to some kind of contagion of the soul. You must recall that the drink that killed Kyle, the homeless man, was handed to him by a woman. Not given by a man, not by Joel Heaney, but by a woman's hand."

"You could have been mistaken, memory can be unreliable, we know that," said Lynch.

"I am not mistaken," said Power firmly.

"Maybe Heaney was in the refuge kitchens at the time. Maybe he was a volunteer there and watched Kyle going into see you and asked another volunteer – some completely innocent lady, totally independent of him – to hand that cup of tea to Kyle?"

"I don't think so," said Power. "As a plan that might go horribly wrong. If the woman was independent of Heaney and knew nothing of the plan . . . imagine if you gave a drink to someone to hand out – someone who didn't know it was poisoned – then they might give it to the wrong person, or even drink it themselves.

"And anyway," said Power. "There is plenty of precedent for families being involved, as a team, in crimes – old East End gangster families, Sicilian mafia families – families where the parents' expectations of their children is that they will just go into the family business of crime when they grow up. They imagine no other way of life for their family. It is merely their way of life – a family custom," said Power.

"But cannibalism!" Lynch protested. "Surely not. Not in this country. Not in the twenty-first century."

"There is a precedent in past centuries, though," said Power. "There was a man called Sawney Beane who was part of such a family in Scotland. His entire family would ambush travellers, like highwaymen, for money, but to ensure they never talked about the family they were killed, and to ensure no waste of the bodies existed, they ate them. They had to send in two hundred soldiers to flush them out of the wild country."

"That was probably a propaganda story, and exactly when was that?" said Lynch. "Hundreds of years ago, in the back of beyond."

"Cannibalism is a way of life in some cultures," said Power. "Papua New Guinea for instance. And recently there was Dahmer and there was Knight."

"Those examples are not the same as this case."

"We like to think these things cannot happen near us geographically, or near us in time. It is unsettling to imagine, I know. Thinking about it is uncomfortable. And when we close our minds to the possible, because it happened somewhere else, or a long time ago – well, it means that thing does become a risk for us, in the here and now. We like to think these bad things happened centuries past – to give ourselves a barrier between then and now. So we can relax in our forgetfulness. We like to think that they are distant in place, too. I find it disturbing to think that children can be abused still. We prefer to think of it all as happening a long time ago, far away. But you and I face reality. In *my lifetime* employees of the Church were actively and systematically abusing my contemporaries." There was real anger in his voice. "The Christian Brothers for example . . . all people who set themselves up as nurturers of children . . . how they have betrayed us all. That is the true discomfort of all this. The real horror amongst us . . . here and now. It could be any of us who is a victim. We cannot deny it, Andrew, because if we deny what is happening we lend it the power to spread unchecked, like a disease without controls. What we must do is be as mindful and vigilant as possible, and fight . . . and never stop."

Lynch heard the impassioned tone of his friend and hung his head. "I know," he whispered, and, thinking of the stack of case files he had back on a shelf at the office, said, "The Foundation is uncovering it. We're working on it." He put his hands up to his forehead and sighed. "You sound so angry. I didn't mean to deny the truth. I get overwhelmed sometimes." He looked at his watch. It was past two. He wondered if there was evensong later this afternoon. He needed some space to pray and clear his troubled mind.

"Maybe we should have coffee," said Power, looking around the restaurant, which had emptied. This was just as well, he thought, as their voices had been raised by the intensity of their conversation. "Or a dessert," he wondered.

"Whatever you will," said Lynch. "We must take the opportunity to make the most of being out, I suppose." Lynch envisaged attending evensong then getting back to the safe house as soon as possible. He was still fearful of a reprisal by Cousins or his agents.

"Well," said Power guiltily, "I was thinking of getting some work done. I have a paper that needs finishing off and there's something else I've been meaning to do."

"Didn't we talk about this earlier? You *are* stubborn. Don't tell me you still intend to go back to Alderley, or confront your fears and go off exploring under the house again . . . don't tell me that . . ." Lynch sounded annoyed. "This is just not the time. It's too risky to go back to the house and not the time to be risking a journey down that stairway. Laura will want you here, surely."

"I won't spend more than a few hours in my study. I will lock all the doors. I'm just getting some academic work done. It will settle my mind to concentrate on something else."

"You're not exploring in the dark, or trying to solve the crime in some mystical way by harnessing the unconscious or whatever you were going on about before? Something I didn't understand."

"I was just referring to the power of the unconscious mind earlier. People need to be creative to generate solutions to problems, like solving a crime. That was all I was saying." A waiter had overheard Power mentioning coffee and desserts and had provided them both with a menu. Power wondered what else the waiter had overheard. The waiter's face remained unmoved, impassive and professional. "And, of course, I won't be doing anything other than a bit of academic work." Power ordered a meringue and raspberries, and an espresso.

"I'm not sure I believe you," said Lynch. "But I am not my brother's keeper, all I can do is advise you. But Cousins is not accounted for and he wants revenge so badly," said Lynch. "We have, from his point of view, taken so much from him – a lucrative position with a corporation, his eye, his brothers."

Power said nothing, but nodded. He finished his coffee and settled their bill. As Power and Lynch left the restaurant they parted company with few words spoken. Lynch turned right to finish his work for the day and afternoon Evensong, and Power turned left to find his car in the car park for the journey to Alderley House.

Chapter Twenty

D r Power struggled to wake. He had been so deeply unconscious that it was a struggle now to recall who he was. He opened his eyes, but it seemed to make no difference. He saw blackness whether his eyelids were closed or open. He wondered whether he had been robbed of sight in the night. Diagnoses such as an occipital lobe stroke or some blockage of the posterior cerebral arteries occurred to the doctor. He had become aware of himself after some sort of sleep, but he couldn't recall going to bed.

What did he remember? He remembered a meal with Lynch, then blankness.

Dr Power had been playing with his self-diagnosis for a moment or so, half in the expectation that his sight would miraculously return. But as the moments slipped by, his sight did not return. This made his heart beat a little faster. He felt the panic urging his pulse faster and felt it bounding in his neck. He was blind.

He called out repeatedly, "Laura!" and "Jo!" There was no response. Power could hear his voice cracking as he shouted out; fear led his breath to snag and strain.

His voice echoed and simply faded away into the distance. His words diminished fruitlessly as their sound waves scattered into the blankness of the all-consuming dark.

He strained to hear the normal sounds of his house. Where were the creaking floor boards, the ticking clocks, the wind rustling the branches of the trees outside, the distant humdrum of the washing machine in the laundry room, the murmur of a radio in the kitchen? He could hear none of that background noise. All he could hear was the almost imperceptible susurration of air as it gently moved around him. He could also hear his breathing relative to the silence of his surroundings, and this told him he was at least not deaf as well as blind, but the almost total silence begged the question: where was he?

To test his hearing again, Power whispered, "Laura," then more confidently, "Laura?" His voice was clear. When he spoke there was a quick echo, a simple reflection from some hard surface, and then the sound faded, like it sank into something vast and undefined.

He was afraid to speak out again, embarrassed by the unknown space beyond him. Some intuition prevented him from letting out another shout.

He became aware, then, of another sound. A trickling, chuckling sound of running water; a small sound, almost tinkling rather than chuckling, but nevertheless distinct. A trickle of water, rather than a stream.

There was a flicker of light on his retina, like a blurred orange flash. It didn't seem to be a record of anything in the real world and Power wondered if his mind had started making things up to occupy itself. People in isolation tanks saw and heard things that weren't there, as their brains, starved of stimulation made up their own sensory content. What else might his understimulated mind imagine in the dark? Voices? Conversations in the dark?

Power felt he was sitting up, not lying down. He was not in some starched clinic bed in a hospital side ward. He was sitting upright against some hard surface with legs stretched out in front of him. His arms were behind his back and his wrists were against something hard, and cold, stiff and unable to move.

He realised he had his boots on and kicked his legs out in front of him. The boots made a gritty, scratching sound as he moved his feet. He felt the cold of the ground against his bottom, permeating through his trousers. The stony chill of the ground seeped into his legs.

Power tried to move his arms to touch his face and found his wrists were bound behind his back by a chain, which rattled gratingly in the gloom.

He realised then that he had not suffered a stroke, rather, that he was in absolute darkness. And, he reasoned, someone wanted him to stay exactly where he was, in the dark.

He sniffed the cool air around him. It smelled fresh, but somehow faintly dusty and there was the whiff of ether. The aromatic smell made him wonder whether he was in a hospital after all.

Power struggled to think back to some time before the eternal night he was in. There was an ache in his head, just over his right forehead and the skin around his eye and cheekbone seemed stiff and moved with difficulty, as if caked in something. Dried blood? Maybe a head injury accounted for his difficulty in orientating himself? Had he had a blow to the head, which might have caused him to forget what had happened? He thought back carefully to try and pick a thread of memory to follow.

He had turned left onto Grosvenor Street after leaving the restaurant where he had dined with his friend. Power had found his car on Pepper Street and driven through Tarvin and Delamere, Davenham and Peover. He remembered the Saab chugging its dogged way through Nether Alderley and up the hill towards Alderley House. He remembered a sense of excitement at the notion of defying the sensible advice of Lynch. Power had reasoned that Cousins would not dare to show himself again, if indeed he was still alive, until his arm was fully recovered. Surely it would take months to recover from a wound like that? He remembered the drive along the roads; the winter sun had been shining after a fall of rain, and the wet metalled surface had gleamed and glistened in the sunlight. All this he remembered.

He recalled the crunch of gravel as he turned into the drive of Alderley House, and walking up to the solid oak front door. The Green Man had looked down upon him from his place on high above the doorway. That day, Power seemed to recall, the Green Man had appeared to be almost frowning, as if in warning, maybe?

Power had assembled a pile of equipment on the kitchen table. He remembered each individual clunk as he put a pair of thick-soled hiking boots on the table, then the helmet, the light, and the heavy battery the caving club secretary had given him. Then, no less than three compact, but solid flashlights, which he checked were working before he took them below. He recalled changing into a warm, thick cotton shirt, a chunky woollen sweater, and heavy-duty cargo trousers. He put on a waterproof cagoule, and over that donned the battery on its belt, the light with its umbilical cord to the battery, and then fixed it onto the helmet he had adjusted to his head size. He did not mean to get cold in the underworld beneath his house. He remembered being too warm in the kitchen. Where were those warm clothes now, Power wondered, as he shivered in the dark?

Power remembered standing there in the warm kitchen, feeling a mixture of anxiety and elation at being on the edge of his own challenge to himself. Then he clumped to the kitchen dresser and heaved it far enough along the wall to give full view of the hidden door, which he then unlocked with a key taken from the dresser drawer.

Then what had happened? There were perhaps only fragments of memory left. The room beyond was merely a short passageway to the stone steps. Sturdy wooden shelves ran round the sidewalls and there was a meat safe on the floor. He remembered being anxious, going through there. His unconscious had screamed at him that something was significant. Something had been different. Something missing. There were a few old tins, but something had changed since he was last there. His conscious mind couldn't fathom the depth of concern produced by his unconscious. Something was gone, and that something had been important. He couldn't recall, even now. He remembered the stairs and the curve as they descended into the dark. Puzzling again as he wondered why a past owner of the house had had these stairs fashioned into the underworld. At the bottom, he encountered the Victorian cast iron gates he had seen before, on his last journey into the dark. The last time they had lain where they had fallen – perhaps their fixings had rusted away over the decades. This time, however, the gates had been lifted and leant against the walls where the steps ended. And here the walls, for a few yards at least, had been smoothed and covered with turquoise tiles, glazed with salts of strontium, nepheline, copper, and cobalt. Why celebrate this underground world? Power had thought.

And the strong beam from his head lamp had pierced the dark tunnels under his house. He remembered once, stumbling one way in the dark and being panicked he might die, and so this time, bolstered by at least three reserve sources of light, he had chosen to walk slowly in the opposite direction along the sandstone tunnel. The circumference of the tunnel was enough to admit two people side by side in places, and in others, narrow and low, to the point he had to duck and his helmet scraped along the rough-hewn roof. The tunnel narrowed towards the roof, and was widest near the floor, thin channels in the edges of the tunnel carried a trickle of water, flowing down into the dark. The rivulets gleamed under the beam of his head lamp. He could see the channels were fed by water that percolated through the porous rock and flowed down the walls in places, and had smoothed and carved the soft stone over the years. He could hear the water running, and echoed plops as occasional drips fell sporadically from the ceiling. The walls of the red sandstone were mottled in places with patches of the most vivid blues and greens. The patches glowed under his light as they were coated in a film of glistening water. He remembered being excited by the brightness of the colour and wondering about the chemical formulae of the pigments therein.

Then there were some more images. He remembered coming across a side shaft in the floor to his right. He threw a pebble into the darkness and it rattled from side to side of the shaft for some seconds before it fell with a 'ploosh' into hidden water at the bottom. He tried to calculate how long the fall had taken and how far it was. If the fall had lasted three seconds how many metres was that? He estimated about forty-four metres. He had skirted the entrance to the shaft with a wary tread.

His last memory was of the tunnel opening out into a space with three possible paths to follow. One was just behind him and had a full height opening, dark and forbidding. He turned to survey another opening at chest height, where if he wanted to go, he would have had to scrambled up a short incline. The last, to his left, was down a short slope. The entrance looked half-height and he would have needed to bend almost double.

And that was it. He had been considering these three options when his memories ended. Had something fallen on him or had he been hit from behind?

That there was a memory trace, and then blankness, told him he had some amnesia, and that as he had formed no memory of how he had got from standing at that junction of tunnels to wherever he was now, meant that he had retrograde amnesia. And it was a mystery to him, how he was now in blind darkness, cold, seated on the hard, unyielding stony ground, and pinioned by his wrists.

The darkness and the silence seemed fathomless, endless, and timeless. The random, dull, red flashes on his retina reminded him that his brain and nervous system sought to imagine something, anything, to populate the silent darkness.

It was into this void of perception that Power began to hear words.

"He's awake."

"I can see him looking round. He looks lost."

Power thought the voices were located over to his right, and ahead of him. But was their origin inside his own mind? Was he finally experiencing third person auditory hallucinations as a result of his sensory deprivation.

The female voice went on, "You have the eyes, but I can feel him stir beside me."

"I thought the blow had smashed his brain," said a male voice directly in front of him.

"Don't be feeling sorry for him," she said. "You know it makes it more difficult when you feel anything for them. He is what he is, meat. Talking meat. Nothing more, nothing less."

Power decided to enter his own voice into the stream of the conversation, no matter whether the conversation were hallucinated or not, and so he asked, "Who is that? Where am I?"

The immediate response was swift and deliberately painful. He felt a waft of air pass his face as an arm swung down and hit him in the thigh.

At first he thought the nearby woman had punched him in the leg, and then he felt the pain as she withdrew the short, sharp knife-blade from his quadriceps muscle. Dr Power's breath was taken away by the sudden viciousness of her attack. "Don't answer him," she hissed. "He's not a person any more."

"I'll do what I like," he said. "I'll say what I like."

Power felt his own blood oozing from the wound and dampening the material of his trousers. He was aware that the woman was nearby. He imagined he could feel the heat of her body and was anxious not to provoke her into any further random acts of violence.

Power thought silence the best option, but then the male voice spoke directly to him.

"My name is Heaney. I thought you were clever. Didn't you figure that out? You want to know where you've ended up, Dr Power?"

And his question demanded a reply in spite of the risk engendered by having the woman with the knife hovering at Power's elbow. "Yes," said Power. "Am I in a basement or a tunnel? Where is this?"

"You're in a mine, Doctor. Deep under the Edge."

"Engine Vein mine?" asked Power.

"The Edge is honeycombed with tunnels, caves, and mineworking. The cavers have only found a couple of the mines, but there were Roman mines, Victorian mines, and other mines they don't know about. There were soldiers from the Napoleonic wars that lived near Lindow and they dug and dug their way into the sandstone, and when they went, well our family owned them tunnels. Our family's been here for generations. We owned a lot of land round here. Farms and the like. Great Granda owned the big house on the hill – he owned the mines for a while . . . till he gambled them away. So we've always known about the mines and, when they closed, well we took them back. And in the mines Granda even found a few soldiers who'd mined down here, under a roof fall. Still in their tatters of uniforms. We've found ways through the flooded parts and the piles of spoil from the minings, and we opened them up when we liked for ourselves. No-one can find you down here. You can do what you like. We always have."

"And what do you do?" asked Power.

"Don't tell him," said the woman.

"I can do what I like down here," said Joel. "And I can say what I like. I'm the King under the hill now."

"So what do you do?" asked Power again. The woman responded by stabbing him again in the thigh. A vicious, sharp, sting of rebuke for going against her wishes and encouraging Joel to spout his boastings.

"We can go unseen here," said Heaney. "Bring victims we find, play with them a bit, kill them, cook them, eat them. We play music loud and we feast as we like."

"But there's only the two of you now?" asked Power, minding his words lest a sudden stab came again out of the dark.

"The family's grown a bit thin, perhaps. But we're all down here. And I'll find someone to join us, and us'll breed a new family. It's up to me now to keep our . . . traditions."

"There was a girl in the house," said Power. "With long, blonde hair. Did you think she might . . . join the family?"

"She had her chance," said Joel. "But she said the wrong things and Mum didn't like her."

"Shhh," hissed the female. "He doesn't need to know." She was close to Power now. He wanted to ask how Joel had lured the girl to his house, what kind of honey he had baited to trap her, and just how much she knew about Heaney's plans for her, or how much Sky had gone along with his ideas before she said 'the wrong things'. Power wondered just how difficult could it be to find a partner who shared your homicidal beliefs? Fred West had managed this task. A task, which would seem insuperably difficult to the rational observer. What had the girl said to alienate the mother? Power thought it wouldn't be difficult to aggravate the jealous mother of this only son.

"Are there many girls who would share your . . . beliefs?" asked Power. The question slipped out before he had chance to censor himself. He thought he had asked too much. He tried to prepare himself in case the blade struck, but the pain never came.

"More than you'd think," said Joel. "There are more outsiders than you'd imagine in your perfect little world. There's more disorder than order. People like you just try to ignore the chaos of nature. Once you open up to chaos, you understand how breathtaking it is. The rules people live by are meaningless. Stop living by them and you set yourself free."

Power wanted to argue, but stopped himself in time. This was not his world.

Instead, Power said, "You said all your family was with you down here, what do you mean?"

"Should we show him?"

"Why bother talking to him?" said the woman. "But I could do with seeing something. You can see us both with the glasses, but I'm as blind as he is; so if you want to switch on the lights for a bit go on."

Power could hear Heaney scrabbling about. The weak light of a torch came on, but to Power's eyes, starved of light for so long, the beam of light looked incredibly bright. Power almost sobbed with relief, for this, if anything, proved that he had not succumbed to some sudden stroke occluding his visual cortex. The torchlight illuminated Heaney's face from below. Power could see he was wearing some kind of goggles.

The female voice had implied Heaney could see. In the absence of any life source, were the goggles picking up infrared? Heaney was peeling the goggles from his face and using the torch to make his way to a tripod about ten feet away. In the periphery of his vision he could just make out the dimly lit figure of the woman. She had her eyes closed against the sudden light. Her eyes were as unaccustomed to light as Power's. How long had she and Joel been with him in the dark?

Then there was an additional burst of light that blinded Power. He shut his eyes tightly against the incandescence. His eyes began their task of accustoming themselves to the new light levels. He peered through half-shut eyes. Power could see that Heaney had switched on an array of double floodlights on tripods. There were six of them set in the space around them. Power tried to take in every detail of his new world. He was seated on the dusty grey-brown ground of a cavern. The roof of the cavern was perhaps only six feet above the ground. The surface of the roof was uneven, jagged rock that was mainly convex, dipping down to a point somewhere above Power's own head. To the edges of the darkness the roof was a little higher and there were alcoves, carved into its walls, and in two of these there were inky black shadows that Power thought might represent tunnels or shafts, potential entrances or exits to the space he was in.

In the space between him and the lights there was an assortment of objects; a large white canister of water, provisions in coolboxes and cardboard boxes full of tinned goods, a jumble of clothes, and a pile of polyester duvets. Power could see his own helmet, lamp, and battery pack sitting atop the mound. Two campbeds sat on the edge of this chaos. Power could see Heaney moving beyond the pile of household goods. He tried to turn his head to see behind him, to try and see the woman. But Power would have needed to rotate himself to see whatever it was behind his back that he was chained to.

"I'm right behind you," said a woman's voice in Power's ear. "I've been here all the time. If you move too much I'll stab you dead as dead." She dropped her voice to a whisper. "I don't know why he's indulging you at all. I'd have you dead and quartered for the pot by now." She chuckled softly. "I suppose he's bored and you're his entertainment, for now. There's no radio or TV under the earth."

She stood up and moved around Power and in her sly way, took the opportunity to stand on Power's hand as it lay on the dust of the cavern. She smiled as she heard his gasp of pain. She went and sat on one of the campbeds. Power noted that her tatty head of grey hair was just a few inches shorter than the cavern roof. She had to duck around a projecting spur of stone that stuck out of the rock. He supposed there was no mirror for her to attend to her hair. She pulled a duvet about herself. "You forced us down here," she said bitterly. "Hunting for us. We had to retreat to our sanctuary." She seemed to draw some comfort from the duvet. Power shivered. "It's always eleven degrees down here," she volunteered. "So you won't die of cold, even if you feel frozen through."

Power's eyes had adjusted to the light better now. He looked at the thin, pinched face and the straggly grey hair. In the photographs her hair had been dark and curly. She still wore glasses, they were no longer horn-rimmed, but rounded frames of thin, gold wire. Her eyes were narrowed and cruel. Her smile was tight and wholly insincere.

Here was the woman Heaney called mother, who had brought him up and offered him such moral guidance as she deemed right. Power was fascinated by her. Whereas most mothers would disown a son so violent and perverse, this mother had steered her son on a different course, entirely outside the ethical boundaries that most of society subscribed to. She had been the sole guiding star for most of his life. Power was altogether horrified, and simultaneously unable to take his eyes off her. He kept asking himself, "What kind of mother **is** she?"

Power searched back through his memories to his time in the homeless centre with Dr Lehman. He was trying to recall the last time he had seen Kyle. The woman now sitting in front of him, Mrs Heaney, had been the volunteer he had seen in the dining hall, handing Kyle the poisoned mug of tea. He was sure of it.

Power watched as she fumbled in a rucksack for a glass and poured a little liquid into it from a brown, glass flask. It looked like a bottle from a laboratory. She added a small amount of water to it from the tap of a canister and then swirled a teaspoon of sugar into the mixture. "We filter the water that runs through the rocks, the stuff that runs through the caves." She took a swig of the cocktail she had made and sighed with pleasure.

"The water from in here?" asked Power. "What is this place? A cave?"

"Mine workings," said Heaney. "There are more mines than people know. The caving club people only know the Victorian mines up near the chemical works. These are older and go down the escarpment and out into the plain. They come up near our farm. The Edge is honeycombed with tunnels. Kilometres of them. My father and all his forefathers, they knew them all."

"What did they mine for?" asked Power, looking at a pile of spoil near one of the alcoves. Some of the rocks seemed coloured with reddish-brown and others the brightest turquoise-blue. "Copper?"

"That's right," said Heaney. "And cobalt."

"Heavy metals," mused Power. "How long have you been drinking the water here?"

"When we come here, that's what we drink," said Heaney.

"And how often do you come here?" asked Power.

"Forever," said Heaney. "To visit our ancestors. To celebrate being family."

Power was thinking about the water, laden with ions of cobalt and copper, heavy metals both, and toxic to the nervous system and brain. How much would you need to drink, and for how long, before you suffered with dementia, he wondered. He thought of the eyes of patients he had seen with Wilson's disease, where excess copper had deposited in their eyes, giving their irises a glittering coppery sheen. He stifled an urge to tell them of the risks of the water they drank, but he didn't know whether volunteering this information might prompt an act of random hostility from Mrs Heaney. He suddenly felt thirsty and wondered whether he would ever have courage enough to ask for a drink, let alone taste their tainted supply.

Mrs Heaney was happily guzzling her drink. Her tiny black eyes shone, and her wrinkled skin smoothed and took on a sunnier disposition. Power sniffed the air for the scent of gin, but there was no hint of juniper. Just a smell reminiscent of hospitals. "What are you drinking?" Power asked, as his curiosity overcame his commonsense resolve to keep quiet in her presence.

"Ethereal spirits," she sniggered. "Like what my Arthur used to bring back from the University."

"Steady on," said Joel. "Don't drink it all, it's difficult for us to get hold of now." He looked at Power. "I was coming back for a few bottles when I first met you in the cellar."

All this time, Heaney had been setting up a series of candles at the entrances to each of the alcoves. As the candles were all lit he switchedthe floodlights off and the cavern descended again into a gloom, lit only by the candles at the entrances to the alcoves.

"I'd take you over to introduce you in person," said Heaney. "But I reckon you're safer kept chained there."

"What am I chained to?" asked Power. He knew he had to watch whatever he said, but this seemed to be an opportune time to ask and glean information about his imprisonment.

"It's a singing post," said Heaney strolling a little closer. Power could see that his hair touched the cavern roof. "Do you know what one is? I bet you don't"

"Can you tell me, maybe?" asked Power, hoping his admission of ignorance might please Joel. "I'd like to know."

"The cavern is very wide. No support for the rock, except at the edges. So the miners put a singing post there. It's probably older than you and me combined."

"It couldn't hold the weight of all this roof surely," said Power.

"It's not meant to," said Heaney. "The post is there to sing. And when it sings and creaks its song – then you know the roof is about to fall. And you run." He laughed, pointing at Power. "Only you can't, can you?"

Dr Power was only too aware that he was completely at the mercy of his captors, so he said nothing in response to this taunt. Instead, he stared at the alcoves as a way of directing Heaney to change the subject and return to his theme.

"You're looking at my ancestors," he said, and there was a trace of pride in his voice.

Power saw a cluster of candles at the foot of each alcove. The candles burned with a smoky, spluttering flame. There was also a smell of animal fat and Power concluded they were tallow candles. Power wondered about the source of the fat for the tallow and felt queasy.

In each curved, carved alcove behind the candles was a large platform, made of heaped up stone chippings. In the concave surface of each platform were a number of long bones: femurs, humerus bones, radius, ulna, tibias and fibulas, and the curved bones of thoracic ribs. The pile of yellowed bones in each alcove represented the bones of a single human, thought Power. Five alcoves, five platforms, five agglomerations of human remains. Each stack of pale bones was sprinkled with yellowy-red and brown ochre. And each pile had a single human skull set at its edge, staring outwards. The dark shadows in the skulls' orbits stared directly at Power, and danced hypnotically in the candlelight.

Joel Heaney walked from alcove to alcove introducing Power to his family.

"This is my granda and this here my granma. This is my uncle, who lived till he was ninety-two. And this was my father, Arthur. The last King under the hill. He looks over us all and protects us. That's why we came here when the plane struck. We knew he'd shelter us. And this is my great grand uncle, who owned your house."

"Owned my house?" Power couldn't control his surprise and a note of alarm crept into his voice and his heart.

"Before he lost it, of course. Seth was his name. Seth built your house. He built it so it connected with the tunnels. So there would be a route in the underworld between his house and all the other places the family owned. We had money once."

"You're telling him too much," said Mrs Heaney. "I'm hungry."

"Not yet," said Heaney. "Eat something else."

"Sooner we start the better. Stun him, bleed him, let him hang for a bit."

"Don't stress him," said Heaney. "Why would you do that? You know it affects the taste."

"How long have you lived like this?" asked Power. "Or has the family always lived like this?"

"Nobody misses a traveller lost in the woods or a homeless person. That's what my grandma used to say. It's a way of life, as you clearly suspect."

"You could choose to live differently," suggested Power. He wanted to keep Heaney talking now. Could he get him to explain, to discuss, to digress. Power wondered if this was what other victims of Heaney and his mother had done. Had Sky kept him talking as long as she could before she ended up in the freezer as the Ice Maiden? Had she cajoled and encouraged him to talk? Had Mrs Heaney urged a swifter ending? When had Sky's attempts at conversation spiralled down into panicked pleading?

"We feed ourselves then we feed the lake," said Heaney. "We respect the spirits in the lake, and give them their share. Head, hands, and feet. They all go in."

"All of them?"

"Most of them," said Heaney. "Some are sacred to other spirits and we bring them down here."

"And you separate the heads from the body, I can see that."

"Of course," said Joel. "Although we love our ancestors, their time is past. We don't want them walking among us again. And you know what, Dr Power? I hear you sneering in every question you ask. You think we are barbarians, but that's just your way of judging something you don't understand."

"There's no need to talk to a meal, let alone argue with him," said Mrs Heaney. "What's the point? Stun him, stick him, hang him to drain out."

"I don't have the stunner unpacked," said Joel. "And I need to fix a hook in the roof."

"And you wouldn't want to do it here, in the sacred cave, would you?" Power suggested.

"He just wants to be unshackled so he can escape," said Mrs Heaney. "That's why he's putting the thought of moving him into your mind. He should shut up!" She jammed the short knife into Power's thigh again, and this time she brutally twisted the blade. Power screamed, and when he stopped he could still hear the echoes of his scream reverberating into the mine shafts.

"Leave him alone, you're spoiling the meat!" shouted Joel. He threw a pebble at his mother, which caught on her chest. "You're always interfering! Like with Sky. You spoiled that. The one girl who wanted to come home with me, who wanted to be with me."

"She wasn't right for you," said Mrs Heaney softly, moaning with her own sudden pain.

"No wonder Dad hit you when he had one too many," Heaney was pacing in front of his ancestors. Power looked at him walking to and fro, his feet crunching on the loose stones that made up the floor of the cavern. "You annoy people. You annoy ME! For no good reason, you ANNOY ME!" And he chose and picked up a heavier stone. "I've got this, so shut up."

"She wouldn't adapt to our ways," said his mother softly, trying to calm him.

"YOU didn't give her chance. I never got to explain our ways. You poisoned her when she came round for tea."

"She didn't like my cooking," said Mrs Heaney quietly. "What girl would understand all this?" she gestured to the bones in their alcoves.

"You understood," said Joel. "Why wouldn't she in time? If she loved me."

"You forget," Mrs Heaney half whispered, half hissed. "I was family. I was born into these ways."

"Then if I can't find someone for me," said Heaney, "then if I can't find a girl, the family ends with me." His pacing became suddenly frantic and he was throwing the stone between his hands in an agitated manner.

"You'll find someone," wheedled his mother, to appease his sudden temper. "You're my handsome boy."

"WHY. DID. YOU. BRING. ME. INTO. THIS. WORLD?" He shouted, and suddenly flung the heavy stone at one of the skulls. The dried out cranium smashed and, in the tallow light,

Power watched a puff of bone dust rise and fall. He couldn't remember which of the skeletons was which. Was it his father's skull he had launched the stone at?

"Now, now," said his mother. "I'm sorry to rile you. There will be someone for you. I'll help you find someone, once all this has calmed down. We'll venture out again into the city. There's all sorts in a city. Someone will share our views. You can even try the Internet, there's all sorts on there. If you want to talk to this man, go on, we've got the time, there's no pressure."

"You said you were hungry," said Joel sulkily.

"You talk all you like, I'll keep my belly quiet," she said sweetly. Power saw her glaring at him. "Why don't you say something interesting?" she asked Power. "It seems your life depends upon it, after all."

But Power found he had been rendered speechless at a time when he needed to have as many tales as Scheherazade. He cudgelled his brain to generate a thought for something, anything, to say or ask, but his mind was filled with the pain in his leg that was throbbing sharply. He felt sick with anxiety, but somehow reasoned that Joel liked talking about himself and his way of life.

"How do you manage down here? How do you heat up your food?" It wasn't the best of questions, under the circumstances, but it was all his reeling brain could suggest.

"There's a small gas hob, over there." Joel pointed to a small hob, supplied by a canister of gas, more or less underneath an opening in the roof. "Air pulls the fumes up and through the shaft that goes up to another level. That's one of the ways we knew you were in the tunnels. You were on the upper level and looked down. We saw your lamplight coming down the shaft."

"Watch what you say, Son," said his mother. "He knows where we are now."

"What does that matter?" asked Joel. "He's not getting away."

Power cast around for anything to talk about that might be a neutral topic.

"The gate," said Power. The words seemed to come slowly and

thickly into his dry mouth. "The iron gate at the bottom of the stairs down from my house. You know them?"

Heaney nodded agreement in a surly fashion. He was looking down at his feet, arms crossed.

Power was careful to use the exact term Heaney had. "Did your 'great grand uncle' put that there?"

"The broken gates?" asked Heaney.

"Yes," said Power, hoping Heaney would talk again.

"There were no gates when Great Grand Uncle built the house. No need for gates. He owned the house. He owned the mine. He could come and go as he liked. The mine has levels, and you go down through the rock. Down through the Edge to levels below the plain, and all along. He kept it all going, with air pumps and water pumps and everything. For years, even after the miners had stopped. One day he thought it might all come back. But he gambled. And he lost the house in a game of cards. And there were witnesses, so he couldn't back out of it. Drink loosened his mind and he gambled it away. Family inheritance. My inheritance. Gone." Joel paced, hugging himself, wild eyed.

"And did the new owners put the gates in?" asked Power. "To stop the family from coming up the steps?"

"No, that's wrong. You got it which ways about," said Heaney. "Granda put the gates up when the house was gambled away. This was our mine, our sacred space, where the family did what it did. So Granda shuttered up the steps and placed those gates there to stop people coming down here."

"Because this is a sacred place?" asked Power.

"That's right. The spirits of past generations of the family look over us from here on the Edge, and they sleep and guard us."

"And the spirits in the Black Lake, they are family too?"

"No, no!" said Heaney most definitely. "They are evil spirits who must be placated, respected always. Sacrifices to them in the lake keep them at bay, satisfied."

A dozen more questions presented themselves to Power's mind. He was tempted to challenge Heaney's ideas to see how firmly he held them. Did he have any doubt, no matter how small, or did he accept everything he had been told by his family? Power looked at Heaney's mother. She maintained a stony-faced silence. There was no clue there. Power could ask, "How certain are you about what you're telling me?" or "Do you think everybody would agree with the idea of spirits?" However, the experiment might go terribly wrong. Who likes their cherished beliefs, ideas they navigate their lives by, probed and challenged? It might be necessary in a clinical interview to establish whether someone's idea is just that, an idea they can discuss and debate with equanimity, or a delusion – an incorrect idea that cannot be swayed by any challenge. In the clinic or ward, Dr Power always had someone to call on if an interview descended into chaos or violence. Here, in the darkened cavern, he was alone, chained, and with two killers. He chose discretion as the better part of survival.

"We, the living, must respect the souls of the dead," said Mrs Heaney. This support for what Heaney said at least confirmed she believed the same ideas as her son. Power itched to challenge her with her lack of respect for the souls of the living, those victims her son had murdered. But he knew that seated on the cold floor of the mine, he was in no position to express any opinion that countered the Heaneys. He wondered about the diagnosis; *folie à deux* or even *folie à famille*? And yet, here was the answer to the problem that had puzzled Power all along. It had always seemed that there were different motives for the murders. And here was the explanation. The murders were owned by a family, with multiple motives. It seemed obvious now. The son living up to a family tradition, removing the unwary lost traveller or homeless person and sacrificing them to the dead, the mother upholding tradition and supporting her kin, recycling the dead's limbs as food. But the jars in the cellar. What was their role.

"And the jars we found in the cellar?" He couldn't bear not to ask.

"Dad's," said Heaney. "And what did you do with them?"

Power noted the warning signal in Heaney's voice. A sign of tension and anger. What was it? Anger that his father's jars had been disturbed? Had he seen they'd been removed and was he affronted? Did he feel bereaved that his father's carefully preserved jars were gone? Power wondered what to say and what might be the consequence, what might be the price to his question.

"They were taken by the police. But they're safe. No-one has done anything to them." This of course was untrue, for the jars had all been opened and examined to a forensic level, but Power was seeking to offer the idea that the treasured possessions were not irretrievably lost to Heaney.

"He kept them from his work, they were special, had power. They were sources of power. Energy, life force, was in them. We drew on them."

Again Power wanted to challenge the ideas behind the belief. But in this brief explanation he had what he wanted to know. Heaney senior had acquired the body parts from his work at the morgue at the University. The parts played some part in the family's belief system.

He had to force himself to ask a question that was all the more difficult, as Power knew his intended fate, "When you eat someone, do you believe you take on their life force?"

Mrs Heaney answered for her son, "What makes them special, we absorb that, yes. An intelligent, tricky person like you . . . we'd absorb that cunning. I know what you're doing, Doctor. You can't put off the inevitable."

And Power felt a wave of despair washing over him. The tallow candles in the alcoves of the dead were burning low and he felt his life, too, was drawing to a close. He thought of how foolish his high spirits were when he had felt elated at defying Lynch and returning to the house. He had escaped Cousins only to fall prey to the Heaneys. He regretted not listening to his friend. And no-one knew where he was. No-one could find him. Laura would think he had just disappeared. Jo would grow up an orphan, losing mother, grandfather, and father in the space of a single year. Who would look after him? Tears pricked at his eyes. He remembered his father's warning. Why do we never listen to our parents? Why do we defy good advice?

Power tried a new tack.

"I think I need to go to the toilet, please can you help?"

Mrs Heaney spoke quickly before her son could respond, "It's a trick, don't untie him!"

"But he's been there ages," said Joel. "It's probably true that he needs to go."

Power sat there wondering whether to exacerbate the differences between mother and son, drive a wedge between them. It could be done. But would it help him? The sorest point in their relationship seemed to be the girl, Sky. Perhaps Joel had lured her back to the farm, or perhaps she had wanted to go with him. He had probably seen the girl as a potential girlfriend or mate. And so she had accompanied him home in all innocence. A date for dinner, rather than being dinner? But perhaps she had challenged the delicate balance of the *status quo* of the relationship between mother and son? Perhaps Mrs Heaney had sensed the girl might never acquiesce to and absorb the family's beliefs? Perhaps she had been instantly jealous. For the first time, maybe her son's eyes were not focused on her, but instead staring adoringly at the girl's Nordic blue eyes? And the jealousy had overwhelmed her. No, Power reasoned, he did not enjoy the luxury of freedom to drive any split between murderous mother and murderous son. He couldn't bring up the topic of the ice maiden again, but still he must try something.

"It would be best if I didn't go to the toilet in here, wouldn't it? This is your sacred place isn't it?"

"Well, that's a point," said Joel.

"He can go where he is," said Mrs Heaney. "It's a trap he's setting for you. When you unchain him and take him into the tunnel where we go, he will attack you."

"I could kill the lights and take him in the dark. I'd have the night-glasses and he couldn't see. I could take a knife too."

"I promise I wouldn't try anything," said Power.

"It would be easier than cleaning up this place," said Joel. "I'd have to lug everything here to clean up after. Easier if he goes to the tunnel we go in."

"It is a ruse, just a trap, my son," said Mrs Heaney. "We didn't have time to think about this. He just appeared. And I didn't expect see him lasting this long . . ."

"Hmm, you may be right about him outliving his welcome," said Heaney. "I can't be lugging extra food and stuff down here for him. Especially if now I have to bring down drinking water for us two, given what he says about cave water and cobalt and copper."

Power was beginning to think, that now whatever he said, he was just making things worse for himself.

"Let me think," said Heaney. "The candles are getting low. I need to start the generator if we want any light when the candles burn out."

Heaney had placed the generator in a passageway to the left of the cavern. The generator powered the lights and fed any extra energy generated to batteries that could be used in reserve. Power watched him pouring some diesel into the fuel tank and pulling the starter cord. The generator chugged into life and Heaney switched the lights on again, flooding the darkness with light. Power watched what little diesel smoke there was, floating out on a stream of air that seemed to waft down the arched passageway. If he could run he would run that way, but he saw no chance of that now.

Heaney switched the various tripod lights off until there was just one alight. He spoke to his mother, "We'll save fuel and charge up the batteries shall we?" He put his night-goggles on top of the supplies pile next to the two camp-beds and sat down opposite her.

"Are you going to find the stunner?" asked Mrs Heaney.

"I suppose so," said Joel. "I'm not arsed about emptying any bed pans, or cleaning up after him or whatever. Although, if we kept him we could use up our more perishable goods first. Save him till later, like." He pulled an electric blue 50 litre rucksack over to himself and rummaged in it. "You'd just know it was at the fucking bottom," he cursed.

"Language," said his mother.

Power laughed. He couldn't stop himself. There was an edge of panic and desperation in his laughter.

"Why are you laughing?" asked Joel.

"Oh, I don't know," said Power. "You swear, and your twisted mother tells you off, but at the same time she's quite happy you're about to murder someone."

Both Heaney and his mother stared at Power, unsmiling.

"I think he's earned it now," said Mrs Heaney.

"OK, let me just find it," and with that, he found what he was searching for and produced a black tube, which he showed to Power.

"What is it? A telescope."

"I suppose it does look like that," said Heaney. "Only telescopes make you see more, and this makes you see less. It's a concussion stunner. Put it to the forehead and it thwacks you with a blunt bolt then retracts. Stuns you."

"I thought you would use electricity," said Power.

"Nah," said Joel, and started inspecting the stunner to see if was working.

Power felt sick.

There was a rumble of thunder.

"What was that?" asked Power.

"Nothing," said Heaney, standing up and stretching himself.

"I felt the ground shake," said Power. "The pole trembled."

"It was nothing," said Heaney.

"I felt something too," said Mrs Heaney. "The bed jittered."

"It was thunder outside," said Heaney.

"You wouldn't hear thunder down here," said Power. "I tell you the pole is vibrating, I can feel it on my back. We should get out now. While we can."

"Hah," said Joel. "You're playing for time and trying to fool us. You know that you're beaten. Admit it." Heaney knew there was no victory without getting the loser to admit their defeat. He had moved a little way away, but was still under the overhanging rock. He had placed the stunner on the dusty floor and was adjusting the tripod light so that it lit Power's body. He angled it so it shone on Power's left side. Then he picked up the bolt gun. He gestured to Power's left-hand side with the stunner. "I'll cut your left carotid so it doesn't splash Mum. Have you got the knife now, Mum?"

"I feel the vibration too," said his mother. Her voice sounded higher; thin and anxious. "I've never felt this down here before. Maybe we should listen to him."

"Nah," said Heaney, and held his hand out for the knife his mother was nursing. "This mine has lasted solid for hundreds of years."

As if in response, the earth let forth another rumble, like thunder again, or a heavy railway wagon being wheeled over a stone floor above their heads. The singing post behind him started to keen and moan. Power pulled at his chains and shouted, "Let me go! We've got to get out now".

Heaney smirked at Power. And with that a large, jagged mass of rock just above him, creaked and detached itself from the cavern ceiling. Against the millions of tons of rock in the mines, this falling piece was just a tiny splinter, but it weighed a ton or more and its newly minted, serrated edge parted from the roof, tumbled over in mid-air and sliced into Heaney's body as it fell. One moment Heaney was standing lording over Power, despising him, the next he was thrown to the floor by the savage rock. Power watched Heaney tumble and crumple mindlessly to the ground like a sack of vegetables. Not even as much as a sigh escaped his lips as the rock pinned him to the ground by his left arm. There was no cry of alarm or pain, so sudden and complete was the fall. He had lost consciousness in an instant as the rock, borne down by gravity, had struck his upper body.

For a moment, Power and Mrs Heaney stared uncomprehendingly at the sprawled mass of Heaney's torso and limbs on the cavern floor. He was dwarfed by the lump of rock that sat across his upper arm and left chest wall. And the silence was absolute. The angry noise of the aftershock and the trembling of the earth had ceased as rapidly as they had started.

And then, compelled to care for her fallen child, Mrs Heaney seemed almost to glide over the surface of the bed, and float over the floor for the short distance that separated her from her son. He lay on his back, with arms outflung. She moaned softly, almost crooning to him as she gently touched and caressed his hair, his forehead, his eyes fast shut.

Power could just see Heaney's chest still moving as he breathed. The breaths were rapid and shallow. He could see, also, a pool of bright red blood was collecting under Heaney's shoulder. The edge of the rock seemed buried in the flesh and meat of his biceps.

"He's haemorrhaging from the brachial artery," said Power softly. "The bleeding must be stopped in the next minute or so, or he will die. It needs pressure immediately, or a tourniquet, or tying off."

Mrs Heaney showed no sign of having heard Power. She started trying to heave the immense rock off her son's arm, trapped beneath its crushing weight. She couldn't make the rock budge a single inch.

"You need to stop the bleeding, then move the rock," said Power.

"I can't move it, Joel," she said to her son. It seemed as if she wasn't hearing Power. "Tell me what to do, Joel."

"He can't hear you," said Power. "I can help him, though."

She looked at him through a veil of tears. She spoke between sobs. "It's a trick you would play on me."

"You can't lift the rock, and he will bleed to death unless I stop the bleeding."

"You'd do that?" she asked. Her eyes fixed on his as if trying to search his soul.

"Of course. If you release me, I will save him." She seemed undecided and there was a brief pause while she considered. "There is not much time for you to think about this," said Power.

"You are a proper doctor . . . ?"

"Yes, yes," said Power. "Trained in medicine and surgery."

She couldn't see any other option and reached within her son's coat pocket for a set of keys. She fumbled for the right one as she hurried to the chains behind Power's back. Power heard her cursing as she tried to unlock the padlock that held the chain fast.

Power had been chained to the post for hours and his muscles shrieked with agony as he tried to raise himself from the hard grit and sharp pebbles he had been sitting upon. The dull ache of his lower limbs became a sharp tingling as blood flowed resurgent through his muscles.

"Hurry up," she said impatiently, as Power battled to stay upright against the feebleness of his cold, blood-starved muscles.

Power stumbled over to Joel's body and knelt unsteadily down beside him. His right arm was partially severed. The hard, uncompromised edge of the rock that had crushed him had sliced through muscle and sinew and cut through the brachial artery, which even now was weakly spurting fresh, bright, arterial blood to sink into the dusty cave floor. From this, Power could deduce that Joel was still alive. He used his right hand to press on a point proximally above the cut artery. In this way Power began to control the blood loss.

Mrs Heaney was now at his side. He would have to ask for help. "I need a torch, please, and do you have anything like a belt or some rope? A sewing kit?"

Mrs Heaney grumbled, and her mean and suspicious-minded nature tempted her to question his requests, but the possibility that he might yet save her grievously wounded son, made her acquiesce with bad grace.

She fetched a torch, which Power took with his left hand, and turned to try and find the things that the doctor had asked for in the ragged pile of goods between the beds. Power looked up at his helmet and battery pack. A symbol of a better time; a time before all this. He thumbed the torch on and played its beam over Joel's face. Joel's eyes were open, but unseeing. Power presumed Heaney was unconscious. Either the falling rock had somehow caught his head or it had brought his body down with such a crash that he had struck his skull against the unyielding stony ground. One pupil, the left, was small and reacted by constricting further when the beam of the torch fell on it. The other pupil, the right, was wide, dilated, and did not react when Power let the edge of its beam touch the right eye.

"What are you doing?" asked Mrs Heaney, standing by him now. The anxiety in her unstable voice was tinged with desperation and rising anger. Power winced as she stabbed his shoulder with the tip of her knife, cutting into his deltoid muscle. The unexpected nature of the assault made him gasp.

"I'm trying to help your son," Power snapped.

"Don't forget who's in charge," she said. "Why are you looking at his eyes? Idiot. You should be looking at his arm. Getting him free. You haven't even tried to move it."

Power used the torch to inspect the severed arm tissue. As much as anything, he did this as a performance to persuade Mrs Heaney that he was doing something, although he had already made up his mind about Heaney's clinical condition when he saw Heaney's pupils. He was considering what to do next.

"The rock is too heavy to move," he said.

"You haven't even tried," she pointed out.

Cold, hungry, tired, and in reaction to hours of fear and stress, Power was close to breaking. His anger welled within him. He struggled to remain calm. "I will in a minute then, but it will take both hands and as you can see I'm controlling the bleeding with the fingers of my right hand – pressing on the artery. I can't move. If I do, he'll start bleeding again." Power needed her to comply with him, to be more co-operative, not less. He made a show of inspecting the arm. "The rock has sliced through muscles and tendons and has bitten deep into the bone of the humerus." An unbidden image of Heaney butchering his victims with a cleaver came into Power's mind. Heaney had intended to butcher him. He had been minutes away from doing so. And now Power was acting as his doctor and struggling with the images that flowed through his brain.

"What are you waiting for? Do something?"

"I'm thinking," said Power.

"Get on with it! Why's he still unconscious?" She was shouting and white-faced. The knife was shaking in her trembling hand.

"I need your help," said Power. "Try and be calm. I know you're worried about Joel. He needs you to be calm and help. I need you to take over and do what I'm doing so I can try and move the stone or operate on him."

"All right, but if you do anything sudden or wrong I will knife you."

"I know you will," said Power. With Mrs Heaney the chance of arbitrary violence was very high. He felt drained by the adrenaline that was coursing through him. How much more could he take? "Do you see where I'm pressing? Can you take my place and press exactly there?"

He shuffled to the right to make way for her as she knelt. Using her left hand she felt for where Power's fingers were. In her right hand she held the sharp knife, which was pointed at Power's neck. Power held the torch so Mrs Heaney could place her fingers in exactly the right spot. There was a spurt of arterial blood as the transfer was made. "Have you got it? Don't move your fingers, even slightly, now you've got control. He has lost an awful lot of blood, and you can't let go or he'll die." Power emphasized the point, "He's entirely depending on you, now," said Power, shifting ever so slowly away to the right, to a new place by the mammoth shard of rock.

"You get that off him!" she said pointing at the rock with her knife.

Power stood up. He put the torch into his pocket as swiftly as he could and turned away from her so that she would not see. He moved just out of range of Mrs Heaney's knife and made a show of bending and placing his two hands firmly on the fallen rock. He grunted and strained and pushed at the rock. His boots slid and scraped along the grit of the floor as he tried to gain purchase. He heaved, but the rock would not move and Heaney's forearm and hand were trapped beneath.

Power imagined the smashed, crushed bones of the forearm and the irreparably mashed hand. "It will not move," said Power. "It must weigh tons. Five men couldn't shift it."

"What are you going to do?" she asked. Her anger and fright was fading and there was despair in her voice.

"We need to move him," said Power. "His arm cannot be repaired. We need to detach him from his arm."

"What are you saying?"

Power looked at the kneeling mother, bent over and tending to her son. He almost felt sorry, but he had felt so afraid of this woman and her son, that he could not bring himself to really own and feel the feeling. He could not retrieve an ounce of genuine sincerity in any sympathy he might feel.

"I need to operate to remove his arm," said Power. He was aware that there was a dispassionate coldness in his voice now. He waited until he was several feet away and stood, looking down at the scene. "I will need the knife you're holding."

"I need it to protect myself," she said.

"Don't let go of the artery," he insisted.

Power picked his helmet off the pile of belongings, and started strapping its battery around his waist.

"What are you doing?" A note of fear in her voice.

"It has a light to operate by," said Power, switching it on. "You see, nice and bright, and it's hands-free so it means that I have both hands free to cut and stitch." She seemed reassured by this. Power came a bit closer, although exercising sufficient care to stay just outside the range of her right arm and the blade of her knife. "And if you give me the knife, I'll go and sterilise it. I think one of the candles is still alight. I can use the flame to sterilise the blade." He held out his hand to take the knife.

"I don't want him to lose his arm," she snivelled.

"But you want him to live?" Power wanted to say 'Trust me', but something prevented him. "Give me the knife and I will go and clean it in the flame."

Most reluctantly she handed the knife to Power. He had disarmed her with words. Power walked over to one of the alcoves where a tallow candle was still burning. The alcove was near the passageway where the generator was, and where Power imagined that fresh air was coming from. He took his bearings as to where he was. He was searching for the shaft he remembered once looking down. Power felt light-headed from lack of food. He fought down waves of agitation, tiredness, and panic. He crouched down by the candle and passed the evil little blade through the flame. Power thought about the number of times Mrs Heaney had used it to pierce his skin. "Don't let go of the artery," Power said as he looked about the cavern; seeing the mother crouched over Heaney's pale body. Life was ebbing away from her son, and in fairness, there was nothing Power could do. The dilated right pupil had told Power all he needed to know about Heaney's prognosis. Power felt he could amputate Heaney's arm, but neurosurgery was beyond his surgical training. Even if Power had had a team of nurses and a fully equipped operating theatre he couldn't save Heaney's life.

And Heaney could never be evacuated from the cave in time to get him to the specialist hospital he needed. The only person that Power could save was himself, and that was what he proposed to do now.

Power stood up. "You need to keep pressing on that artery," he said. He kicked over the candle and its evil wax soaked into the gravel floor as the flame sputtered and died. He moved to the entrance of the tunnel where the generator was.

"What are you doing?" asked Mrs Heaney. "You said you would save him."

"Yes, I did say that," said Dr Power sorrowfully. "Maybe I shouldn't have."

"You are betraying the Hippocratic Oath," she hissed.

"You were going to kill me," said Power. "I don't owe you anything. You were going eat me. I think anybody would agree I'm entitled to my escape."

Power switched off the generator. The tripod light blinked off. Only the light from Power's helmet now existed to dispel the darkness.

"I will phone the authorities," said Power. "They'll come and find you." He turned and the light shone up the passageway. The ground rose, leading him out of the cavern and away from gloom of the darkest night. He called back over his shoulder. "They might help you, if I find my way out."

She screamed obscenities at Power as he left, and as his footsteps receded, she wondered when, if ever, she could bear to let go of her son.

Chapter Twenty-One

Dr Power had been staring out from the office window into the gardens of the hospital, taking pleasure in the winter sunlight on the grass, and the golden gleams of the evening's light as they played through the branches of the tall oak trees. He had enjoyed a good lunch of grilled vegetables at home, washed down by intense black coffee. He had driven across to his afternoon clinic with a relish that he never usually felt prior to a clinic crammed with patients. The experience in the cave with the Heaneys had rendered every moment of life in the light dear to him. Even the temporary safe house accommodation provided by the Foundation had appeared palatial to him, and he had found it difficult to stop grinning at his partner, Laura, and son, Jo. At his father's return, Jo had initially been solemn and stood apart, until his eyes suddenly swam with tears and he threw his arms about Power. For the next twenty-four hours Jo had seemed unwilling to leave Power for a second, even insisting on sleeping on a couple of chairs at the bottom of their bed.

Power had been dreading the admonishments of his friend, Lynch, for venturing into the tunnels alone, but there were none. Lynch explained that it had been quite obvious to him that Power intended to challenge himself in this way. "I knew when you accepted the gift of the miner's helmet and lamp that you would go it alone. Because you didn't ask to borrow a set for me." He also put his finger on the motivation for Power's journey underground, "You couldn't have known consciously that Heaney was there, but somehow, unconsciously, I think you pieced it all together. And then you felt compelled, didn't you?"

Power protested that he had always meant to return to the underworld beneath his house, to still any fears he had acquired from his first trip down there. It was, he said, "a classic exposure technique to conquer fear – face what you fear and try to relax yourself in its presence . . ."

Lynch chuckled at that idea. "'Relaxing in the face of danger', I don't think so. Well," he said. "I tried to stop you, but here you are anyway. Something was protecting you, I like to think it was a prayer answered."

They had sent a squad into the tunnels as soon as Power had surfaced and raised the alarm. Power had stood in the kitchen and watched the team of body-armoured agents, with their lights and carbines, descend into the darkness through his house and down into the mines beneath. They had gone swiftly and in silence. Power did not stay long enough to see them return, carrying the thin, limp rag of a body that had once been Heaney. He had felt unable to stay in the house a moment longer and had slammed the front door behind him and sped to the safe house to find his family.

And today, working in his clinic, as ever, Power glanced at a copy of *The Times* newspaper, recently gone shrunken and tabloid. The front page exploded with the story of the discovery of Heaney's cave. On inner pages there was more about the Heaneys, and other stories about Saddam Hussein retrieved from a bunker in Tikrit, and the conviction of the Soham murderer. On an inner page, mercifully tucked away, Power read an article about himself, and the press conference that Beresford had implored him to attend. At last Beresford had been able to announce definitive news in his investigation. And after the vilification and criticism Beresford had endured, Power had felt partially glad to attend and see Beresford bask in the good news of the end of Heaney's spree of death.

In the warmth of his hospital office, Power felt uneasy at the article and how it honoured his role in discovering Heaney. It treated him as a hero, but Power felt he was nothing but an impostor. The sentence about a source close to the Foundation explaining his method, worried him. Power didn't feel he could, or should, pretend to any method. He

A Quiet Genius

Jessica Smyth;
Crime Correspondent

- **Front Page:** The End of a Cannibal
- **Page 2:** The list of identified victims

Professor Power is a quiet, unassuming man. At the press conference after the discovery of Heaney's body he sat at the edge of the panel and made little eye contact. He made very few comments and seemed almost embarrassed at the publicity surrounding his vital contribution to bringing Heaney's reign of terror to a very final close.

Power is a consultant psychiatrist who has brought his forensic expertise to the assistance of the police in previous murders such as the Ley Man case and the murder of Government Minister Sir Ian McWilliam.

Professor Power is believed to have profiled Joel Heaney after examining the Heaney farmhouse and heroically tracked the cannibal into a mine system that honeycombs a sandstone escarpment near Manchester. Heaney found many of his victims amongst the homeless in Manchester city centre and lured them back to the deserted farm where they were killed and butchered, (see page 2 for list of known victims).

Power personally explored the labyrinth of tunnels, which extends for kilometres inside the earth. Characteristically modest, Power described his discovery of Heaney as 'the result of coincidence'.

Power was also nearly trapped underground when an aftershock, from a recent earthquake in the region, dislodged rocks in the old mine. Heaney was killed by the roof fall and Power summoned help.

When asked for further detail of his heroism underground Power declined to comment.

A private team of armed personnel, led and co-ordinated by ex-Superintendent Lynch entered the tunnel system. Heaney's body was found alone in the cavern, pinioned to the ground by the rock. He was surrounded by his supplies and a grisly set of full skeletons, believed to be his dead relatives (see front page report).

This was the first complex case where the police team, led by Inspector Beresford, turned to the Howarth-Weaver Foundation for consultancy help. Professor Power has a prominent role in this Foundation, set up to promote justice and provide assistance in complex or hitherto unsolved crimes. A source close to the Foundation described Power's methods as "thorough and insightful, often melding conscious and unconscious processes."

Professor Power declined to comment.

recalled a psychologist who had trumpeted his geographical method of finding serial killers. No one mentioned the miscarriages of justice it had caused. In Power's philosophy of life, caution was everything. Precision was important. And in any case, thought Power, wasn't such hagiography in the newspaper, an invitation to hubris and just the perfect way to tempt Fate?

The truth was, that Power had, he thought, gone into the mines to cure his own fears – to expose himself to his irrational fear of the darkness and conquer this fear – however, this article sought to portray this solitary journey as some kind of mission. And yet, had his unconscious mind somehow been urging him to journey into the depths? Was there a vestige of truth in the myth described by 'a source close to the Foundation'? Power concluded that the source who had spoken about to the press was clearly Lynch himself.

And another truth Power had to face was that in seeking to rid himself of a fear of the darkness beneath his house, he had merely acquired another greater fear, that filled him with sadness. His house, a source of stability, seemed somehow tainted by the Heaneys. Power felt unhomed. Just as the Heaneys had been unhomed by the air crash and driven out of their farmhouse. Or at least he worried that he might have been unhomed; he would have to test his real feelings when he returned. And unfortunately, he didn't yet feel like trying to go home.

There was a knock at the office door. Power turned from the window to answer it. There was a bespectacled medical student outside, staring away down the corridor. He hadn't noticed the door was open yet. He stood sideways on to his Professor, and Power looked down on the top of his curly brown hair. He had earphones dangling from his ears and Power could just hear a tinny rendition of 'Seven Nation Army' emanating from his iPod. He seemed shocked when he turned and saw Power in front of him and fumbled as he pulled the earphones out. "Professor Power?"

"The one and only," said Power. He glanced at the student's photo ID, which hung on a lanyard round his neck. He was a student attached to the hospital, from a medical school at a different University to Power's. The ID looked genuine enough. "And you are?"

"Jeremy Cooper, I'm here for your clinic, Professor."

Power welcomed him in and sat him down in a comfortable chair. Power took care that the student's chair was out of the eyeline of the patient's chair, so that the student could observe the consultation, but not distract either patient or Dr Power. Power noticed there was a vague smell of mothballs about Cooper's yellow waffle-weave cardigan.

"It is a full clinic this afternoon, Mr Cooper. My Senior Registrar is seeing half of the patients, though, so there should be time to do some teaching." Power handed a referral letter to the student. The letter concerned the first patient of the clinic. "This is about our first patient, someone new to me. He turned up in the emergency department and saw our Dr Proctor. Read this through, please."

Cooper took the letter and read. Dr Proctor wrote as follows:

Dear Professor Power,

Thank you so much for offering to see Mr Susskind when I phoned this morning. I am writing to give you some background details of his case before you see him in clinic.

Mr Susskind is a 42-year-old man. Married but with no children. He is employed as a physics lecturer at Manchester University.

History of Presenting Complaint

Mr Susskind complained that he felt 'unhomed', and that he felt the world had become 'unfamiliar' after he had crossed the wooden floor of the Royal Exchange in Manchester. One minute all had been as usual, and the next he 'went through a bubble wall' and 'things were different'. His wife, who had been out that evening attending a play with him, looked like his wife, except her hair style had changed. The front door of his flat was a different shade of grey when they walked home.

At this point in the interview, Mr Susskind became upset and said he felt guilty that he could not find love for his wife any more as 'some essential spark was lost'. He referred to there being other important differences, but he seemed too upset to tell me these.

My initial thought was that he had developed some paranoid delusional system, but there was something very rational about him and he seemed to have some insight into the way he might appear to others; apologising for his 'outlandish' ideas and how they might sound to me. He said he became certain that something was wrong when he overheard someone in the theatre passing on the news that Johnny Cash had just died. In 'his' reality Johnny Cash had died in 1998.

He described alternate universes touching each other – like the surfaces of bubbles kissing each other, and said his theory was that people can slip between by accident.

He denied any hallucinations or thought interference.

He said his sleep and appetite were poor and that he had not been able to concentrate on his work. With regard to his life at the University he said his namesake had been at work on a different physics paper and that some of his students were different.

He said he had been anxious and low in mood, but emphasized that this was because of his change in circumstances and that he had been perfectly happy prior to 'moving between bubbles'.

Past Psychiatric History

Mr Susskind denied ever having had stress at work, previous depression, or psychosis, and said he had never sought help from his family doctor for his mental health.

Family History

Mr Susskind said he had been brought up by his mother after his father died of a stroke when he was 12. His mother is 69 and well. His father died at the age of 42. There is no family history of psychiatric disorder in his parents, but his paternal grandfather had PTSD after his role in liberating Belsen at the end of World War Two.

Social History

Mr Susskind is married and owns a flat in the city centre. He is off work at present, having self-certified as sick. He is not in debt. He does not smoke and is teetotal. He denied using street drugs.

Personal History

Mr Susskind was born in North Manchester and educated at Manchester Grammar School. He said he had been happy as a child and had fond memories of his father. He remembers being sad and lonely after his father died and had suffered some emotional bullying by fellow pupils. He took A levels in Physics, Maths, and Chemistry. He went to study physics at Trinity College, Cambridge. He met his wife, Janet, there. She was also studying, for an English degree. They have no children.

His hobbies include watercolours and hillwalking.

He described himself as an atheist after his father died.

He has no forensic history, although he was brought to the emergency department by the police, having been found wandering in the city centre in a distressed state.

Mental State Examination

Mr Susskind was somewhat untidy, but seemed clean. He was dressed in shirtsleeves and jeans. He attended to the interview and was co-operative, but was mildly agitated and tearful at times. He was orientated in time, place, and person, but seemed perplexed. He was low in mood, but denied suicidal ideation or plans. He had some unusual ideas that he had moved through alternate universes and gave various reasons for this – his observations – his wife's hair style was suddenly different, a different decoration to his flat door, differences at work, and different 'facts' such as the date of Johnny Cash's death. He said there were other differences between the realities but these were too upsetting to relate, although I did try to ask him what these were. When I challenged his ideas he replied that many scientists now accept that alternate universes are theoretically possible. He sounded rational. He said that he had been walking in the night air to clear his head. He apologised for his beliefs, which he seemed to know sounded unusual, and from this I assessed that he had some insight. At the end of the interview I could not be sure if he was deluded or not and thought I should refer him on. He had no ideas to harm himself or anyone else.

Formulation
Mr Susskind is a 42 year old man presenting for the first time, with a history of recent ideas he has passed through the boundaries of alternate universes, and has beliefs that although elements of his world are very similar – his wife, flat, and job – there are subtle differences which lead him to suspect this is a different universe. He seems perplexed, but denies other psychotic experiences such as hallucinations and does not have thought disorder. I considered whether he might have a paranoid delusional psychosis (ICD10 F22), or some rare psychiatric syndrome such as Capgras syndrome.

I wondered about admitting him, but he was reluctant and you and I decided he was not detainable under the Mental Health Act.

Thank you again for seeing Mr Susskind. I'd be interested to hear what you think of him. Perhaps you can tell me, if we meet at the trainee's Journal Club? I know you often attend.

Yours sincerely,
Dr Judith Proctor

Cooper looked up at Power as he finished the letter. "Schizophrenia," he announced.

"Isn't it a bit early to be jumping to conclusions?" suggested Professor Power. "Wouldn't we be better off seeing Mr Susskind and giving him the benefit of allowing us his version of events and conducting a full mental state examination before we make a diagnosis?"

"Maybe," said Cooper. He looked as if he'd much prefer to be listening to his iPod. "But it seems to me that there are only a few diagnoses in psychiatry; schizophrenia, depression, anxiety disorder, and dementia. It's an easy subject."

"Thank you for the tutorial," said Power, growing irritable. "Shouldn't we listen to his ideas and test them out – for instance, his ideas about different realities – are they correct or incorrect?"

"Incorrect," said Cooper.

"If they are incorrect, as you say, are they held with unshakeable conviction, even though they are wrong? Surely we need to ask Mr Susskind?"

"People don't slip between universes or dimensions," said the student with conviction.

Power tried his best not to sigh in frustration. "If you have that approach to patients – making your mind up before you've even seen them – why bother seeing them at all?" Cooper's expression looked like he might consider this a reasonable approach for psychiatric patients. Power felt his annoyance was in danger of bursting forth. Not every student he trained was sympathetic to mental disorder, but Mr Cooper seemed to approach the subject with contempt. To him psychiatry was merely one of the compulsory attachments all students had to complete. Power issued a warning. "If you don't take a reasoned approach and spend some time listening to your patient, then you don't learn from your patient and you make mistakes. And mistakes can cost the patient and their family – and cost you too. A wrong diagnosis matters in psychiatry just as much as it does in surgery or medicine. You need to keep an open mind. Imagine what would happen if a young woman came in to your surgery for help and said that a priest had been abusing her. Would you instantly jump to the conclusion that a priest couldn't behave like that and so she must be deluded?"

"But sexual abuse is possible, isn't it? But these ideas of slipping between realities are impossible, so insane," argued the student.

"Well," said Power, feeling that the student judged his Professor to be far less than a genius, no matter what *The Times* said. "I'll go and fetch Mr Susskind and take a history from him myself, and we'll test out your hypothesis." Power stood up and went to the door. Power mused as to the relative standing of psychiatry amongst the specialties. How did Cooper rate it against surgery or medicine, say? Some students rated psychiatry as little more than bogus. Cooper seemed to be one such critic.

Power walked into the clinic waiting area and looked round for a man of Mr Susskind's age. There was no male waiting, but there was a diminutive young woman with long blonde hair and blue eyes. "Excuse me," said Power, "Are you with Mr Susskind? Has he gone out for a moment?" Sometimes patients found it difficult to wait and slipped out for a cigarette or the toilet.

"I'm Mrs Susskind, are you the Professor?"

"Professor Power, yes." He held out his hand to shake.

"I'm afraid I've come on my own," she said. "Can I have a word with you about my husband?" This was an unusual occurrence. Power felt there was no reason why he could not hear her out. He said he could listen to anything she wanted to tell him, of course, but that he couldn't necessarily divulge any confidential information. He led her to his office, and warned her he had a medical student with him.

He seated her so he could see her and the student doctor at the same time and asked, "Tell me about your husband. Did he not want to come to see me himself?" Power was wondering whether he would be required to visit Mr Susskind at home. Some patients would not come to see a psychiatrist.

"He couldn't come," said Mrs Susskind, smoothing out her skirt on her lap. "He's no longer here."

Power felt his stomach sinking. "He's dead?"

Whereas a physician might be accustomed to the inevitability of a proportion of their patients dying each week, a psychiatrist's work is infrequently marked by the death of a patient. The rarity of death in a psychiatrist's professional life makes each death an exquisitely sensitive matter, and every suicide comes as a shock to a good psychiatrist.

"He's no longer here," she repeated to correct the Professor.

"I'm sorry," said Power. "I don't understand. I thought maybe he had harmed himself?"

"Well, he wasn't himself, for sure. How much do you know of his case?" She lifted her gaze from the pink embroidered flowers on her light-blue percale dress, and fixed her blue eyes on Power's face.

"I have read a referral letter, and a junior doctor discussed him over the phone with me when he came to the hospital. I have never met him, though, and so if you want to tell me something, please do."

"We've been married for ten years. My husband used to work at the University. What he did was a mystery to me. Research on light particles, the nature of light. A super laser project, allied to the Astra project, I think it was. Not the Astra car," she smiled. "It was something altogether more fundamental, about particles . . . curtains of light . . . I didn't understand. I am afraid that I just switched off when he started talking about it. I have studied at University level myself, but English literature is not physics. Every day of our lives was the same, he'd cycle to work with sandwiches in a box and a flask of juice, and every day he'd be back at six – unless he had an experiment on and he might stay late. He liked music, and we ate out. We had been trying for a baby. Everything was 'normal'. And then one Friday he didn't come home at six.

"Then a man arrived at 9 p.m. He arrived in a taxi and said he'd found the house because our home address was on a wage slip. And this man standing on the threshold of my home looked like my husband. Very much like my husband. But he smelled different. And his hair was parted on the other side. And he looked at me differently, as if I was a stranger. If it had been my husband I would have thrown my arms around him, but I didn't feel like I should be doing that. He came in, and you could tell he didn't know where things were, or what rooms were where. He was trying not to upset me, so he didn't say that he felt things were odd, and I didn't say what I was thinking either. I was just so puzzled, because he looked like George.

"And we didn't touch. He lay on his side of the bed and I lay on mine, but neither of us slept. Neither of us felt safe that first night. Then in the morning when I made him porridge he said he was troubled, and he cried and asked me where our son was! And I said we didn't have one and he broke down. We both cried."

"He seemed to believe he had a son? He genuinely believed that?" asked Power.

"Yes, he was distraught." Even now she had a tear in her eye. "His distress was so real it upset me. I asked if maybe he'd woken up after a dream where he'd had a child and been upset to find it was just a dream. You know how sometimes dreams are very real? But he said that this was no dream he had woken up from, but a whole life he had woken up from. He said nothing more about it and on Monday he went off to work at the University, but they were puzzled because he didn't seem to know about the course he was supposed to be teaching. And when he came home and tried to do some work on his teaching for the next day, I noticed he was writing with his left hand. And my husband was right handed. And as I watched him writing with the wrong hand, I was fascinated, and frightened. As he worked away, the news came on, and someone had died, and he seemed puzzled and asked me questions about the news. He didn't seem to know the things I knew about current affairs. So I cried, and said we had to talk about what had happened, and we tried to work it out, work out what had changed for both of us."

"And what did you both decide?" asked Power cautiously.

"Everything had changed. This was not my husband. He looked like my husband, but he wasn't. We both had to face that. My husband had gone to work in the morning and someone else had come back in the evening. He told me that he had been puzzled by my husband's research. He'd read his notebooks to try and get up to speed on it, and it was as if their respective researches were the mirrors of each other. And they'd both been working on a crucial experiment to test their hypotheses at the same time. He talked about creating bubbles in the fabric of everything and that the two experiments, somehow . . . the bubbles had overlapped or that the experiments had worn down the boundaries between this place and that place and had worn so thin that they had swapped places. He showed me two equations in his little notebook; I remember they were so neatly written, in small black handwriting, sitting neatly on the notebook page on green ruled lines, but the equations meant nothing to me."

"So you were both sure that there had been some . . . slippage between worlds? That this man was not your real husband?" asked Power.

"Absolutely," said Mrs Susskind. "He looked like him, but something didn't smell right about him. He went off, in distress, after we talked some more. I assume he found his way to the hospital. He did return, after he'd seen the doctor. For a while anyway."

"So Mrs Susskind, the man who came to the emergency department, where is he now do you think?"

"Before he left that last time he said that he could use his equations and correct for the passage of time and the rotation of the earth to find the place where the bubbles touched, where there was the thinning. He said he thought the thinning would have some permanence for a few weeks, and that if he could just locate the place there was a chance – a small chance – that he could slip through back to his own space.

And I remember crying, because I knew then I would lose even him. Even though he wasn't my husband . . . I didn't want to lose the reminder . . . do you understand?"

Power nodded, "So what happened?"

"I said it was too risky. Surely he couldn't predict things precisely enough. If the thinning place moved round in this universe, well maybe it would move round in the other universe too. He might slip through into some different time or place. Maybe he'd emerge onto the fast lane of a motorway, or in the midst of a furnace. He said he was very sorry, but that he had to try, he had to go. He couldn't live without his son. And we both broke down. I felt so raw."

In the consulting room, she began to sob. "It felt like he was rejecting me, because we had no child." It took a moment for her to recover, then she went on. "He said he would buy a mobile phone before he went and carry it as he went through into the other world. He would give it to my husband, if he could find him, and let him phone me. Maybe it would work? He would try and get my husband back to me, by helping him find the place he had come through. He tried to comfort me by saying that maybe my husband was in his world, working out how to get back to me, even as we spoke, and that maybe my husband would reappear as he disappeared."

"So what happened next?" asked Power.

"He announced early one morning that he'd worked out where the thinning place would be at noon. A journey of about two hours from ours, in the Peak District. And although I started crying, he just left, coldly like that. Two hours later he phoned me and said he was there and that he would do what he could to get my husband back to me, and the line fizzed and went fuzzy and then went dead. You know you can track these phones? I tried and it couldn't be found."

"Maybe he just switched it off?" said Power.

She looked at him and frowned sceptically. "My friend works in a cell phone company. Even when you turn them off, you can find out where they are. This phone blinked out of existence."

Power didn't know whether her claim about being able to locate switched off phones was, or was not, credible, so he chose not challenge her on this point. Instead, he asked, "And you haven't heard anything more? Your own husband did not reappear?"

"I wouldn't be here if he had," she said.

"How do you want me to help?" asked Power.

"I wanted someone to talk to," she said. "It sounds pathetic, but I wanted someone to hear my hurt."

"Are you sleeping all right?" Power asked.

"I'm sleeping all the time," she said. "Sleep seems to blot it out for a bit. And when I'm awake, I'm worrying about him. Whether he'll ever phone or come back. And the mortgage. Who will pay that?"

"If you would like me to see you again, to treat you, I would be happy to," said Power. "It sounds like you might have more to tell me if we met another time? I'd just need to know your family doctor's name so I can be reassured they are happy for me to see you. That would be the professional etiquette, you see."

"Maybe I could come and see you again," she agreed. "You've been kind listening to me, I watched your face, I didn't think you were judging me."

"No," said Power, "I can tell you've been through a very stressful time. Maybe things will seem clearer if we meet in clinic next week?" He handed her a form. "It's tiresome, I know, but please could you fill this out and leave it with the reception so I have the details to register you? And I will ask my secretary to ring you about the appointment."

They said their goodbyes and Power closed the door. He took a swig of cold coffee and looked at the medical student. "What do you think?"

"She's as mad as her husband," Cooper said. There was a dismissive curl of his lip as he spoke that Power particularly disliked.

"Do you disbelieve her?" Power asked.

"That a mobile phone being traced when it's switched off? That people move through bubbles in space? He was just dumping her. He left her for someone else. The same old story, just dressed up in some rubbish about space-time equations."

"So you think Mr Susskind is a cynical manipulator of women, perhaps an old-style bigamist?"

"Yes," said Cooper. "And his wife has fallen for his story. It's the old 'just going out for a pint of milk' scenario."

"Then does Mrs Susskind have a diagnosis?" asked Power. "Is it worthwhile my seeing her again in clinic?"

"I don't know why you bothered," said Cooper. "She'll work out what he's done in a few days, when her joint bank account is cleared out."

Power sighed. "Could you be wrong, do you think? Could there be another explanation?"

"Like what?"

"Well, her distress is clear; she may be developing a depression no matter how or why her husband has disappeared, so it's worth seeing her at least one more time, with her GP's consent. And if we consider that she genuinely believes her husband's account of travel between universes, and if he too was a genuine individual who believed what he said, what then?"

"But he was just a liar," said Cooper.

"That's your construct, your hypothesis. But imagine if Susskind genuinely believed what he told his wife. Because people with delusions do believe they are right, they are convinced, so when they speak about things you think are impossible, they are being genuine, they are not lying to you even if they are incorrect. If we entertain the idea he is ill and deluded . . . then what? What if the final phone call was him actually jumping off a crag in the Peak District, imagining he was going through some portal? Maybe he's lying in bony splinters at the bottom of a ravine?"

"Then you are saying they are both mad?"

"I would never use that terminology," said Power delicately. "Have you ever heard of *folie à deux*?" Cooper shook his head. Dr Power explained, "It's a condition where two individuals develop aberrant ideas. Close people like husband and wife, or mother and son." Power paused, reflecting on his recent experience with the Heaneys. "Usually the couple is somewhat isolated from society. Imagine that one of the couple has a psychosis, say the husband has paranoid delusions about the neighbours listening in, and being spies, and keeps repeating this thinking for months and months. The other person in the couple – the wife maybe – starts sympathizing with him and takes his paranoid mindset on board. Maybe then the couple both start to avoid speaking near the party wall, or both keep whispering together. And so the paranoid ideas become common currency in the household. So when the couple comes to medical attention, both individuals seem to hold these unusual ideas. But if somehow the couple is separated, and the non-psychotic person mixes with others, socializes again, then the paranoid ideas gradually diminish. Whereas, in the psychotic person – the husband – the delusions just keep running on and on. So, only one of the couple – the husband – needs treating with antipsychotic drugs. In the case we are considering, perhaps Mr Susskind was, or is, ill, and Mrs Susskind developed *folie à deux*. I'll reserve my decision till I see her next.

"It's fascinating how couples work," said Power. "How one person interacts with the other in the *dyad*. We now recognise that in families where a mother has postnatal depression, the father can suffer with this too."

"Men with postnatal depression?" Cooper snorted derisively.

"All I'm saying, is that perhaps you could keep a more open mind," said Power. "Don't rush to make a judgment. Because not every person is how they seem."

There was a knock on the door. The rhythm of the knock was sharp and insistent. Before Power could answer, his Senior Registrar, Dr Wootton, stuck his head round the door.

"Professor? There's an urgent phone call for you at reception. From Laura."

"Urgent? Laura . . . are you sure?" Power stood up and the patient notes he had been writing in, fell, scattering on to the floor.

"Yes," said Wootton, holding the door open and accompanying Power as he hurried to the phone. "Don't worry about the clinic, Professor. I will take over. I think you will need to leave."

"Thanks," said Power.

He hurried down the corridor worrying about what Wootton had said. The idea that Wootton and the reception staff already knew there was an emergency which would force Power to abandon his clinic, sank inside him like lead in his stomach.

The receptionist was holding the receiver of the phone cupped in her hand as she waited for Power to rush over. Her face looked full of sympathy and this made Power feel even worse. He couldn't bear any more bad news.

Power took the phone and pressed the receiver to his ear, "Hello?"

"Carl? It's Laura. It's about Jo." Power groaned and he suddenly felt unsteady, like a ship yawing in the trough of a wave. "He's disappeared."

"How do you mean? You mean Jo's gone?" asked Power. His mouth was dry and the inner surface of his lips stuck to his teeth. "Taken?" Power thought guiltily about how much risk he had visited upon his family. The loss of his father sprang into his thoughts and his eyes welled up.

"I don't know," said Laura. "He's been asking about you all afternoon since lunch. Really worried. He was saying he thought something was about to happen to you. I tried my best to reassure him, I tried to distract him with painting and making some rhubarb pies. I'm sorry, but while we were doing things there was a phone call from my mum, and when I put the phone down, he was gone. The front door of the flat was wide open."

"Maybe he's just gone to the shop," suggested Power, but he knew this wasn't so.

"It's getting dark," said Laura. "I don't think he's gone on an errand – he didn't mention sweets or anything. His rucksack has gone, and his jacket. And, Carl, he took about thirty pounds from my purse. He's gone on a journey."

"I don't think he knows where the hospital is," said Power. "I don't even think I've told him which hospitals I work in. He wouldn't know where my office was in the University either."

"I don't think I mentioned your clinic or the University, certainly not the hospital. So where has he gone? Would he try and get back to his grandfather?"

"Have you told Andrew?" asked Power.

"Yes, but he says that the police wouldn't usually act yet – Jo's only been gone forty minutes at the most. Andrew has been brilliant. He's dropped everything and is going to the bus station in town, then the train station."

"I suppose Jo could be there. If he took money it would be for a journey."

"Do you want me to do anything? I feel so guilty." He heard the catch in her voice. She was holding back the tears.

"Can you stay there in case he just comes straight back? I never thought he'd do anything like this. Maybe he's gone home to Alderley?"

"But if he knows it isn't safe, why would he go there?"

"He's being brave," said Power. "Maybe he heard about me facing down my fears. He thinks I'm in danger and he's set off to find me. I don't know whether to stay here, in case . . . or go to Alderley."

"How would he get to Alderley? He's only seven," said Laura.

Power wondered what route anyone would take to reach Alderley from Chester by public transport. "Would you get a train to Manchester and then Alderley?" He wondered half to himself and half to Laura.

"You get a train from Chester to Crewe," said Laura. "Change at Crewe and travel to Alderley."

"Then maybe I should go to Crewe?" said Power. "Wait there for him?"

"Unless you miss him and he gets on the Alderley train before you get there."

"Well, I have to do something," Power snapped at her, and immediately regretted being irritable. "I'm sorry. I didn't mean to say it like that."

"Don't worry about it," said Laura. "It's just that the whole journey by road will take longer. You could take a chance that you're right about his going to Alderley and drive straight there. Be at Alderley station to meet him if he arrives."

"**If**," said Power. "If." And he felt sadness inside, a feeling of uselessness sapping at his very core. "I can't lose him, Laura. Not now."

"Oh, Carl, you won't!" said Laura. "Stay calm. I'll stay here. Andrew is searching Chester. You go to Alderley Station and then the house. I'll tell Andrew what your plan is, maybe he'll join you later."

"OK," said Power. "I'd better go, I need to hurry."

"Good luck. Drive carefully. Keep your mind on the road as you drive. I love you."

And she was gone. Power felt all alone in the clinic although he was in the midst of a group of people all looking at him. "I've got to go," he said softly. "I'm so sorry."

"Don't worry about us," said Dr Wootton. "Go. We can cope." And Dr Wootton always did, thought Power thankfully, as he ran from the clinic to find his car.

* * *

Sparked into sudden life Power's Saab gave an angry roar and sped out of the hospital car park. Power's vision became a tunnel focused on the road ahead. His aim was simply to go as fast as his driving, the road, and the V4 engine could contrive. Nevertheless, as much as he tried hard to focus, his mind was afflicted by intermittent images of what might be happening to his son. He fought down waves of panic by plotting his journey east to Alderley and the small village station. Power even worked out how long he would stand waiting there if he didn't find Jo at once. He planned in detail what he would do, to keep the overwhelming blur of panic at bay. Power would stay for about half an hour or so, or for enough time to meet a sequence of two trains from Crewe. He would check each platform. (There were only two). There was a ticket office and waiting room. It was after 1 p.m. and so he knew that the station would be unstaffed – thus there would be no station manager to ask if they had seen a small boy arrive unaccompanied. It would be a long wait if Jo were not there. An hour between trains so at least an hour to wait for two trains. How would Power manage to keep a lid on his agitation? It was growing darker now. By half past four it would be a dark winter night. The crescent moon was already beginning to glow in the sky as Power drove on along the country roads.

Power wondered if Jo was wearing light clothes. He knew that the boy's coat was black as night, and cursing his lack of foresight, Power worried about Jo on any long walk to Alderley House; if walking that very long way up the hill had indeed had been Jo's plan.

As Power drove, he looked occasionally over at the silent mobile lying on the car seat by his side. The phone was dark – there was no message.

Power revised his plan again as he drove; he decided he could wait no more than forty minutes at the station, and then he should drive through the village and up the long hill, scanning the pavements for his son. If he still didn't see him, then he would phone Laura and Lynch and begin his long wait at Alderley House.

* * *

She rose up from the depths, having sensed that the house was now occupied again. The place had been quiet and still, and she had faced a long wait with determination. Her life had been on pause for many long hours waiting for him to return. Her life on pause, perhaps, but then, she had nothing else to do now. Her son was dead. And that was *his* fault. She was sure that he could have helped her son far more than he did. He was a doctor, and after all, he was trained to save life. Joel had been breathing when Power had walked out on mother and son. Joel had been alive! She was convinced that Power had walked out on his vocation too. He had tricked her into a position where she could not afford to move without harming Joel, and then left. And then, when Joel's pulse finally stopped, she had faced the anguish of separating from her boy. Once she knew her boy had stopped breathing and his heart had stilled, his mother had faced the dilemma of whether to stay with her son, or leave his dead body. He was, she thought, at least at rest in the presence of the bones of his ancestors, in front of his father and his grandfather. It had been a wrench to leave, like splitting herself in two. But if she stayed with her son in the darkness, then eventually the lights would come. The bright lights of the helmeted ones, with their uniforms and guns, and she would be shot, or worse still, arrested to face their ignorant scrutiny and petty judgment. And so she had let go of Joel's cooling body and cast about her for the pile of goods in the middle of their cavern. Plunged into darkness by Power leaving them, the tomb of her son and his predecessors was darker then the night. She scrabbled about with her hands to find the bed, and the pile of clothes and provisions nearby. In the pile she fumbled about for one of the torches they had taken from Power when he was unconscious.

The clinical blue light of the torch had revealed to her the drained body of her son. How pale he was, and how lifeless and dry his cloudy eyes were. She let out a wail of distress and grief, and the silence of the tomb swallowed it whole.

She moved on, with a gathered hoard of temporary supplies, to distant, secret spaces in the mine, to wait for the arrival and inevitable departure of the police force. They took her son from her, and disturbed the bones of her family as they rested, robbing them from their eternal tomb for their 'urgent' analysis.

When Mrs Heaney returned the cavern was bare, as if her family had never been there. Some traces of powdered ochre from the bones scattered on the cave floor were all that remained of the Heaney ancestors. The singing post where Power had been shackled was bare. Her possessions were gone. All that remained was her loss, her burning anger and her unquenched thirst for revenge.

She had retraced Power's route to his house, along the galleries and tunnels of the mine up to the steps that ascended into his world. And the house, his house, was as empty as her world and her heart.

Although she could not have known he had retreated to a safe house, it seemed to her that Dr Power had fled.

The agents of the law, the police and their ilk, hadn't even locked or barred the doors that could have shielded his kitchen from her world. Did they rate her so low that they dismissed her so easily? Their search for her in the darkness of the mine had been timid and unimaginative. Still, she reasoned, there were many kilometres of tunnels under the earth. She suspected their fears would affect their decisions about the thoroughness of the search. They might rationalise their lack of resolution on a belief she had escaped, but really, she knew, all men were afraid of the dark.

And so she had food, and she waited, just below the house, ready to run if the search began again, or to do what needed to be done if Power returned alone. And logic dictated what he would do, it was his house, he *would* return. It was just a matter of patience and waiting for his return. And return he had, as his heavy male footsteps in the kitchen above clearly announced to her.

She carried her knife in her hand.

She had honed its blade on the stone steps beneath Power's kitchen. Its edge was razor sharp, ready for him.

She took infinite care to place her stockinged feet squarely on the steps to minimize the chance of any noise that might alert him.

With each step upwards she thought about her son. Joel had never been as clever as his parents. He had needed watching through childhood and beyond. She had pretended otherwise, so that his pride and self-esteem were not too damaged, but Joel would never have had the idea of their working together in the homeless centre and her feeding the vulnerable ones to him. And even then he would have gone for the thin girls, the quirky, clever, interesting ones; whereas she would steer the best candidates to him. The bigger girls, dull mountains, whose muscles were marbled with lard; she thought the taste was superior. Joel was, however, the only link to the future for the family. With Joel dead, the family and their unique set of traditions were finished.

Silent tears ran down her cheeks as she climbed. She deliberately channelled her thoughts away from grief towards anger. It was necessary to be in the right frame of mind when she met Power, so she could kill him.

She had even thought of how to deal with him, depending on how he stood when they met. If he faced her she would stab upwards through his belly into his heart from beneath. If he had his back to her she could aim for the sixth intercostal space, for his heart, to slice through his heart strings and bring the thread of his life to an end, like *Atropos*, or she could aim five inches lower for two stabs to the kidneys – the renal arteries would provide rapid bleeding, or there was another way to reach round and quickly sever his windpipe and carotid. She had taught Joel all these techniques the way her husband, Arthur, had taught her. The advantages of him working in the anatomy lab at the University . . .

Mrs Heaney glided silently through the short hallway that separated the stairs from the kitchen. She smiled again at how boneheaded the police had been not to seal off the steps down into the mine. Had they totally discounted her? Had they assumed that poor Joel was the brain and motivation behind the killings? Had they assumed she would run in feminine fear and never come back? Had they assumed she was too weak in character and strength to avenge her boy?

She paused at the doorway into the kitchen to assess her prey. She knew he was in there. For some reason, he had not switched on the house lights. The sun had gone down and kitchen was dark, but nowhere as dark as the depths she had risen from. She saw him now. He was there at the far corner of the kitchen, standing at the sink, and staring out of the window into the garden. The window framed him in silhouette against the moonlit night. She could hear his breathing. She could feel the change from cold stone to warm wood on her feet as she crept onto the kitchen floor. She moved noiselessly into the room to a position just behind the kitchen table.

She was sure that she still had the advantage of surprise. He had not so much as flinched as she successfully attained a hunting spot not more than six feet from his back. He had not heard her soft footfall, nor her light breath. She knew that sooner or later he would inevitably sense he was being looked at. Soon he would shift and turn and jump as he saw her standing there. To preserve her advantage she must act now.

She thrust her arm clutching the knife, out in front of her, and using her body's weight behind the steel tip, ran forward at him. He was catapulted forward by the force of her attack and gasped as he was rammed into the sink. He had not even felt the blade go inside him, so cleanly and deeply had it plunged. She twisted the blade in the space between his ribs and pulled it out again, ready to strike another blow. His knees sagged beneath him and he sank down, but then he began to react to the attack and half turned, lifting his right arm to fend her off. The ferocity of her onslaught knew no limit, though, and she jabbed the knife into him again, under the ribcage on the right side of his back. She was aiming, successfully, for his kidney. She raked the blade leftwards, causing the tip to slice through cortex, renal pelvis, and artery. He staggered again, and fell to his knees on the floor, mortally wounded. She was on him now, like an animal in frenzy, sinking her teeth into his neck. Biting again and again as his life ebbed swiftly away.

She felt a punch in her back, and she let out a muffled cry through a mouthful of his muscle and blood. Then another punch to her side. She was surprised at how light the punches were and felt puzzled as to how the dying man had landed them upon her when he was crumpling beneath her.

She suddenly felt inordinately tired. She fought the waves of fatigue washing over her. There was a sense of perplexity as she wondered what was happening to her. It was a battle with the inevitable. She was alarmed to be losing the battle, as the night around her grew darker still and an endless sleep engulfed her.

* * *

Dr Power parked his Saab on the drive of Alderley House and got out. He switched on a torch and played it about the bushes and trees. Of Jo there was no sign. He realised that in his panic to leave the hospital he'd forgotten to ask Laura whether Jo had taken the keys for Alderley House. That would have guided his strategy. If Jo had not taken the keys, then maybe he hadn't been heading here at all. Why would Jo travel all this way without the keys? Nevertheless, Power thought, he was here now and the logical thing to do would be to check the house. Power looked at his phone. There were no messages to say whether Lynch or Laura had already found Jo. And so, Power must search Alderley House. The air smelt of recent rain on the earth. All was quiet except for the occasional sound of cars passing on the Macclesfield Road. Gravel crunched beneath his feet as he walked all around the drive and the outside of the property. He made a circuit of the house and ended up by the front door. The Green Man looked down upon him benevolently, giving Power no sense of the danger that awaited him within the house.

The first thing Power noticed when he opened the door was a difference to the comforting smell of home. He closed the front door behind him and stood inside the familiar hall. The usual scents of the place had changed. He wondered if the altered smell could be explained by traces left behind by the many officers and workers who'd been through the house to empty the caves beneath. Maybe it would take a little while for the normal smell of the house to return. The reassuring aromas of his family, of bread and cakes and coffee, and the familiar smells of Laura and Jo were not there; how long would it take to get them back? He felt a prickling on his neck, a deep unease. The smell was not just that of strangers passing through. There was something else. Not quite the smell of putrescine and cadaverine molecules he associated with long-dead corpses, but something else; something sweet, the early smell of death, mixed with the smell of iron that came from blood.

Heart in mouth, Power advanced through the hall to the kitchen, where the smell seemed to intensify, and switched on the light.

There was blood. A pool of it was running over the polished oak floorboards near the sink; half congealed and half still seeping into the cracks between the boards.

Power suddenly felt icy cold. He steadied himself against the table and looked at the two bodies that lay in the blood. Immediately, he took in that the two bodies were clearly adult sized. Jo was not here. Bodies of a man and a woman grasping at each other, entwined in death. Their eyes already seemed sunken, skin waxy and white through blood loss. Jaws agape. Mouths open in now silenced screams.

The teeth in Mrs Heaney's mouth, her face, and chin were covered in blood.

Mrs Heaney had the handle of a knife protruding from her back. Power looked and saw the slit of another wound alongside the one that the knife now resided in. Two stab wounds. Power mused on the fact that that particular kitchen knife had always been one of his favourites. It had been good at slicing tomatoes.

Underneath her corpse was the body of a man. It was a bit difficult to see how he had managed to get the kitchen knife into her as he was seemingly collapsed beneath Mrs Heaney's body. Power shifted in his stance to get a different viewpoint, and moved carefully over the kitchen floor, avoiding the blood thereon. Nevertheless, he still couldn't see past Mrs Heaney's body to detect the fatal injuries the man must have sustained. Power could see there was a sizable chunk of his neck bitten away. His face was visible.

The man's eye patch had slipped, and Power found himself looking into the man's empty eye socket. The empty hollow of his orbit, an old injury, stared balefully up at Power.

Looking at them both, Power began to understand that somehow he had escaped death. Both of these people had sought to kill him and now both lay dead at his feet. Both had been in the darkness wanting to kill Power, and Mrs Heaney had mistaken the other person for Power and killed him.

She had killed Cousins.

Epilogue

Power examined the scene in the kitchen for a moment longer before retreating into the hall, unable to bear the sight of both bodies any more.

The house was so still and quiet in the aftermath of such violence. The sounds of the struggle for life between Joel's mother and Cousins must have been loud, desperate ones. And yet the house bore no trace, no echo of that frenzy.

Power wondered if he could ever shrug off the memory of this dual death in his house? Could he ever see the house of his childhood, his home, in quite the same way as before? Or would the image of what he had seen there on the kitchen floor haunt him forever? Every time he chose to enter the room to cook a meal or make a cup of tea would he see and smell the bodies? Could the ghost of those murderous events ever be exorcised? Or could he push those thoughts away, shut the tunnels off, build stout brick walls at the top and bottom of the steps, and safely seal off the past forever?

The thought of Alderley House as it had been, a family home, urgently reminded him of Jo. He might arrive back here at any time. Power couldn't let him see what was lying in the kitchen. The image would scar the boy for life.

Power phoned Lynch first, then Beresford. There was the reassurance that the emergency services would soon be here. The drive in front of his house would be bathed in blue light, and the chatter of radios and sounds of heavy feet would fill his house once again.

Where *was* Jo? A thought grew and settled in his heart like lead. What if Jo had arrived earlier and had met with Cousins or Joel's mother when they were alive? What if they had already attacked Jo, before they killed each other? Was Jo's body lying unattended in the house?

Power felt paralysed and unable to move from the spot he stood in. If he moved he would disturb this moment of unknowing, and break into some unwelcome future where Jo lay downstairs, lifeless, in the living room, or his study perhaps.

For just a second, Power thought he would rather never know, and then, heart thudding fast in his chest, he went from room to room downstairs, throwing every light switch on to dispel the gloom and searching behind and under every seat, couch, or table for his son. Then he mounted the stairs and searched every room on the first floor, in his and Laura's bedroom, in bathrooms, behind every shower curtain, in every linen cupboard.

Finally, Power climbed the steps up into the tower where Jo's bedroom was. Power's legs felt heavy and numb. His hands shook.

And there, in Jo's own bedroom, he found his son.

Jo lay under the bed, half obscured behind a duvet, as still as the grave. His eyes were open, unmoving, and staring at the bedstead above him.

Power looked at the boy, and at his chest to see if it was still moving with the breath of life.

"It's me, Jo," said Power, softly.

The boy's head did not turn. "I prayed that it was you," he said. "I knew you would come some time."

"Are you all right?" asked Power, reaching out to his son's hand under the bed.

Jo held his father's hand tightly, but he kept staring at the bottom of his bed, chin quivering, his eyes awash with tears.

"Not really," said Jo. "I came here to find you. I had this idea you were in danger from . . . the man that Pam shot." His breath came in shuddering gasps as he tried not to cry. "I got here and searched for you. I came here to my room. Then, when I was upstairs, I heard him come through the front door. I nearly shouted out, because it could have been you, but I just felt . . . something stopped me. He just unlocked the front door and came in. I saw him through the bannisters and I held my breath. He went into the kitchen." It was worse than Power had feared. Cousins had been alone with Jo in the same place at the same time. And Cousins would have been determined to kill Jo if he had found him. If Jo had only shouted down thinking it was his father come home . . .

"It's all right, it's all right," said Power, trying to reassure himself as much as his son. "It's all right. He's gone. There was a fight and he's dead."

"There **was** a fight," said Jo. "I saw."

"You saw?" The words caught guiltily in Power's throat.

"The woman and the man. I saw. She attacked him. He was dead, and she was biting him. I thought she would turn on me. She was worse than him. I thought she would kill me next. So I had to do something."

""Oh Jo, I'm so sorry you saw that," said Power softly.

"I know, Dad . . . I killed her."

Commentary on Son of Darkness

This commentary contains spoilers, so please make sure you read the chapters first.

CHAPTER ONE

The Foundation, a private organisation, is introduced here, but was pre-figured in *Schrodinger's God*. Superintendent Lynch becomes disenchanted with the police after a lifetime of working for them. He feels his methods are no longer supported and that his faith – which he sees as the essence of his being – makes him a target of unhealthy skepticism. The offer of a huge grant from the Howarth-Weaver Corporation allows him to direct his efforts towards justice as he sees fit and with almost unlimited resources. The Foundation can assist with consultancy work or follow its own direction, just as Lynch and Power wish. Whilst Lynch is the prime director of operations, Power can follow his clinical and teaching work as a psychiatrist, coming in to work on cases for the Foundation as he sees fit. The establishment of the fictional Foundation coincides with the real world shedding of senior detectives from UK police forces, essentially to save the higher salaries associated with the length of service that tallies with such experience. Such cost-cutting has led to impairments in the quality of detective work and a rise in expensive mistakes that have in turn marred prosecutions. Inspector Beresford raises this point in Chapter Two.

CHAPTER TWO

The emergency services are drawn to the farm near the Black Lake by the tragedy of a plane crash. Once there, by chance, they discover Mr Heaney's lair and the toxic family legacy he has left behind. There are a few clues as to the current inhabitant of the farm, but some residual traces of old Mr Heaney. It is Beresford's investigation as senior investigating officer (SIO), and his role to develop an investigative strategy. Level 3 investigations are usually led by at least a Detective Inspector (DI), like Beresford, attached to a specialist unit such as a Major Crimes Unit.

Beresford welcomes having Dr Power's input as he has worked with him several times before and Power is no threat, clearly being outside the police force, by dint of his being from the medical profession. He feels somewhat anxious, or even ambivalent about Lynch's involvement. Although Lynch has never been anything other than a positive figure in Beresford's career, Beresford feels at Lynch may encroach on what he sees as *his* case. To compound this niggling feeling of inadequacy, Beresford neglects to notice that the freezer contains the remnants of more than one body.

Lynch arrives at the farmhouse murder scene and immediately refers to it as 'Cain's lair'. There are several references to Cain through the book. Cain is, of course, the first documented murderer – for his slaughter of his brother Abel in the Book of Genesis, motivated possibly by jealousy. Cain is interpreted by Biblical scholars as the originator of evil and father of a tainted line, including all manner of mythical monsters, including Grendel.

The chapter mentions the humble, orangey-yellow and black Sexton Beetle *(Nicrophorus vespilloides).* This is a kind of undertaker beetle found in the UK which buries dead animals like mice and birds. The beetle feeds on the corpses and breeds there. The carcass is prepared and buried in a lengthy process over eight hours or so sometimes by both the male and female beetles. Hair is removed. Beetles leave secretions on the carcass to delay decay and limit the smell of decomposition that might attract other predators. The parent beetles thus create a kind of crypt for the corpse, which doubles as a nursery for their offspring. The beetles stay around after the eggs are laid and hatched, to rear their offspring in the crypt. In *Son of Darkness* the Sexton Beetle is meant to be attracted into the house by the scent of death.

CHAPTER THREE

Mystery novels that focus in police investigations are often called 'police procedurals'. Police procedurals don't always follow strict police procedure. Some novels stray further from reality than others and in the balance between documentary and fiction, place characters and plot first. *Son of Darkness* includes many elements that you would have found in a real police investigation in 2003, but does not follow the process slavishly, as the necessary, detailed routine in any investigation would slow the plot down. Readers who like detail may like to acquaint themselves with the techniques of the time which are glancingly mentioned – such as HOLMES2 – the computer database which was being rolled out. HOLMES 2 was the acronym for the Home Office Large Major Enquiry System 2 and was instrumental in some successful inquiries such as the murder of Danielle Moorcroft in 2002. Other acronyms are scattered through the chapter and the book to lend verisimilitude, and credibility to characters like Lynch – acronyms like TIE and NAFIS. Some of these investigational details are actually also relevant to the later plot, such as the extremely dull-sounding SIO Investigation Policy File, which contains details of the investigations strategy and would include key details of advisers such as Dr Power. The loss of this key police file, as we find out in later chapters, puts Dr Power's safety in jeopardy.

CHAPTER FOUR

Dr Power wanders across the Edge for an evening walk with Laura. The Edge is a nature reserve and landscape with a dramatic, red sandstone escarpment managed by the National Trust. There is a car park for visitors and a pub, The Wizard, so named after the legends surrounding the Edge and the Wizard. Dr Power's house is on the Macclesfield Road almost within the woods on the Edge.

Paul Gent's illustration shows Power and Laura standing on Castle Rock, overlooking the plain. The description of trees and wildlife, such as the insects, is accurate. Power retells another local legend besides that of the Wizard; a ghost story.

CHAPTER FIVE

Although he is a professor, Power does not use the title more than he wants to, he chooses not to use it when booking the table at the *Dysart Arms*.

Power and Lynch discuss the meaning of trophies kept in Kilner jars and potential motives for the murders including sacrifice. The notion of a spiritual dimension to the motivation irritates Power and this resurfaces later in the book when he discusses how often 'religion or superstition' is invoked as sufficient explanation for our ancestors' behaviour.

To Lynch, who is strongly motivated by his Faith, such motivation is more comprehensible. Lynch is troubled by a change in how society views religion, with the rise of a secular society.

Power reflects on his teaching of psychiatry – how a man with psychosis killed his mother when he thought she was a witch, citing Exodus 22.18 – *'thou shalt not suffer a witch to live'*, now seen perhaps as an anachronistic and decidedly judgemental point of view.

The book touches several times on the strange phenomenon of cultural change and how what is deemed reasonable in society at one time (e.g. witch finding and their punishment) becomes seen as unreasonable. Whatever beliefs motivated the society that built neolithic stone circles and sustained such endeavours for thousands of years are lost to us, and can only be surmised. Local history testimony of the Edge from a man called Alastair Clay-Egerton described a coven allegedly meeting in the Alderley Edge woods and mines in the nineteenth and twentieth centuries; when this was more widely discovered the members of the coven were supposed to have received death threats.

CHAPTER SIX

The chapter describes how Dr Power cares for the wife of his closest friend. There is a professional dilemma here. Purists would argue that a doctor should not treat his friends or relatives. There are all sorts of pitfalls that could occur. The doctor might over-treat, or under-treat, or act outside his field of expertise and be a real interfering nuisance to other doctors. Friends might prevail upon the doctor for prescriptions that he might not normally give – like addictive drugs. Or the doctor might come under pressure to provide euthanasia at the end of life. But there is also the burden of guilt that a doctor might have to live with, if he does not intervene. For instance, in this situation where Dr Power finds Mrs Lynch is severely depressed, what if he had earlier refused to see her when Lynch asked him and she had later died by her own hand? How could he have lived with the knowledge that he had the training and skills to help her? I think Power negotiates his way through a minefield here, trying to do his best for his friend and Pamela Lynch. Ultimately, he defers to the GP to act and to actually prescribe, though.

Lynch is trying to develop the Foundation to be a legitimate and useful agency, and to do so he seeks a mutual co-operation with the security services. Having previously relied on the internal intelligence network provided by the police, he is seeking strategic alliance so that the Foundation can act in this and other cases. He can only do so through his good reputation, links with sympathetic politicians, and the 'clout' that comes from an almost unlimited supply of money through the Howarth-Weaver Corporation. Nevertheless, Lynch is initially viewed with suspicion by his handler, and clearly Lynch will have to build on this relationship if the Foundation is to grow.

Dr Power returns to the farmhouse, believing the scene to be a cold one, devoid of action and a place he can reflect in. He is particularly keen to try and isolate the motives behind Heaney's actions. He explores the unpleasant motive of cannibalism. He is clearly struggling with many aspects of the case. His plunge into the water is an external symbol of threat that mirrors the Lake outside, is an urgent real physical threat and also represents the conflict of ideas in his unconscious.

CHAPTER SEVEN

'Looks were deceiving for this was clearly a portal into a different realm; Heaney's world'. The water that marks a transition into 'Heaney's world' symbolizes both the amniotic world and the world of spirits that Heaney and his kin also see in the lake at Lindow. It is a transition point, between Power's world and Heaney's, and there the two men grapple in the darkness. There is another distant echo of something in *Beowulf*, but we will consider this later.

The journalist, John Lovett, is an impostor, and is the same man who stole Beresford's file. He uses the details in the file to try and tempt Power into a meeting, on his own.

The visit to see his father is Power's last ever meeting with him, although neither know this explicitly. It is by luck that they manage to express something of the feelings father and son share.

At the end of the chapter, Power and Lynch again discuss the motives of Heaney – discussing, rather obliquely at times, as their discussion is over breakfast, the subjects of Heaney's cannibalism and trophy keeping. Power's final comment is "You are what you eat." And in this he is partially alluding to Lynch's omnivorous diet as Power himself is a vegetarian.

CHAPTER EIGHT

Lynch undertakes to visit a number of funeral parlours in the vicinity of Lindow Common to try and find out if these might be a source of the body parts, and also to see if Mr Heaney works there. His visit is ultimately not profitable and he is dismayed by the secular nature of the funeral directors, and comforts himself with an ancient hymn, which he sings softly, "Still be Thy care, O God, our shield; Still may Thy wisdom guide us"

In a parallel search to Lynch, Dr Power visits Dr Lehman, a volunteer doctor, who runs a psychiatric drop-in clinic for the homeless. Power's hunch is that the victims of the Lindow murderer may be from this homeless population. Dr Lehman mentions the frightening statistic that the average age of death for a man on the city streets is about 47 and 43 for a woman. The cynical and profoundly unwise closure of the asylums (the UK now has fewer psychiatric beds than in the 1800s when the population was less than a third of what it is now) and the grim results of austerity programs have resulted in an itinerant population of which studies indicate over 24% have drug problems and over 37% alcohol problems. Over 12% have psychosis and over 11% have major depression. 23% have personality disorder (Fazel et al, 2008). [N.B. It is possible for some individuals to have more than one diagnosis]. Only the coldest of hearts would not be filled with anger at society's abandonment of these people.

Professor Rose is the friendly archeologist first mentioned by Laura in Chapter Four as the professor who took her school group round the University Museum. Professor Rose is a composite figure and not based on any unique individual. She adds a glimpse of the distant past to the story, talking about Neolithic mining and smelting on the Edge. The character is there to remind Dr Power that what happens in the present often has roots in history long-gone. She also implies that Power should explore these roots in the tunnels below his house. Power hesitates as he remembers his experience in the dark below his house (see *Dr Power's Casebook*).

The phenomenon of the preserved remains of the bog people throughout Europe is both fascinating and disturbing. Were these people victims of a single murderer who deliberately disposed them of where they would never be found, or sacrificial victims committed to the spirits of dark water by a society? Historically, Mr Reyn-Bardt did murder his wife and dispose of her in the bog in the 1960s. Ironically Reyn-Bardt confessed to the police when a body of a woman was discovered, (although this was of a woman who had actually died nearly two thousand years before). Other ancient bog people from Tollund, Dätgen, Worsley Moss and Holland also met violent deaths.

Professor Rose is open to Power's idea that these bodies were the result of murders that perpetrators wished to cover up, but also talks wistfully of ancient beliefs that such a watery places were gates to the underworld, returning to a theme in the book (see Chapter Twenty-One) that certain places offer thin boundaries to allow an exchange between different worlds.

The paragraphs of Dr Power's visit to the University of Manchester also contain a reference to Alan Turing who taught at the University in the 1950s (and whose memory features in the story 'Magpies' in *Dr Power's Casebook*).

Finally, Lynch is described at prayer in Chester Cathedral, where a Deacon preaches on Cain, the murderous son of Adam, and God's curse on Cain's family. The Deacon makes an elliptical remark about how we sometimes get glimpses of the truth, just at the edge of our perception. What she means is left unsaid, but might refer to how difficult it is to see the hand of God in our everyday lives, and Lynch is left in a reflective mood.

CHAPTER NINE
The chapter begins with a rail journey between Manchester and Alderley Edge. Alderley Edge really only emerged as an entity after the coming of the railway and the development of commutable suburbs and villas. The station features a couple of times in the book.

The journey also allows Power to reflect on his frustrated ambition to be a father. He is judgmental about a mother's focus on her mobile phone to the detriment of her baby. He imagines he would not make the same decision if he was a parent, but is he being fair?

On his journey Power reflects on his earlier visit to the Museum and the conversation with the archaeology professor. The dialogue about the Neolithic peoples of the Edge, and the long history of mining in the area contains some of the themes of heredity in the book. I am indebted to the University of Manchester's own Professor Prag for answering my queries about ancient or Neolithic peoples on the Edge and his successor Professor Sitch for his indirect recommendations via John Prag:

- *Lindow and the Bog Warriors* Matthew Hyde and Christine Pemberton (Wilmslow: Rex, 2002)

- *Lindow Common as a peat bog: its age and its people* by William Norbury

- *The Story of Alderley: Living with the Edge* (Prag)

One of the sound inspirations for some of the writing was the song by Manchester band, *Everything Everything*, called 'Distant Past' (2015). Their lead singer Jonathan Higgs, described the song – "'Distant Past' is about primal human nature, and no matter how far we progress in our civilisations, we can never escape it." This theme is relevant to the Heaney family, who say they have always lived near the Edge, and is developed later in the book. Our actions are derived from a complex mixture of effects from genetics, early environment, and experience. How much are our behaviours determined by these factors? Can we escape from the past and our family traditions?

Sometimes our identity is guided by our perceptions of our heritage. People living in the British Isles might, for instance, identify with the builders of Stonehenge, or, say, the Romans, whose empire we were part of for the best part of four hundred years. However, should we lend such cultural identities so much power over us?

Recent genetic studies challenge the notion of continuity and are consistent with successive sweeps of immigration from places like Iberia or Anatolia, and the rise and fall of various peoples in tandem with innovations in farming, and decimations by infections such as plague. Those whom we perceive to be our forebears may not be. The builders of Stonehenge who replaced earlier hunter gatherers, may themselves have been succeeded by the Beaker people, who replaced 90% of the British gene pool in a few hundred years. (See for instance the work of Professor Reich and others in *Nature*).

There have been copper and cobalt mines under the massive outcrop of sandstone that is Alderley Edge. There are miles of tunnels, explored and unexplored. Several of the mines have been rendered relatively safe for the public to venture into with guides, and the Derbyshire Caving Club holds occasional tours and Open Days. Visits can be booked on-line for those who can tolerate the cold, the wet, the dark, low ceilings, and some enclosed spaces . . . the author benefited from several tours underground in Wood Mine and at Engine Vein.

I should note that the Caving Club characters depicted in the novel are entirely fictional.

Looking at the Edge today, an epitome of a National Trust woodland landscape, it is difficult to envisage it was once a semi-industrial landscape with mines, and brick buildings which housed large scale processes to crush the mined rock and treat it in huge vats of acid to free the deep-dwelling minerals from the earth.

"Born all in the dark wormy earth, cold specks of fire, evil lights shining in the darkness. Where fallen archangels flung the stars of their brows."

In the book Dr Power occasionally muses on the nature and purpose of ritual – psychiatrists are familiar with the rituals we all engage in to allay our anxieties. Some rituals are more extreme and time consuming than others – for example, the elaborate undoing rituals seen in obsessive compulsive disorder – e.g. lengthy handwashing rituals to overcome a fear of contamination. Power expressed some frustration with academics who perhaps overly resort to the concept of religious ritual as an explanation for inexplicable aspects of archaeological sites or phenomena. His interest in ritual is particularly piqued in this book as he is endeavouring to explore the motives for the various murders in the novel. In considering the historical deaths of European bog people he rails against the formulaic reliance on ritual as a motive, when more prosaic motives could be employed.

In Chapter Nine, and in a few other places in the book, Power discourses about the various types of cannibalism, again to illustrate the mental exploration he is engaged in to ensure he is covering all possible avenues before discounting any.

CHAPTER TEN

Hospitals are now large organisations, employing thousands of staff. It would be possible to assume an identity and walk unchallenged through its corridors. The staff group is diverse, and the hierarchy from the most menial employee and the Chief Executive is extensive, with the pay of the latter exceeding the poorest paid member of the staff by over ten times. In such a complex organisation the average Chief Executive has become far removed from the nursing staff and patients. The staff of a hospital would not know a modern-day Chief Executive either by face or name. Some areas of a hospital are protected by electronic and conventional security – the Chief

Executive's suite perhaps and wards such as maternity (as a result of past experiences with baby theft) and psychiatry (to prevent absconsion), so the absence of a security card would be a temporary deterrent to a determined criminal, but confidence and cunning can run rings even round the tightest security systems.

In Chapter Ten the Matron is, of course, an impostor. Modern Matrons were being newly introduced across UK NHS hospitals from 2001 onwards and staff would be unfamiliar with the role, and possibly fearful of their power.

Those who doubt that impostors can get very far in the modern NHS should look at the example of Dr Levon Mkhitarian, who posed as a locum doctor, and treated 3,363 patients in two years. He successfully convinced people in seven NHS Trusts across various specialties including oncology, cardiology, and surgery. He was caught out when he applied for a security pass in the name of another doctor. He was convicted in 2015 and sentenced to six years in prison.

In the latter part of the chapter Power mourns his father and becomes introspective, focusing on small details such as the carving of a Green Man in his house. The long history of the Green Man is interesting and this figure is glimpsed everywhere in Europe on buildings. He is seemingly ubiquitous. He is often identified as Adam. There is an apocryphal story of how Adam became the Green Man involving a desire to return to Eden at the end of his days, sending his son Seth to ask for permission for Adam's return, God's refusal, the provision of three seeds from the Garden, which are placed in Adam's mouth on his death, and the prolific growth of greenery from his body which in turn becomes the tree that provides the wood, upon which Christ is crucified. The appearance of the Green Man is a sign, perhaps, that Power is being watched over, but also links symbolically to Cain, the other son of our original family, whose story is told elsewhere in the *Son of Darkness*.

CHAPTER ELEVEN

This chapter explores the nature of Power's father's death. The initial assumption that his father died a natural death is challenged by a crude note received by Power, clearly from Cousins, a man who has himself seemingly risen from the grave to act out a revenge against Power and his kith and kin. Power refers to the ancient Law of Hammurabi, the Babylonian king, when he says "An eye for an eye, the death of a relative for the death of his brother".

Power reacts with a mixture of disbelief (he initially noted the pathological petechiae on his father's face when he visited the hospital but chose to be reassured by the imposter pretending to be Matron, rather than listen to any internal suspicions), despair, swiftly followed by anger and guilt. The chapter ends with him battling against the earth itself, digging frantically in the rain and darkness.

CHAPTER TWELVE

Power is challenged morally and physically during a working day despite wanting a peaceful time; the tests he faces are unbidden and unwelcome.

This chapter shows Power resisting temptation, even though he is encouraged to fall by Dr Shacklin. Shacklin is a very senior figure in the University that Power has moved into. Shacklin acts purely in his own interests, and notes that there is no hard and fast rule against employees having a relationship with other members of staff or students. Shacklin, despite his seniority and our expectations of a more moral stance in such a figure, interprets the lack of a prohibitory rule as being a green light to enjoying such relationships. Power is baffled by Shacklin's viewpoint, but before he can protest, Shacklin is gone.

Dr Shacklin is introduced here ahead of a more substantial appearance in the next Dr Power mystery.

The chapter ends with Dr Power receiving a further communication from Cousins, who is stalking him and motivated by revenge, to seek what he sees as balance. This quest for revenge is perceived as justifiable from Cousins's viewpoint, but as Power has always acted in terms of justice from a societal point of view, few would agree with Cousins about his justification.

CHAPTER THIRTEEN

This chapter is about transition from one reality to another. Mr Susskind, the patient discussed by Dr Power when he is on call claims to have suddenly moved from one universe to another – like slipping between bubbles. Dr Power also slips suddenly between one world in which he is childless, to another where he gains a son. Both Susskind and Power have to come to terms with these sudden transitions.

There are a number of events, which illustrate a theme of universal balance in the book – for instance Power loses his father but also gains a son. There is also homeostasis occurring Susskind's universes – a balanced like for like exchange of people between universes. And there is a kind of balance in terms of revenge – which motivates some of the villains – notably Cousins and Mrs Heaney, as they seek to maintain a kind of balance in their eyes.

In early forms of the manuscript there was a recognition that Power had gone through two major life events – the death of his father and the sudden arrival of a son. It would be predictable that he would succumb to depression, but after reflection, his descent into despair is short-lived and he quickly channels his anger. This acknowledges readers' expectations that heroes will necessarily be active, rather than passive, or perhaps that a hero's mask cannot slip for long. Detectives such as Sherlock Holmes and Harry Hole may dabble with substance misuse, but such idiosyncrasies are temporary, even if recurrent.

Mr Susskind's experience is revisited later in the book, and Dr Power reviews the clinical possibilities, but his complaint could be seen as an example of a false memory, as per early work by Freud and Janet, and revisited by other researchers such as Elizabeth Loftus and populist author Broome, who coined the term "Mandela Effect'.

CHAPTER FOURTEEN

Power tries to build a relationship with his suddenly acquired son, Jo. His house is not adapted to cater to the sudden arrival. The bedroom he is given in the tower is no nursery, and is initially poorly provided – without a side lamp – and Jo is unprepared to live in a vegetarian household. Despite Power's long-term hope for a child, particularly a son, the sudden arrival of Jo is highly stressful for him. He is unprepared and caught off guard. Laura acts as an initial bridge between father and son, and lends Power useful observations.

The situation is probably more stressful for Jo – his mother has died and his ailing grandfather has landed him with his father and disappeared. He brings some of his beliefs with him, like a game he and his mother might have shared about protecting people or things by walking three times around them. Power is not critical of this, but suggests improvements (changing the direction Jo walks) and thus fails to enter the spontaneous spirit or fun of the moment.

Jo was conceived in the context of a flying visit Power made to Dublin where he met a PhD student, Penny Ferrer. A short story called 'The Fallen Man' features their meeting and pre-figures Jo's appearance in *Son of Darkness*. The story is in *Dr Power's Casebook*.

Another tale in this collection of short stories prefigures *Son of Darkness*. This story, 'The Dark', features Dr Power's first foray into the dark realm underneath his house. This realm is also symbolic of Power's unconscious and analogous to a Jungian viewpoint of how a house is symbolically structured. The theme of the unconscious is also woven into *Son of Darkness*. Power even refers to how he relies upon creatively listening to his unconscious as a method in his solving problems. Dr Power books and stories, and even the illustration, often contain clues as to other stories in the series. For instance in the *Fire of Love,* an illustration of a chapel includes a reference to the next Dr Power book, *The Good Shepherd*. If you care to carefully look for it 'The Dark' also includes the first appearance of the Heaneys.

The chapter also highlights that Power and Lynch face a dual threat. There is Heaney, and there is Cousins. Both threats coincide. Cousins first appeared in *The Good Shepherd*, and was thought to have died at the end of that book. Cousins's simultaneous absence, and seemingly ghostly-presence, haunts Power throughout *Schrödinger's God*. His more definite re-appearance in *Son of Darkness* through mortal threats and actions resolves the ambiguous nature of his disappearance in *The Good Shepherd*.

Power meditates on the phrase 'Death cannot be experienced' in a personal sense. This is because if there is no after-life, then to experience death would require an individual to perceive it before and after the event, which would be impossible. It is perhaps because of this that Cousins decides to wreak havoc upon the lives of Power and Lynch by targeting their loved ones (rather than killing them) in revenge for his brothers' deaths (in *Schrödinger's God).* He believes they must suffer by experiencing the pain caused by their relatives' demise. From Cousins's warped perspective, Power and Lynch hounded his brothers to their respective deaths. That Power and Lynch were seeking justice for the lives damaged by the brothers does not register in Cousins's *weltanschauung.*

In Chapter Fourteen Power also briefly confronts his guilt about his father's death. The thought occurs to him and he refuses to give it life and explore its meaning immediately. It is too much and too soon.

The two stanzas quoted in Chapters Thirteen and Fourteen are by James Joyce from the poem *Ecce Puer*. The poem neatly describes a man in mid-life – between two generations – considering his feelings for, and responsibilities to, his father and his son. With the sudden arrival of Jo and the murder of his father, Power faces the same conflict of emotion:

> A child is sleeping:
> An old man gone.
> O, father forsaken,
> Forgive your son!
> *Ecce Puer,* Joyce, 1932

The process of Power getting to know his son and vice versa contains some surprises. Power is alarmed when his son kills two magpies using a slingshot. Power cannot understand why any son of his would indulge in this cruelty. Jo cannot understand why his father does not applaud a demonstration of such skill and accuracy. Magpies from Power's garden previously appeared in a short story in *Dr Power's Casebook*.

CHAPTER FIFTEEN

A train station has been on the site of Manchester Piccadilly since 1842, and it is the major station in Manchester. At the time *Son of Darkness* is set it had been going through an expensive process of renovation costing some £100 million by 2002. There is an undercroft beneath the main station, but the description of the area visited by Power and Lynch is entirely fictional.

The Willow Tea Rooms, modelled on designs by Charles Rennie Mackintosh, are at 97 Buchanan Street, Glasgow and very fine tea and light meals can be enjoyed there.

The tearoom is very close to the Central Station in Glasgow and it is quite conceivable that Lynch and Power could run between the two locations in a few minutes.

The foray north is a red herring, devised by Cousins to take Power and Lynch away from home. Cousins designs his trap using the SIO Policy File which he stole from Beresford, knowing that Power and Lynch were working on the case. The Policy File would give Cousins the definitive record of critical policy decisions in the case, and documents the progress of an investigation, naming key figures, contact details, suspects, victims, listing priorities, strategies, tactics, investigations, and so on. The record would include details of the crime scene, forensics, pathology, witness details, elimination enquiries, searches, etc. The record is used by the SIO to account for any decisions he or she makes.

The Policy File also records the plan for the investigation. Its theft would be a grave matter for Beresford. And it gives Cousins a vital insight into what is currently occupying the minds of Power and Lynch and would suggest ways he might entrap them. Using the Policy File he can decide what bait to use to lure them far enough away from home so he can act.

CHAPTER SIXTEEN

Power and Lynch venture north to talk to Mrs Kilty about a potential lead to Mrs Heaney. Mrs Kilty set up a meeting in the Willow Tea Rooms – like the Matron in an earlier chapter Mrs Kilty is an impostor, creating a simple trap to lure Power and Lynch away from those they love – the use of a place to eat as a venue, is a deliberate choice that ironically mocks Power and Lynch's penchant for good food and drink.

Later in the chapter Power and Lynch discuss altruism and why people put themselves at risk for the sake of others. Power takes an evolutionary approach, pointing out the advantages to the individual as well as society – 'if we help society, society will help us, reciprocally. And altruism is an attractive trait, biologically speaking, if a person demonstrates altruistic behaviour, then a potential mate might think them kind; a good provider for any children. And altruists have more life satisfaction. Research finds they are less likely to be depressed or anxious.'

Lynch's contrasting approach is that to be altruistic is to express love for one's fellow man, which in turn brings one closer to God, quoting *I John 4*.

Altruism, as a term, is not that old, being coined by the French philosopher Auguste Comte, from the latin *alteri*, meaning another [person]. Comte developed the term in contrast to egoism.

Altruism was a major theme in the Dr Power mystery, *The Good Shepherd*.

Acts of altruism vary from the everyday acts of kindness towards others as demonstrated, say, by Leopold Bloom and his everyday altruism in *Ulysses* – in the course of his day Bloom attends a funeral he strictly does not need to, visits the sick, helps someone across a road, and even puts himself in jeopardy to save the son of a friend from some irate soldiers.

The chapter closes as Cousins acts out his long-planned revenge, stalking outside Alderley House and watching its occupants. The house itself seems to recognise the threat and even the Green Man glares ominously down on Cousins as he broods before the front door.

CHAPTER SEVENTEEN

According to a newspaper article, quoted in *Schrödinger's God*, Cousins began his career as a trainee priest. He left the seminary after a scandal, however, and thereafter always told people that he focused his efforts on becoming a solicitor. He left his two brothers behind at the seminary and they completed their studies and were ordained. Whether Cousins ever applied himself to the lengthy years required at University and obtained a training contract is an entirely different matter. Cousins would see little point in investing his time in years of study when professional systems can be bypassed or hacked, CVs forged, and identities acquired in a few days. At some point he then became an agent for an international pharmaceutical corporation working for one of the elderly Howarth-Weaver brothers. It is not likely that he applied for any such position, rather that he attracted the attention of the brothers for his ability to operate without the narrow confines of legality and regulation. He is likely to have been recommended to them as someone who can fix unpleasant matters or inconvenient truths without fuss.

For those naïve enough to believe that public institutions and corporations only operate openly in a transparent fashion within a strictly regulated arena, slumber on. Industrial espionage has a venerable tradition, and is infinitely better funded than the machinations of the state, being funded to a level commensurate with the profits achievable.

This is Cousins's world, which we explore in *The Good Shepherd*. Cousins's world is an unpleasant one, parallel with our own, and sharing few of our values. As historical example of industrial espionage, consider the eighteenth century French Bureau of Commerce which obtained English technology in plate glass and steel industries. (Holt, J R (1985) Industrial Espionage in the Eighteenth Century, Industrial Archaeological Review 7.2, 127-138.)

Cousins would be a prime example of a sociopathic personality disorder. He has narcissistic and sadistic traits and harbours a deep-seated resentment against Power for an injury sustained in *The Good Shepherd*. After the death of his two brothers in the course of Power and Lynch's enquiries Cousins determines to come out of hiding and destroy their lives. First, he takes Power's father. Power never vocalises his deepest fears after he learns his father was murdered, but he is tortured by the idea that Cousins was alone with the old man before he died and hates to think what words of gall and spite Cousins might have spoken to his father before suffocating him.

Cousins deeply repellent sadism is again demonstrated by an allusion to his arousal at seeing the fear in the eyes of Power's son, hinting at a more perverse motive for the murders he has committed over the years. Krafft-Ebbing was one of the first to describe such sadistic homicides in 1898. The general reader is spared many of the details of this element of Cousins's psychopathology. Some readers might fuel further academic interest by reading Malmquist's 2006 book, *Homicide: a psychiatric perspective*.

CHAPTER EIGHTEEN

The Pamela of Chapter's Seventeen and Eighteen is markedly different to the depressed Pamela that Dr Power visited at home in Handbridge. Such is the contrast between a depressed and well state. In her depressed and passive state Pamela's attention was focused on her inner anger and helplessness, but by Chapter Seventeen she is well again, active and able to direct her anger outwards, appropriately, and take on the threat to her, and her friends' lives.

Ironically Pamela uses exactly the same model of firearm, a SIG P226, to shoot Cousins that he was intending to use to murder her, Laura and Jo.

Lynch arranged firearms training for Pamela in the same way he arranged training for Power in the story *The Shooting Range* in *Dr Power's Casebook*

CHAPTER NINETEEN

In this chapter Lynch asks Power to mimic the thinking used by profiles and Power considers how such profilers work from the crimes backwards looking at factors like whether serial killers are 'organised' or 'disorganised' and making *thematic inferences* – looking at the dominant themes of the criminal style – like stealing from the victim, leading to the conclusion that the perpetrator might have prior convictions for burglary; this process of inference guides the police to extrapolate from known convictions to find their offender. Working this way – backwards from the crimes – does not accord with Power's medical training, which is to work forwards from the patient, and so he struggles with this process. Throughout this case, Power is puzzled by the varying themes and how he can resolve various different motives into the psyche of one individual.

There is reference to the case of Sawney Beane and his cannibalistic family, who were all mentioned in the *Newgate Calendar*. Some believe the account is 'embellished'. I am grateful to Judith Eddles for bring the case to my attention. You can find the original report in the calendar at:

http://tarlton.law.utexas.edu/lpop/etext/newgate/beane.htm

The case is from Elizabethan times and led to the execution of Beane and his children and grandchildren at Leith, in Scotland. The Beane family lived far away from civilisation in 'a cave', and stole from travellers who passed their territory, and then disposed of their victims by eating them. They would 'pickle the mangled limbs'. They lived deep in a cave system and would not hesitate to kill any spies or investigators of the missing. The gothic cruelty of the family is described in detail with regard to a husband and wife attacked after a fair. Four hundred of King James's men were needed to subdue and arrest the clan.

CHAPTER TWENTY

Power regains consciousness after a head injury and is in darkness. Amnesia initially prevents him from a perfect understanding of how he came to be in darkness. The darkness under the earth is unlike the darkness of night, and is so profound that Power wondered whether he had gone blind, or had a stroke affecting the parts of his brain that allow him to see. Sensory deprivation of this sort can lead to hallucinosis as the brain attempts to fill the sensory void and so when Power hears the conversation about him he wonders whether this is real or imaginary. Eventually he pieces together an understanding of what happened to him and the alarming position he is now in, trapped in the mines below the Edge and entirely within the power of two serial killers. He must somehow outwit the Heaneys and overturn his helpless position.

The chance occurrence of an earthquake allows Power to bargain with Mrs Heaney by implicitly offering her the hope of saving her son. (There was such an earthquake leading to roof falls in the Alderley mines in 2002. Using artistic license I have moved the earthquake from 2002 to 2003). Mrs Heaney is outraged that Power manipulates the situation after she releases him, reversing their circumstances, so that he can escape, leaving her and her dying son in darkness. She lacks insight and expects Power to live by his Hippocratic Oath and save her son (an impossible task given the nature of his injuries), even though she clearly intended Power to die when he was her captive.

Heaney's injury to his arm parallels that of Grendel in Beowulf, and Mrs Heaney rises from the depths to seek revenge on Power in a parallel to Grendel's mother rising from her sea-cave.

The Heaney family members clearly share, and act upon, some overvalued, or even delusional, ideas about society. The closest diagnosis to a condition that would fit the mother and son is *folie à deux*. This is a condition where the psychosis of one individual becomes shared by another. The madness can extend beyond a pair of family members to three or even more. Recent examples would include twin sisters Ursula and Sabina Eriksson in May 2008, or in 2016 a family of five from Australia who suddenly fled the family home travelling more than 1,000 miles across the country, living off-grid (like the Heaneys), because one member had become convinced someone was out to kill and rob them all. The first three reports of *folie à deux* were published in 1877 by two French psychiatrists, Charles Lasègue and Jean-Pierre Falret.

Of course in terms of Grendel and his mother, they come from a work of fiction, ancient though that tale may be. It might be interesting to speculate as to whether the author based these monsters, albeit loosely, on a historical case of *folie à deux*.

The Heaneys' case is more complex still though, because the family's off ideas have persisted, possibly due to their deliberate isolation from society across generations, as the speech by Joel Heaney in the mines indicates that the family's tradition of behaviours including the veneration of the bones of past generations of ancestors have proceeded in exactly the same way for many years, and that much of the current generation's behaviour was taught to it by the father and husband, Arthur Heaney (b.1904), with other statements implying that the family has always behaved in this way.

CHAPTER TWENTY-ONE

The chapter starts with a consideration of different realties; with Dr Power seeing Mrs Susskind in clinic and listening to her description of her husband's scientific work and his beliefs he has somehow crossed over from an alternate universe. Before clinic though, Dr Power reads *The Times* for December 18th 2003 – in 'his' alternate fictional Universe *The Times* was preoccupied with the death of Joel Heaney and the paper devoted an article to Dr Power himself, to Power's discomfort. He shuns publicity. In the non-fictional world of our 'reality' the news that week focused on the Old Bailey trial of the Soham child murderer, Ian Huntley, and his girlfriend Maxine Carr. Other events of that week included the film release of the final instalment of *The Lord of the Rings* and the capture of the dictator Saddam Hussein, discovered in an underground bunker.

Dr Power tries to teach a medical student, Mr Cooper, using the case of Mr Susskind, but comes up against a singularly closed mind. There is a discussion as to whether Mr Susskind's ideas regarding alternate universes could satisfy the definition of a delusion or not. Mrs Susskind clearly sympathises with her husband's ideas . . . is she colluding with him to avoid thinking about the possibility he just chose to leave her? Or does she share his delusion? This possible case of *folie à deux* deliberately echoes the mother and son case of the Heaneys.

In his fictional research, Mr Susskind seeks to detect alternate realities – as Dr Power points out to his medical student that some scientists do consider there are alternate Universes. Susskind thinks he has caused some anomaly and has slipped through this thin space between universes. Experiments to detect elements of such alternate realities, to the extent of creating some kind of portal, have been devised by US scientists at Oak Ridge National Laboratory, (*The Independent*, 2019). This element of human scientists trying to engage with another realm, parallels the sacrifices made to spirits in the 'thin places' like the lake at Lindow. These 'thin places' are sites in the landscape where the boundary between the sacred and profane worlds is thinnest. At these places the Heaneys continue their family traditions of sacrifice.

Later in the chapter, Mrs Heaney rises from the depths to avenge her son's death, perhaps to create some kind of balance. Mrs Heaney's revenge is targeted at Power, but in the event she mistakes Cousins for Power and kills him instead.

The story of Beowulf is the oldest surviving work of English literature, and dates from the last millennium. Beowulf offers himself as a hero to kill the monster Grendel who has killed dozens of the king's men as they slept in King Hrothgar's hall. Beowulf slays the monster by tearing off his arm. Grendel's mother rises from the watery depths of her cave to slay the men of Hrothgar's hall again and avenge her son's death. This ancient tale is both a horror story and an epic account of heroism.

Surely the most chilling aspect of the Grendel element of Beowulf is that Grendel's mother, rather than disapproving of her son's senseless slaughter, shares his murderous capacity. Her revenge is every bit as violent and terrible as her son's repeated massacres. Whilst one might expect Grendel's mother to balance his rage with her reason and temper his savagery with some maternal mercy, she shows that both of them share the same scalding fury and hatred for the world of men.

What makes the idea of Grendel's mother so chilling and so horrific to us? Perhaps it is the notion we carry inside that mothers and, by extended inference, all women are predominantly nurturing by their very nature. Beowulf tells us that this cosy generalization is plain wrong, and this is what hurts and surprises us. Grendel's mother not only supports her son, she condones and reprises the evil acts he wrought.

Lest the reader think the behaviour of Grendel's mother is pure fantasy, we have unfortunate examples of women supporting murderous men in recent history such as Rosemary West, (convicted in 1995) or, as mentioned above, Maxine Carr (convicted in 2003).

Mrs Heaney, like Grendel's mother, brought her son up in a particular way, grooming him towards a series of murders that he enacts in his own particular style, but still very much according to a family tradition. It is the case, that Mrs Heaney enables her son's murderous activities. When Kyle talks to Dr Power she senses that he will lead the inquisitive outsider to their door. As Kyle represents a threat to the Heaney family's strange existence she deals with him herself, administering poison. It is her hand that Power witnesses, giving Kyle the poisoned tea. And it is Mrs Heaney who cooks and serves the joint of meat from the family freezer, and who poisoned the girl (the 'Ice Maiden') in the freezer through jealousy at the thought of losing her son to her.

In the commentary above there is some consideration of whether Joel Heaney and his mother share a *folie à deux*, and we could speculate as to whether Grendel and his mother represent the first possible description of this psychopathology.

The use of the underground world in *Son of Darkness* is a metaphor for Carl Power's unconscious, in a way that echoes a dream that psychiatrist Carl Jung published in 1909. The unconscious is a truly ancient world, born early in our evolution. The theme of the distant past is imbued within the family traditions of the Heaneys who are fully at home in the underground tunnels and caverns of the mines under the Edge.

Jung's dream is as follows:

"I was in a house I did not know, which had two storeys. It was "my house". I found myself in the upper storey, where there was a kind of salon furnished with fine old pieces in Rococo style. On the walls hung a number of precious old paintings. I wondered that this should be my house and thought "not bad". But then it occurred to me that I did not know what the lower floor looked like. Descending the stairs, I reached the ground floor. There everything was much older. I realised that this part of the house must date from about the fifteenth or sixteenth century. The furnishings were mediaeval, the floors were of red brick. Everywhere it was rather dark. I went from one room to another thinking "now I really must explore the whole house." I came upon a heavy door and opened it. Beyond it, I discovered a stone stairway that led down into a cellar. Descending again, I found myself in a beautifully vaulted room which looked exceedingly ancient. Examining the walls, I discovered layers of brick among the ordinary stone blocks, and chips of brick in the mortar. As soon as I saw this, I knew that the walls dated from Roman times. My interest by now was intense. I looked more closely at the floor. It was of stone slabs and in one of these I discovered a ring. When I pulled it, the stone slab lifted and again I saw a stairway of narrow stone steps leading down to the depths. These, too, I descended and entered a low cave cut into rock. Thick dust lay on the floor and in the dust were scattered bones and broken pottery, like remains of a primitive culture. I discovered two human skulls, obviously very old, and half disintegrated. Then I awoke."

At various times in the book, Power is unconsciously attracted to the mines – both as a means of solving the crime and facing his own fears after losing his father and gaining a son, he also needs to find courage after nearly losing Laura/Jo and dealing with his guilt. His unconscious mind has already combined all the information that points to the underground world as the solution.

The underworld/unconscious contains a combination of Jungian archetypes – there is Power himself as hero, plus shadow, animus, anima, and mother in varying positive and negative qualities and amounts.

EPILOGUE
As he searches his house Power confronts the fear of losing the son he gained so recently. He doesn't know if his son is alive or dead, only that he is missing and that Cousins, and Mrs Heaney too, for that matter, would happily have killed Jo.

Power finds Jo. Initially, Power is overwhelmed with relief, but in the midst of that emotion Jo tells Power that he believes that he stabbed Mrs Heaney whilst she was distracted in her fight with Cousins. Up to this point, the reader may have assumed that Joel Heaney was the son referred to in the title Son of Darkness, but could this refer to someone else in the book?

Readers may be interested in a Spotify playlist of eclectic music chosen to accompany *Son of Darkness* as a soundtrack.

https://open.spotify.com/playlist/3dGAKFNqclQVVvhqFYvi6k

Printed by Amazon Italia Logistica S.r.l.
Torrazza Piemonte (TO), Italy

11130059R00192